LARGE PRINT   4 WEEKS

WITHDRAWN

BLUE-EYED DEVIL

This Large Print Book carries the
Seal of Approval of N.A.V.H.

BLUE-EYED DEVIL

LISA KLEYPAS

THORNDIKE PRESS
A part of Gale, Cengage Learning

Detroit • New York • San Francisco • New Haven, Conn • Waterville, Maine • London

GALE
CENGAGE Learning™

Thorndike Press® Large Print Core.

The text of this Large Print edition is unabridged.

Other aspects of the book may vary from the original edition.

Set in 16 pt. Plantin.

Printed on permanent paper.

LIBRARY OF CONGRESS CATALOGING-IN-PUBLICATION DATA

Kleypas, Lisa.
  Blue-eyed devil / by Lisa Kleypas.
    p. cm.
  ISBN-13: 978-1-4104-0610-1 (hardcover : alk. paper)
  ISBN-10: 1-4104-0610-5 (hardcover : alk. paper) 1. Rich people — Fiction. 2. Texas —
  Fiction. 3. Large type books. I. Title.
  PS3561.L456B55 2008b
  813'.54—dc22

                                                                    2008000674

Published in 2008 in arrangement with St. Martin's Press, LLC.

Printed in the United States of America
1 2 3 4 5 6 7 12 11 10 09 08

To my husband, Greg . . .
A gentleman, and a gentle man
Love always,
L.K.

ACKNOWLEDGMENTS

I have many people to thank for their contributions to my work and to my life, during what has turned out to be a challenging but joyful year.

Mel Berger, a man of strength and wisdom, and an extraordinary literary agent.

(And thanks to Evan Goldfried for his patience, efficiency, and great sense of humor.)

Jennifer Enderlin, who is a magnificent person and an absolute dream of an editor.

Sally Richardson, Matthew Shear, Sara Goodman, John Karle, George Witte, Matt Baldacci, John Murphy, Dori Weintraub, and my other friends at St. Martin's Press who have helped to make my dreams come true.

My parents-in-law, Ireta and Harrell Ellis, for their unconditional love, their wisdom, and for the abundant happiness they bring to our lives. And for being the perfect grandparents.

My brother, Ki, who always understands,

and who will always be close to my heart.

Christina and Scott for being wonderful in every way.

Christina, Connie, Mary, Terri, and Liz . . . I carry you all in my heart, always. (I know I repeated your name, Xtina, but you're worth a second mention.)

The board of the Romance Writers of America, not only for the work they do on behalf of the romance genre but also for giving me the opportunity to speak at this past year's conference — it was an experience I will always treasure. So a huge thank-you to: Jill Limber, Sherry Lewis, Kelley St. John, Stephanie Feagan, Terri Brisbin, Michelle Monkou, Peggy Emard, Dorien Kelly, Linda Howard, Linda Winstead Jones, Karen Fox, Terri Reed, Geralyn Dawson, Donna Grant, Teresa Carpenter, Diane Pershing, Nicole Burnham, Julie Hurwitz, and Trish Milburn.

And thanks to the staff of RWA, who are the most charming, hardworking, and talented group of women you could ever meet: Allison Kelley, Nicole Kennedy, Judy Scott, Erin Fry, Stephani Fry, Dionne Cockrell, Kathleen Adey, Paula Levron, and Aronika Horne.

To Geralyn and Susan for being fantastic women and beloved friends.

Sheila Clover, Michael Miller, and Circle

of Seven Productions for their gorgeous work on my book trailers.

Michelle Buonfiglio, who is beautiful, understanding, and smart about everything.

Cindy Blewett, and Truly Texan, for her terrific Web design, and for being an altogether fabulous person.

To Rick Kittinger for his technical advice and for finding us the perfect new home, and, together with his wife, Amy, for the gift of friendship. Thanks from Greg and me in advance for all the memories we'll make in the future.

To Sybil Cook, Jane Litte, and Kristie Jenner for a special lunch I will always treasure.

And most of all, to my son and daughter, for being patient while I work, giving me the best hugs and kisses, and just for being you. No matter where you go or what you do, I'm proud of you. Love forever from Mom.

CHAPTER ONE

I first saw him at my brother's wedding, at the back of the reception tent. He stood with the insolent, loose-jointed slouch of someone who'd rather spend his time in a pool hall. Although he was well dressed, it was obvious he didn't make his living sitting behind a desk. No amount of Armani tailoring could soften that build — big framed and rugged — like a roughneck or a bull rider. His long fingers, clasped gently around a champagne flute, could have snapped the crystal stem with ease.

I knew from a glance that he was a good ol' boy, able to hunt, play football and poker, and hold his liquor. Not my type. I was interested in something more.

Even so, he was a compelling figure. He was good-looking, handsome if you overlooked the crook in a nose that had once been broken. His dark brown hair, as thick and lustrous as mink fur, was cut in short layers. But it was the eyes that seized my attention, blue even at a distance, a volatile color you could never forget once you'd seen it. It gave me a little shock when his head turned and he stared right at me.

I turned away immediately, embarrassed to have been caught staring. But awareness continued to spread over my skin, a heat so insistent that I knew he was still looking. I drank my champagne in fast swallows, letting the arid fizz soothe my nerves. Only then did I risk another glance.

Those blue eyes glinted with an uncivilized suggestion. A faint smile was tucked in one corner of his wide mouth. *Definitely wouldn't want to be alone in a room with that guy,* I thought. His gaze moved downward in a lazy inspection, returned to my face, and he gave me one of those respectful nods that Texan men had raised to an art form.

I deliberately turned away, giving full attention to my boyfriend, Nick. We watched the newlyweds dance, their faces close. I stood on my toes to whisper in Nick's ear. "Our turn next."

His arm slid around me. "We'll see what your father has to say about it."

Nick was going to ask Dad for permission to marry me, a tradition I thought was old-fashioned and unnecessary. But my boyfriend was being stubborn.

"What if he doesn't approve?" I asked. Given our family history, of me rarely doing anything that warranted parental approval, it was a distinct possibility.

"We'll get married anyway." Drawing back a little, Nick grinned down at me. "Still, I'd like to convince him I'm not such a bad deal."

"You're the best thing that's ever happened to me." I snuggled into the familiar crook of Nick's arm. I thought it was a miracle that someone could love me the way he did. No other man, no matter how good-looking, could ever interest me.

Smiling, I looked to the side one more time, wondering if the blue-eyed guy was still there. I wasn't sure why I was so relieved that he was gone.

My brother Gage had insisted on a small wedding ceremony. Only a handful of people had been allowed inside the tiny Houston chapel, which had once been used by Spanish settlers in the seventeen hundreds. The service had been short and beautiful, the air suffused with a hushed tenderness you could feel down to the soles of your feet.

The reception, by contrast, was a circus.

It was held at the Travis family mansion in

River Oaks, an exclusive Houston community where people told a lot more to their accountants than their ministers. Since Gage was the first of the Travis offspring to get married, my father was going to use the occasion to impress the world. Or at least Texas, which in Dad's view was the part of the world most worth impressing. Like many Texans, my father firmly believed if our state hadn't been annexed back in 1845, we probably would have ended up in charge of North America.

So in light of the family reputation and the fact that the eyes of Texas would be upon us, Dad had hired a renowned wedding planner and given her a four-word instruction: "The checkbook is open."

As all creation knew, it was a big checkbook.

My father, Churchill Travis, was a famous "market wizard," having created an international energy index fund that had nearly doubled in its first decade. The index included oil and gas producers, pipelines, alternative energy sources, and coal, represented by fifteen countries. While I was growing up, I never saw much of Dad — he was always in some far-off place like Singapore, New Zealand, or Japan. Often he went to D.C. to have lunch with the Federal Reserve chairman, or to New York to be a roundtable commentator on some financial show. Having breakfast with my father had meant turning on CNN and watching him analyze the market while we ate our toaster waffles.

With his full-bodied voice and outsized personality, Dad had always seemed big to me. It was only in my teens that I came to realize he was a physically small man, a bantam who ruled the yard. He had contempt for softness, and he worried that his four children — Gage, Jack, Joe, and me — were being spoiled. So when he was around, he took it upon himself to give us doses of reality, like spoonfuls of bitter medicine.

When my mother, Ava, was still alive, she was an annual cochair of the Texas Book Festival and went for smoke breaks with Kinky Friedman. She was glamorous and had the best legs of any woman in River Oaks, and gave the best dinner parties. As they said in those days, she was as fine as Dr Pepper on tap. After meeting her, men would tell Dad what a lucky bastard he was, and that pleased him to no end. She was more than he deserved, he announced on more than one occasion. And then he would give a sneaky laugh, because he always thought he deserved more than he deserved.

■■■■

Seven hundred guests had been invited to the reception, but at least a thousand had shown up. People milled inside the mansion and out to the enormous white tent, which was webbed with millions of tiny white fairy lights and blanketed with white and pink orchids. The humid warmth of the spring evening brought out the pillowy-sweet fragrance of the flowers.

Inside the air-conditioned house, a main buffet room was divided by a thirty-two-foot-long ice bar laden with all kinds of shellfish. There were twelve ice sculptures, one of them formed around a champagne fountain, another featuring a vodka fountain studded with pockets of caviar. White-gloved waiters filled frosted crystal cylinders with biting-cold vodka, and ladled caviar onto tiny sour cream blinis and pickled quail eggs.

The hot buffet tables featured tureens of lobster bisque, chafing dishes filled with slices of pecan-smoked tenderloin, grilled ahi tuna, and at least thirty other entrées. I'd been to many parties and events in Houston, but I had never seen so much food in one place in my life.

Reporters from the *Houston Chronicle* and *Texas Monthly* were there to cover the reception, which included guests like the former governor and mayor, a famous TV chef, Hollywood people, and oil people. Everyone was waiting for Gage and Liberty, who had stayed behind at the chapel with the photographer.

Nick was a little dazed. Coming from a respectable middle-class background, this was a shock to his system. I and my fledgling social conscience were embarrassed by the excess. I had changed since going to Wellesley, a women's college with the motto *non ministrari sed ministrare.* Not to be served, but to serve. I thought it was a good motto for someone like me to learn.

My family had gently mocked that I was going through a phase. They — especially my father — thought I was a living cliché, a rich girl dabbling in liberal guilt. I dragged my attention back to the long tables of food. I had made arrangements for the leftovers to be taken to a number of Houston shelters, which my family had thought was a fine idea. I still felt guilty. A faux liberal, waiting in line for caviar.

"Did you know," I asked Nick as we went to the vodka fountain, "that you have to sift through the equivalent of a ton of dirt to find a one-carat diamond? So to produce all the diamonds in this room, you'd have to excavate most of Australia."

Nick pretended to look puzzled. "Last time I checked, it was still there." He ran his fingertips over my bare shoulder. "Take it easy, Haven. You don't have to prove anything. I know who you are."

Although we were both native Texans, we'd found each other in Massachusetts. I had gone to Wellesley and Nick went to Tufts. I'd met him at an around-the-world party that was held in a big rambling house in Cambridge. Each room was designated a different country, featuring a national drink. Vodka in Russia, whiskey in Scotland, and so forth.

Somewhere between South America and Japan, I'd staggered into a dark-haired boy with clear hazel eyes and a self-confident grin. He had a long, sinewy runner's body and an intellectual look.

To my delight, he spoke with a Texas accent. "Maybe you should take a break from your world tour. At least until you're steady on your feet."

"You're from Houston," I'd said.

His smile had widened as he heard my accent. "No, ma'am."

"San Antonio?"

"No."

"Austin? Amarillo? El Paso?"

18

"No, no, and thank God, no."

"Dallas, then," I said regretfully. "Too bad. You're practically a Yankee."

Nick had led me outside, where we'd sat on the doorstep and talked in the freezing cold for two hours.

We had fallen in love very fast. I would do anything for Nick, go anywhere with him. I was going to marry him. I would be Mrs. Nicholas Tanner. Haven Travis Tanner. No one was going to stop me.

When I finally had my turn to dance with my father, Al Jarreau was singing "Accentuate the Positive" with silky cheerfulness. Nick had gone to the bar with my brothers Jack and Joe, and he would meet me in the house later.

Nick was the first man I'd ever brought home, the first man I'd ever been in love with. Also the only one I'd ever slept with. I had never dated much. My mother had died of cancer when I was fifteen, and for a couple of years after that I'd been too depressed and guilty even to think about having a love life. And then I'd gone to a women's college, which was great for my education but not so great for my love life.

It wasn't just the all-female environment that kept me from having relationships, however. Lots of women went to parties off campus, or met guys while taking extra courses at Harvard or MIT. The problem was me. I lacked some essential skill for attracting people, for giving and receiving love easily. It meant too much to me. I seemed to be driving away the people I most wanted. Finally I had realized that getting someone to love you was like trying to coax a bird to perch on your finger . . . it wouldn't happen unless you stopped trying so hard.

So I'd given up, and as the cliché went, that was when it happened. I met Nick, and we fell in love. He was the one I wanted. That should have been enough for my family. But they hadn't accepted him. Instead I found myself answering questions they hadn't even asked, saying things like "I'm really happy," or "Nick's majoring in economics," or "We met at a college party." Their lack of interest in him, in the history or future of our relationship, aggravated me beyond bearing. It was a judgment in itself, this ominous silence.

"I know, sweetie," my best friend, Todd, had said when I called to complain. We had known each other since the age of twelve, when his family had moved to River Oaks. Todd's father, Tim Phelan, was an artist who'd been featured at all the big museums, including MoMA in New York and the Kimbell in Fort Worth.

The Phelans had always mystified the residents of River Oaks. They were vegetarians, the first ones I had ever met. They wore wrinkly hemp garments and Birkenstocks. In a neighborhood where two decorating styles predominated — English Country and Tex-Mediterranean — the Phelans had painted each room of their house a different color, with exotic stripes and swirling designs on the walls.

Most fascinating of all, the Phelans were Buddhist, a word I'd heard even less often than "vegetarian." When I asked Todd what Buddhists did, he said they spent a lot of time contemplating the nature of reality. Todd and his parents had even invited me to go to a Buddhist temple with them, but to my chagrin, my parents said no. I was a Baptist, Mother said, and Baptists didn't spend their time thinking about reality.

Todd and I had always been so close that people assumed we were dating. We hadn't ever been romantically involved, but the feeling between us wasn't strictly platonic either. I'm not sure either of us could have explained what we were to each other.

Todd was probably the most beautiful human being I had ever seen. He was slim and athletic, with refined features and blond hair, and his eyes the opulent blue-green of the ocean in Caribbean travel brochures. And there was a feline quality about him that set him apart from the big-shouldered swagger of other Texan men I knew. I had asked Todd once if he was gay, and he had said he didn't care if someone was a man or a woman, he was more interested in the person's inside.

"So are you bisexual?" I had asked, and he had laughed at my insistence on a label.

"I guess I'm bipossible," he had said, and pressed a warm, careless kiss on my lips.

No one knew me or understood me as well as Todd did. He was my confidant, the person who was always on my side even when he wasn't taking my side.

"This is exactly what you said they would do," Todd said when I told him that my family was ignoring my boyfriend. "So, no surprise."

"Just because it's not a surprise doesn't mean it's not aggravating."

"Just remember, this weekend's not about you and Nick. It's about the bride and groom."

"Weddings are never about the bride and groom," I said. "Weddings are public platforms for dysfunctional families."

22

"But they have to *pretend* it's about the bride and groom. So go with it, celebrate, and don't talk to your dad about Nick until after the wedding."

"Todd," I had asked plaintively, "you've met Nick. You like him, don't you?"

"I can't answer that."

"Why not?"

"Because if you don't already see it, nothing I say could make you see it."

"See what? What do you mean?"

But Todd hadn't answered, and I hung up feeling mystified and annoyed.

Unfortunately, Todd's advice went by the wayside as soon as I started a foxtrot with Dad.

My father was flushed from champagne and triumph. He'd made no secret of wanting this wedding to happen, and the news about my new sister-in-law's pregnancy was even better. Things were going his way. I was pretty sure he had visions of grandchildren dancing in his head, generations of malleable DNA all at his disposal.

Dad was barrel-chested, short-legged, and black-eyed, with hair so thick you could hardly find his scalp beneath. All that and his German chin made him a striking man, if not a handsome one. He had some Comanche blood on his mother's side, and a

23

bunch of German and Scottish ancestors whose futures had been hamstrung back in their native countries. So they had come to Texas looking for cheap, winterless land that only needed their labor to bring forth prosperity. Instead they got droughts, epidemics, Indian raids, scorpions, and boll weevils the size of their thumbnails.

The Travises who had survived were the most purely stubborn people on earth, the kind who relied on their backbones when their wishbones were broken. That accounted for Dad's stubbornness . . . and for mine too. We were too much alike, Mama had always said, both of us willing to do anything to get our way, both of us eager to hop over a line the other one had drawn.

"Hey, Dad."

"Punkin." He had a gravelly voice, edged with the perpetual impatience of a man who never had to ingratiate himself with anyone. "You look pretty tonight. You remind me of your mama."

"Thanks." Compliments were rare from Dad. I appreciated it, even though I knew my resemblance to my mother was, at best, slight.

I was wearing a light green satin sheath, the shoulder straps fastened with two crystal buckles. My feet were strapped in delicate silver sandals with three-inch heels. Liberty had insisted on doing my hair. It had taken her about fifteen minutes to twist and pin the long inky locks up into a deceptively simple updo that I could never hope to reproduce. She was only a little older than I, but her manner had been maternal, gentle, in a way my own mother had seldom been.

"There," Liberty had murmured when she was finished, and picked up a powder brush to dust my nose playfully. "Perfect."

It was really hard not to like her.

As Dad and I danced, one of the photographers approached. We leaned close and smiled into the blinding white flash, and then resumed our previous distance.

"Nick and I are going back to Massachusetts tomorrow," I said. We were flying commercial — I had put two first-class tickets on my credit card. Since Dad paid my Visa bill, and went over it personally, I knew he was aware that I'd bought Nick's ticket. He hadn't said anything about it. Yet.

"Before we leave," I continued, "Nick's going to have a talk with you."

"Looking forward to that."

"I'd like you to be nice to him," I said.

"Sometimes I'm not nice for a reason. It's a way to find out what someone's made of."

"You don't need to test Nick. You just need

to respect my choices."

"He wants to marry you," Dad said.

"Yes."

"And then he reckons he'll have a first-class ticket for life. That's all you are to him, Haven."

"Have you ever thought," I asked, "that someone could actually love me for myself, and not for your money?"

"He's not the one."

"I get to decide that," I shot back. "Not you."

"You've made up your mind," Dad said, and although it wasn't exactly a question, I said yes, I had. "Then don't ask for my permission," he went on. "Make your choice and accept the consequences. Your brother sure as hell didn't ask what I thought about him marrying Liberty."

"Of course he didn't. You've done everything possible to push them together. Everyone knows you're crazy about her." Appalled by the edge of jealousy in my own voice, I continued quickly. "Can't we just do this the normal way, Dad? I bring my boyfriend home, you pretend to like him, I go on with my life, and you and I call each other on all the major holidays." I made my mouth into the shape of a smile. "Don't stand in the way, Dad. Just let me be happy."

26

"You won't be happy with him. He's a nonstarter."

"How would you know? You've never spent more than an hour in Nick's company."

"I've been around long enough to know a nonstarter when I see one."

I didn't think either of us had raised our voices, but we were getting a few curious glances. I realized our mutual haranguing didn't have to be loud for other people to notice. I struggled for calm, and kept my feet moving in a "dancing out of rhythm but by God still dancing" kind of shuffle. "Any man I wanted would be a nonstarter to you," I said. "Unless you got to pick him."

I thought there was just enough truth in that to make my father mad. "I'll give you a wedding," he said, "but you'll have to get someone else to walk you down the aisle. And don't come to me later when you need money for a divorce. You marry him, I'm cutting you off. Neither of you will get a plug nickel from me, you understand? If he has the balls to talk to me tomorrow, I'm going to tell him that."

"Thanks, Dad." I pulled away from him just as the music ended. "You do a mean foxtrot."

As I left the dance floor, I passed Carrington, who was running to my father with her arms outstretched. She was Liberty's little sister. "My turn," she cried, as if dancing with Churchill Travis were the best thing in the world.

When I was nine, I thought bitterly, I'd felt that way about him too.

I pushed my way through crowds of people, and all I could see were mouths and more mouths . . . talking, laughing, eating, drinking, air-kissing. The accumulated noise was mind-numbing.

I glanced at a wall clock in the hallway, an antique Ball regulator that had once belonged to the Buffalo Bayou, Brazos, and Colorado Railway. Nine o'clock. In about a half hour, I was supposed to meet Liberty in one of the upstairs bedrooms to help her change into her going-away outfit. I couldn't wait to get through that particular ritual. There was only so much misty-eyed happiness I could take in one evening.

The champagne had made me thirsty. I went to the kitchen, filled wall to wall with caterers and their staff, and managed to find a clean tumbler in one of the cabinets. Filling it with water from the sink, I drank in big quenching gulps.

"Excuse me," a waiter said urgently, trying to push by me with a steaming chafing dish.

28

I shrank back to let him pass, and wandered into the oval dining room.

To my relief, I saw the familiar outline of Nick's head and shoulders near the dark arched doorway that led to the dine-in wine cellar. He had gone through the small wrought-iron gate and left it ajar. It looked like he was heading into the vault, which was lined with oak barrel stays that sweetened the air. I figured Nick must have gotten tired of the crowds and had come early to meet me. I wanted him to hold me. I needed a moment of peace in the middle of the cacophony.

Skirting around the dining table, I went to the wine cellar. The gate closed behind me with a smooth clack. Reaching for the light switch, I flipped it off and went into the cellar.

I heard Nick mutter, "Hey —"

"Just me." I found him easily in the darkness, giving a low laugh as my palms slid over his shoulders. "Mmmn. You feel nice in a tux."

He started to say something, but I tugged his head down until my half-open mouth skimmed the edge of his jaw. "I missed you," I whispered. "You didn't dance with me."

His breath caught, and his hands came to my hips as I wobbled a little in my high heels. The wine-sweet air filled my nostrils, and something else . . . the scent of male skin, fresh like nutmeg or ginger . . . a sun-warmed spice. Exerting pressure on the back of his neck, I urged his mouth to mine, finding softness and heat, the tang of champagne melting into the intimate taste of him.

One of his hands traveled up my spine, coaxing out a shiver, a sweet shock, as the warmth of his palm met my bare skin. I felt the strength of his hand, and the gentleness, as it closed over my nape and tilted my head back. His mouth barely grazed mine, more a promise of a kiss than an actual one. I made a little sound at the brush of his lips and kept my face upturned, straining for more. Another lush descent, a dizzying pressure as he opened my mouth with his. He reached deeper, his tongue finding ticklish places that drew a shivering laugh from my throat.

I tried to curl around him, holding him with my arching body. His mouth was slow and searching, the kisses hard at first, then loosening as if unraveling from their own heat. The pleasure thickened, hard flushes rising through me, bringing the desire to full-slip ripeness. I wasn't aware of moving backward, but I felt the frame of the tasting table high against my bottom, the sharp edge digging into my flesh.

Nick lifted me with astonishing ease until I sat on the chilled table. He took my mouth again, longer, deeper, while I tried to catch his tongue, tried to draw him as far inside as possible. I wanted to lie back on the table, an offering of aching flesh on sterile marble, and let him do anything he wanted. Something had been cut loose in me. I was saturated with excitement, drunk with it, and part of it was because Nick, who always seemed so in control, was fighting for self-restraint. His breath came in ragged puffs, his hands gripping my body.

He kissed my throat, tasting the thin, susceptible skin, his lips stroking the throb of my pulse. Panting, I slid my hands up to his hair, so soft and thick, layers of heavy silk in my palms.

Not at all like Nick's.

A cold shot of horror went down to my stomach. "Oh, God." I was barely able to force the words out. I touched his face in the darkness, encountering hard, unfamiliar features, the scrape of shaven bristle. The corners of my eyes stung, but I wasn't sure whether the imminent tears were caused by embarrassment, anger, fear, disappointment, or some unholy combination of all of them. "Nick?"

My wrist was caught in a powerful hand,

and his mouth dragged softly over the insides of my fingers. A kiss burned the center of my palm, and then I heard a voice so smoky and deep I would have sworn it belonged to the devil.

"Who's Nick?"

CHAPTER TWO

The stranger didn't release me in the scalding darkness, only stroked my back in an effort to loosen the tight chain of my vertebrae.

"God, I'm sorry," I said through chattering teeth. "I th-thought you were my boyfriend."

He sounded rueful. "At the moment, I wish to hell I was." His hand moved up to the bare nape of my neck and squeezed with gentle pressure, relieving the cramp of tiny muscles. "Should I turn on the lights?"

"No!" I clutched at him.

He held obligingly still. A smile colored his voice as he asked, "Mind telling me your name?"

"Absolutely, positively *no.* No names."

"Okay, boss." He eased me down from the table, steadying my balance with his hands.

My heart pounded violently. "I've never done anything like this before. I — I feel like I should pass out or scream or something —"

"I'd rather you didn't."

"I *really* don't want anyone knowing about this. I wish *I* didn't know about it. I wish —"

"You talk fast when you're nervous," he observed.

"I talk fast all the time. And I'm not nervous. I'm in shock. I wish I could undo this. I feel like one of those error pages you get on the computer . . ."

"A Four-Oh-Four?"

"Yes. This is a major Four-Oh-Four."

He made a quiet sound of amusement. "It's okay," he said, easing me closer. The proximity of his body was so comforting that I couldn't bring myself to push him away. And his voice was soothing enough to stop a herd of stampeding cattle in their tracks. "Everything's okay. No harm done."

"You won't tell anyone?"

" 'Course not. If Nick found out, he'd kick my ass."

I nodded, even though the idea of Nick kicking this guy's ass was laughable. Even through the layers of his tux I could feel the contours of a body so hard and powerful it seemed invulnerable. In a flash, I remembered the guy in the reception tent, and my eyes widened in the darkness. *"Oh."*

"What is it?" He'd bent his head low, and

his hot breath stirred the hair at my temple.

"I saw you at the tent, standing in the back. You're the one with the blue eyes, aren't you?"

He went very still. "You're the bridesmaid in the green dress." A low, ironic laugh escaped him, the sound so delicious that every hair on my body stood up. "Shit. You're a Travis, aren't you?"

"I admit nothing." I struggled to catalogue the shame and excitement that stung the insides of my veins. His mouth was so close. I wanted more of those sweltering kisses. I felt terrible about that. But the warm sunny fragrance of him . . . he smelled better than any human being I'd ever met. "Okay," I said unsteadily, "forget what I said about not exchanging names. Who are you?"

"For you, honey . . . I'm trouble."

We were both still and silent, caught in a half-embrace as if every forbidden second had formed a link in a chain around us. The part of my brain that was still functioning urged me to pull away from him with all due haste. And yet I couldn't move, paralyzed by the sensation that something extraordinary was happening. Even with all the noise outside the wine cellar, the hundreds of people so close by, I felt as if I were in some faraway place.

One of his hands came up to my face, fingertips exploring the curve of my cheek. Blindly I reached up and felt the backs of his fingers, searching for the hard band of a ring.

"No," he murmured, "not married."

The tip of his little finger found the outside rim of my ear and traced delicately. I found myself slipping into a strange, pleasant passivity. *I can't do this,* I thought, even as I let him pull me closer, his hand tucking my hips into his. My head felt heavy, tipping back as he nuzzled into the soft space beneath my jaw. I had always thought I was pretty good at resisting temptation. But this was the first time I'd ever felt the pull of serious lust, and I wasn't at all equipped to handle it.

"Are you a friend of the groom," I managed to ask, "or friend of the bride?"

I felt him smile against my skin. "Wouldn't say I'm popular in either quarter."

"My God. You crashed the reception, didn't you?"

"Honey, half the people here crashed the reception." He traced one of the straps that held my dress up, and my stomach gave an excited leap.

"Are you in the oil business? Or ranching?"

"Oil," he said. "Why'd you ask?"

"You're built like a roughneck."

A laugh rustled in his chest. "I've stacked my share of drill pipe," he admitted. His breath was soft and hot against my hair. "So . . . you ever go out with a blue-collar guy? I bet not. Rich girl like you . . . you'd stick with your own kind, wouldn't you?"

"You're wearing a nice tux for a blue-collar guy," I countered. "Armani?"

"Even roughnecks get to dress up now and then." He braced his hands on either side of me, lightly gripping the edge of the table. "What's this for?"

I leaned back to preserve the small but crucial distance between our bodies. "The tasting table?"

"Yeah."

"It's for uncorking and decanting. We keep wine accessories in the drawers. Also white cloths to drape over the top, so you can judge the color of the wine."

"I've never been to a wine tasting before. How do you do it?"

I stared at the outline of his head, now dimly visible in the heavy shadows. "You hold the glass by the stem, and you stick your nose right into the bowl and breathe in the scent."

"In my case, that's a considerable amount of nose."

I couldn't resist touching him then, my fingers stealing up to his face, investigating the assertive line of his nose. I touched the crook near the bridge. "How did you break it?" I asked in a hushed voice.

His warm lips slid over the heel of my hand. "That's one of the stories I only tell when I'm drinking something a lot stronger than wine."

"Oh." I pulled my hand away. "Sorry."

"Don't be sorry. I wouldn't mind telling you someday."

Doggedly I steered the conversation back on course. "When you take a sip of wine, you hold it in your mouth. There's a place in the back of your mouth that leads to smell receptors in your nasal cavity. It's called retro-olfaction."

"Interesting." He paused. "So after you taste and smell the wine, you spit it out in a bucket, right?"

"I'd rather swallow than spit."

As the double meaning of the words occurred to me, I flushed hard enough I was certain he could see it in the darkness. Mercifully he didn't comment, although I heard the flick of amusement in his voice. "Thanks for the pointers."

"You're welcome. We should go now. You leave first."

"Okay."

But neither of us moved.

And then his hands found my hips, skimming upward, a callus on his finger catching at the fragile fabric of my dress. I was aware of every shift of his weight, the subtle movements of bone and heavy muscle. The sound of his breathing was electrifying.

The long, work-roughened hands didn't stop until he was cradling my face with a tenderness that made my throat tight. His mouth sought mine, all hot silk and sweetness. But for all the gentleness of the kiss, there was something so raw about it that by the time he drew back, my nerves were pleasure-stung and unbearably alive. A whimper emerged from my throat, the sound embarrassing me, but there was no controlling it. No controlling anything.

I reached up to hold on to his heavy wrists, mostly to keep from toppling over. My knees were shot. I had never felt anything so explosive, or insidious. The world had shrunk to this small wine-scented room, two bodies in the darkness, the ache of desire for someone I could never have. He moved his mouth to my ear, and I felt the moist heat of his breath, and I leaned against him in a daze.

"Listen, honey," he whispered. "There've only been a couple times in my life when something felt so good I didn't give a damn about the consequences." His lips slid over my forehead, my nose, my trembling eyelids. "Go tell Nick you're not feeling well, and come away with me. Right now. There's a strawberry moon out tonight. We'll go somewhere and find a patch of soft grass, and share a bottle of champagne. And I'll drive you to Galveston to watch the sun rise over the bay."

I was amazed. Men never propositioned me like that. And I never would have thought to be so insanely tempted. "I can't. That's crazy."

His lips caught at mine in a gently biting kiss. "Maybe it's crazy not to."

I squirmed and pushed back from him until I'd managed to put some distance between us. "I have a boyfriend," I said shakily. "I don't know why I just . . . I don't know why I let that happen. I'm sorry."

"Don't apologize. At least, not for that." His footsteps came closer, and I tensed. "What you should really be sorry for," he continued, "is that for the rest of my life, I'll have to avoid wine cellars to keep from thinking about you."

"Why?" I asked, woeful and shamed. "Was kissing me that bad?"

A devil-soft whisper. "No, sweetheart. It was that good."

And he left first, while I leaned against the tasting table with raggedy balance.

I went back out into the clamor and stole away to the grand staircase leading to the second-floor bedrooms. Liberty was waiting for me in the room Gage had occupied in childhood. I had barged in there a thousand times, wanting attention from the one person who always seemed to have time for me. I must have been a royal pain, chattering to him while he did his homework, dragging in my broken toys for him to fix. But Gage had tolerated it with what was, in retrospect, remarkable patience.

I remembered the time I'd been about Carrington's age, maybe a little younger, when Jack and Joe had dropped my favorite doll out the window and Gage had rescued her. I had gone into Jack's room, a chaos of toys and books and discarded clothes, and I'd seen him and Joe kneeling by the open window.

"Whatcha doing?" I had asked, venturing nearer. The two dark heads turned at the same time.

"Get outta here, Haven," Jack had commanded.

"Daddy says you have to let me play with you."

"Later. Get lost."

"What are you holding?" I had gone closer, my heart clutching as I saw something in their hands, tied up with strings. "Is that . . . is that *Bootsie?*"

"We're just borrowing her," Joe had said, his hands busy with string and some kind of plasticky fabric.

"You can't!" I had felt the panic of the thoroughly powerless, the outrage of the dispossessed. "You didn't ask me. Give her back! Give her —" My voice shredded into a scream as I saw Bootsie being dangled over the windowsill, her naked pink body harnessed with a contraption of strings and tape and paper clips. My baby doll had been recruited on a mission as a parachute jumper. *"Dooooooooon't!"*

"For Pete's sake," Jack had said in a disgusted tone. "She's just a hunk of plastic." And, adding injury to insult, he'd given me a mean look and dropped her.

Bootsie had gone down like a stone. I couldn't have been more upset if the boys had dropped a real baby out the window. Howls ripped from my throat as I'd raced from the room and down the big staircase. And I kept howling as I tore outside to the side of the house, paying no attention to the voices of my parents, the housekeeper, the gardener.

Bootsie had fallen into the middle of a massive ligustrum bush. The only thing visible had been the crumpled parachute caught on a top branch, my doll hanging unseen in the green and white thicket. Since I was too short and small to reach into the branches, I could only stand there crying, while the heat from the Texas sun had settled on me with the weight of a wool blanket.

Alerted by the racket, Gage had come and rummaged through the ligustrum until he found Bootsie. He had dusted away the powdering of scurf from ligustrum leaves, and held me against him until my tears were blotted against his T-shirt.

"I love you more than anybody," I had whispered to him.

"I love you too," Gage had whispered back, and I could feel him smiling against my hair. *"More than anybody."*

As I entered Gage's room now, I saw Liberty sitting on the bed in a heap of shimmering organza, her shoes on the floor, her veil a rich froth floating on the mattress. It seemed impossible that she could have been any more stunning than she had been earlier at the church. But she looked even better this way, glowing and smudged. She was half Mexican with a butter-smooth complexion

43

and big green eyes, and a figure that made you think of the old-fashioned word "bombshell." She was also shy. Cautious. You got the sense that things hadn't come easy for her, that she'd had close acquaintance with hardship.

Liberty made a comical face as she saw me. "My rescuer. You'll have to help me out of this dress — it has a thousand buttons and they're all in the back."

"No problem." I sat on the bed next to her, and she turned her back to make it easier for me. I felt awkward, struggling with unspoken tensions that no amount of niceness on her part would dispel.

I tried to think of something gracious to say. "I think today was the best day of Gage's life. You make him really happy."

"He makes me happy too," Liberty said. "More than happy. He's the most incredible man, the most . . ." She paused and lifted her shoulders in a little shrug, as if it were impossible to put her feelings into words.

"We're not the easiest family to marry into. A lot of strong personalities."

"I love the Travises," she said without hesitation. "All of you. I always wanted a big family. It was just Carrington and me after Mama died."

I'd never reflected on the fact that both of

us had lost a mother while we were in our teens. Except it must have been much scarier for Liberty, because there'd been no rich father, no family, no nice house and cushy life. And she'd raised her little sister all by herself, which I had to admire.

"Did your mother get sick?" I asked.

She shook her head. "Car wreck."

I went to the closet and took down the white pantsuit hanging over the back of the door. I brought it to Liberty, who shimmied out of her wedding dress. She was a vision of sumptuous curves contained in white lace, the swell of her pregnancy more developed than I would have expected.

Liberty dressed in white pants and matching blazer, and low-heeled beige pumps. Going to the dresser, she leaned close to the mirror and neatened her smudged eyeliner with a tissue. "Well," she said, "this is as good as it's going to get."

"You look gorgeous," I said.

"Droopy."

"In a gorgeous way."

She looked over her shoulder with a dazzling grin. "All your lipstick's gone, Haven." She motioned me to the mirror beside her. "Nick caught you alone in a corner, didn't he?" She handed me a tube of something shimmery and pale. Mercifully, before I had to answer, there was a knock at the door.

Liberty went to open it, and Carrington came in, accompanied by my aunt Gretchen.

Aunt Gretchen, my father's older sister and only sibling, was hands down my favorite relative from either side of the family. She had never been elegant like my mother. Gretchen was country born and as tough as any pioneer woman who ever crossed the Red River on the Cherokee Trace. Back then Texas women had learned to take care of themselves because the men were always gone when you needed them. The modern versions were still like that, iron-willed beneath their coating of Mary Kay cosmetics.

By all rights Aunt Gretchen should have been a tragic figure. She'd been engaged three times, and had lost all three fiancés, the first in the Korean War, the second in a car accident, and the third to an undiagnosed heart ailment. Each time Aunt Gretchen had confronted the loss, grieved, and accepted. She said she would never consider marriage again — it was clear she wasn't meant to have a husband.

But Aunt Gretchen found all the fun she could out of life. She wore bright shades of coral and red, and always matched her lipstick to her clothes, and she wore jewelry on every appendage. Her hair was always teased and ratted into a puffy silver-white ball. When I was little, she had traveled a lot and nearly always brought presents for us.

Whenever Aunt Gretchen dropped in to stay for a week or so, it had never been a convenient time for Mother. Putting two strong-minded women in the same house was like setting two trains on one track and waiting for the collision. Mother would have liked to limit Aunt Gretchen's visits, but she hadn't dared. One of the few times I ever heard my father speak sharply to my mother was when she was complaining about his meddlesome sister.

"I don't give a damn if she turns the whole house upside down," Dad said. "She saved my life."

When Dad was still in grade school, his father, my Pappaw, had left the family for good, telling people his wife was the meanest woman who ever lived, and crazy too, and while he could have put up with a crazy woman, there was nothing worse than being married to a mean one. He disappeared from Conroe, where they had lived, and was never heard from again.

A person might have hoped Pappaw's leaving would have given Mammaw cause for reflection, and maybe inspired her to be a little nicer. Instead Mammaw went the other way. She wore her arm out on her two children, Gretchen and Churchill, whenever she was provoked. And apparently just about everything provoked her. She'd reach for kitchen utensils, garden tools, anything she could get a hold of, and she'd beat her children half to death.

Back then people were more tolerant of such things, so there was no public interference in what was viewed as the family's private business. Gretchen knew she and her little brother were in for certain death if she didn't get them both out of there.

She saved up money from taking in extra washing and sewing, and just after her sixteenth birthday, she got Churchill up in the middle of the night, packed their clothes in a cardboard suitcase, and walked him to the end of the street, where her boyfriend met them with his car. The boyfriend drove them forty miles from Conroe to Houston and dropped them off with the promise he'd visit soon. He never did. That was fine with Gretchen — she hadn't expected him to. She had supported herself and Churchill with a job at the telephone company. Mammaw never found them, and it was doubtful she had even looked.

Years later when they figured Mammaw was too old to do them any harm, Gretchen had someone check on her. They found out she was living in a pitiful mess, with piles of trash and varmints all in her house. So Gretchen and Churchill had her put in a nursing home, where she happily bullied the other residents and the staff for about ten years until she passed. Churchill never did go visit her, but Gretchen had from time to time. She would take Mammaw out to the local Luby's, maybe off to Beall's to buy some new housedresses, and return her to the nursing home.

"Was she nice to you when you took 'er places?" I once asked Aunt Gretchen.

The question had made her smile. "No, honey. She didn't know how to be nice. Anything you did for her, she felt she was entitled and deserved even more."

"Well, why'd you go take care of Mammaw and visit her, after all she'd done? I'd have just let 'er rot."

"Well . . ." Gretchen had pursed her mouth thoughtfully. "I figured she couldn't help the way she was. She was broke when I got her."

The past few years had slowed Gretchen down quite a bit. She'd become a little forgetful, a little querulous. She moved as if her joints weren't banded together as tight as they should have been. There was a new translucent quality to her thinned-out skin,

blue veins showing underneath like a dia-
gram sketch that hadn't been fully erased.
She had come to live with us since Mother
had died, which pleased Dad since he
wanted to keep an eye on her.

Bringing Carrington into the house
seemed to have given Gretchen a much-
needed jump start. No one could doubt the
two of them adored each other.

Dressed in pink and purple, her pale
golden hair caught in a high ponytail with a
huge sparkly bow, Carrington was the picture of nine-year-old haute couture. She was
carrying the bridal bouquet, the smaller version that had been made for Liberty to
throw. "I'm gonna toss this," Carrington announced. "Liberty can't throw near as good
as me."

Gretchen came forward, beaming. "You
were the prettiest bride I've ever seen," she
said, hugging Liberty. "What are you going
to wear for your going-away outfit?"

"This is my going-away outfit," Liberty
replied.

"You're wearing pants?"

"It's an Escada suit, Aunt Gretchen," I
said. "Very stylish."

"You need more jewelry," Gretchen told
Liberty. "That outfit's too plain."

"I don't have much jewelry," Liberty

50

said, smiling.

"You've got a diamond ring the size of a doorknob," I remarked. "That's a great start." I grinned at Liberty's wince of embarrassment over the engagement ring she thought was too big. Naturally my brother Jack had compounded her discomfort by nicknaming the diamond the "pet rock."

"You need a bracelet," Gretchen said decisively, holding out something in a little velvet pouch. "Take this, Liberty. A little something jangly to let people know you're in the neighborhood."

Liberty opened the pouch carefully, and my heart contracted as I saw what it was: the gold charm bracelet Gretchen had worn forever, strung with charms from all the exotic places she had gone in her life.

She had promised it to me when I was five years old.

I remembered the exact day — she had brought me a junior tool kit complete with a leather belt with loops and pockets. They were real working tools, including a C-clamp, an awl, saw, pliers, level, hammer, eight wrenches, and a set of Phillips-head screwdrivers.

As soon as Mother had seen me strapping on the tool belt, she had gone bug-eyed. She had opened her mouth, and before a single

51

syllable came out, I knew she was going to tell Aunt Gretchen to take the gift back. So I clutched a handful of tools and ran to Dad, who was just coming into the family room. "Look what Aunt Gretchen brung me!"

"Well, isn't that nice," Dad had said, smiling first at Gretchen, then at my mother. The smile had ossified as he saw her face.

"Gretchen," Mother had said crisply, "I'd like to be asked the next time you buy a gift for my daughter. I'm not planning on raising a construction worker."

My heels had stopped bouncing. "I'm not giving 'em back."

"Don't sass your mother," Dad said.

"Land's sake," Gretchen had exclaimed. "They're toys, Ava. Haven likes to make things. Nothing wrong with that."

Mother's voice had been full of prickly burrs. "I'm the one to decide what's best for my own daughter, Gretchen. If you know so much about children, you should've had one of your own." She had stalked from the room, past me and Dad, leaving a chill of silence in her wake.

Gretchen had sighed, shaking her head as she looked at Dad.

"Can I keep the tool kit?" I had asked.

Dad had thrown me an exasperated glance and gone after Mother.

I had gone to Gretchen slowly, my hands clenched tight in front of me. She was quiet, but I knew what I had to do. I unstrapped the tool belt and laid it carefully back into the box. "I guess you should have gotten me a tea set," I said glumly. "Take it back, Aunt Gretchen. She'd never let me play with it anyway."

Gretchen had patted her knee, and I crawled into her lap, snuggling into the scents of powder and hair spray and Rive Gauche perfume. Seeing how intrigued I was by her charm bracelet, she took it off and let me look at it. She'd bought herself a charm every time she went to a new place. I found a tiny Eiffel Tower, a pineapple from Hawaii, a Memphis bale of cotton, a matador with a little swirling cape, crossed snow skis from New Hampshire, and too many others to name.

"Someday," Gretchen had said, "I'm going to give this bracelet to you. And you can add your own charms."

"Will I go as many places as you, Aunt Gretchen?"

"You may not want to. People like me only travel because they don't have enough reasons to stay put."

"When I'm big," I'd said, "I'll *never* stay put."

Gretchen had forgotten that promise, I thought. It wasn't her fault. She'd forgotten a lot of things lately. *It's okay,* I told myself. *Let it go.* But I knew the story behind every charm. And it seemed as if Gretchen were taking those handfuls of memories away from me and bestowing them on Liberty. Somehow I forced a smile and held it.

My aunt made a show of fastening the bracelet on Liberty's wrist. Carrington danced around the two of them with excitement, demanding to see the charms. My smile didn't feel like it was part of my face. It hung there like a picture on a wall, suspended by tacks and wires.

"I think I'm supposed to be doing something with this," I said lightly, picking the veil up from the bed, draping it over my arm. "I'm a lousy maid of honor, Liberty. You should fire me."

She threw me a quick glance. Despite my cheerful mask, she saw something that caused her to look troubled.

When we all left the room, Carrington and Gretchen went first and Liberty stopped me with a light touch on my arm. "Haven," she whispered, the bracelet jingling, "were you supposed to have this someday?"

"Oh, no, no," I said at once. "I'm not a fan of charm bracelets. They catch on things."

We walked downstairs, while Gretchen and Carrington waited for the elevator.

As we got to the bottom step, someone approached in a long, relaxed stride. I looked up and saw a pair of startling blue eyes. A thrill of alarm ran through me as he stopped beside the newel post and leaned against it comfortably. My face turned aspirin-white. It was him, the guy from the wine cellar, Mr. Blue-Collar-in-a-Tux, big and sexy and as cocky as a junkyard dog. He gave me a brief and impersonal glance, his attention focusing immediately on Liberty.

To my astonishment, Liberty regarded him with no awe or curiosity whatsoever, only a resigned grin. She stopped and folded her arms across her chest. "A pony, for a wedding present?"

A smile touched his wide mouth. "Carrington liked him when we went riding." His accent was a little more pronounced than it had been in the wine cellar, melting into the hot-tar drawl you mostly heard in small towns or trailer parks. "Figured you already have everything you need, so I got a little something for your sister."

"Do you know what it costs to stable that 'little something'?" Liberty asked without heat.

"I'll take him back if you want me to."

"You know Carrington would never forgive us. You've put my husband in a difficult position, Hardy."

His smile turned gently mocking. "You know how I hate to hear that."

Hardy.

I turned my face away and closed my eyes sickly, just for a second. Shit. Just . . . shit. Not only had I kissed someone other than my boyfriend, he also happened to be an enemy of the family. My brother's worst enemy, who had deliberately ruined a huge biofuel deal that had meant a lot to Gage personally and professionally.

From what little I knew, Hardy Cates had once been in love with Liberty, but he'd left her and broken her heart, and now he'd come back to make trouble.

That kind always did.

It was humiliating to realize that he hadn't been attracted to me at all, that his proposition in the wine cellar had been designed as another strike against the Travises. Hardy Cates wanted to embarrass the family, and he had no problem using me to do it.

"Haven," Liberty said, "this is an old friend of mine. Hardy Cates, this is my sister-in-law, Haven Travis."

"Miss Travis," he said softly.

I braced myself to look at him. His eyes were an astonishing blue-upon-blue in his sun-cured complexion. Although he was expressionless, I noticed the tiny laugh lines that whisked outward from the corners of those eyes. He extended a hand, but I couldn't take it. I was actually afraid of what might happen, how I might feel, if I touched him again.

Smiling at my hesitation, Hardy spoke to Liberty while his gaze remained locked on mine. "Your sister-in-law's a mite skittish, Liberty."

"If you're here to make a scene —" she began calmly.

His gaze moved to her. "No, ma'am. Just wanted to give you my best wishes."

Something softened in her face, and she reached out to clasp his hand briefly. "Thank you."

A new voice entered the conversation. "Hey, there." It was my brother Jack, looking relaxed. But there was a glint in his hard black eyes that silently warned of trouble to come. "Mr. Cates. I've been told you weren't included on the guest list. So I have to ask you to leave."

Hardy gave him a measuring glance.

In the silence that followed, I went tense in

every muscle, praying silently that a fistfight wouldn't break out at Gage's wedding. Glancing at Liberty, I saw she had turned pale. I thought vengefully that Hardy Cates was a selfish bastard, turning up at her wedding like that.

"No problem," Hardy said with soft insolence. "I got what I came for."

"Let me show you out," Jack said.

Liberty and I both let out our breaths as they departed. "I hope he's gone before Gage sees him," Liberty said.

"Believe me, Jack will make sure of that." Now I understood why she had chosen my brother over that rascal. "Cates is obviously a guy on the make," I said. "He could probably sell butter to a cow."

"Hardy's ambitious," Liberty admitted. "But he came from nothing. If you knew some of the things he had to overcome . . ." She sighed. "I bet within a year, he'll marry some River Oaks debutante who'll help take him to the top."

"He'd need a lot of money for that. We River Oaks debutantes are expensive."

"Of all the things he wants," Liberty said, "money's the easiest to get."

Carrington ran up to us, having finally emerged from the elevator. "Come on," she said in excitement. "Everyone's going outside. The fireworks are about to start!"

Just what I need, I thought. *More fireworks.*

The next morning I was packing a suitcase in my room when Nick came in. We had occupied separate bedrooms during our stay in River Oaks, which Nick had said was just fine because there was no way he was going to touch me when we were under the same roof as my father.

"He's old, and he's only half your size," I had told Nick, laughing. "What do you think he's going to do, beat you up or something?"

"It's the 'or something' that scares me," Nick had said.

As soon as Nick came into the room, I knew he had talked to my father. The stress showed on his face. He was hardly the first to come away looking like that after a heart-to-heart with Churchill Travis.

"I told you," I said. "Dad's impossible. He wouldn't accept you no matter how wonderful you were."

"Were?" He gave me a comical look.

"Are." I put my arms around him and laid my head on his chest. "What did he say?" I whispered.

"Basically a variation on the 'not a plug nickel' theme." Nick eased my head back and looked down at me. "I told him I was going to put you first, always. That I will earn enough to take care of you. I told him I just wanted his approval so there wouldn't be conflict between you and your family."

"Travises love conflict," I said.

A smile entered Nick's hazel eyes, all green and gold and brown. There was a touch of color on his high cheekbones, a remnant of the confrontation with my bulldog of a father. The smile vanished from his eyes as he smoothed my hair back, his hand curving gently over the back of my skull. He was handsome, grave, concerned. "Is this what you want, Haven? I couldn't live with myself if I did something to hurt you."

Emotion made my voice unsteady. "The only thing that would hurt is for you to stop loving me."

"That's not even possible. You're the one, Haven. You're the one for me, always." He bent his head, his mouth taking mine in a long, slow dream of a kiss. I responded avidly, lifting against him.

"Hey," he said softly. "What do you say we get out of here and go get married?"

CHAPTER THREE

Contrary to my expectations of elopement as a furtive Elvis-supervised ceremony in Las Vegas, there were hotels in Florida, Hawaii, and Arizona that offered "elopement packages" including the wedding service, the hotel stay, massages, and a meal plan. Gage and Liberty paid for our elopement to the Keys — it was their wedding present to me and Nick.

Having taken a stand against my marriage to Nick, Dad went through with his threat to cut me off entirely. No money, no communication. "He'll come around," my brothers told me, but I said emphatically that I didn't want Dad to come around, I'd had enough of him and his controlling ways for a lifetime.

Liberty and I had our first argument when she tried to tell me that Churchill still loved me and always would.

"Sure he does," I told her curtly. "As a

pawn. As a child. But as an adult with my own opinions and preferences . . . no. He only loves people when they spend their lives trying to please him."

"He needs you," Liberty persisted. "Someday —"

"No he doesn't," I said. "He's got you." It was unfair of me to lash out at her, and I knew it, but I couldn't stop myself. "You be the good daughter," I said recklessly. "I've had enough of him for a lifetime."

It was a long time before Liberty and I spoke again.

Nick and I moved to Plano, north of Dallas, where Nick worked as a cost estimator at a construction firm. It wasn't something he wanted to do forever, but the pay was good, especially the overtime. I got an entry-level position as a marketing coordinator for the Darlington Hotel, which meant I assisted the director of communications with PR and marketing projects.

The Darlington was a sleek, modern hotel, a single elliptical-shaped structure that would have looked phallic enough, except it had also been covered in a skin of pink granite. Maybe that subliminal suggestion was partly responsible for the Darlington having been voted as the most romantic hotel in Dallas.

"You Dallasites and your architecture," I told Nick. "Every building in town looks like a penis or a cereal box."

"You like the red flying horse," Nick pointed out.

I had to admit he was right. I had a weakness for that neon Pegasus, an iconic sign that had perched on top of the Magnolia Building since 1934. It lent a lot of personality to an otherwise sterile skyline.

I wasn't sure what to make of Dallas. Compared to Houston, it was squeaky-clean, cosmopolitan, tightly hinged. Fewer cowboy hats, much better manners. And Dallas was a lot more politically consistent than Houston, which had drastic public policy swings from election to election.

Dallas, so tasteful and composed, seemed to feel it had something to prove, like a woman who was too concerned about what to wear on the second date. Maybe that had something to do with the fact that unlike most great cities of the world, it had no port. Dallas had become a player in the 1870s when two railroads, the Houston and Texas Central and the Texas and Pacific, both met and crossed at a ninety-degree angle, thereby making the city a big commercial center.

Nick's family all lived in or around Dallas.

His parents had divorced and married other people when he was still a kid. Between all the stepsisters and stepbrothers, and half sisters and half brothers, and the full-blood siblings, I had trouble figuring out who belonged to whom. It didn't seem to matter, though, because none of them were close.

We bought a small condo with two parking spaces and access to a community pool. I decorated the condo with cheap, brightly colored contemporary furniture, and added some baskets and Mexican ceramics. In our living room, I hung a huge framed reprint of an old travel poster, featuring a dark-haired girl holding a basket of fruit beneath a huge banner reading, VISIT MEXICO: LAND OF SPLENDOR.

"It's our own special style," I told Nick when he complained that our furniture was crap and he didn't like Southwestern decor. "I call it 'Ikea Loco.' I think I'm onto something. Soon everyone will be copying us. Besides, it's all we can afford."

"We could afford a fucking palace," Nick replied darkly, "if your father wasn't such an asshole."

I was taken aback by the flash of animosity, a lightning strike that had come out of nowhere. My pleasure in the condo was an irritant to Nick. I was just playing house, he told me. When I'd lived like middle-class people for a while, he'd like to see if I was still so happy.

"Of course I will be," I said. "I have you. I don't need a mansion to be happy."

It seemed at times that Nick was a lot more affected by my changed circumstances than I was. He resented our small budget for my sake, he said. He hated that we couldn't afford a second car.

"I really don't mind," I said, and that made him angry because if he minded it, so should I.

After the storms had passed, however, the peace was all the sweeter.

Nick called me at work at least twice a day just to see how things were going. We talked all the time. "I want us to tell each other everything," he said one night, when we were halfway into a bottle of wine. "My parents always had secrets. You and I should be completely honest and open."

I loved that idea in theory. In practice, however, it was hard on my self-esteem. Complete honesty, it turned out, was not always kind.

"You're so pretty," Nick told me one night after we'd made love. His hand moved over my body, coasting up the gentle slope of my chest. I had small breasts, a shallow B cup at most. Even before we were married, Nick had laughingly complained about my lack of endowment, saying he'd buy me implants except a pair of big boobs would look ridiculous on a woman as short and slight as me. His fingertips moved up to my face, tracing the curve of my cheek. "Big brown eyes . . . cute little nose . . . beautiful mouth. It doesn't matter that you don't have a body."

"I have a body," I said.

"I meant boobs."

"I have those too. They're just not big ones."

"Well, I love you anyway."

I wanted to point out that Nick didn't have a perfect body either, but I knew that would start a fight. Nick didn't react well to criticism, even when it was gentle and well meant. He wasn't used to anyone finding fault with him. I, on the other hand, had been raised on a steady diet of critiques and evaluations.

Mother had always told me detailed stories about her friends' daughters, how well behaved they were, how nice it was that they would sit still for piano lessons, or make tissue-paper flowers for their mothers, or show off their latest ballet steps on cue. I had wished with all my heart that I could have been more like those winsome little girls, but I hadn't been able to keep from rebelling against being miscast as a smaller version of Ava Travis. And then she had died, leaving me with a mountain of regrets and no way to atone.

Our holidays — the first Thanksgiving, the first Christmas, the first New Year's — were quiet. We hadn't joined a church yet, and it seemed that all Nick's friends, the ones he said were his family, were occupied with their own families. I approached cooking Christmas dinner as if it were a science class project. I studied cookbooks, made charts, set timers, measured ingredients, and dissected meat and vegetables into the appropriate dimensions. I knew the results of my efforts were passable but uninspired, but Nick said it was the best turkey, the best mashed potatoes, the best pecan pie he'd ever eaten.

"It must be the sight of me in oven mitts," I said.

Nick began stringing noisy kisses along my arm as if he were Pepe Le Pew. "You are ze goddess of ze keetchen."

The Darlington had been so busy during the holidays that I had had to work overtime, while Nick's job had eased up until after New Year's. With our unsynchronized schedules, it was frustrating and time-consuming for him to drive back and forth all the time. Nothing was ever finished . . . the condo was always a mess, the fridge was seldom stocked, there were always piles of dirty laundry.

"We can't afford to take all my shirts to the dry cleaner's," Nick said the day after Christmas. "You'll have to learn how to do them."

"Me?" I had never ironed anything in my life. The proper pressing of a shirt was a mystery of the universe akin to black holes and dark matter. "How come you can't do your own shirts?"

"I need you to help. Is it too much to ask for you to give me a hand with my clothes?"

"No, of course not. I'm sorry. I just don't know how. I'm afraid I'll screw them up."

"I'll show you how. You'll learn." Nick smiled and patted me on the backside. "You just have to get in touch with your inner Martha Stewart."

I told him I had always kept my inner Martha Stewart chained in the basement, but for his sake I would set her loose.

Nick was patient as he took me step by step through the process, showing me exactly how he liked his shirts starched and ironed. He was particular about the details.

At first it was sort of fun, in the same way grouting is fun when you first do it . . . until you face an entire bathroom full of tiles. Or a laundry basket crammed with unwashed shirts. No matter how I tried, I could never seem to get the shirts exactly the way Nick liked them.

My ironing technique became the focus of a near-daily inspection. Nick would go to our closet, file through the row of pressed garments, and tell me where I'd gone wrong. "You need to iron the edges more slowly to get all the little creases out," or, "You need to redo the armhole seams." "You need to use less starch." "The back's not smooth enough."

Exasperated and defeated, I finally resorted to using my personal money — we each had the same amount to spend each week — to have Nick's shirts professionally laundered and pressed. I thought it was a good solution. But when Nick found a row of shirts hanging in plastic coverings in the closet, he was pissed.

"I thought we agreed," he said shortly, "that you were going to learn to do them."

"I used my own money." I gave him a placating smile. "I'm ironing deficient. Maybe I need a multivitamin."

He refused to smile back. "You're not trying hard enough."

I found it hard to believe we were having an argument over something as trivial as shirts. It wasn't really about the shirts. Maybe he felt I wasn't contributing enough to the relationship. Maybe I needed to be more loving, more supportive. He was going through stress. Holiday stress, work stress, newlywed stress.

"I'll try harder," I said. "But sweetheart . . . is there anything else bothering you? Something we should talk about besides ironing? You know I'd do anything for you."

Nick gave me a cold stare. "All I need is for you to fucking get something right for a change."

I was angry for approximately ten minutes. After that, I was suffused with fear. I was going to fail at marriage, the most important thing I had ever tried to do.

So I called Todd, who sympathized and said everyone had stupid arguments with their partner. We agreed it was just part of a normal relationship. I didn't dare talk to anyone in my family, because I would have rather died than let Dad suspect the marriage wasn't going well.

I apologized abjectly to Nick.

"No, it was my fault," he said, wrapping his arms around me in a warm, firm hug. His forgiveness was such a relief, I felt tears spring to my eyes. "I'm asking too much of you," he continued. "You can't help the way you were brought up. You were never expected to do things for other people. But in the real world, it's the small gestures, the little things, that show a guy you love him. I'd appreciate it if you'd make more of an effort." And he rubbed my feet after dinner, and told me to stop apologizing.

The next day, I saw a new can of spray starch in the laundry closet. The ironing board had been unfolded and set up for me, so I could practice while Nick started dinner.

We went out one night with two other couples, who were guys from the construction firm Nick worked at, and their wives. I was excited about doing something social. It had been a surprise to discover that although Nick had grown up in Dallas, he didn't seem to have any old friends to introduce me to. They had all moved away, or weren't worth bothering with, he had told me. I was eager to make some friends in Dallas, and I wanted to make a good impression.

At lunch hour I went to the hotel salon and had one of the stylists trim several inches of my long hair. When she was finished the floor was littered with wavy black locks, and my hair was medium-length and sleek. "You should never let your hair get longer than this," the stylist told me. "The way you had it before was too much for someone as petite as you. It was overwhelming your face."

I hadn't mentioned to Nick that I was getting a haircut. He loved it long, and I knew he would have tried to talk me out of it. Besides, I thought once he saw how flattering it was, not to mention easier to care for, he would change his mind.

As soon as he picked me up, Nick started to frown. "Looks like you've been busy today." His fingers were tight on the steering wheel.

"Do you like it? It feels great." I shook my head from side to side like a hair model. "It was about time I had a good, healthy trim."

"That's not a trim. Most of your hair is gone." Every word was edged with disapproval and disappointment.

"I was tired of my college look. I think this is more polished."

"Your long hair was special. Now it looks ordinary."

I felt as if someone had just emptied a syringe of liquid anxiety into my veins. "I'm sorry if you don't like it. But it was too much work. And it's my hair, anyway."

"Well, I'm the one who has to look at you every day."

My skin seemed to shrink until my body was compressed in a tight envelope. "The stylist said it was overwhelming my face."

"I'm glad you and she think the world needs to see more of your goddamn face," he muttered.

I endured about fifteen minutes of thick, choking silence while Nick maneuvered through the six o'clock traffic. We were going straight to the restaurant to meet his friends.

"By the way," Nick said abruptly, "just so you won't be surprised, I've told people your name is Marie."

I stared at his profile in complete incomprehension. Marie was my middle name, the one no one had ever used unless I was in trouble. The sound of "Haven Marie" had always been a sure sign that something had hit the fan.

"Why didn't you tell them my first name?" I managed to ask.

Nick didn't look at me. "Because it makes you sound like a hick."

"I like my regular name. I don't want to be Marie. I want —"

"Jesus, can't I just have a normal wife with a normal name?" He was turning red, breathing hard, the air clotted with hostility.

The whole situation felt unreal. I was married to a man who didn't like my name. He'd never said anything about it before. *This isn't Nick,* I told myself. The real Nick was the guy I'd married. I glanced at him covertly. He looked like an ordinary, exasperated husband. He was asking for normal, and I wasn't altogether certain what that was.

I worked to steady my own breathing. We were almost at the restaurant — we couldn't walk in there looking like we'd just had a fight. My face felt as if it had been coated with glass. "Okay," I said. "So we'll be Nick and Marie tonight."

"Okay." He seemed to relax a little.

After that evening, which had gone well, Nick hardly ever called me Haven, even when it was just the two of us. He said it would be too confusing when we went out with other people, if I wasn't used to being called Marie. I told myself it could be a good thing, this name change. I would let go of my past baggage. I could become whoever I wanted, a better person. And it pleased Nick, which I wanted desperately to do.

I'm Marie, I told myself. *Marie, the married woman who lives in Dallas and works at the Darlington and knows how to iron a shirt.* Marie, whose husband loved her.

■ ■ ■ ■

Our marriage was like a machine I learned how to operate but never understood the inner mechanisms that made it work. I knew how to do the things that kept it running smoothly, all the minor and major requirements that kept Nick on an even keel. When Nick was happy, I was rewarded with affection. But when something had set Nick off, he would become sullen or irritable. It could take days to coax him back into a good temper. His changeable mood was the thermostat that regulated our household.

By the time our first anniversary approached, I realized that Nick's bad days, the days I was required to sympathize and compensate for every small injustice done to him, were outnumbering the good days. I didn't know how to fix that, but I suspected it was my fault. I knew other people's marriages were different, that they didn't constantly worry about how to anticipate their husbands' needs, they weren't always walking on eggshells. Certainly my own parents' marriage hadn't been like this. If anything, the household had revolved around my mother's needs and wants, while my father showed up every now and then to appease her.

Nick maintained a steadily percolating anger toward my family, blaming my father for not giving us money to buy a house. He pushed me to make contact with my father and brothers, to ask for things from them, and he got angry when I refused.

"It wouldn't do any good," I told him, even though that wasn't true. Regardless of my father's attitude, my brothers would have given me anything I asked for. Especially Gage. The few occasions we had talked on the phone, he had asked if there was anything he could do for me and Nick, and I had said no, absolutely not, things were fantastic. I was afraid to give Gage any hint of how things really were. One pulled thread and I might unravel completely.

"Your dad will have to start doing things for us when we have kids," Nick told me. "It would be a public embarrassment for him to have grandchildren living in a damn shack. He'll have to cough up some money then, the stingy bastard."

It worried me that Nick seemed to regard our future children as tools that would be used to pry open the Travis family coffers. I'd always planned to have children when I felt ready, but this situation couldn't begin to accommodate a fussy, demanding infant. It was all I could do to keep my fussy, demanding husband happy.

I had never had problems sleeping, but I began having dreams that woke me up at night, leaving me exhausted the next day. Since my tossing and turning kept Nick awake, I often went to the sofa in the middle of the night, shivering beneath a throw blanket. I dreamed of losing my teeth, of falling from tall buildings.

"It was so weird," I told Nick one morning while he was drinking his coffee, "this new one I had last night. I was in a park somewhere, just walking by myself, and my right leg fell off. No blood or anything. It was like I was a Barbie doll. I was so upset, wondering how I was going to get around without that leg, and then my arm broke off at the elbow, and I picked it up and tried to hold it in place, and I was thinking, 'I need this arm, I've got to find someone to reattach it.' So then —"

"Did you take your pill yet this morning?" Nick interrupted.

I had been on birth control ever since we had started sleeping together. "No, I always take it after breakfast. Why? Do you think the hormones may be giving me bad dreams?"

"No, I think you're giving yourself bad dreams. And I asked because it's time for you to go off the pill. We should start having kids while we're still young."

I stared at him. A huge wave of unwillingness went through me, every cell in my body resisting the idea of a great big hormone-fueled helplessness that would make everything impossible. But I couldn't say no. That would set off a bad mood that might last for days. I had to work Nick around to changing his mind. "Do you really think we're ready?" I asked. "It might be better to put away some money first."

"We won't need to. Your dad will be a lot more reasonable once he finds out Gage and Liberty aren't the only ones who can pop out a kid."

I realized Nick had less interest in the baby itself than in its usefulness as a way to manipulate Churchill Travis. Would he feel differently when the baby was born? Would he be one of those fathers who melted at the sight of the small person he had helped to bring into the world?

As hard as I tried to imagine it, I couldn't see Nick summoning the patience to deal with a screaming infant, a messy toddler, a needy child. It frightened me, thinking of how tightly I would be bound to him, how dependent I would be once we had a baby together.

I went into the bathroom to get ready for work, brushing mascara onto my lashes, slicking on lip gloss. Nick followed, rummaging through the assortment of cosmetics and hair products I had set out on the counter. He found the round plastic container my birth control pills came in, and flipped it open to reveal the wheel of pastel-colored tablets.

"You don't need these anymore." He tossed the pills into the trash.

"I need to finish the cycle," I protested. "And usually before you try to get pregnant, you go in to get a checkup —"

"You're healthy. You'll be fine." He put a hand on my shoulder, forcing me up as I bent to retrieve the pills. "Leave them."

A disbelieving laugh bubbled from my throat. I had been conditioned over months to tolerate Nick's whims for the sake of harmony, but this was too much. I was not going to be forced into having a baby neither of us was ready for.

"Nick, I'd rather wait." I picked up a hairbrush and began to drag it through my tangled hair. "And this really isn't a good time to talk about having children, with both of us getting ready for work and —"

"I'll decide what we talk about and when!" The explosive intensity of his voice startled me into dropping the hairbrush. "I didn't realize I had to make a goddamn appointment with you to talk about our personal life!"

I went white with alarm, my heart kicking into a violent rhythm. "Nick —"

"Do you ever think about anyone or anything besides yourself?" Anger had knotted his throat and the tiny muscles of his face. "It's always about what *you* want . . . you selfish bitch, what about what *I* want?"

He leaned over me, towering and furious, and I shrank against the mirror. "Nick, I just . . ." My mouth had gone so dry, I could barely force the words out. "I'm not saying no. I just want . . . would like . . . to talk about it later."

That earned a look of soul-shredding contempt. "I don't know. It may not be worth talking about. This whole marriage may not be worth a shit pile. You think you did me some big fucking favor, marrying me? I was the one who did you a favor. You think anyone else would put up with your crap?"

"Nick —" Panicky and confused, I watched him walk to the bedroom. I started to follow, but I hung back, fearful of maddening him further. The men in my family were generally slow to anger, and once they worked up to an explosion, it was over soon. Nick's temper was different, a fire that fed on itself, growing until its proportions had far outstripped the cause. In this case, I wasn't sure what the best strategy should be . . . If I went after him to apologize, it might pour fuel on his rage. But if I stayed in the bathroom, he might take new offense at being ignored.

I settled for hovering at the doorway, straddling both rooms, watching for a sign of what Nick wanted. He went to the closet and pushed through the clothing with quick, vicious movements, hunting for a shirt. Deciding to retreat, I went back into the bathroom.

My cheeks looked white and stiff. I brushed on some pink blush in light strokes, but the tinted powder seemed to sit on top of my skin, not blending. The brush caught at the mist of nervous sweat and made ruddy streaks. I reached for a washcloth, about to clean it all off, and that was when the world seemed to explode.

Nick had come back, cornering me, clutching something in one fist. Screaming. I'd never had someone scream into my face like that before, certainly not a man, and it was a kind of death. I was reduced to the level of an animal under attack, unable to slip beyond the whiteness of fear, frozen in mute incomprehension.

The thing in his hand was a striped shirt . . . I had ruined it somehow . . . a mistake . . . but Nick said it was sabotage. I had done it on purpose, he said. He needed it for an important meeting this morning, and I said *no, I didn't mean to I'm so sorry* but every word brought murderous heat to his face and his arm drew back and the world caught fire.

My head snapped to the side, my cheek blazing, and droplets of sweat and tears went flying. A burning stillness settled. The veins in my face felt huge and pumping.

I was slow to comprehend that Nick had hit me. I stood swaying, blank, using my fingertips to explore where the heat had turned to numbness.

I couldn't see through the blur in my eyes, but I heard Nick's voice, thick with disgust. "Look what you made me do."

He went back into the bedroom.

No retreat. I couldn't run from the apartment. We had only one car. And I didn't know where I would go. I held the washcloth under cold water, sat on the closed toilet seat and held the dripping mass against my cheek.

There was no one I could tell. This was something Todd or my other friends couldn't comfort me about, couldn't say it was part of a normal relationship. Shame spread through me, leaking from the marrow of my bones . . . the feeling that I must have deserved it, or it wouldn't have happened. I knew that wasn't right. But something in me, in the way I had been formed, made it impossible to escape that spreading shame. It had lurked inside me forever, waiting to surface. Waiting for Nick, or someone like him. I was stained with it, like invisible ink . . . in the right light, it would show.

I waited without moving while Nick finished getting ready for work. I didn't stir even when I heard him call the Darlington and tell them I wouldn't be in that day. His wife was sick, he said regretfully. The flu or something, he didn't know what. He sounded compassionate and concerned. He chuckled a little at something the other person on the line said. "Yes," he said, "I'll take good care of her."

I waited until I heard the jangle of the keys, and the front door closing.

Moving like an old woman, I reached into the trash and pulled out my pills. I took one, and scooped water into my mouth with my hand, and downed it with a painful swallow.

I found the striped shirt on the floor of the bedroom, and I laid it out on the mattress. I couldn't see anything wrong with it. I couldn't find the flaw that had driven Nick berserk. "What did I do?" I asked aloud, my fingers trailing down the stripes as if clawing through iron bars. What had I done wrong?

The urge to please was a sickness in me. I knew that, and I did it anyway. I washed and starched and ironed the striped shirt all over again. Every thread in the cotton weave was pressed perfectly flat, every button gleaming and pristine. I hung it in the closet and I checked all the other shirts, and aligned his shoes and hung all his ties so the bottoms were all at the same level.

When Nick got home, the condo was clean and the table was set, and I had put a King Ranch casserole in the oven. His favorite dinner. I had a hard time looking at him.

But Nick came in contrite and smiling, bringing a bouquet of mixed flowers. He handed me the fragrant offering, petals rustling in layers of tissue and cellophane. "Here, sweetheart." He leaned down to kiss my cheek, the one he had struck earlier. The side of my face was pink and swollen. I held still while his mouth touched my skin. I wanted to jerk away from him. I wanted to hit him back. Mostly I wanted to cry.

Instead I took the flowers to the sink and began to unwrap them mechanically.

"I shouldn't have done that this morning," Nick said behind me. "I thought about you all day."

"I thought about you too." I put the bouquet into a vase and filled it with water, unable to face the prospect of cutting and arranging the flowers.

"It was just the last straw, seeing what you'd done to my shirt."

I wiped the counter slowly, moving a paper towel in tight circles. "I don't understand what was wrong with it."

"It had about ten times too much starch. I mean, I could have cut a slice of bread with one of those sleeves." A long pause, and then he sighed. "I overreacted. I know that. But like I said, it was the last straw. So much other stuff has been driving me crazy, and seeing what you'd done to my shirt was too much."

I turned to face him, gripping the edges of my long sleeves over my fingers until they were shrouded like cat paws. "What other stuff?"

"Everything. The way we live. This place is never clean and organized. We never have home-cooked meals. There's always piles of crap everywhere." He raised his hands as if in self-defense as he saw me start to speak. "Oh, I know, it looks great right now. And I can see you've put dinner in the oven. I appreciate that. But it should be like this all the time. And it can't be, with both of us working."

I understood right away what Nick wanted. But I didn't understand why he wanted it. "I can't quit my job," I said numbly. "We can't afford to lose my salary."

"I'm about to get a promotion. We'll be fine."

"But . . . what would I do all day?"

"Be a wife. Take care of the house. And me. And yourself." He came closer. "And I'll take care of you. You're going to get pregnant soon anyway. You'd have to quit then. So you may as well do it now."

"Nick, I don't think —"

"We're both stressed, sweetheart. This would help take the pressure off, for you to handle all the stuff that never gets done." Reaching out, Nick took one of my hands gently, and brought it to his face. "I'm sorry about what I did this morning," he murmured, nuzzling into my palm. "I swear it'll never happen again. No matter what."

"You scared me, Nick," I whispered. "You weren't yourself."

"You're right. You know that's not me." With infinite care, he brought me against him. "No one could love you as much as I do. You're everything to me. And we're going to take care of each other, right?"

"I don't know." My voice was scratchy and tight. I had never been so torn, wanting to stay and wanting to leave, loving and fearing him.

"You can always get another job if you want," Nick said reasonably. "But let's try it this way. I want you to be free for a change."

I heard myself whisper, "Please don't do it again, Nick."

"Never," he said at once, kissing my head, my ear, my neck. His fingers came very gently to my reddened cheek. "Poor baby," he murmured. "I'm so glad I did it open-handed, or you'd have a hell of a bruise."

CHAPTER FOUR

Little by little our marriage closed around me. At first it seemed like heaven when I stopped working. I had all the time I needed to make the condo look perfect. I vacuumed the carpet so the polyester nap was arranged in symmetrical stripes. Every square inch of the kitchen was sparkling and clean. I spent hours poring over recipes, improving my cooking skills. I arranged Nick's socks in color-coordinated rows in the drawer.

Just before Nick came home from the office, I put on makeup and changed my outfit. I had started to do that after he'd told me one night he hoped I wasn't one of those women who let themselves go after they'd caught a husband.

If Nick had been a jerk all the time, I wouldn't have been so compliant. It was the in-between moments that kept me with him, the evenings when we cuddled in front of the TV and watched the news, the impromptu slow dance after dinner when our favorite song came on. He could be affectionate and funny. He could be loving. And he was the first person in my life who had ever needed me. I was his audience, his reflection, his solace, the person without whom he could never be complete. He had found my worst weakness: I was one of those people who was desperate to be needed, to matter to someone.

There was a lot about our relationship that worked. The part that I had a hard time dealing with was the constant sense of being off balance. The men in my life, my fathers and brothers, had always been predictable. Nick, however, reacted differently at different times to the same behavior. I was never certain when I did something if it would be received with praise or displeasure. It made me anxious, always hunting for clues about how I should behave.

Nick remembered everything I had ever told him about my family and childhood, but he colored it all differently. He told me I had never really been loved by anyone but him. He told me what I really thought, who I really was, and he was so authoritative on the subject of me that I began to doubt my own perceptions. Especially when he echoed the standard phrases from my childhood . . .

"You need to get over it." "You're overreacting." "You take everything too personally." My own mother had said those things to me, and now Nick was saying them too.

His temper exploded without warning when I made the wrong sandwich for his lunch, when I'd forgotten to run a particular errand. Since I didn't have a car, I had to walk or bike a quarter mile to the grocery store, and I didn't always have time to accomplish all I needed to do. Nick never hit me after that first time. Instead he broke possessions I valued, jerking a delicate gold necklace from my throat, throwing a crystal vase. Sometimes he would push me against the wall and shout into my face. I dreaded that more than anything, the force of Nick's voice blowing all circuitry, shattering parts of me that couldn't be reassembled.

I began to lie compulsively, afraid to reveal some little thing I had said or done that Nick wouldn't like, anything that might set him off. I became a sycophant, assuring Nick he was smarter than everyone else put together, smarter than his boss, than the people at the bank, than anyone in his family or mine. I told him he was right even when it was obvious he was wrong. And in spite of all that, he was never satisfied.

Our sex life went downhill, at least from

my perspective, and I was fairly certain Nick didn't even notice. We had never been all that successful in the bedroom — I'd had no experience before Nick, and I had no way of knowing what to do.

In the beginning of our relationship, I'd found some pleasure in being with him. But gradually he had stopped doing the things he knew I liked, and sex became a slam-bam deal. Even if I had known enough to explain to Nick what I needed, it wouldn't have made a difference. He had no interest in the possibilities of sex beyond the simple matter of one body entering another.

I tried to be as accommodating as possible, doing what was necessary to get it over with quickly. Nick's favorite position was from behind, driving into me with straight, selfish thrusts that gave me no stimulation. He praised me for being one of those women who didn't make a big deal about foreplay. In truth, I was fine without foreplay — it would only have prolonged an act that was messy, often uncomfortable, and not at all romantic.

I realized that I was not a sexual person. I was not moved by the sight of Nick's well-exercised body, toned from spending most of his lunch hours at the gym. When we went out, I saw the way other women stared at my handsome husband and envied me.

I got a call one night from Liberty, and from the sound of her voice, I knew instantly that something was wrong. "Haven, I've got some bad news. It's about Gretchen . . ." As she went on, I felt weighted with shock and despair, and I strained to understand her, as if she were speaking in a foreign language. Gretchen had had a headache for about two days, and had fallen unconscious in her room — Dad had heard the thud from down the hall. She was dead by the time the paramedics arrived. A cerebral aneurism, they said at the hospital.

"I'm so sorry," Liberty said, her voice tear-clotted. I heard the sounds of her blowing her nose. "She was such a wonderful person. I know how much you loved each other."

I sat on the sofa and leaned my head back, letting tears run in a hot trail down the sides of my face. "When is the funeral?" I managed to ask.

"In two days. Will you come? Will you stay with Gage and me?"

"Yes. Thanks. I . . . How is Dad?" No matter what the state of our relationship was, I ached with sympathy for my father. Losing Gretchen would be hard for him, one of the hardest things he would ever face.

"I guess as well as could be expected." Liberty blew her nose again. She added in a constricted whisper, "I've never seen him cry before."

"I haven't either." I heard the key in the front door lock. Nick was home. I was relieved, wanting the comfort of his arms. "How is Carrington?" I asked, knowing that Liberty's little sister had been close to Gretchen.

"You're so sweet to ask . . . she's really torn up about it, but she'll be okay. It's hard for her to understand how everything can change so suddenly."

"It's hard even for grown-ups to understand." I pressed my sleeve over my wet eyes. "I don't know whether I'll drive or fly down. I'll call you after I talk to Nick and figure things out."

"Okay, Haven. Bye."

Nick came into the apartment, setting down his briefcase. "What's up?" he asked, frowning as he came to me.

"My aunt Gretchen died," I said, and started to cry again.

Nick came to sit beside me on the sofa, and put his arm around me. I nestled against his shoulder.

After a few minutes of consolation, Nick stood and went to the kitchen. He got a beer from the fridge. "I'm sorry, baby. I know this is tough for you. But it's probably a good thing that you can't go to the funeral."

I blinked in surprise. "I can go. If we don't have the money for a plane ticket, I can —"

"We only have one car." His voice changed. "I guess I'm supposed to sit in the apartment all weekend while you're in Houston?"

"Why don't you come with me?"

"I should have known you'd forget. We've got something going on this weekend, Marie." He looked at me hard, and I gave him a blank stare. "The company's annual crawfish boil, at the owner's house. Since this is my first year, there's no way I can miss it."

My eyes widened. "I . . . I . . . you want me to go to a crawfish boil instead of my aunt's funeral?"

"There's no choice. Jesus, Marie, do you want to cost me any chance of a promotion? I'm going to that crawfish boil, and I'm damn well not going to go alone. I need to have a wife there, and I need you to make a good impression."

"I can't," I said, more bewildered than angry. I couldn't believe my feelings about Gretchen would mean so little to him. "I need to be with my family. People will understand if you tell them —"

"*I'm* your family!" Nick threw the beer, the full can hitting the edge of the sink with an explosion of foam. "Just who is paying your bills, Marie? Who's keeping a roof over your head? *Me.* No one in your fucking family is helping us. I'm the breadwinner. You do what I say."

"I'm not your slave," I shot back. "I have the right to go to Gretchen's funeral, and I'm going to —"

"Try it." He sneered, reaching me in three angry strides. "Try it, Marie. You've got no money and no way to get there." He clenched my arms and shoved me hard, and I went stumbling back against the wall. "God knows how such an idiot managed to graduate from college," he said. "They don't give a shit about you, Marie. Try to get that through your thick head."

I sent Liberty an e-mail telling her I couldn't go to the funeral. I didn't explain why, and there was no reply from her. Since there were no calls from the rest of my family, I was pretty sure I knew what they thought of me for not going. Whatever they thought, however, it wasn't nearly as bad as the things I was thinking about myself.

I went to the crawfish boil with Nick. I

smiled the whole time. Everyone called me Marie. And I wore elbow-length sleeves to cover the bruises on my arms. I didn't cry one tear on the day of Gretchen's funeral.

But I did cry on Monday, when I got a small package in the mail. Opening it, I found Gretchen's bracelet with all its jaunty, jingly little charms.

"Dear Haven," read Liberty's note, "I know you were meant to have this."

Halfway through our second year of marriage, Nick's determination to get me pregnant had become all-consuming. I half suspected he would kill me if he knew I was still secretly taking birth control pills, so I hid them in one of my purses shoved back in a corner of our closet.

Convinced that the problem was me — it couldn't possibly be him — Nick sent me to the doctor. I cried in the doctor's office for an hour, telling him I felt anxious and miserable and had no idea why, and I came home with a prescription for antidepressants.

"You can't take that crap," Nick said, crumpling the slip of paper and tossing it into the trash. "It might be bad for the baby."

Our nonexistent baby. I thought guiltily of the pill I took every morning, a secret act that had become my last desperate bid for autonomy. It was difficult on the weekends, when Nick watched me like a hawk. I had to dash into the closet when he was in the shower, fumble for the cardboard wheel, pop a pill out and take it dry. If he caught me . . . I didn't know what he'd do.

"What did the doctor say about getting pregnant?" Nick asked, watching me closely.

"He said it could take up to a year."

I hadn't mentioned a word to the doctor about trying to get pregnant, only asked for my birth control prescription to be renewed.

"Did he tell you when the best days were? The days you're most fertile?"

"Right before I ovulate."

"Let's look at the calendar and figure it out. How long into the cycle do you ovulate?"

"Ten days, I guess."

As we went to the calendar, which I always marked with an *X* on the days my period started, my reluctance didn't seem to matter to Nick. I was going to be invaded, impregnated, and forced to go through the birthing process simply because he had decided so.

"I don't want it," I heard myself say in a sullen tone.

"You'll be happy once it happens."

"I still don't want it. I'm not ready."

Nick slammed the calendar onto the counter with such force, it sounded like the crack of a gunshot. "You'll never be ready. It'll never happen unless I push you into it. For God's sake, Marie, will you grow up and be a woman?"

I started to shake. Blood rushed up to my face, adrenaline pumping through my overworked heart. "I am a woman. I don't have to have a baby to prove that."

"You're a spoiled bitch. A parasite. That's why your family doesn't give a damn about you."

My own temper exploded. "And you're a selfish jerk!"

He slapped me so hard it whipped my face to the side, and my eyes watered heavily. There was a high-pitched whine in my ears. I swallowed and held my cheek. "You said you'd never do that again," I said hoarsely.

Nick was breathing heavily, his eyes crazy-wide. "It's your fault for driving me nuts. Damn it all, I'm going to straighten your ass out." He grabbed me by one arm, his other hand fisting in my hair, and he hauled me into the living room. He was shouting filthy words, shoving me facedown over an ottoman.

"No," I cried, smothered in the upholstery. *"No."*

But he jerked down my jeans and panties and drove into my dry flesh, and it hurt, a fierce pinching pain that turned to raw fire, and I knew he had torn something inside me. He thrust harder, faster, easing only when I stopped saying no and fell silent, my tears sliding in a hot salty trail down to the cushion. I tried to think beyond the pain, told myself it would be over soon, *just take it, take it, he'll be done in a minute.*

One last bruising thrust, and Nick shuddered over me, and I shuddered too as I thought of the swimming liquid inside me. I wanted nothing to do with his babies. I wanted nothing to do with sex either.

I gasped with relief as he pulled out, heat trickling down my thighs. There were the sounds of Nick zipping and fastening his pants.

"Your period's started," he said gruffly.

We both knew it was too early for my period. That wasn't where the blood had come from. I said nothing, only lifted myself from the ottoman and pulled my clothes in place.

Nick spoke again, sounding more normal. "I'll finish cooking dinner while you clean yourself up. What do I need to do?"

"Boil the pasta."

"How long?"

"Twelve minutes."

I hurt from my waist to my knees. I'd never had rough sex with Nick before. *It was rape,* a small voice said inside, but I immediately told myself that if I had only relaxed a little more, been less dry, it wouldn't have hurt nearly as much. *But I didn't want it,* the voice persisted.

I stood and flinched at the brutal throbbing soreness, and began to hobble to the bathroom.

"A little less drama, if you don't mind," I heard Nick say.

I was silent as I continued to the bathroom and closed the door. I started the shower, made it as hot as I could stand it, and I undressed and got in. I stood in the spray for what seemed like forever, until my body was stinging and clean and aching. I was in a fog of bewilderment, wondering how my life had come to this. Nick would not be pacified until I'd had a baby, and then he would want another, and the unwinnable game of trying to please him would never end.

This was not a matter of trying to sit down and talk honestly with someone about your feelings. That only worked when your feelings mattered. Nick, even when he seemed to be listening, was only gathering points to be used against me later. Someone else's pain, whether emotional or physical, didn't register with him. But I had thought he loved me. Had he changed so much since we'd gotten married, or had I made a fatal misjudgment?

Turning off the shower, I wrapped a towel around my sore body and went to the mirror. I used my hand to wipe a circle in the fogged mirror. My face was distorted, one eye swollen at the outside corner.

The bathroom door rattled. "You've been in there too long. Come out and eat."

"I'm not hungry."

"Open the goddamn door and stop sulking."

I unlocked the door and opened it, and stood facing him, this angry man who looked ready to tear me apart. I was afraid of him, but even more than that, I was utterly defeated. I had tried so hard to play by his rules, but he kept changing them.

"I'm not going to apologize this time," he said. "You were asking for it. You know better than to talk to me like that."

"If we had children," I told him, "you would hit them too."

Fresh rage began to color his face. "Shut your mouth."

"You would," I insisted. "You would knock them around whenever they did something you didn't like. That's one of the reasons I don't want your baby."

Nick's lack of reaction scared me. It became so quiet that the drip-drip from the showerhead made me flinch. He stared at me without blinking, his hazel eyes flat and shiny like buttons. Drip. Drip. Drip. Gooseflesh rose over my naked body, the towel damp and cold around me.

"Where are they?" he asked abruptly, and pushed past me. He started rummaging through the bathroom drawers, tossing out compacts and hairpins and brushes, everything clattering to the wet tile floor.

"Where are what?" I asked, my heart kicking into overdrive, going so wild that it made my rib cage hurt. I was amazed at how calm I sounded when terror was corroding my insides like battery acid. "I have no idea what you're talking about."

He threw an empty water glass to the floor, smashing it. And he continued to empty out drawers like a madman. "You know exactly what I'm asking."

If he found the birth control pills, he would kill me. A strange, sickening resignation settled beneath the fear, and my pulse quieted. I was light-headed and freezing. "I'm going to get dressed," I said, still calm, even as he broke, ripped, threw, destroyed, liquids and powders spilling, running together in oozing pastel puddles.

I went to my dresser, pulled out jeans and underwear and a T-shirt even though it was late and I should have reached for pajamas. I guess my subconscious had already figured out I wouldn't be sleeping that night. As I finished dressing, Nick stormed into the bedroom and shoved me aside. He pulled out drawers and upended them, emptying my clothes into piles.

"Nick, stop it."

"Tell me where they are!"

"If you're looking for an excuse to hit me again," I said, "just go ahead and do it." I didn't sound defiant. I wasn't even scared anymore. I was weary, the kind of weary you get to when your thoughts and emotions dry up to nothing.

But Nick was determined to find proof that I had betrayed him, and punish me until I would forever be afraid. Finishing with the drawers, he went into the closet and started throwing my shoes and ripping open my purses. I didn't try to run or hide. I just stood there, numb and expectant, waiting for the execution.

He came from the closet with the pills in hand, hell in his face. I dimly understood that he was no more in control of his actions than I was. There was a monster in him that had to be fed, and he wouldn't stop until it was satisfied.

I was grabbed and slammed against the wall, my head filled with white noise as the back of my skull struck the hard surface. Nick hit me harder than he ever had before, his hand closed this time, and I felt my jaw crack. I only understood a few words, something about the pills, and I was going to have all the goddamn pills I wanted, and he tore some from the package and shoved them into my mouth, and tried to hold my jaw shut as I spat and sputtered. He hit me in the stomach and I doubled over, and he dragged me through the first-floor apartment to the front door.

I went hurtling to the ground, landing hard on the edge of the front doorstep. A piercing agony shot through me as his foot connected with my ribs. "You stay there till morning," he snarled. "You think about what you've done."

The door slammed shut.

I lay outside on the pavement, the sun-heated asphalt smoking like a stove plate even though it was dark. October in Texas was as hot as high summer. Cicadas creaked and teemed, the vibration of their tymbals filling the air. After a long time I sat up and spat out a mouthful of salty liquid, and evaluated the damage. I hurt in my stomach and ribs and between the legs, and in the back of the head. My mouth was bleeding, and there was searing pain in my jaw.

My biggest fear was that Nick might open the door and drag me back in.

Trying to think above the violent pounding in my head, I considered my options. No purse. No money. No driver's license. No cell phone. No car keys. No shoes either. I looked down at my bare feet, and I had to laugh even though it hurt my swollen mouth. Shit, this was not good. It occurred to me that I might actually have to wait outside all night like a cat Nick had thrown out. Come morning, he would let me in, and I would crawl back, chastened and defeated.

I wanted to curl up and start crying. But I found myself lurching to my feet, fighting for balance.

To hell with you, I thought, glancing at the closed door. I could still walk.

If I could have gone to anyone at that moment, it would have been my best friend, Todd. I needed his understanding and comfort. But in these circumstances, there was only one person who could really help me. Gage. Everyone from McAllen to El Paso either owed him favors or wanted to do him favors. He could solve a problem quickly, efficiently, with no fanfare. And there was no one in the world I trusted more.

I walked to the grocery store a quarter mile away, barefoot. As the darkness thickened, a full orange moon rose in the sky. It wavered before my eyes as if it were a set decoration in a high school play, hanging on hooks. A hunter's moon. I felt foolish and scared as the lights of passing cars crossed over me. But soon my accumulated aches and pains grew to the point that I stopped feeling foolish. I had to concentrate on putting one foot in front of the other. I was afraid I might pass out. I kept my head low, not wanting anyone to stop by the side of the road. No questions, no strangers, no police. They might take me back to my husband. Nick had become so powerful in my mind that I thought he might explain everything away, take me back to that condo and possibly kill me.

The ache in my jaw was the worst. I tried to match my teeth together to see if it was broken or askew, but even the slightest movement of my mouth was agony. By the time I reached the grocery store, I was seriously considering offering my wedding band as a trade for some Tylenol. But there was no way I was going into that brightly lit store with all the people coming and going. I knew how I looked, the attention it would draw, and that was the last thing I wanted.

I found a pay phone outside, and I made a collect call, pushing each button with fierce concentration. I knew Gage's cell phone number by heart. *Please answer,* I thought, wondering what I would do if he didn't. *Please answer. Please . . .*

And then I heard his voice, and the operator asked if he would accept the call.

"Gage?" I held the receiver with both hands, gripping as if it were a lifeline.

"Yeah, it's me. What's going on?"

The task of answering, explaining, was so overwhelming that for a moment I couldn't speak. "I need you to come get me," I managed to whisper.

His voice became very calm, gentle, as if he were speaking to a child. "What happened, darlin'? Are you all right?"

"No."

A brief, electric silence, and then he asked urgently, "Where are you, Haven?"

I couldn't answer for a moment. The relief of hearing my own name, spoken in that familiar voice, melted through the numbness. My throat worked hard, and I felt hot tears gush down my face, stinging my abraded skin. "Grocery store," I finally managed to choke out.

"In Dallas?"

"Yes."

"Haven, are you by yourself?" I heard him ask.

"Uh-huh."

"Can you take a cab to the airport?"

"No." I sniffled and gulped. "I don't have my purse."

"Where are you?" Gage repeated patiently.

I told him the name of the grocery store and the street it was on.

"Okay. I want you to wait near the front entrance . . . is there a place you can sit?"

"There's a bench."

"Good girl. Haven, go sit on that bench and do not move. I'll have someone there as soon as possible. Don't go anywhere, do you understand? Sit there and wait."

"Gage," I whispered, "don't call Nick, 'kay?"

I heard him draw an unsteady breath, but when he spoke, his voice was even. "Don't worry, sweetheart. He's not coming near you again."

As I sat on the bench and waited, I knew I was garnering curious glances. My face was bruised, one eye was almost swollen shut and my jaw was huge. A child asked his mother what was wrong with me, and she hushed him and told him not to stare. I was grateful that no one approached me, that people's natural instincts were to avoid the kind of trouble I was obviously in.

I wasn't aware of how much time passed. It could have been a few minutes or an hour. But eventually a man approached the bench, a young black guy wearing khakis and a button-down shirt. He lowered to his haunches in front of me, and I looked blearily into a pair of worried brown eyes. He smiled as if to reassure me. "Miss Travis?" His voice was as soft and rich as sorghum syrup. "I'm Oliver Mullins. A friend of your brother's. He called and said you needed a ride." Staring at me, he added slowly, "But now I'm wondering if maybe you don't need to go to the emergency room."

I shook my head, panicking. "No. No. Don't want that. Don't take me there —"

"Okay," he soothed. "Okay, no problem. I'll take you to the airport. Let me help you to my car."

I didn't move. "Promise we're not going to the emergency room."

"I promise. I absolutely promise."

I still didn't move. "Can't get on a plane," I mumbled. It was getting really hard to talk. "Don' have my driver's license."

"It's a private plane, Miss Travis." His gaze was kind and pitying. "You won't need your license, or a ticket. Come on, let's —" He broke off as he saw my torn, bleeding feet. "Christ," he whispered.

"No hospital," I muttered.

Without asking permission, Oliver sat beside me. I watched as he took off his shoes and socks, slipped his bare feet back into the loafers, and carefully put his own socks on me. "I'd give you the shoes," he said, "but there's no way you could keep 'em on. Will you let me carry you to the car?"

I shook my head. I was pretty sure I couldn't tolerate being held by anyone, for any reason, no matter how briefly.

"That's all right," Oliver murmured. "You just take your time, then." He stood and waited patiently while I struggled up from the bench, his hands half raised as if he had to stop himself from reaching for me. "Car's over there. The white Cadillac."

Together we walked slowly to the car, a gleaming pearl-colored sedan, and Oliver held the door open as I crawled in. "Would you be more comfortable with the seat back lowered?" he asked.

I closed my eyes, too exhausted to answer. Oliver leaned down, pressed a button, and eased the seat back until I was half reclining.

He went to the other side, got in and started the car. The Cadillac purred smoothly as we pulled out of the parking lot and onto the main road. I heard the sound of a cell phone being flipped open, and a number being dialed. "Gage," Oliver said after a moment. "Yeah, I got her. Headed to DFW right now. Have to tell you, though . . . he knocked her around pretty good. She's a little out of it." A long pause, and Oliver answered quietly. "I know, man." More talking on the other end. "Yeah, I think she's okay to travel, but when she gets there . . . Uh-huh. I think so, definitely. I'll let you know when she takes off. No problem."

There was no softer ride than a Cadillac — the closest thing to a mattress on wheels — but every delicate bounce sent fresh aches through my body. I tried to grit my teeth against the pain, only to gasp at the burst of fire in my jaw.

I heard Oliver's voice between the loud throbs of the pulse in my ears. "Feel like you're going to get sick, Miss Travis?"

I made a small negative sound. No way was I going to do that — it would hurt too much.

A small plastic trash receptacle was settled carefully in my lap. "Just in case."

I was silent, my eyes closed, as Oliver maneuvered carefully through the traffic. Lights from passing cars sent a dull red glow through my lids. I was vaguely worried by the difficulty I had in thinking coherently . . . I couldn't seem to come up with any idea of what would happen next. Trying to grab hold of a coherent thought was like standing under a big cloud and trying to catch raindrops with a teaspoon. I felt like I would never be in control of anything again.

"You know," I heard Oliver say, "my sister used to get beat up by her husband. Pretty often. For no reason. For any reason. I didn't know about it at the time, or I would have killed the son of a bitch. She finally left him and brought her kids to my mama's house, and stayed there till she got her life back together. Saw a shrink and everything. My sister told me the thing that helped her the most was to hear it wasn't her fault. She needed to hear that a lot. So I want to be the first one to tell you . . . it wasn't your fault."

I didn't move or speak. But I felt tears leak from beneath my closed eyelids.

"Not your fault," Oliver repeated firmly, and drove me the rest of the way in silence.

I dozed a little and woke a few minutes later when the car had stopped and Oliver was opening the door. The roar of a departing jet tore through the cushioned quiet of the Cadillac, and the smells of fuel and equipment and humid Texas air drifted over me. Blinking and sitting up slowly, I realized we were on the tarmac.

"Let me help you out," Oliver said, reaching for me. I shrank from his outstretched hand and shook my head. Clasping an arm across the place on my ribs where Nick had kicked me, I struggled from the car by myself. When I got to my feet, my head swam and a gray mist covered my eyes. I swayed and Oliver caught my free arm to steady me.

"Miss Travis," he said, continuing to grip my arm even as I tried to shake him off. "Miss Travis, please listen to me. All I want to do is help you get on that plane. You've got to let me help you. If you fall trying to get up those steps by yourself, you'd have to go to the hospital for sure. And I'd have to go there with you, 'cause your brother would break both my legs."

I nodded and accepted his hold, even as my instincts screamed to throw him off. The last thing I wanted was to be touched by another man, no matter how apparently trustworthy or friendly. On the other hand, I wanted to be on that plane. I wanted to get the hell out of Dallas, away from Nick.

"Okay, now," Oliver murmured, helping me shuffle toward the plane. It was a Lear 31A, a light jet made to accommodate up to six passengers. With four-foot-high winglets and delta fins attached to the tail cone, it looked like a bird poised for flight. "Not far," Oliver said, "and then you'll get to sit again, and Gage will be there to pick you up at the other end." As we ascended the stairs with torturous slowness, Oliver kept up a running monologue as if he were trying to distract me from the agony of my jaw and ribs. "This is a nice plane. It belongs to a software company headquartered in Dallas. I know the pilot real well. He's good, he'll get you there safe and sound."

"Who owns the company?" I mumbled, wondering if it was someone I'd met before.

"Me." Oliver smiled and helped me to one of the front seats with great care, and buckled me in. He went to a minibar, wrapped a few pieces of ice in a cloth, and gave it to me. "For your face. Rest now. I'm gonna talk to the pilot for a minute and then you'll be on your way."

"Thanks," I whispered, holding the shifting icy weight of the bag against my jaw. I settled deeper into the seat, gingerly molding the ice bag to the swollen side of my face.

The flight was miserable but mercifully short, landing in southeast Houston at Hobby Airport. I was slow to react when the plane stopped on the tarmac, my fingers fumbling over and over with the seat belt fastener. After the Jetway stairs were brought to the plane, the copilot emerged from the cockpit and opened the entrance door. In a matter of seconds, my brother was on the plane.

Gage's eyes were an unusual pale gray, not like fog or ice, but lightning. His black lashes and brows stood out strongly on his worry-bleached face. He froze for a millisecond as he saw me, then swallowed hard and came forward.

"Haven," he said, sounding hoarse. He lowered to his knees and braced his hands on either chair arm, his gaze raking over me. I managed to free myself from the seat belt, and I leaned forward into his familiar smell. His arms closed around me tentatively, unlike his usual firm grip, and I realized he was trying to keep from hurting me. I felt the trembling beneath his stillness.

Overwhelmed with relief, I laid my good cheek on his shoulder. "Gage," I whispered. "Love you more than anybody."

He had to clear his throat before he could speak. "Love you too, baby girl."

"Don' take me to River Oaks."

He understood at once. "No, darlin'. You're coming home with me. I haven't told Dad you're here."

He helped me out to his car, a sleek silver

115

Maybach. "Don't go to sleep," he said sharply as I closed my eyes and leaned back against the headrest.

"I'm tired."

"There's a lump on the back of your head. You probably have a concussion, which means you shouldn't sleep."

"I slept on the plane," I said. "I'm fine, see? Jus' let me —"

"You're not fine," Gage said with a savagery that made me flinch. "You're —" He broke off and modulated his tone at once as he saw the effect it had on me. "Hell, I'm sorry. Don't be afraid. I won't yell. It's just . . . not easy . . . to stay calm when I see what he's done to you." He took a long, uneven breath. "Stay awake until we get to the hospital. It'll only be a few minutes."

"No hospital," I said, pulling out of my torpor. "They'll want to know how it happened." The police would be told, and they might file assault charges against Nick, and I wasn't nearly ready to deal with all of that.

"I'll handle it," Gage said.

He would too. He had the power and money to circumvent all the usual processes. Palms would be greased, favors would be exchanged. People would look the other way at precisely the right moment. In Houston the Travis name was a key to open all doors —

or close them, if that was preferable.

"I want to go somewhere and rest." I tried to sound resolute. But my voice came out blurred and plaintive, and my head throbbed too much for me to keep up an argument.

"Your jaw might be broken," Gage said quietly. "And hell knows what he did to the rest of you." He let out an explosive sigh. "Can you tell me what happened?"

I shook my head. Sometimes a simple question could have a complicated answer. I wasn't really sure how or why it had happened, what it was about Nick or me or both of us together that had resulted in such damage. I wondered if he realized I was gone yet, if he'd gone out to the front doorstep and found it empty. Or if he was sleeping comfortably in our bed.

Gage was silent during the rest of the drive to the Houston Medical Center, the biggest medical district in the world. It consisted of many different hospitals, academic and research institutions. I had no doubt my family had donated new wings or equipment to at least a couple of them.

"Was this the first time?" Gage asked as we pulled up to the emergency room parking lot.

"No."

He muttered a few choice words. "If I'd

117

ever thought the bastard would raise a hand to you, I'd never have let you go with him."

"You couldn' have stopped me," I said thickly. "I was determined. Stupid."

"Don't say that." Gage looked at me, his eyes filled with anguished fury. "You weren't stupid. You took a chance on someone, and he turned out to be . . . Shit, there's no word for it. A monster." His tone was grim. "A walking dead man. Because when I get to him —"

"Please." I'd had enough of angry voices and violence for one night. "I don't know if Nick realized how much he hurt me."

"One small bruise is enough to warrant me killing him." He got me out of the car, picking me up and carrying me as if I were a child.

"I can walk," I protested.

"You're not walking through the parking lot in your socks. Damn it, Haven, give it a rest." He carried me to the emergency room waiting area, which was occupied by at least a dozen people, and set me gently beside the reception desk.

"Gage Travis," my brother said, handing a card to the woman behind the glass partition. "I need someone to see my sister right away."

I saw her eyes widen briefly, and she nodded to the door on the left of the reception desk. "I'll meet you at the door, Mr. Travis. Come right in."

"No," I whispered to my brother. "I don' want to cut in front of everyone. I want to wait with the other people."

"You don't have a choice." The door opened, and I found myself being pushed and pulled into the pale beige hallway. A wave of anger rushed over me at the man-handling from my brother. I didn't give a shit how well intentioned it was.

"It's not fair," I said fiercely, while a nurse approached. "I won't do it. I'm no more important than anyone else here —"

"You are to me."

I was outraged on behalf of the people in the waiting room, all taking their turn while I was whisked right on through. And I was mortified at playing the role of privileged heiress. "There were a couple of children out there," I said, pushing at Gage's restraining arm. "They need to see a doctor as much as I do."

"Haven," Gage said in a low, inexorable tone, "everyone in that waiting room is in better shape than you. Shut up, settle down, and follow the nurse."

With a strength fed on adrenaline, I jerked away from him and bumped against the wall.

Pain, too much of it, too fast, came at me from various sources. My mouth watered, my eyes began to stream, and I felt a rising pressure of bile. "I'm going to throw up," I whispered.

With miraculous speed, a kidney-shaped plastic bowl was produced as if by sleight of hand, and I bent over it, moaning. Since I hadn't eaten dinner, there wasn't much to disgorge. I vomited painfully, finishing with a few dry heaves.

"I think she's got a concussion," I heard Gage tell the nurse. "She has a lump on the head, and slurred speech. And now nausea."

"We'll take good care of her, Mr. Travis." The nurse led me to a wheelchair. From that point on, there was nothing to do but surrender to the process. I was X-rayed, run through an MRI, checked for fractures and hematomas, then disinfected and bandaged and medicated. There were long periods of waiting between each procedure. It took most of the night.

As it turned out I had a middle rib fracture, but my jaw was only bruised, not broken. I had a slight concussion, but not enough to warrant a stay in the hospital. And I was dosed with enough Vicodin to make an elephant high.

I was too annoyed with Gage, and too exhausted, to say much of anything after I'd been checked out. I slept during the fifteen-minute ride to Gage's condo at 1800 Main, a Travis-owned building made of glass and steel. It was a mixed-use structure with multimillion-dollar condos at the top and offices and retail space at the base. The distinctive glass segmented-pyramid surmounting the building had earned 1800 Main a semi-iconic status in the city.

I had been inside 1800 Main a couple of times to eat at one of the downstairs restaurants, but I had never actually seen Gage's place. He had always been intensely private.

We rode a swift elevator to the eighteenth floor. The condo door was open before we even made it to the end of the hallway. Liberty was standing there in a fuzzy peach-colored robe, her hair in a ponytail.

I wished she weren't there, my gorgeous, perfect sister-in-law who'd made all the right choices, the woman everybody in my family adored. She was one of the last people I would want to see me like this. I felt humiliated and troll-like as I lurched down the hallway toward her.

Liberty drew us both into the condo, which was ultramodern and starkly furnished, and closed the door. I saw her stand on her toes to kiss Gage. She turned to me.

"Hope you don' mind —" I began, and fell silent as she put her arms around me. She was so soft, smelling like scented powder and toothpaste, and her neck was warm and tender. I tried to pull back, but she didn't let go. It had been a long time since I'd been held this long by an adult woman, not since my mother. It was what I needed.

"I'm so glad you're here," she murmured. I felt myself relaxing, understanding there was going to be no judgment from Liberty, nothing but kindness.

She took me to the guest bedroom and helped me change into a nightshirt, and tucked me in as if I were no older than Carrington. The room was pristine, decorated in shades of pale aqua and gray. "Sleep as long as you want," Liberty whispered, and closed the door.

I lay there dizzy and dazed. My cramped muscles released their tension, unraveling like braided cord. Somewhere in the condo a baby began to cry and was swiftly quieted. I heard Carrington's voice, asking where her purple sneakers were. She must have been getting ready for school. A few clanks of dishes and pans . . . breakfast being prepared. They were comforting sounds. Family sounds.

And I drifted gratefully to sleep, part of me

wishing I would never wake up.

After you've been systematically abused, your judgment erodes to the point where it's nearly impossible to make decisions. Small decisions are as tough as big ones. Even choosing a breakfast cereal seems filled with peril. You are so scared about doing the wrong thing, being blamed and punished for it, you'd rather have someone else take the responsibility.

For me there was no relief in having left Nick. Whether or not I was still with him, I was buried in feelings of worthlessness. He had blamed me for causing the abuse, and his conviction had spread through me like a virus. Maybe I had caused it. Maybe I had deserved it.

Another side effect of having lived with Nick was that reality had acquired all the substance and stability of a jellyfish. I questioned myself and my reactions to everything. I didn't know what was true anymore. I couldn't tell if any of my feelings about anything were appropriate.

After sleeping about twenty-four hours, with Liberty checking on me occasionally, I finally got out of bed. I went to the bathroom and inspected my face in the mirror. I had a black eye, but the swelling had gone down. My jaw was still puffy and weird on one side, and I looked like I'd been in a car wreck. But I was hungry, which I thought was probably a good thing, and I was definitely feeling more human and less like road-kill.

As I shuffled into the main living area, groggy and hurting, I saw Gage sitting at a glass table.

Usually he was impeccably dressed, but at that moment he was wearing an old T-shirt and sweatpants, and his eyes were underpinned by dark circles.

"Wow," I said, going to sit by him, "you look terrible."

He didn't smile at my attempt at humor, just watched me with concern.

Liberty came in carrying a baby. "Here he is," she said cheerfully. My nephew, Matthew, was a chubby, adorable one-year-old with a gummy grin, big gray eyes, and a thatch of thick black hair.

"You gave the baby a Mohawk?" I asked as Liberty sat beside me with Matthew in her lap.

She grinned and nuzzled his head. "No, it just sort of fell off the sides and stayed on the top. I've been told it'll grow back in eventually."

"I like it. The family's Comanche streak is

coming through." I wanted to reach for the baby, but I didn't think my cracked rib could take it, even with the support of the elastic rib belt around my midsection. So I settled for playing with his feet, while he giggled and crowed.

Liberty looked at me appraisingly. "It's time for your medicine again. Do you think you could eat some toast and eggs first?"

"Yes, please." I watched as she settled Matthew in a high chair and scattered some Cheerios on the surface. The baby began to rake the cereal bits with his fist, transferring them to his mouth.

"Coffee?" Liberty asked. "Hot tea?"

I usually preferred coffee, but I thought it might be tough on my stomach. "Tea would be great."

Gage drank his own coffee, set the cup down, and reached over to cover my hand with his. "How are you?" he asked.

As soon as he touched me, a nasty threatened feeling came over me. I couldn't stop myself from jerking my hand away. My brother, who had never done violence to a woman, looked at me with openmouthed amazement.

"Sorry," I said, abashed as I saw his reaction.

He tore his gaze away, seeming occupied

with a fierce inner struggle, and I saw that his color was high. "You're not the one who should be sorry," he muttered.

After Liberty had brought me tea and my prescription pills, Gage cleared his throat and asked gruffly, "Haven, how did you get away from Nick last night? How did you end up with no purse and no shoes?"

"Well, he . . . he sort of . . . threw me out. I think he expected me to wait on the doorstep until he let me back in."

I saw Liberty pause temporarily as she came to pour more coffee for him. I was surprised by how shocked she looked.

Gage reached for a glass of water, nearly knocking it over. He took a few deliberate gulps. "He beat you up and threw you out," he repeated. It wasn't a question, more a statement he was trying to make himself believe. I nodded yes and reached over to nudge one of Matthew's Cheerios more closely within reach.

"I'm not sure what Nick's going to do when he sees I'm gone," I heard myself say. "I'm afraid he might file a missing persons report. I guess I should call him. Although I'd rather not tell him where I am."

"I'm going to call one of our lawyers in a few minutes," Gage said. "I'll find out what we need to do next." He continued talking in a measured tone, about how we might need to take photos of my injuries, how to get the divorce over with as quickly as possible, how to minimize my involvement so I wouldn't have to face Nick or talk to him —

"Divorce?" I asked stupidly, while Liberty set a plate in front of me. "I don't know if I'm ready for that."

"You don't think you're ready? Have you looked in the mirror, Haven? How much more of a pounding do you need to be ready?"

I looked at him, so big and decisive and strong-willed, and everything in me rebelled.

"Gage, I just got here. Can I have a break? Just for a little while? Please?"

"The only way for you to get a break is to divorce the son of a" — Gage paused and glanced at his attentive baby — "gun."

I knew my brother was trying to protect me, that he wanted what was best for me. But his protectiveness felt like bullying. And it reminded me of Dad. "I know that," I said. "I just want to think about things before I talk to a lawyer."

"God help me, Haven, if you're actually considering going back to him —"

"I'm not. I'm just tired of being told what to do and when to do it. All the time! I feel like I'm on a runaway train. I don't want you making decisions about what I should do next."

"Fine. Then you make them. *Fast.* Or I will."

Liberty intervened before I could reply. "Gage," she murmured. Her slim fingers went to the taut surface of his clenched bicep and stroked lightly. His attention was instantly diverted. He looked at her, the lines on his face smoothing out, and he took a deep breath. I had never seen anyone wield that kind of power over my authoritative brother, and I was impressed. "This is a process," she said gently. "I know we want Haven to skip over the middle part and get right to the end . . . but I think the only way for her to get out of it is to go through it. Step by step."

He frowned but didn't argue. They exchanged a private glance. Clearly there would be more discussion later, out of my hearing. He turned back to me. "Haven," he said quietly, "what would you say if one of your friends told you her husband had thrown her out on the doorstep one night? What would your advice be?"

"I . . . I'd tell her to leave him right away," I admitted. "But it's different when it's me."

"Why?" he asked in genuine bewilderment.

"I don't know," I answered helplessly.

Gage rubbed his face with both hands. He stood from the table. "I'm going to get dressed and go to the office for a while. I won't make any calls." He paused deliberately before adding, "Yet." Going to the high chair, he lifted Matthew and held him aloft to make him squeal with delight. Lowering the wriggling body, Gage kissed his neck and cuddled him. "Hey, pardner. You be a good boy for Mommy while I'm gone. I'll come back later and we'll do some guy stuff."

Settling the baby back in the chair, Gage leaned down to kiss his wife, sliding his hand behind the back of her neck. It was more than a casual kiss, turning harder, longer, until she reached up and stroked his face. Breaking it off, he continued to look into her eyes, and it seemed an entire conversation passed between them.

Liberty waited until Gage had gone to take a shower before telling me gently, "He was so upset after he brought you home. He loves you. It drives him crazy, thinking of someone hurting you. It's all he can do to stop himself from going to Dallas and . . . doing something that's not in your best interests."

I blanched. "If he goes to Nick —"

"No, no, he won't. Gage is very self-controlled when it comes to getting the results he wants. Believe me, he'll do whatever is necessary to help you, no matter how hard it is."

"I'm sorry for involving you in this," I said. "I know it's the last thing you or Gage need."

"We're your family." She leaned over and gathered me into another of those long, comfortable hugs. "We'll figure it out. And don't worry about Gage — I'm not going to let him bully you. He just wants you to be safe . . . but he's got to let you be in charge of how it's handled."

I felt a wave of affection and gratitude for her. If there was any lingering trace of resentment or jealousy in my heart, it vanished in that moment.

Once I started talking, I couldn't stop. I told Liberty everything, the way Nick had controlled the household, the shirts I'd had to iron, the way he called me "Marie." Her eyes widened at that last, and she said in a low voice, "Oh, Haven. It's like he was trying to erase you."

We had laid out a big quilt with a barnyard design, and Matthew had crawled among the hand-stitched animals until he drifted to sleep on top of a flock of sheep. Liberty opened a bottle of chilled white wine. "Your prescription instructions say that alcohol may magnify the effects of the medication," she warned.

"Good," I said, holding out my glass. "Don't be stingy."

Lounging on the quilt with the sleeping baby, I tried to find a comfortable position on the pile of pillows Liberty had set out for me. "What's confusing," I told her, still pondering my relationship with Nick, "are the times when he's okay, because then you think everything is getting better. You know what buttons not to push. But then there are new buttons. And no matter how sorry you are, no matter how hard you try, everything you say and do builds up the tension until there's an explosion."

"And the explosions get worse each time," she said with a quiet certainty that got my attention.

"Yeah, exactly. Did you ever date a guy like that?"

"My mother did." Her green eyes were distant. "His name was Louis. A Jekyll and Hyde type. He started out charming and nice, and he led Mama step by step into the relationship, and by the time things got bad enough for her to leave, her self-esteem was shredded. At the time I was too young to understand why she let him treat her so badly."

Her gaze wandered over Matthew's slumbering body, limp and heavy as a sack of flour. "I think the thing you've got to figure out is if Nick's behavior is something that could be helped with counseling. If your leaving him would be enough to make him want to change."

I sipped my wine and considered that for a while. Was Nick's abusiveness something that could be peeled away like an orange rind? Or was it marbled all the way through?

"I think with Nick, it's always going to be about control," I finally said. "I can't see him ever admitting something is his fault, or that he needs to change in any way. The fault is always mine." Setting aside my empty wine glass, I rubbed my forehead. "I keep wondering . . . did he ever love me at all? Was I anything more than just someone to push around and manipulate? Because if he never cared about me, it makes me even more of an idiot for having loved him."

"Maybe he cared about you as much as he was capable," Liberty said.

I smiled without humor. "Lucky me." I realized we were talking about my relationship with Nick as if it were already in the past tense. "If I had known him longer," I continued, "dated him longer, maybe I would have seen through the façade. It was my fault for rushing into marriage so quickly."

"No it wasn't," Liberty insisted. "Sometimes an imitation of love can be pretty damn convincing."

The words reminded me of something I'd heard her say a long time ago on her wedding night. A lifetime ago. "Like the imitation you had with Hardy Cates?"

She nodded, her expression turning thoughtful. "Yes, although I wouldn't care to put Hardy in the same company as Nick. He would never hurt a woman. In fact, Hardy had the opposite problem . . . always wanting to rescue someone . . . I forget the name for it . . ."

"A white knight complex."

"Yes. But after the rescue was done, that was Hardy's cue to leave."

"He wasn't such a white knight when he ruined Gage's business deal," I couldn't resist pointing out.

Liberty's smile turned rueful. "You're right. But I think Hardy considered that a shot against Gage, not me." She shook her head dismissively. "About you and Nick . . . it's not your fault that he went after you. I've read that abusers choose women they can easily manipulate — they have a kind of radar for it. Like, if you filled the Astrodome with people and put one abusive man and

133

one vulnerable woman in there, they'd find each other."

"Oh, great." I was indignant. "I'm a walking target."

"You're not a target, you're just . . . trusting. Loving. Any normal guy would appreciate that. But I think someone like Nick probably thinks of love as a weakness he can take advantage of."

Regardless of what I wanted to hear, that got to me. It was a truth I couldn't get over, under, or around . . . it stood right in my way, blocking any possible path back to Nick.

No matter how much I loved him, or what I did for him, Nick wouldn't change. The more I tried to please him, the more contempt he would have for me.

"I can't go back to him," I said slowly, "can I?"

Liberty just shook her head.

"I can imagine what Dad will say if I got a divorce," I muttered. "Starting with a big, fat 'I told you so.' "

"No," Liberty said earnestly. "Really. I've talked with Churchill more than once about the way he behaved. He's sorry about having been such a hard-ass."

I wasn't buying that. "Dad *lives* to be a hard-ass."

Liberty shrugged. "Whatever Churchill says or thinks is not important right now. The point is what *you* want."

I was about to tell her it might take a long time to figure that out. But as I lowered myself next to the baby's warm body and snuggled close, a few things had become very clear. I wanted to never be hit or yelled at again. I wanted to be called by my own name. I wanted my body to belong to me. I wanted all the things that anyone deserved by virtue of being human. Including love.

And I knew deep down it wasn't love when one person had all the power and the other person was completely dependent. Real love was not possible in a hierarchy.

I nuzzled Matthew's scalp. Nothing in the world smelled as good as a clean baby. How innocent and trusting he was in sleep. How would Nick treat a helpless creature like this?

"I want to talk to the lawyer," I said sleepily. "Because I don't want to be the woman in the Astrodome."

Liberty draped a throw blanket gently over the two of us. "Okay," she whispered. "You're in charge, Haven."

CHAPTER FIVE

In Texas there is an obligatory sixty-day waiting period after you file a petition for divorce. At some point someone in the state legislature had decided that a legally mandated cooling-off period was a good idea for people who wanted a divorce. I'd rather they had left it up to me to decide whether I needed cooling off or not. Once the decision had been made, I wanted to get it over with quickly.

On the other hand, I made pretty good use of those two months. I healed outwardly, the bruises fading, and I started going twice a week to a therapist. Having never been to a therapist before, I expected I was going to have to lie back on a sofa and talk while some impersonal white-coated professional took notes.

Instead I was welcomed into a small, cozy office with a sofa upholstered in flowered yellow twill, by a therapist who didn't seem all that much older than me. Her name was Susan Byrnes, and she was dark-haired and bright-eyed and sociable. It was a relief beyond description to unburden myself to her. She was understanding and smart, and as I described things I had felt and gone through, it seemed she had the power to unlock the mysteries of the universe.

Susan said Nick's behavior fit the pattern of someone with narcissistic personality disorder, which was common for abusive husbands. As she told me about the disorder, it felt as if she were describing my life as it had been for the past year. A person with NPD was domineering, blaming, self-absorbed, intolerant of others' needs . . . and they used rage as a control tactic. They didn't respect anyone else's boundaries, which meant they felt entitled to bully and criticize until their victims were an absolute mess.

Having a personality disorder was different from being crazy, as Susan explained, because unlike a crazy person, a narcissist could control when and where he lost his temper. He'd never beat up his boss at work, for example, because that would be against his own interests. Instead he would go home and beat up his wife and kick the dog. And he would never feel guilty about it, because he would justify it and make excuses for himself. No one's pain but his own meant anything to him.

"So you're saying Nick's not crazy, he's a sociopath?" I asked Susan.

"Well . . . basically, yes. Bearing in mind that most sociopaths are not killers, they're just nonempathetic and highly manipulative."

"Can he ever be fixed?"

She shook her head immediately. "It's sad to think about what kind of abuse or neglect might have made him that way. But the end result is that Nick is who he is. Narcissists are notoriously resistant to therapy. Because of their sense of grandiosity, they don't ever see the need to change." Susan had smiled darkly, as if at some unpleasant memory. "Believe me, no therapist wants a narcissist to walk in the door. It only results in massive frustration and a waste of time."

"What about me?" I brought myself to ask. "Can I be fixed?" At that point my eyes stung and I had to blow my nose, so Susan had to repeat her answer.

"Of course you can, Haven. We'll work on it. We'll do it."

At first I was afraid I was going to have to work on forgiving Nick. It was an indescribable relief to hear Susan say no, I didn't need to stay trapped in the cycle of abuse and forgiveness. Victims of abuse were often burdened with the so-called responsibility of forgiving, even rehabilitating, their tormentors. That wasn't my job, Susan said. Later we could find some level of resolution so the poison of my relationship with Nick wouldn't spill into other areas of my life. But right now there were other things to concentrate on.

I discovered I was a person with weak boundaries. I had been taught by my parents, especially my mother, that being a good daughter meant having no boundaries at all. I had been raised to let Mother criticize and have her way all the time, and make decisions for me that she had no business making.

"But my brothers didn't have that kind of relationship with her," I told Susan. "They had boundaries. They didn't let her mess with their personal lives."

"Sometimes a parent's expectations of sons and daughters are very different," Susan replied wryly. "My own parents insist that I'm the one who should take care of them in their old age, but they would never think of demanding that from my brother."

Susan and I did a lot of role-playing, which felt mortifyingly silly at first, but as she pretended by turns to be Nick, my father, a friend, a brother, even my long-gone mother, I practiced standing up for myself. It was hard, muscle-knotting, perspiration-inducing work.

"No is a vitamin." That phrase became my mantra. I figured if I told it to myself often enough, I would start believing it.

Gage handled as much of the divorce proceedings as I would allow. And, possibly because of Liberty's softening influence, he changed his approach to me. Instead of telling me how things were going to be, he patiently laid out choices and explained them, and didn't argue with my decisions. When Nick had dared to call the condo and demanded to talk to me, and I'd said all right, Gage had forced himself to hand the phone to me.

It had been quite a conversation, mostly one-sided, with Nick talking and me listening. My husband poured it on, progressing from guilt to fury to pleading, telling me it was my fault as much as his.

You couldn't just give up on a marriage when you hit a rough spot, he said.

It was more than just a rough spot, I said.

People who loved each other found a way to work things out, he said.

You don't love me, I said.

He said he did. Maybe he hadn't been the

best husband, but I damn sure hadn't been the best wife.

I'm sure you're right, I told him. But I don't think I deserve getting a cracked rib.

He said there was no way he'd cracked my rib, that must have happened accidentally when I fell.

I said he'd pushed me, hit me.

And I was astonished when Nick said he didn't remember hitting me. Maybe one of his hands had slipped.

I wondered if he really didn't remember, if he could actually rewrite reality for himself, or if he was just lying. And then I realized it didn't matter.

I'm not coming back, I said. And every comment he made after that, I repeated it. I'm not coming back. I'm not coming back.

I hung up the phone and went to Gage, who had been sitting in the living area. His hands had clenched so hard in the arms of the leather chair that his fingertips had riveted deep gouges in the smooth hide. But he had let me fight my battle alone, as I had needed to.

I had always loved Gage, but never so much as then.

I filed for a divorce on the grounds of insupportability, meaning the marriage had become insupportable because of personality conflicts that had destroyed "the legitimate ends of the marriage relationship." That was the quickest way to end it, the lawyer said. If Nick didn't contest it. Otherwise there would be a trial, and all kinds of nastiness and humiliation in store for both parties.

"Haven," Gage said to me in private, his gray eyes kind, the set of his mouth grim. "I've tried my best to hold back and do things your way . . . but I have to ask you for something now."

"What is it?"

"You and I both know there's no way Nick's going to let the divorce go uncontested unless we make it worth his while."

"You mean pay him off," I said, my blood simmering as I thought of Nick getting a financial reward after the way he'd treated me. "Well, remind Nick that I've been disinherited. I'm —"

"You're still a Travis. And Nick will play his part to the hilt . . . a poor hardworking guy who married a spoiled rich girl, and now he's being tossed aside like a bartender's rag. If he wants, Haven, he can make this process as long and difficult and public as possible."

"Give him my share of the condo, then. That's all the community property we've got."

"Nick will want more than just the condo."
I knew what Gage was leading up to. He wanted to pay Nick off, to keep him quiet long enough to let the divorce go through. Nick was about to get a big fat reward, after all he'd done to me. I got mad enough to start shaking. "I swear," I said with blistering sincerity, "if I manage to get rid of him, I will *never* get married again."

"No, don't say that." Gage reached for me without thinking, and I shrank back. I still didn't like to be touched, especially by men, which Susan had said was a protective mechanism and would get better in time. I heard Gage utter a quiet curse, and he dropped his arms. "Sorry," he muttered, and heaved a sigh. "You know, putting a bullet in his head would be a lot cheaper and quicker than a divorce."

I glanced at him warily. "You're kidding, right?"

"Right." He made his expression bland, but I didn't like the look in his eyes.

"Let's stick with the divorce option," I said. "I'd prefer Matthew and Carrington not to have to visit you in prison. What kind of terms are you thinking? And am I supposed to go crawling to Dad for money to give to Nick? . . . Because I sure don't have any."

"You let me worry about the terms. We'll settle up later."

Realizing my brother was not only going to assume the expenses of my divorce, but also the settlement, I gave him a wretched look. "Gage —"

"It's okay," he said quietly. "You'd do it for me. You're not causing hardship for anyone, sweetheart."

"It's not right for you to pay for my mistakes."

"Haven . . . part of being strong is being able to admit you need help sometimes. You went into this marriage alone, you suffered through it alone, you damn sure don't have to get out of it alone. Let me be your big brother."

His quiet certainty made the ground beneath my feet feel solid. Like someday everything might actually be okay.

"I'm going to pay you back someday."

"Okay."

"I guess the only time I've ever felt more grateful," I told him, "is when you pulled Bootsie out of the ligustrum bush."

I swallowed my pride and called Dad the day after my divorce was final in February. To my profound relief, Nick hadn't appeared at

144

court when the judge signed the decree. Two people had to show up to get married, but only one had to for a divorce. Gage had assured me that Nick would stay far away from court that day. "What'd you do, threaten to break his legs?" I asked.

"I told him if I caught sight of him, his guts would be strung on the courthouse gate within five minutes." I had smiled at that until I realized Gage hadn't been joking.

Gage and Liberty had let my family know that I was back in Houston, but that I wouldn't be ready to see anyone or do any telephone-talking for a while. Naturally Dad, who wanted to be in the center of whatever was going on, took offense at my elusiveness. He told Gage to tell me that any time I was ready to get off my high horse, he would like for me to come see him.

"Did you tell him I was getting a divorce?" I asked Gage.

"Yes. I can't say he was surprised."

"But did you tell him why?" I didn't want anyone to know about what had occurred between Nick and me. Maybe in time I would tell Jack or Joe, but for now I needed it to be kept private. I didn't want to be seen as weak or helpless, a victim, ever again. Most of all I didn't want to be pitied.

"No," Gage said, his tone reassuring. "I

just told Dad it didn't work out — and if he wanted any kind of relationship with you at all, to keep his mouth shut about it."

So I finally called Dad, my sweaty hands gripping the phone. "Hey Dad." I tried to sound casual. "Been a while since I talked to you. Just thought I'd check in."

"Haven." The sound of his gravelly voice was familiar and comforting. "You took your sweet time. What have you been doing?"

"Getting a divorce."

"I heard about that."

"Yeah, well . . . it's all over between me and Nick." Since my father couldn't see me, I wrinkled up my face as if I'd chomped on bitter dandelion greens as I forced myself to admit, "It was a mistake."

"There are times I take no pleasure in being right."

"Like hell," I said, and was rewarded by his scratchy chuckle.

"If you really got rid of him," Dad said, "I'll call my lawyer this afternoon and have you put back in the will."

"Oh, good. That's why I called."

It took him a moment to realize I was being sarcastic.

"Dad," I said, "you're not going to hold that will over my head the rest of my life. Thanks to you, I've gotten a great education, and there's no reason I can't hold down a job. So don't bother calling the lawyer — I don't want to be in the will."

"You'll be in the will if I say so," Dad retorted, and I had to laugh.

"Whatever. The real reason I'm calling is to say I'd like to see you. It's been way too long since I've had a good argument with someone."

"Fine," he said. "Come on over."

And with that, our relationship was back on track, as flawed and frustrating as it had ever been. But I had boundaries now, I reminded myself, and no one was going to cross them. I would be a fortress of one.

I was a new person in the same world, which was a lot more difficult than being the same person in a new world. People thought they knew me but they didn't. With the exception of Todd, my old friends were no longer relevant to the new version of me. So I turned to my brothers for support, and I discovered that adulthood had done nice things for their personalities.

Joe, a commercial photographer, made a point of telling me that he had a big house and there was plenty of room if I wanted to stay with him. He said he was gone a lot of the time, and we wouldn't infringe on each other's privacy. I told him how much I appreciated the offer, but I needed my own place. Still, it wouldn't have been bad at all, living with him. Joe was an easygoing guy. I never heard him complain about anything. He took life as it came, which was a rare quality in the Travis family.

But the real surprise was Jack, the brother I'd never gotten along with — the one who'd given me a bad haircut when I was three, and scared the wits out of me with bugs and garden snakes. The adult Jack turned out to be an unexpected ally. A friend. In his company I could fully relax, the haunted, anxious feeling burning away like water drops on a smoking griddle.

Maybe it was because Jack was so straightforward. He claimed to be the least complex person in the Travis family, and that was probably true. Jack was a hunter, comfortable with his status as a predatory omnivore. He was also an environmentalist and saw no conflict in that. Any hunter, he said, had better do his best to protect nature since he spent so much time out in it.

With Jack, you always knew where you stood. If he liked something, he said so without hesitation, and if he didn't, he'd tell you the truth about that too. He stayed on the right side of the law while admitting that some things were just more fun when they were illegal. He liked cheap women, fast cars, late nights, and hard liquor, especially all together. In Jack's view, you were obliged to sin on Saturday night so you'd have something to atone for Sunday morning. Otherwise you'd be putting the preacher out of business.

After Jack had graduated from UT, he'd gone to work at a small property management company. Eventually he'd gotten a loan, bought the company, and expanded it to four times its original size. It was the perfect occupation for Jack, who liked to fix things, to tinker and problem-solve. Like me, he had no interest in investment lingo and all the sophisticated financial strategies that Gage and Dad so relished. Jack preferred the nuts-and-bolts issues of working and living. He was good at backroom deals, cutting through legal bullshit, talking man-to-man. To Jack, there was nothing more powerful than a promise made over a handshake. He would have died — literally chosen death — before breaking his word.

In light of my hotel experience at the Darlington, Jack said I'd be perfect working for the residential side of his management company, which was headquartered at 1800 Main. His current on-site manager was leaving on account of pregnancy — she wanted to spend the first few years of her child's life at home.

"Thanks, but I couldn't," I said when Jack first broached the idea of my taking the job.

"Why not? You'd be great at it."

"Reeks of nepotism," I said.

"So?"

"So there are other more qualified people for the position."

"And?"

I began to smile at his persistence. "And they'll complain if you hire your sister."

"See," Jack said easily, "that's the whole point of having my own company. I can hire Bozo the fucking clown if I want."

"That's so flattering, Jack."

He grinned. "Come on. Give it a shot. It'll be fun."

"Are you offering to employ me so you can keep an eye on me?"

"Actually, we'll hardly see each other, we'll both be so damn busy all the time."

I liked the sound of that, being busy all the time. I wanted to work, to accomplish things, after the past couple of years of being Nick's personal slave.

"You'll learn a lot," Jack coaxed. "You'd be in charge of the money stuff — insurance, payroll, maintenance bills. You'd also negotiate service contracts, purchase supplies and equipment, and you'd work with a leasing agent and an assistant. As the on-site manager, you'd live in a one-bedroom unit in the building. But you wouldn't be stuck in the office all the time . . . you'll have a lot of outside meetings. Later, when you're ready, you could get involved in the commercial side of things, which would be a help since I'm planning to branch out into construction management and then maybe —"

"Who'd be paying my salary?" I asked suspiciously. "You, or Dad?"

Jack looked affronted. "Me, of course. Dad doesn't have shit to do with my management company."

"He owns the building," I pointed out.

"You're employed by me and my company . . . and believe me, 1800 Main is *not* the only client we've got. Not by a long shot." Jack gave me a look of exaggerated patience. "Think it over, Haven. It'd work out great for both of us."

"It sounds great," I said. "And I can't tell you how much I appreciate it. But I can't start out at the top, Jack. I don't have enough experience. And it doesn't look good for either of us, for you to give me a job like that when I haven't paid any dues. What if I start out as the manager's assistant? I could learn

151

from the ground up."

"You don't have to pay dues," Jack protested. "You ought to get something for being a Travis."

"Being a Travis means I should pay extra dues," I said.

He looked at me and shook his head, and mumbled something about liberal Yankee shit.

I smiled at him. "You know it makes the most sense. And it's only fair to give the manager's job to someone who's really earned it."

"This is business," Jack said. "Fairness doesn't have crap to do with it."

But he relented eventually, and said far be it from him to keep me from starting at the bottom, if that was what I really wanted.

"Hack it all off," I told Liberty, sitting in her bathroom, draped in plastic. "I'm so sick of all this hair. It's hot and tangly and I never know what to do with it."

I wanted a new look to go with my new job. And as a former hairstylist, Liberty knew what she was doing. I figured anything she did to me was bound to be an improvement.

"Maybe we should go in stages," Liberty said. "It may be a shock if I take too much off at once."

"No, you can't donate it if it's less than ten inches long. Just go for it." We were going to give the foot-long rope of hair to the Locks of Love program, which made wigs for children who suffered from medical hair loss.

Liberty combed my hair deftly. "It's going to release some curl once I shorten it," she said. "All this weight is dragging your hair down."

She plaited it and sawed the entire length off at the nape. I held the braid while Liberty brought a Ziploc bag, and I dropped it inside the plastic pouch and sealed it with a kiss. "Good luck to whoever wears it next," I said.

Liberty spritzed my hair with water and moved all around my head with a straight razor, slicing off angled pieces until there were heaps of hair on the floor. "Don't be nervous," she said as she caught me examining a lock that had fallen onto my plastic-covered lap. "You're going to look great."

"I'm not nervous," I said truthfully. I didn't care how I looked, as long as it was different.

She blow-dried my hair using a round brush, ran her fingers through it to make it piecey, and beamed in satisfaction. "Take a look."

I stood and got a mild shock — a nice one — at my reflection. Liberty had given me long bangs that swept across my forehead, and a short layered bob, the feathered ends turning up gently. I looked stylish. Confident. "It's flippy," I said, playing with the layers.

"You can turn the ends under or out," she said, smiling. "Do you like it?"

"I love it."

Liberty turned me around so we could both see the cut in the mirror. "It's sexy," she said.

"You think so? I hope not."

She smiled at me quizzically. "Yes, I do think so. Why don't you want to look sexy?"

"False advertising," I said.

The manager that Jack brought over from the other office was named Vanessa Flint. She was one of those highly groomed and put-together women who had probably looked thirty-five when she was twenty-five, and would still look thirty-five even when she was fifty-five. Although she was only medium height, her slimness and good posture fooled you into thinking she was a lot taller. Her face was fine-boned and serene beneath a sweep of ash-blond hair. I admired the composure she wore like a high-buttoned blouse.

There wasn't much substance to her voice,

which was crisp and soft, like ice wrapped in velvet. But somehow it forced you to pay more attention, as if you shared in the responsibility of Vanessa making herself understood.

I liked her at first. At least, I wanted to like her. Vanessa was friendly, sympathetic, and when we went out for drinks after our first day at work, I found myself confiding more about my failed marriage and divorce than I should have. But Vanessa had recently been divorced too, and there seemed to be enough similarities between our two exes that it was a pleasure to compare notes.

Vanessa was frank about her concern over my relationship with Jack, and I appreciated her honesty. I reassured her that I had no intention of coasting by, or running to Jack just because he was my brother. Just the opposite, in fact. I was going to work a lot harder, because I had something to prove. She seemed satisfied by my earnest declarations, and said she thought we would work well together.

Vanessa and I were both given apartments at 1800 Main. I felt a little guilty about it, knowing that no other manager's assistant would have gotten an apartment, but it was the one concession I'd made to Jack. He had insisted on it, and the truth was, I liked the security of living so close to my brother.

The other employees lived off-site and came in each day, including a petite blond office manager named Kimmie; the leasing agent, Samantha Jenkins; the marketing agent, Phil Bunting; and Rob Ryan in accounting. We contacted Jack's commercial office whenever there was a need for legal resources, tech questions, or something we weren't equipped to handle on our own.

It seemed that everyone who worked for Jack at the commercial office had acquired his personal style . . . everyone was relaxed and almost jovial, in comparison to our office. Vanessa ran a tighter ship, which meant no casual-dress Fridays, and a "zero error tolerance" policy that was never exactly spelled out. However, everyone seemed to regard her as a good boss, tough but fair-minded. I was ready to learn from her, follow her example. I thought she was going to be a great new influence in my life.

But in a matter of days, I realized I was being gaslighted.

I was familiar with the tactic, since Nick had done it a lot. A bully or someone with a personality disorder needs to keep their victims confused, off balance, perpetually unsure of themselves. That way he — or she — could manipulate you more easily. Gaslighting could be anything that made you doubt yourself. For example, a bully would make a statement about something, and when you'd agree with it, he'd disagree with his own original statement. Or he'd make you think you'd lost something when you hadn't, or accuse you of forgetting something when he'd never asked you to do it in the first place.

What worried me was that I seemed to be Vanessa's only target. No one else seemed to be having a problem with her.

She would misplace a file and tell me to get it for her, turning up the tension until I was scrambling to find it. If I couldn't come up with it, she accused me of hiding the file somewhere. And then the file would turn up in some weird place, like beneath a plant on top of a cabinet, or wedged between the printer cart and her desk. She gave people the impression that I was scatterbrained and disorganized. And I had no proof of her mischief-making. The only thing that kept me from doubting myself was my own shaky sense of sanity.

There was no predicting Vanessa's moods or requests. I learned to save everything, after she asked me to write three different drafts of a letter and then decided on the first version after I'd deleted it. She would tell me to be at a meeting at one-thirty, and when I arrived, I was a half hour late. And she swore she'd told me one o'clock. She said I must not have paid attention.

Vanessa let it drop to me that she'd had an assistant named Helen for years, and she would have brought Helen with her to the new job, except that I'd already been given the position. It hadn't occurred to me that I would have broken up a long-running professional partnership, and robbed someone of a position they deserved. When Vanessa had me call Helen, who was still at the old office, to find out the name and number of Vanessa's favorite manicurist, I took the opportunity to apologize to Helen.

"God, don't be sorry," Helen said. "It was the best thing that ever happened to me."

I wanted to quit right then. But I was stuck, and Vanessa and I both knew it. With my skimpy résumé, I couldn't quit a job right after starting one. And I didn't know how long it would take me to find something else. Complaining about Vanessa was out of the question — it would make me look like a prima donna, or paranoid, or both. So I decided I would stick it out for a year. I would make some contacts and dig my own way out.

"Why me?" I asked my therapist, Susan,

after describing the situation with Vanessa. "She could focus on anyone in that office as a target. Do I give off 'victim' signals or something? Do I seem weak?"

"I don't believe so," Susan said gravely. "In fact, it's most likely that Vanessa sees you as a threat. Someone she has to subdue and neutralize."

"Me, a threat?" I shook my head. "Not to someone like Vanessa. She's confident and put-together. She's —"

"Confident people aren't bullies. I'll bet Vanessa's apparent confidence is really nothing but a front. A false self she's constructed to cover her deficiencies." Susan smiled at my skeptical expression. "And yes, you could be a big threat to an insecure person. You're bright, educated, pretty . . . and there's the little matter of your last name. Conquering someone like you would be a big bolster to Vanessa's sense of superiority."

My first Friday after starting at Travis Management Solutions, Jack came to my cubicle carrying a large shopping bag tied with a bow. "Here," he said, handing it to me over a mountain of paper on my desk. "A little something to celebrate your first week."

I opened the shopping bag and unearthed a briefcase made of chocolate-colored leather. "Jack, it's beautiful. Thank you."

"You're coming out with me and Heidi tonight," he informed me. "That's the other part of the celebration."

Heidi was one of a virtual harem of women that Jack dated interchangeably. Since he was so open about not wanting to be tied down, none of them seemed to expect any form of commitment from him.

"I don't want to be a third wheel on your date," I protested.

"You won't bother us," he said. "And you're not even a full-sized wheel. More like a training wheel."

I rolled my eyes, having already accepted a long time ago that being the target of short jokes from my towering brothers was an inescapable fact of life. "I'm tired," I said. "Trust me, I'm not up to partying with you and Heidi. One drink and I'll probably pass out."

"Then I'll put you into a cab and send you home." Jack gave me an inexorable look. "I'll haul you out of here if I have to, Haven. I mean it."

Even though I knew he would never use force on me, I felt myself blanch, and I went stiff in my chair. *Don't touch me,* I wanted to say, but the words were locked behind my teeth, thrashing like caged wild birds.

Jack blinked in surprise, staring at me. "Hey . . . I was just kidding, honey. For God's sake, don't look at me like that. It makes me feel as guilty as shit, and I don't even know why."

I forced myself to smile and relax. "Sorry. Bad memory." I reflected that Nick wouldn't have wanted me to go out tonight, having fun, meeting people. He would have wanted me to stay at home, isolated. Just for that, I decided, I would go out to spite him.

"Okay," I heard myself say. "Maybe for a little while. Is what I'm wearing all right?" I was dressed in a black turtleneck and a simple skirt and pumps.

"Sure. It's just a casual bar."

"It's not a meeting-people type of bar?"

"No. This is an after-work bar where you get a drink to unwind. After that, you leave for the meeting-people type of bar. And if you pick up someone good there, you go to a nice, quiet gonna-get-laid bar, and if that works out, you take her home with you."

"That sounds like a lot of work," I said.

Vanessa came to the opening of the cubicle, slim and sleek and poised. "What fun," she said, her gaze moving from Jack to the present on the desk. She confused me with a warm smile. "Well, I guess you deserve a reward, Haven . . . you did a great job this week."

"Thanks." I was surprised and gratified that she would praise me in front of my brother.

"Of course," she added, still smiling, "we'll have to work on using your time more productively." She winked at Jack. "Someone likes to e-mail friends when she should be working."

That wasn't true — I was outraged — but I couldn't argue with her in front of Jack. "I don't know how you got that idea," I said mildly.

Vanessa gave a gentle laugh. "I noticed the way you click on the minimizer whenever I walk by." She turned to Jack. "Did I hear you say you two were going out?"

My heart sank as I realized she wanted to be invited along.

"Yeah," Jack said easily. "We need a little family time together."

"That's nice. Well, I'll be home, resting up and getting ready for next week." She gave me a wink. "Don't be too much of a party girl, Haven. I'll need you to get up to full speed by Monday."

Implying, I thought darkly, that I hadn't been at full speed so far. "Have a nice weekend," I said, and closed my laptop.

Jack had been right — it was a fairly casual

bar, even if the parking lot did look like an impromptu luxury-car show. The interior was trendy, unromantic, and crowded, with dark paneling and low lighting. I liked Jack's girlfriend Heidi, who was bubbly and giggly.

It was one of those winter evenings when the Houston weather couldn't make up its mind about what it wanted to do. It rained on and off for a while, a few sideways gusts hitting us beneath the shelter of an umbrella as Jack guided us inside. I gathered Jack was a regular at this place — he appeared to know the bouncer, two of the bartenders, a couple of waitresses, and pretty much everyone who passed by our small table. In fact, Heidi seemed to know everyone too. I was introduced to a steady parade of overworked Houstonites who were all desperate for their first Friday-evening cocktails.

A couple of times Heidi nudged me under the table when a nice-looking guy had stopped by. "He's cute, isn't he? I know him — I could fix you up. And that one over there — he's cute too. Which one do you like better?"

"Thank you," I said, appreciating her efforts, "but I'm still not over the divorce."

"Oh, you've got to get a rebound guy," Heidi said. "Rebound guys are the *best*."

"They are?"

"They never even think of getting serious, because everyone knows you don't jump into a relationship right after a divorce. They just want to be your welcome wagon when you start having sex again. It's your time to *experiment,* girl!"

"The world is my petri dish," I said, raising my drink.

After slowly drinking one and a half vodka martinis, I was ready to go home. The bar was getting more crowded, and the groups of bodies moving by our table reminded me of upstreaming salmon. I looked at Jack and Heidi, who appeared in no hurry to go anywhere, and I felt the kind of loneliness that can happen in a roomful of people when everyone but you seems to be in on the good time.

"Hey, you two . . . I'm heading out."

"You can't," Jack said, frowning. "It's not even eight o'clock."

"Jack, I've had two drinks and met three hundred and twenty-eight people" — I paused to grin at Heidi — "including a couple of potential rebound guys."

"I'll fix you up with one of 'em," Heidi said enthusiastically. "We'll go on a double date!"

When hell and half of Texas freezes over, I thought, but I smiled. "Sounds great. Let's talk later. Bye, y'all."

Jack began to stand. "I'll help you get a cab."

"No, no . . . stay with Heidi. I'll ask one of the door guys to help me." I shook my head in exasperation as he still looked concerned. "I can find the front door and get a cab. In fact, 1800 Main is close enough I could even walk."

"Don't even think about it," he said.

"I'm not *planning* to walk, I was just pointing out . . . Never mind. Have fun."

Relieved at the prospect of going home and taking off my high-heeled pumps, I plunged into the mass of jostling bodies. It gave me a clammy feeling, being close to so many people.

"I don't think it's an outright phobia," Susan had said when I'd told her I thought I'd developed sexophobia. "That would put it on the level of a disorder, and I'm not convinced the problem is that deep-seated. What happens is, after an experience like you had with Nick, your unconscious mind says 'I'll attach feelings of aversion and anxiety to the opposite sex, so I'll avoid ever being hurt again.' It's just a matter of rewiring."

"Well, I'd like to wire around it, then. Because I don't think I have it in me to go gay."

"You don't have to go gay," Susan had

said, smiling. "You just have to find the right man. It'll happen when you're ready."

In retrospect, I wished I'd had sex with someone before Nick, some positive association that would help me get back in the saddle, so to speak. Bleakly I wondered how many men I was going to have to sleep with before I started to like it. I wasn't good at acquired tastes.

The mass of people inched by the bar. Every stool was occupied, hundreds of drinks set along the expanse of glittering mosaic tabletop tiles. There was no way to get to the door other than follow along with the herd. Revulsion spiked in my stomach every time I felt another impersonal brush of someone's hip, someone's stomach, someone's arm. To distract myself, I tried to calculate how many people beyond the acceptable fire code level had been admitted to the bar.

Someone in the herd stumbled or staggered. It was a domino effect, one person falling into another until I felt the impact of a shoulder against mine. The momentum pushed me into the line of barstools, causing me to drop my purse. I would have bumped hard into the bar if someone sitting there hadn't reached out to steady me.

"Sorry, ma'am," someone called from the

crowd.

"It's okay," I said breathlessly, hunting for my purse.

"Here, let me get that," the guy on the barstool said, bending down to retrieve it.

"Thanks."

As the guy straightened and handed me the purse, I looked up into a pair of blue eyes, and everything stopped, the sound of voices, the background music, every footstep, blink, breath, heartbeat. Only one person I'd ever met had eyes that color. Dazzling. Devil-blue.

I was slow to react, trying to jump-start my heart back into action, and then my pulse hammered too hard, too fast. All I could think of was that the last time — the only time — I'd seen Hardy Cates, I'd been wrapped around him in my family's wine cellar.

CHAPTER SIX

People were pressing behind me, trying to get the bartender's attention. I was about to be trampled. With a murmur, Hardy Cates guided me to the stool he'd been occupying, helping me up. I was too dazed to object. The leather seat was warm from his body. He stood with one hand on the counter, the other on the back of my chair, sheltering me. Trapping me.

Hardy was a little leaner than I remembered, a little more seasoned, tempered by maturity. The look of experience suited him, especially because somewhere deep in those eyes, there still lurked a dangerous invitation to play. He had a quality of masculine confidence that was a thousand times more potent than mere handsomeness. Perfect good looks could leave you cold, but this kind of sexy charisma went straight to your knees. I had no doubt every available woman at the bar had been drooling over him.

In fact, just beyond the outline of his shoulder, I saw the leggy blonde in the next chair glaring at me. I had stumbled, literally, into the middle of their conversation.

"Miss Travis." Hardy looked at me as if he couldn't quite believe I was there. "Pardon. I mean Mrs. Tanner."

"No, I'm . . . it's Travis again." Aware that I was stammering, I said baldly, "I'm divorced."

There was no change in his expression except for a slight widening of those blue-on-blue eyes. He picked up his drink and tossed back a swallow. When his gaze returned to mine, he seemed to be looking right inside me. I flushed hard, remembering the wine cellar again.

The blonde was still giving me the evil eye. I gestured to her awkwardly and babbled, "I'm sorry to interrupt. I didn't mean to . . . please, you go on with your . . . it was nice seeing you, Mr. —"

"Hardy. You're not interrupting anything. We're not together." He glanced over his shoulder, the yellow bar light sliding over the layers of his shiny dark hair. "Excuse me," he said to the woman. "I have to catch up with an old friend."

"Sure," she said with a dimpled smile.

Hardy turned back to me, and the

169

woman's face changed. From the look she gave me, I should have dropped dead on the spot.

"I'm not going to take your chair," I said, beginning to slide off the barstool. "I was just heading out. It's so crowded in here —" My breath caught as my legs touched his, and I scooted up onto the stool again.

"Give it a minute," Hardy said. "It'll thin out soon." He gestured for a bartender, who appeared with miraculous speed.

"Yes, Mr. Cates?"

Hardy looked at me, one brow lifting. "What'll you have?"

I've really got to go, I wanted to tell him, but it came out as, "Dr Pepper, please."

"Dr Pepper — extra cherries," he told the bartender.

Surprised, I asked, "How did you know I like maraschinos?"

His mouth curved with a slow burn of a smile. For a moment I forgot how to breathe. "Just figured you for the type who likes extra."

He was too big. Too close. I still hadn't rid myself of the habit of assessing a man in terms of how much damage he could do to me. Nick had left bruises and fractures — but this guy could kill a normal person with a swipe of his hand. I knew that someone like me, with all my baggage and my possible case of sexophobia had no business being around Hardy Cates.

His hands were still on either side of me, braced on the chair arm and the countertop. I felt the tension of opposing urges, the desire to shrink away from him, and an attraction that prickled like sparks inside me. His silver-gray tie had been loosened and the top button of his shirt was unfastened, revealing the hint of a white undershirt beneath. The skin of his throat was smooth and brown. I wondered for a second what his body felt like beneath the layers of thin cotton and broadcloth, if he was as hard as I remembered. A tumult of curiosity and dread caused me to fidget on the chair.

I turned gratefully as the bartender brought my drink, a highball of sparkling Dr Pepper. Bright red cherries bobbed on the surface. I plucked one from the drink and pulled the fruit from its stem with my teeth. It was plump and sticky, rolling sweetly on my tongue.

"Did you come here alone, Miss Travis?" Hardy asked. So many men his size had incongruously high voices, but he had a deep voice, made to fill a big chest.

I considered telling him to call me by my first name, but I needed to keep every possible barrier between us, no matter how slight.

"I came with my brother Jack and his girl-friend," I said. "I work for him now. He has a property management company. We were celebrating my first week." I picked out another cherry and ate it slowly, and found that Hardy was watching me with an absorbed, slightly glazed expression.

"When I was little, I could never get enough of these," I said. "I stole jars of maraschinos from the fridge. I ate the fruit like candy and poured the juice into my Coke."

"I bet you were a cute little girl. A tomboy."

"Absolutely a tomboy," I said. "I wanted to be like my brothers. Every Christmas I asked Santa for a tool set."

"Did he ever bring you one?"

I shook my head with a rueful smile. "Lots of dolls. Ballet outfits. An Easy-Bake Oven." I washed down another cherry with a swallow of Dr Pepper. "My aunt finally gave me a junior tool kit, but I had to give it back. My mother said it wasn't appropriate for little girls."

The corner of his mouth quirked. "I never got what I wanted either."

I wondered what that was, but getting into personal subjects with him was out of the question. I tried to think of something mundane. Something about work. "How's your EOR business going?" I asked.

From what I knew, Hardy and a couple of other guys had started a small enhanced oil recovery company that went into mature or spent fields after the big companies were through with them. Using specialized recovery techniques, they could locate leftover reserves, called "bypassed pay." A man could make a lot of money that way.

"We're doing okay," Hardy said easily. "We've bought up leases for some mature fields, and got some good results with CO_2 flooding. And we bought an interest in a nonoperated property in the Gulf — we're getting some good play out of it." He watched as I drank my Dr Pepper. "You cut your hair," he said softly.

I lifted a hand and scrubbed my fingers through the short layers. "It was in the way."

"It's beautiful."

It had been so long since I'd gotten a compliment of any kind that I was desperately tongue-tied.

Hardy was watching me with an intent stare. "I never thought I'd have a chance to say this to you. But that night —"

"I'd rather not talk about that," I said hastily. "Please."

Hardy fell obligingly silent.

My gaze focused on the hand resting on the countertop. It was long-fingered and capable, a workman's hand. His nails were clipped nearly to the quick. I was struck by the scattering of tiny star-shaped scars across some of his fingers. "What . . . what are those marks from?" I asked.

His hand flexed a little. "I did fencing work after school and during summers while I was growing up. Put up barbed wire for the local ranchers."

I winced at the thought of the wicked barbs digging into his fingers. "You did it with your bare hands?"

"Until I could afford gloves."

His tone was matter-of-fact, but I felt a twinge of shame, aware of how different my privileged upbringing had been. And I wondered about the drive and ambition it must have taken for him to climb from a trailer-park life, the aluminum ghetto, to where he'd gotten in the oil business. Not many men could do that. You had to work hard. And you had to be ruthless. I could believe that about him.

Our gazes caught, held, the shared voltage nearly causing me to fall off the barstool. I flushed all over, heat gathering beneath my clothes, inside my shoes, and at the same time I was overtaken by a nervous chill. I had never wanted to get away from anyone so fast.

"Thanks for the drink." My teeth were chattering. "I have to go, I'm . . . It was nice to see you. Good luck with everything." I got off the chair and saw with relief that the crowd had thinned out, and there was a negotiable path to the door.

"I'll walk you to your car," Hardy said, tossing a bill on the counter. He picked up the jacket of his business suit.

"No, thanks, I'll get a taxi."

But he walked with me anyway.

"You'll lose your place at the bar," I muttered.

"There's always another place at the bar." I felt the casual pressure of his hand at the small of my back, and I recoiled instinctively. The light touch was instantly withdrawn. "Looks like it's still raining," he said. "Do you have a coat?"

"No," I said abruptly. "It's fine. I don't mind getting wet."

"Can I drive you somewhere?" His tone had gentled, as if he recognized my increasing distress even if he didn't understand the reason for it.

I shook my head violently. "A taxi's fine."

Hardy said a few words to one of the door-

175

men, who went out to the curb. "We can wait inside," he said, "until a car pulls up."

But I couldn't wait. I had to escape him. I was so full of anxiety standing beside him, that I was afraid I was going to have a panic attack. The side of my jaw was throbbing for no reason at all, and my ribs ached where Nick had kicked me, even though I was all healed now. The resonance of old wounds. *I'm going to fire my therapist,* I thought. *I shouldn't be nearly this screwed up after all the time I've spent with her.*

"Bad divorce?" Hardy asked, his gaze falling to my hands. I realized I was clutching my purse in a death grip.

"No, the divorce was great," I said. "It was the marriage that sucked." I forced a smile. "Gotta go. Take care."

Unable to stay inside the bar any longer, I dashed outside even though the taxi wasn't there yet. And I stood there in the drizzle like an idiot, breathing too hard, wrapping my arms around myself. My skin felt too tight for my body, like I'd been shrink-wrapped. Someone came up behind me, and from the way the hairs on the back of my neck lifted, I knew Hardy had followed me.

Without a word he draped his suit jacket around me, cocooning me in silk-lined wool. The feeling was so exquisite that I shivered.

The scent of him was all around me, that sunny, soft spice I had never forgotten . . . God, it was good. Comforting and stimulating at the same time. Absolute world-class pheromones. I wished I could take his jacket home with me.

Not him, just the jacket.

I turned to look up at him, at the raindrops glittering in the rich brown locks of his hair. Water fell in tiny cool strikes on my face. He moved slowly, as if he thought a sudden move might startle me. I felt one of his palms curve along the side of my face, his thumb wiping at the raindrops on my cheek as if they were tears.

"I'd ask if I could call you," I heard him say, "but I think I know the answer." His hand moved to my throat, caressing the side with the backs of his fingers. He was touching me, I thought, dazed, but at that moment I didn't give a damn. Standing in the rain, wrapped in his jacket, was about the best feeling I'd had in a year.

His head lowered over mine, but he didn't try to kiss me, just stood looking into my face, and I stared up into intense blue. His fingertips explored the underside of my jaw and wandered to the crest of my cheek. The pad of his thumb was slightly callused, sandpapery like a cat's tongue. I was filled with mortified fire as I imagined what it might feel like if he —

No.

No, no . . . it would take *years* of therapy before I'd be ready for that.

"Give me your phone number," he murmured.

"That would be a bad idea," I managed to say.

"Why?"

Because there's no way I could handle you, I thought. But I said, "My family doesn't like you."

Hardy grinned unrepentantly, his teeth white in his tanned face. "Don't tell me they're still holding that one little business deal against me?"

"The Travises are sort of touchy that way. And besides" — I paused to lick a raindrop from the corner of my mouth, and his gaze followed the movement alertly — "I'm not a substitute for Liberty."

Hardy's smile vanished. "No. You could never be a substitute for anyone. And that was over a long time ago."

It was raining harder now, turning his hair as dark and slick as otter's fur, his lashes spiking over brilliant blue eyes. He looked good wet. He even smelled good wet, all clean skin and drenched cotton. His skin looked warm beneath the mist of droplets. In fact, as we stood there surrounded by the city, and falling water and lowering night, he seemed like the only warm thing in the world.

He stroked a sodden curl back from my cheek, and another, his face still, severe. For all his size and strength, he touched me with a gentleness Nick had never been capable of. We were so close that I saw the texture of his close-shaven skin, and I knew that the masculine smoothness would be delicious against my lips. I felt a sharp, sweet ache somewhere beneath my rib cage. Wistfully I thought of how much I wished I had gone with him that night at the wedding, to drink champagne under a strawberry moon. No matter how it might have ended, I wished I had done it.

But it was too late now. A lifetime too late. A million wishes too late.

The taxi pulled up.

Hardy's face remained over mine. "I want to see you again," he said in a low voice.

My insides turned into a mini-Chernobyl. I didn't understand myself, why I wanted so much to stay with him. Any rational person would know that Hardy Cates had no real interest in me. He wanted to annoy my family and get my sister-in-law's attention. And if doing that meant screwing a girl from the other side of the tracks, so much the better. He was a predator. And for my own sake, I had to get rid of him.

So I plastered a disdainful smile over the panic, and gave him a look that said *I've got your number, pal.* "You'd just love to fuck a Travis, wouldn't you?" Even as I said it, I cringed inwardly at my own deliberate crudeness.

Hardy responded with a long stare that fried every brain cell I possessed. And then he said softly, "Just one little Travis."

I went scarlet. I felt myself clenching in places I didn't even know I had muscles. And I was amazed that my legs still worked as I went to the taxi and got in.

"Where do you live?" Hardy asked, and like an idiot, I told him. He handed a twenty to the cabbie, a huge overpayment since 1800 Main was only a few blocks away. "Drive careful with her," he said, as if I were made of some fragile substance that might shatter at the first bump on the road.

"Yes, sir!"

And it wasn't until the cab pulled away that I realized I was still wearing his jacket.

The normal thing would have been to have the jacket dry-cleaned immediately — there was a service in the building — and have someone take it to Hardy on Monday.

But sometimes normal just isn't happening. Sometimes crazy feels too good to resist. So I kept the jacket, uncleaned, all weekend. I kept stealing over to it and taking deep breaths of it. That damned jacket, the smell of Hardy Cates on it, was crack. I finally gave in and wore it for a couple of hours while I watched a DVD movie.

Then I called my best friend, Todd, who had recently forgiven me for not talking to him in months, and I explained the situation to him.

"I'm having a relationship with a jacket," I said.

"Was there a sale at Neiman's?"

"No, it's not mine, it's a guy's jacket." I went on to tell him all about Hardy Cates, even going so far as to describe what had happened at Liberty and Gage's wedding almost two years ago, and then about meeting him in the bar. "So I just put on the jacket and watched a movie in it," I concluded. "In fact, I'm wearing it right now. How far outside of normal is that? On a scale of one to ten, how crazy am I?"

"Depends. What movie did you watch?"

"Todd," I protested, wanting a serious answer from him.

"Haven, don't ask me to define the boundaries of normal. You know how I was raised. My father once stuck strands of his own pubic hair onto a painting and sold it for a million dollars."

I had always liked Todd's father, Tim Phelan, but I'd never understood his art. The best explanation I'd heard was that Tim Phelan was a revolutionary genius whose sculptures exploded conventional notions of art and displayed common materials like bubble gum and masking tape in a new context.

As a child I had often wondered at the perplexing role reversal of the Phelan household, in which the parents seemed like children, and their only child, Todd, had been the grown-up.

It had only been at Todd's insistence that the family kept standard hours for eating and sleeping. He had dragged them to parent/teacher conferences even though they didn't believe in the grading system. Todd had no luck, however, in curbing their wild house decorating. Sometimes Mr. Phelan would pass through the hallway, pause to sketch or paint something right on the wall, and continue on his way. Their house had been filled with priceless graffiti. And at holiday time, Mrs. Phelan would hang the Christmas tree, which they called a bodhi bush, upside down from the ceiling.

Now Todd had become an enormously successful interior designer, mostly because of his ability to be creative without going too far. His father disdained his work, which pleased Todd tremendously. In the Phelan family, Todd had once told me, beige was an act of defiance.

"So," Todd said, returning to the subject of the jacket. "Can I come over and smell it?"

I grinned. "No, you'd take it for yourself, and I have to give it back. But not until tomorrow, which means I have at least twelve hours left with it."

"I think you need to talk with Susan this week about why you're so afraid of a guy you're attracted to that you can't handle anything more than fondling his jacket. While he's not in it."

I was instantly defensive. "I already told you, he's a family enemy and I —"

"I call bullshit," Todd said. "You didn't have any problem telling your family to go to hell when you wanted to be with Nick."

"Yeah, and as it turned out, they were all right about him."

"Doesn't matter. You have the right to go after any guy who appeals to you. I don't think you're afraid of your family's reaction. I think it's something else." A long, speculative pause, and then he asked gently, "Was it that bad with Nick, sweetheart?"

I had never told Todd that my husband had physically abused me. I wasn't at the point that I could talk about it with anyone other than Gage, Liberty, or the therapist. The concern in Todd's voice nearly undid me. I tried to answer, but it took forever to force a sound from my tight throat.

"Yeah," I finally whispered. My eyes flooded, and I wiped them with my palm. "It was pretty bad."

Then it was Todd's turn to wait a while, before he could manage to speak. "What can I do?" he asked simply.

"You're doing it, you're being my friend."

"Always."

I knew he meant it. And it occurred to me that friendship was a lot more dependable, not to mention long-lasting, than love.

CHAPTER SEVEN

When an apartment at 1800 Main became available, it never lasted long despite the multimillion-dollar price tag. No matter whether your place was a thousand square feet — the size of my manager's apartment, which I loved for its coziness — or four thousand square feet, you got the best views in Houston. You also had the benefits of twenty-four-hour concierge and valet service, designer kitchens loaded with granite and quartz, Murano glass light fixtures, bathrooms with travertine floors and Roman soaking tubs, closets you could park a car in, and membership to a sixth-floor club featuring an Olympic-sized pool, a fitness center, and your own personal trainer.

Regardless of all those amenities, Gage and Liberty had moved out. Liberty was not much on high-rise living, and she and Gage had both agreed that Matthew and Carrington needed to live in a house with a yard.

They had a ranch north of Houston, but it was too far from the city and Gage's offices to be their main residence. So they had found a lot in the Tanglewood subdivision and had built a European-style home there.

Once the apartment was empty, our leasing agent, Samantha, began to show it to prospective buyers. But before anyone was able to see a place in 1800 Main, Samantha had to get a reference from a bank or law firm to make sure they were legit. "You'd be amazed," she told me, "how many weirdos want a peek at a big fancy apartment." She also revealed that about a third of our residents had paid cash for their apartments, at least half were business executives, and almost three quarters of them were what Samantha considered "new money" people.

About a week after I had messengered Hardy's dry-cleaned jacket to his office, I got a call from Samantha.

She sounded tense and distracted. "Haven, I can't make it in today. My dad had some chest pains over the weekend, and he's in the hospital and they're doing tests."

"Oh, I'm so sorry to hear that. Is there anything I can do?"

"Yes." She gave a groan. "Would you please tell Vanessa for me? I feel terrible. She made it clear we were supposed to give twenty-four-hours' notice before taking a day off."

"Vanessa's gone," I reminded her. "She took a long weekend, remember?" From what I knew, Vanessa was having a long-distance affair with a guy from Atlanta, and she went to visit him at least once a month. She wouldn't tell anyone his name or what he did, but she had dropped heavy hints to me that he was extremely rich and powerful, and she had him wrapped around her finger, of course.

I couldn't have cared less about who Vanessa was dating, but I tried to look impressed to keep from offending her. Vanessa seemed to expect me to be fascinated by the mundane details of her life. Sometimes she repeated the same stories, like the one about being caught in traffic, or what her masseur had said about what great shape she was in, two and three times, even when I reminded her she'd already told me. I was certain it was deliberate, although I couldn't figure out why she did it, or why I seemed to be the only one she did this to.

"Is there anything else, Sam?" I asked.

"I would really appreciate it if you could go to my computer and print out the latest marketing plan file for Mr. Travis — he was coming by today, and he really needs to take a look at it."

"I'll make sure he gets it," I said.

"And one more thing . . . there's a guy coming to the office at nine to look at the condo. Could you show him around for me? Tell him I'm sorry I couldn't make it, and I'll be available by cell to answer any questions."

"Sure. Is he qualified?"

"He's so qualified it sort of makes me dizzy to be in the same room with him." A dramatic sigh. "Single and loaded. Damn it! I was really looking forward to this showing. The only thing that makes me happy is knowing Vanessa won't get to meet him either."

I chuckled. "I'll make sure to say some nice things to him about you."

"Thanks. And make sure he has my cell number."

"Got it."

As I mulled over the phrase "single and loaded," a funny shiver chased down my spine, and somehow . . . I knew. I *knew* who Mr. Single-and-Loaded was, and I wondered what the hell he was up to.

"Samantha," I asked suspiciously, "what's his —"

"Call waiting," she said. "It's Dad — I gotta go."

The connection terminated, and I put

down the phone. I went to Samantha's computer and pulled up her schedule, just as the concierge, David, beeped on the intercom. "Samantha, Mr. Cates is here in the lobby."

As my suspicion was confirmed, I found myself out of breath. I was simultaneously stunned, worried, and oddly amused. My voice sounded strange to my own ears. "Samantha's not here today," I told David. "Tell Mr. Cates that Miss Travis will be doing the showing. I'll be down in just a minute."

"Yes, Miss Travis."

I did a quick, discreet check in a compact mirror, applied some tinted lip balm, and pushed the long bangs back from my forehead. I was wearing dark brown wool trousers and a matching V-neck wrap sweater. Unfortunately I had chosen flats for comfort that day. If I'd known I would see Hardy Cates, I would have worn my tallest heels to give him less of a height advantage.

I looked into Samantha's file on Hardy and skimmed the prequalification report, and nearly dropped it as I saw the numbers. When Hardy said his company was doing "okay," he had neglected to mention that he was in the process of becoming obscenely rich. That property in the Gulf they were getting "good play" out of must have been a major find. A *really* major find.

Hardy Cates was on his way to becoming a big-time oilman. I was certainly the last person who could hold that against him. My father had huge ties to the oil industry. And even my oldest brother, with his alternative energy company, hadn't cut fossil fuels entirely from his repertoire. Sighing, I closed the file and took the elevator to the residential lobby.

Hardy was sitting in a black leather chair near the concierge's desk, talking with David. He saw me and stood, and my heart began to thump so hard that I felt a little light-headed.

I put on a business face, a business smile, and extended a hand as I reached him.

"Mr. Cates."

"Hello, Miss Travis."

A hard, impersonal grip of our hands, and we stood facing each other. We might have been strangers. But there was a glint in Hardy's eyes that drew heat to the surface of my skin.

"I'm sorry Samantha wasn't available this morning," I said.

"I'm not." He swept a quick, thorough glance over me. "Thanks for returning the jacket. You didn't have to have it cleaned."

That certainly got David's attention. He

looked from one of us to the other with indiscreet interest.

"I'm afraid all I'm going to be able to do," I said to Hardy briskly, "is take you on an initial walk-through so you can get an idea of what the apartment looks like. I'm not a leasing agent, so Samantha's the only one who can answer your questions definitively."

"I'm sure you'll be able to answer any questions I've got."

We went to the elevator, and a pair of women walked out, one older, one around my age. They looked like a mother and daughter heading out to do some shopping. As I got into the elevator and turned to face out, I saw that both women had glanced back for a better look at Hardy.

I had to admit, the man looked amazing in jeans. The ancient denim clung lightly to his hips and followed the long lines of some remarkable thigh muscles. And although I made a point of *not* checking out his rear view, my peripheral vision was having a very good day.

I pushed the button for the eighteenth floor. As the elevator whooshed up, we occupied separate corners.

Hardy studied me with frank interest. His blue cashmere sweater lay softly over the hard lines of his torso. "I appreciate you taking some time out for me today, Miss Travis."

I decided we had to go on a first-name basis. He'd started to say "Miss Travis" with a touch of overdone respect that bordered on mockery. "You can call me Haven," I muttered.

"Haven," he repeated. The sound of my name in that melted-tar drawl gave me a pang of uneasy pleasure.

"What are you doing here?" I asked tersely. "Are you really interested in this condo?"

"Why wouldn't I be?"

"I saw your address on the prequalification form. You're at Post Oak right now. I don't see why you'd want to move from there."

"I'm only leasing that place," he said evenly. "I haven't bought it. And I like this location better."

I narrowed my eyes. "You know who used to live in this apartment, right?"

"Your brother and sister-in-law. So what?"

"So I think there's something weird about you wanting to move into Gage and Liberty's old place."

"You got another apartment available, I'll look at that one too."

We stepped out of the elevator into the H-shaped layout of corridors, all serene in varying shades of cream and gray. I turned to face Hardy, the air between us nearly crackling with challenge. "Eighteen hundred Main isn't that much better than Post Oak," I said. "In fact, in terms of bang for the buck, you're probably better off staying where you are."

Hardy lifted a brow, looking amused. "Are you trying out some new kind of sales tactic on me?"

"No. I'm wondering what your ulterior motive is."

"What's your best guess?"

I stared straight into those fathomless eyes. "I think you've got some leftover hang-up about my sister-in-law."

Hardy's smile fled. "You're way off on that one, honey. We never even slept together. I wish Liberty all the best, but I don't want her that way." He stepped closer, not touching me, but I felt like he was just about to . . . well, I didn't know what. I felt a nervous chill chase down my back. "So take another guess," he said. "You can't keep me out of here if you can't come up with a good reason for it."

I stepped back from him and took a shaky breath. "You're a hell-raiser," I said. "That's a pretty good reason."

The corner of his mouth twitched. "I got all that out of my system in my twenties."

"You look like you've still got some left in you."

"No, ma'am. I'm completely tame."

I had an inkling of what he must have been like as a naughty schoolboy, trying to convince his teacher of his innocence. And his sneaky charm was so irresistible that I had to turn away to hide a smile. "Sure you are," I said, leading him to the apartment.

Stopping at the door, I began to punch numbers into the combination touch pad. I was suffused with an intense awareness of Hardy, so big and solid beside me. There was that scent again, insanely distracting.

I punched the last button, barely aware of what I was doing. Although I had used the combination pad a thousand times while I'd stayed there with Gage and Liberty, I must have hit a wrong number. Instead of clicking open, the lock emitted a series of beeps.

"Sorry," I said breathlessly, trying to look anywhere but at him. "I pushed the wrong buttons. When that happens, it takes a few seconds to clear and reset. You can change the combination to any number you —"

"Haven," he said quietly, and waited until I could bring myself to look up at him.

I gripped the door handle as if hanging on for dear life. I had to clear my throat before I could make a sound. "Wh-what?"

"Why do I make you so nervous?" His voice was soft, reaching inside me to a raw, tender place. A mocking smile touched his lips. "You afraid I'm going to make a move on you?"

I couldn't answer. *I can't stand this,* I thought desperately. Heat washed over me, color layering on color. My heart worked in painful beats. All I could do was stare at Hardy without blinking, my back pressing against the door while he bent over me. He moved closer, imparting the pressure of his body until I felt the touch of hard muscle in several places at once. I closed my eyes, mortified by the rapid gusts of my breathing.

"Then let's get it over with," Hardy murmured, "so you'll stop worrying."

His dark head bent. He eased his mouth over mine. I put my fists between us, my arms clasped over my chest in a tight blockade. I couldn't make myself push him away, but neither could I let him hold me full-on. His arms went around me, the embrace firm but gentle, as if he were being mindful not to crush me. Our breath mingled, heat surging in restless rhythms.

His mouth shifted, catching at my top lip, then the lower one, opening them. Every time I thought the kiss might stop, it went on longer, deeper, and the back of my throat tingled as if I were being fed something sweet. I felt the silken stroke of his tongue . . . a soft taste . . . another . . . I went weak against him, dissolving in sensation.

His tenderness disarmed me until I almost forgot about the knot of fear in my stomach. I stood there breathing him, feeling him . . . but he was all around me, he could overpower me so easily if he chose. I couldn't handle feeling that defenseless, no matter how gentle he was. Turning my mouth away from his, I broke the kiss with a whimper.

Hardy's lips grazed the top of my head, and he released me slowly. He looked down at me, blue heat in his eyes.

"Now show me the apartment," he whispered.

Purely by luck — I couldn't yet pull a coherent thought from my brain — I managed to dial the right combination and open the door.

Since I wasn't certain how far I could walk without staggering, I let Hardy do his own exploring. He wandered through the three-bedroom apartment, checking out the finishes, the appliances, the views from every room. In the main living area, a wall of nothing but windows revealed a spectacular view of Houston, the unzoned city sprawling outward in a mix of offices and strip malls and mansions and shacks, the cheap and the great mingling freely.

Watching Hardy's long, lean form silhouetted against those windows, I thought the apartment suited him. He wanted to show people he'd arrived. And you couldn't blame him for that. In Houston, if you wanted a place at the table, you had to have the clothes, the cars, the high-rise apartment, the mansion. The tall blond wife.

Needing to break the silence, I finally found my voice. "Liberty told me you used to work on a drilling rig." I leaned against the kitchen counter as I watched him. "What did you do?"

He glanced at me over his shoulder. "Welder."

No wonder, I thought, and I didn't realize I'd said it aloud until he replied.

"No wonder what?"

"Your . . . your shoulders and arms," I said, abashed.

"Oh." He turned to face me, his hands still tucked in his pockets. "Yeah, they usually get the bigger guys to do the onboard welding, the stuff they can't do in shore-based shops. So I had to carry a seventy-pound power-con all around the rig, up and down stairs and ladders . . . that whips you into shape real fast."

"A power-con is some kind of generator?"

He nodded. "The newer models are built with the handles farther apart, so two people can carry them. But the older version, the one I had to lug around, could only be carried by one guy. Hell, my muscles would get so sore . . ." He grinned and rubbed the back of his neck, as if recalling long-ago discomforts. "You should have seen the other rig welders. They made me look puny."

"I honestly can't imagine that," I said.

His smile lingered as he approached me, coming to lean on the other side of the counter.

"Did you like being a rig welder?" I asked hesitantly. "I mean, was it what you wanted to do?"

"I wanted to do anything that would get me out of Welcome."

"That's the town you grew up in?"

He nodded. "Blew out one of my knees playing football — so no chance of a scholarship. And in Welcome, if you don't make it to college, your options are limited. I knew how to weld, from my fence work. It didn't take much to get certified. And I had a buddy who worked as a rig roustabout — he told me the welders made eighty bucks an hour."

"Did you ever think you'd go on to . . .

this?" I gestured at the gleaming, pristine apartment around us.

"No," Hardy said at once. "I never imagined I —" But as he stared into my eyes, he paused. It seemed as if he were weighing the consequences of his words, wondering how I'd react if he told me the truth. "Yeah, I knew," he finally said, his voice soft. "I always knew I'd do whatever it took. Living in a trailer park, running in a pack of barefoot kids . . . my whole life was already set out for me, and I sure as hell didn't like the looks of it. So I always knew I'd take my chance when I got it. And if it didn't come, I'd make something happen."

As I began to comprehend what a tremendous drive he possessed, I was surprised by the hint of something like shame or defensiveness secreted deep in the quiet admission. "Why does it make you uncomfortable to admit you're ambitious?"

He gave me an arrested glance, as if it were a question he'd never been asked before. A wary pause, and then he said, "I learned to keep quiet about it early on. Folks make fun of you otherwise."

"Why?"

"It's like crabs in a box." Seeing my incomprehension, he explained, "You can keep a bunch of crabs in a shallow container, and none of them will escape. Because as soon as one of 'em tries to climb out, the others pull him back in."

We faced each other directly, our forearms resting on the counter between us. It felt too close, too strong, as if some incinerating current had opened between us. I pulled back and looked away, breaking the connection.

"What did you do in Dallas?" I heard him ask.

"I worked at a hotel for a little while. Then I stayed at home for about a year."

Hardy's eyes held a mocking glint. "Doing what? Being a trophy wife?"

Since I would have died before ever letting him know the truth, I said casually, "Yes. It was pretty boring."

"Is that why your marriage ended? You got bored?"

"More or less." Reading his expression, I said rather than asked, "You think I'm spoiled, don't you?"

He didn't bother to deny it. "I think you should have married someone who could have done a better job keeping you entertained."

"I should never have gotten married at all," I said. "I'm not cut out for it."

"You never know. You may want to give it another try someday."

I shook my head. "No man will ever have that power over me again."

The barest trace of contempt crept into his voice. "You had all the power, sweetheart. You're a rich man's daughter."

Of course. That was how it looked from the outside. No one could know that I'd had no power at all, over anything.

"The entire subject of marriage is boring," I said. "Especially mine. And I'd rather you not call me 'sweetheart.' " I walked out from behind the counter, my arms folded across my chest. "What do you think about the apartment?"

"I like it."

"A lot of space for a single guy, isn't it?"

"I grew up in a family of five living in a single-wide. After that, I can handle a lot of space."

I tried to remember what Liberty had told me about his family. "Two brothers and a sister, right?"

"Yes. Rick, Kevin, and Hannah." A shadow crossed his face. "My sister died last year from breast cancer. Fought it real hard. Double mastectomy, four months of chemo. She went to M. D. Anderson . . . I'd have taken her anywhere in the world, but everyone said that was the best place. Near the end they put her on Arimidex, which she said was worse than the chemo. Nothing stopped the tumor markers from going up."

"I'm sorry." I wanted to convey how much I understood, even the things he hadn't said. I found myself moving toward him, now leaning on the same side of the counter as he was. "I know what it's like to lose someone that way. My mother died of breast cancer too. Except she never went through the chemo. They caught it too late. She was at stage four with lung dissemination. Mother chose to have a shorter, better quality of life, as opposed to dragging it out and going through all the surgery and treatments, which wouldn't have worked anyway."

"How old were you?" he asked gently.

"Fifteen."

Staring at me, he reached out to stroke back my bangs, which had fallen over one eye. "Haven . . . tell me not to take the apartment, and I won't. Otherwise, I want it. It's up to you."

My eyes widened. "I . . . I . . . your decision has nothing to do with me. Don't make me part of it."

"Would it bother you if I lived here?"

"Of course not," I said, a little too quickly.

He smiled lazily. "I'm not a man of many talents . . . but the few I've got are good ones. One of them being, I can always tell when someone's lying to me."

I had no choice but to admit the truth. "Okay. It might bother me a little."

"Why?"

He was good at throwing me off balance. I could feel my pulse kicking up with agitation. I didn't know what it was about Hardy that broke through my defenses. Damn, he was wily. Aggressive, pushy, but smart enough to cover it with easy charm. He was ten times the man Nick was, and he was just too much, too much in every way. If I ever let him close to me, I would deserve whatever I got, and the results wouldn't be pretty.

"Look," I said sharply, "whether you move here or not, I'm not interested in any kind of . . . whatever . . . with you."

His gaze didn't move from mine. His eyes were darker than a blueprint. "Define 'whatever.' "

"In this case it means sex."

"That's one of my other talents," he volunteered.

As distraught as I was, I almost smiled. "I'm sure that will make some of the female residents of 1800 Main very happy." I paused for emphasis. "But I won't be one of them."

"Understood. So where do I end up, Haven? . . . Here, or Post Oak?"

I made an impatient gesture to indicate it was of no consequence. "Move here if you want. It's a free country."

"Okay. I will."

I didn't like the way he said it. As if we had just made some kind of bargain.

CHAPTER EIGHT

"Like hell he's gonna live here," Jack said indignantly, pacing around my office later that day. He had dropped by for a quick visit to see how things were going. Although he would never admit it, I thought that Jack was mildly relieved that Vanessa was gone. Whenever she was around, she sent out discreet signals that she was angling for some kind of relationship that went beyond business. Thankfully, he didn't seem interested.

While Jack fumed about Hardy, I sat behind my desk, trying to figure out some new software that had gone contrary on me.

"Here's the way I'm looking at it," I said, looking up from my laptop. " 'Keep your friends close, keep your enemies closer.' What better way to find out what Hardy Cates is up to, than have him in our building?"

That made Jack pause. "I guess there's some sense in that. But why does he want to live *here?* If this is some whack deal about Gage and Liberty —"

"No, I honestly don't think that's it. I think he would have taken another apartment if it were available."

Jack sat on the edge of my desk. "He's got something up his sleeve. I guarantee it."

He sounded so certain that I gave him a questioning glance. "Have you met him before?"

"Yeah, about a year ago. He was going out with a girl I used to date and I happened to see her at a club, and we all talked for a few minutes."

"What did you think about him?"

A wry smile curved his lips. "Hate to admit it, but if it weren't for the shit he pulled with Gage's biofuel deal, and crashing the wedding, I might have liked the guy. We talked some hunting and fishing, and he struck me as a good ol' boy. And like him or not, you've got to hand it to him — that company of his is kicking ass."

"Why do you think that is?"

"He's pulled together a great team, and he can negotiate a tight deal. But mostly he's got the knack for finding oil. Call it luck, call it skill, but some people got it and some don't. Maybe he's not college-smart, but he's smart in a way they can't teach. Man, I wouldn't underestimate him." Jack dragged his hand through his dark hair, looking thoughtful. "Joe's met him."

I blinked in surprise. "What? Our brother Joe?"

"Yeah. Joe took his picture for that thing they did on him in *Texas Monthly* last year."

"What a coincidence," I said slowly. "What did Joe say about him?"

"Can't remember. I'll have to ask him." Jack frowned. "You think Cates has some kind of revenge thing going on against the Travises?"

"For what?"

"Because Gage married his old girlfriend?"

"That would be taking things a little far," I said skeptically. "I mean, they never even slept together."

Jack's brows rose. "How do you know?"

"He said so."

"You were talking about sex with Hardy Cates?" he asked in the same tone he would have used for *et tu, Haven?*

"Not like that," I said uncomfortably. "It was sort of a casual reference."

Jack gave me a long, hard stare. "If he so much as glances in your direction, I'm going to wipe the floor with his ass —"

"Jack, *hush* —"

"— and I'm gonna make that *real* clear to

him before the contracts are signed."

"If you embarrass me that way, I'm going to find a new job. I swear it, Jack. Not a word to Hardy."

A long silence, while my brother stared at me. "Are you interested in Cates?" he asked.

"No!"

"Good. Because — and don't take this personal — I have no confidence in your ability to pick a decent guy for yourself. If you like someone, he's probably scum."

"That is a *huge* boundary violation," I said indignantly.

"A what?"

"That means I don't make any comments about the kind of women you date, and you have no right to judge my choices."

"Yeah, but —" Jack stopped and scowled. "You're right. It's none of my business. It's just . . . I'd like you to find some nice guy with no weird fuckin' baggage."

I had to laugh. My irritation vanished, and I reached over to pat his hand. "If you ever meet one," I said, "let me know."

My cell phone rang, and I fished it out of my purse. "Bye, Jack," I said, and flipped the phone open. "Hello?"

"Haven."

The sound of Hardy's voice gave me a subtle, pleasurable jolt. "Hi," I said, and damned myself for sounding breathless.

Jack, who'd been in the process of leaving, stopped at the doorway and shot me a curious glance. I waved for him to go on, but he stayed where he was, watching and listening.

I adopted a brisk, professional tone. "Do you have a question about the apartment? I'll give you Samantha's number —"

"I've already got her number. I want to talk to you."

"Oh." I fiddled with a pen on the desk. "How can I help you?"

"I need a recommendation for someone who can come in and fix up the apartment — pick out the furniture, colors, that kind of stuff."

"An interior decorator?"

"Yeah, but a good one. The one I hired for my last apartment charged a fortune, and it ended up looking like a Fort Worth bar."

"And that's not your style?"

"No, it's exactly my style. That's the problem. I need an image upgrade."

"You don't need to worry about that," I said. "The formal look is out. Casual and comfortable is fine."

"I have a sofa that once roamed the open range."

I couldn't help laughing at that. "You mean cowhide? Oh, God. You do need help."

I thought of Todd. "I know someone — but he's not cheap."

"That's okay, as long as he's good."

"Would you like me to call him for you and set up something?"

"Thanks. That would be great. And as a favor — would you be there with me when I meet him?"

I hesitated, my fingers tightening on the pen. "I don't think I'd be much help."

"I need your opinion. My kind of decorating usually involves fur, skins, and horns. You have no idea what I could be talked into."

"All right," I said reluctantly. "I'll be there. When are you free?"

"I'm tied up the rest of today and tomorrow, finishing up an AFE. So the next day or anytime after that would be fine."

"What's an AFE?"

"Authority for expenditure form. Basically it's all the estimates for drilling and completing a well, including salaries, services, and equipment. You can get screwed six ways to Sunday if you don't get the AFE right and make sure everyone follows it. It's real important for a smaller company with a limited budget."

"So are you the one who makes sure everyone follows the AFE?"

"Yeah, I'm the heavy," Hardy admitted.

"Neither of my partners are good at it — one's a geophysicist and sticks to the science stuff, and the other one can't handle confrontation. So it's up to me. I figure I haven't managed a project right unless I get a few death threats along the way."

"I bet you're good at confrontation," I said.

"I have to be, sometimes. But I'm not that way by nature."

"Sure," I told him, smiling skeptically. "I'll call you later with the appointment time."

"Okay, boss."

The smile was still tucked in the corners of my lips as I looked up and saw Jack there. I couldn't tell if he was frowning or scowling — but it was not a happy expression.

"Don't tell me you were just talking to Hardy Cates," Jack said.

"I was just talking to Hardy Cates. What about it?"

"I haven't heard you giggle like that since high school."

"I wasn't giggling," I said defensively. "I never giggle. And before you say anything else, remember my personal boundaries."

"You make sure Cates remembers about your personal boundaries," Jack muttered, and left my cubicle.

■ ■ ■ ■

"You know," Todd said, "I've had lots of clients who have crappy taste in decorating. But they never want to admit it. They hire me and then they waste a lot of time arguing over the design scheme. This is the first client who's ever admitted he has crappy taste."

"I think he may actually be proud of it," I said.

We were riding up in the elevator to the eighteenth floor, where we were going to meet Hardy at his new apartment. "Did I tell you what Beebe Whitney said when I told her that I was doing his apartment?" Todd asked.

Back in high school, Beebe had been the most beautiful girl at Lamar, not to mention head cheerleader and class princess. She had been married in one of Houston's biggest weddings ever and had divorced eleven months later.

"No, what?"

"She said, 'You may be doing his apartment, Todd, but I've done *him*.' "

My mouth fell open. "Beebe Whitney slept with Hardy Cates?" I whispered, scandalized.

Todd's blue-green eyes sparkled with relish. "A one-night stand. They met on her divorce-moon."

"What's a divorce-moon?"

"It's the trip you take after your divorce . . . you know, like a honeymoon. You didn't have one?"

I remembered lying in Gage and Liberty's apartment with a rib brace and a concussion, and I smiled grimly. "Not exactly."

"Well, Beebe did. She went to Galveston, and there was this great party, and Hardy Cates was there. So after they talked for a while, they went to her hotel room. According to Beebe, they had sex all night in every possible position, and by the time it was over she felt like a cheap whore. She said it was fabulous."

I put a hand over my midriff, where nerves were jumping. The idea of Hardy having sex with someone I knew was strangely upsetting.

"Too bad he's straight," Todd said. "Heterosexuality is so limiting."

I gave him a dark glance. "Do me a favor and don't pull anything with Hardy."

"Sure. You calling dibs?"

"No. Not at all. I just don't want you to make him nervous. He is definitely not bi-possible."

As we got out of the elevator and went to

the apartment, I wondered what Hardy would make of Todd. My friend wasn't in the least effeminate, but he still gave off the vibe of being able to play it any way. People usually liked Todd — he had a sense of effortless cool, of being comfortable in his own skin.

"I think you'll get along with Hardy," I said. "I'll be interested to hear your opinion of him later."

Todd had an unerring ability to read people, to ferret out the secrets they gave away without even knowing it. Body language, verbal hesitations, the minute changes in expression . . . Todd saw it all with an artist's sensitivity to detail.

As we got to the door, we saw that it was already open. "Hello?" I said tentatively as we went inside the apartment.

Hardy came to meet us, his gaze flicking over me, then settling on my face. "Hi." He smiled and reached for my hand. He held it a little too long, his thumb sliding into the cup of my palm before I tugged free.

He was wearing a designer suit, a beautiful dress shirt, a good watch. His tie was a little loose, as if he'd been tugging at it, and his hair fell in mink-brown layers that practically begged to be touched and played with. He looked good in the civilized attire, but there was still a touch of the bruiser about him, a sense that he was not meant be bound up in a suit and tie.

"Can I help you with that?" he asked Todd, who was burdened with a stack of materials including a portfolio, sample books, sketches, and folders.

"Nope, I've got it." Todd set the stack on the gray quartz countertop. He gave Hardy a pleasant smile and extended a hand. "Todd Phelan. Great place you've got here. I think we can come up with something really spectacular for it."

"Hope so." Hardy shook his hand firmly. "I'll do my best to stay out of your way."

"You don't have to stay out of the way. I intend to take your likes and dislikes into account." Pausing, Todd added with a grin, "We may even be able to work in the cowhide sofa if you're attached to it."

"It's damn comfortable," Hardy said with a touch of wistfulness. "I have some good memories of that sofa."

"We'll all be better off if you keep those to yourself," I said crisply.

Hardy grinned at me.

"In the absence of furniture," Todd said, "this will have to be a kitchen counter meeting. If you'll come around here, Hardy, I'll show you some ideas I've already come up with. I have a copy of the floor plan, so I'm familiar with the layout . . ."

As Hardy walked around the counter to join him, Todd turned to me and mouthed a silent *Wow,* his turquoise eyes sparkling with glee. I ignored him.

The two men bent over the sample book. "See this color palette . . . ?" Todd was saying. "Earth tones, caramels, botanical greens, some pumpkin orange here and there for pop. This would be a really comfortable environment. And it would definitely soften the sterility of the finish in here."

They agreed on natural textures and tones, and furniture with tailored lines. The only preference Hardy had was that he didn't want a lot of little tables and chairs scattered around. He liked solid furniture that wouldn't make him feel cramped.

"Of course," Todd said. "Big guy like you . . . what are you, six one, six two . . . ?"

"Six two."

"Right." Todd slid me a glance of bright mischief. Clearly he found Hardy as delicious as I did. But unlike me, Todd was not at all conflicted about it.

"What do you think?" Hardy asked me as they pulled some sample pages from a book and laid them side by side. "Do you like the way this looks?"

As I moved next to him, I felt the gentle brush of his hand on my back. Heat raced along my spine, up to the base of my skull. "I do," I said. "I still object to the cowhide, however."

"It adds a touch of whimsy," Todd protested. "It'll work. Give it a chance."

"No cowhide if she doesn't like it," Hardy told him.

Todd arched his brow sardonically as he looked at me. "What about orange, Haven? Can we have orange, or is that too much for you to handle?"

I studied the palette and touched a sample of chocolate-colored velvet. "I like this brown, actually."

"I'm already using that for the chair," Todd argued.

"Then make the chair orange and the sofa brown."

Todd considered that and made some notes.

I heard the ring of a cell phone. Hardy glanced at both of us. "Excuse me. Do you mind if I take this one? I'll make it as fast as possible."

"Take your time," Todd said. "We're fine."

Hardy flipped it open, wandering to the next room for privacy. "Cates here." He paused while the person on the other end of the line spoke. "Make sure they drill slower when they go in sliding mode . . . and I want them to build that angle tight, got it? The equipment can handle it. Especially since we're not drilling deep, no more than medium radius . . ."

There was no business with more phallic terminology than the oil business. After being exposed to three minutes of conversation about drilling, holes, fluids, and pumping, even a Benedictine nun would have dirty thoughts. Todd and I were silent, listening avidly.

". . . tell them we're going long and horizontal . . ."

"I'd like to go long and horizontal with him," Todd commented.

I smothered a laugh. "I'll admit, he's cute."

"Cute? No. Sexy as hell. Unfortunately, also very straight, so . . . he's yours."

I shook my head. "It's too soon after the divorce. I don't want him. Besides, he can be a jerk, and I've had enough of that."

"You let him touch you," Todd observed idly.

My eyes widened. "I do not."

"Yes you do. Just little touches here and there. He puts his hand on your arm or back, he stands close to you, getting you used to him . . . it's a mating ritual. Like *March of the Penguins*."

"It has nothing to do with mating rituals. It's a Texas thing. People are touchy-feely here."

"Especially when they want to bone you into the middle of next week."

"Todd, *shut up,*" I muttered, and he snickered.

We both looked hastily down at the sample book as Hardy came back into the room.

A few more minutes of discussion, and then Hardy glanced down at his watch. "I'm sorry to have to ask this . . . but would either of you mind if we cut this a few minutes short?"

"Not at all," Todd said. "I've got more than enough to start with."

"Thanks. I appreciate it." Hardy loosened his tie and unbuttoned his shirt collar. "Time to change out of the monkey suit. We're having some drilling issues with a deviated well, and I need to go on-site to check on it." He picked up a briefcase and a set of keys, and grinned at me. "So far it's a dry hole. But I have a feeling we've got a wildcat on our hands."

I didn't dare look at Todd. "Good luck," I said. "By the way, is it okay if Todd and I stay here a few minutes?"

"Of course."

"I'll lock up when we leave."

"Thank you." Hardy passed by me, his fingers brushing lightly over my hand as it rested on the counter. The warm touch caused a ripple of sensation to run up my arm. His gaze connected with mine in a flash of unholy blue. "Bye." The door closed behind him.

I lent my weight to the counter, trying to think straight. But my brain had evacuated the premises.

It was a good half minute before I looked over at Todd. His eyes were slightly foggy, like he was waking up — reluctantly — from a lascivious dream. "I didn't know they still made them like that," he said.

"Like what?"

"Cool, tough, retro-manly. The kind who only cries if someone just ran over his dog. The big-chested guy we can indulge our pathetic daddy complexes with."

"I don't have a pathetic daddy complex."

"Oh? Tell me you haven't imagined sitting on his lap." Todd grinned as I flushed. "You know what it is you smell on him, Haven? Testosterone. It's leaking out of his pores."

I covered my ears with my hands, and he broke out laughing. He waited until I had taken my hands from my ears before he said in a more serious tone, "You need to be care-ful with him, sweetheart."

"Careful? Why?"

"I get the sense that beneath that all-American, blue-eyed exterior, he's a little twisted."

I felt my eyes go as round as quarters. "Sick twisted?"

"No, twisty twisted. Like, bending-the-rules, foxy, conniving twisted."

"I don't agree at all. He's like Jack. Straightforward."

"No, that's what he wants you to think. But don't believe it for a minute. It's a front, that aw-shucks-I'm-just-a-redneck routine. He does it to set people up. And then he goes in for the kill."

"You're saying Hardy's some kind of mas-ter manipulator or something?" I asked skeptically. "He's from a trailer park, Todd."

"The only person I've ever seen who's al-most as good at that kind of calculated un-derplaying . . . *almost* . . . is your father."

I gave a disbelieving laugh, but I felt a chill run down my back. "Do you think he's a bad guy?"

"No. But there's a lot going on under the surface. You watch his eyes. Even when he's doing his regular-guy routine, he's taking measure, learning, every damn second."

"You got all that from talking about sofas with him?"

Todd smiled. "People reveal a lot when discussing their personal taste. And I picked up a lot by watching him watch you. I think you're in for a time of it with him, sweetheart."

"Do you think I should stay away from him?" I asked in a scratchy voice.

Todd took a long time to answer. "My advice is, if you're inclined in that direction, go with your eyes open. It's okay to let someone play you, Haven, as long as you know what's going on."

"I don't want to be played."

"Oh, I don't know." A smile touched his lips. "With a guy like that . . . it could be fun."

When my lunch break was over, I returned to my cubicle and Vanessa's soft, crisp voice rose from my intercom pad.

"Haven, come to my office, please."

I immediately reasoned that I hadn't done anything wrong, I couldn't possibly be in trouble, but each word pierced me like I'd been shot through the heart with a nail gun.

I was pretty sure Vanessa's romantic long weekend hadn't gone well, because she'd come back in a bitch of a mood. She wore the same serene mask as always, but when it was just the two of us in her office, she had "accidentally" knocked over her pencil holder and asked me to pick all of them up. And then she dropped a file folder, and asked me to collect the papers that had flown everywhere. I couldn't accuse her of doing it on purpose. After all, everyone had moments of clumsiness. But I knew it hadn't been accidental. And the sight of me on my hands and knees had definitely improved her mood. She seemed almost jovial by the time I'd finished putting the file back together.

I realized that in a very short period of time, I had acquired a new person in my life to be afraid of. "She does that same self-absorbed, grandiose, bullying thing that Nick does," I had told Susan during our last session. "Except she's sneakier about it. She's a stealth narcissist. God, how many of these jerks are out there?"

"Too many," Susan said ruefully. "I've heard varying statistics, but I could make an argument that three to five percent of the population has either strong tendencies or the full-blown disorder. And although I've read that three quarters of all narcissists are men, I personally think it runs about fifty-fifty."

"Well, how do I stop being an N-magnet?"

I had demanded, and Susan had smiled.

"You're not an N-magnet, Haven. None of us can escape having to deal with a narcissist now and then. But I'd say you're better equipped than most to handle it."

Yes . . . I knew how to handle a narcissist. You could never disagree with one. You had to look awed by everything they did, and miss no opportunity to flatter or praise them. Basically, you had to sell out in every conceivable way, until there was nothing left of your dignity, self-respect, or your soul.

Vanessa didn't bother looking up from her desk as I entered the open door to her office. "I'd like you to knock before coming in," she said, still concentrating on her computer screen.

"Oh. Sure." I went back to the doorway, knocked on the doorjamb, and waited for a response. Vanessa said nothing, only kept typing. I stood in the doorway and waited for a full two minutes until she finally paused to glance at me.

"Come in."

"Thank you," I said with exquisite politeness.

"Have a seat."

I took the chair across from her desk and looked at her expectantly. It was unfair that someone so rotten on the inside could be so pretty. Her eyes were round and light in her oval face, and her hair was a perfect pale sweep across her shoulders.

"I'd like you to straighten the coffee area and clean out the machine," Vanessa said.

"I cleaned the machine yesterday," I said.

"I'm afraid you need to clean it again. The coffee doesn't taste right." Her brows lifted. "Unless you feel it's beneath you? I don't want you to do anything that makes you uncomfortable, Haven."

"No, it's fine." I gave her a shallow, innocuous smile. "No trouble. Anything else?"

"Yes. About your lunch hour activities."

I didn't reply, only stared at her innocently.

"You were doing something with the new tenant in his apartment this afternoon."

"I introduced him to an interior decorator," I said. "He asked me to."

"You didn't clear it with me."

"I didn't realize I had to," I said slowly. "It was more of a personal favor."

"Well, I have a rule that I should have explained before, Haven. There is no 'getting personal' with any of the tenants in this building. It can lead to trouble, and it can get in the way of doing your job effectively."

"Believe me, I wouldn't —" I stopped,

completely thrown off guard. "There is absolutely *nothing* going on between me and Mr. Cates."

Some of my genuine consternation must have gotten through to Vanessa, because it was obvious she was pleased. Her face softened with the kind concern of an older sister. "I'm glad to hear that. Because someone with your history of failed relationships could make a huge mess of things."

"I . . ." My *history* of failed relationships? I'd only had one. One failed marriage. I burned with the desire to remind Vanessa that she'd been through a divorce too, and she was hardly one to talk. But somehow I managed to keep my mouth shut, while my face flooded with red.

"So," Vanessa said with a gentle smile, "no more private meetings with Mr. Cates, right?"

I looked into those clear eyes, at her smooth, tranquil face. "Right," I half whispered. "Anything else?"

"As a matter of fact . . . I noticed one of the vending machines near the conference room wasn't working. I'd like you to read the service number on the machine and call for it to be fixed."

"I'll do it right away." I forced my lips

into a smile and stood. "Okay if I go now?"

"Yes."

I left her office and went to clean the coffee machine, thinking grimly that anything Vanessa Flint could dish out, I could take.

CHAPTER NINE

Vanessa's warning about staying away from the tenants hadn't been necessary. I had already decided to take Todd's assessment of Hardy to heart. I wasn't going anywhere near him. My rebound guy, when and if I found one, was not going to be manipulative or twisty twisted. He was going to be someone I could handle, someone who wouldn't overwhelm me. And although Hardy was only about seven or eight years older than me, he'd had infinitely more experience in just about every way. As far as sex was concerned, he'd gone "around the sugar bowl," as Aunt Gretchen would have put it, just a few too many times.

But the day after Hardy had moved into 1800 Main, I found a wrapped package on my desk, tied with a neat red ribbon. Since it wasn't my birthday or any gift-giving holiday I could think of, I was mystified.

Kimmie stood at the entryway of my cubicle. "It was dropped off a few minutes ago," she said, "by one of the cutest guys I've ever seen. All blue eyes and bronzy muscles."

"I think it was the new tenant," I said, approaching the package like it might contain a bomb. "Mr. Cates."

"If that's the kind of tenant we're attracting," Kimmie said, "I will work here forever. For no pay."

"I'd steer clear of him if I were you." I sat at my desk. "He's no respecter of women."

"One can only hope so," she said.

I shot her a distracted glance. "Did Vanessa see him bring it in? Did she meet him?"

Kimmie grinned. "Not only did she meet him, she was smacking her lips over him, like Samantha and I were. And she tried her best to find out what was in that package, but he wouldn't tell her."

Great, I thought, and repressed a sigh. It didn't take a genius to figure out I'd be cleaning the coffee machine at least ten times that day.

"Well . . . aren't you going to open it?"

"Later," I said. God knew what was in that box — I was going to wait until I could unwrap it in private.

"Haven . . . you're crazy if you think you can take that present out of the office without letting Vanessa know what it is." Although Kimmie seemed to like our boss, it was common knowledge that no detail of what went on in the office escaped Vanessa's notice.

I set the wrapped box on the floor. It was heavy, with a metallic rattle coming from inside. Was it an appliance of some kind? God, please let it not be some bizarre sex toy. "I don't have to let her pry into the details of my private life."

"Uh-huh." Kimmie gave me a skeptical glance. "Wait until Vanessa gets back from lunch. Your privacy will last about as long as an ice cube in Brownsville."

It was no surprise, of course, when Vanessa came straight to my cubicle when she returned. She was dressed in a pristine white skirt suit, with an ice-pink blouse that matched her nails and delicately glossed lips. I tensed as she half sat on the edge of my desk, looking down at me.

"We had a visitor while you were out," she remarked with a smile. "Apparently you and Mr. Cates have gotten friendly."

"I'm friendly to all the tenants," I said.

She looked amused. "How many of them are you exchanging gifts with, Haven?"

I stared at her without blinking. "Mr. Cates and I are not exchanging gifts."

"Then what is that?" She pointed to the

box beside my desk.

"I assume it's a thank-you gesture. Because I recommended the interior decorator."

"You *assume*?" She laughed gently. "Well, let's stop assuming and find out what it is."

I fought to keep the desperation from my voice. "I'm too busy to deal with that right now. I've got a lot of —"

"Oh, there's always time for presents," Vanessa said brightly. "Go on, Haven. Open it."

Silently I damned her, myself, and most of all Hardy Cates for putting me in this position. Reaching for the box, I hefted it to my lap. At the first sound of ripping paper, the other employees, including Kimmie, Rob, and Phil, appeared at the entrance to my cubicle. I now had an audience.

"Hey," Kimmie said with a grin, "you're finally opening that thing."

Grimly I tore off the wrapping, wadded it up and deposited it in the wastebasket. The gift, whatever it was, was inside an innocuous white box. If it was something embarrassing, I thought, I was going to kill Hardy Cates within the hour. Holding my breath, I lifted the lid and discovered a case of sturdy pink molded plastic.

There was a tag tied to the handle, with a

few words:

HOPE THIS WILL COME IN HANDY.
— H

"Is it bath stuff?" Kimmie prompted. "Makeup? Jewelry?"

"Jewelry, in a box *this* big?" I unfastened the silver latches.

"This is Texas," Kimmie said reasonably.

"Go on," Vanessa prompted, as I hesitated before lifting the lid.

Before I could stop myself, a huge, irrepressible smile spread across my face as I opened the case. It was a tool kit complete with a pink-handled hammer, a tape measure, a screwdriver, and a set of wrenches.

"A *tool kit?*" Kimmie asked blankly. "Well. That's different."

Even Vanessa looked disappointed. No doubt she had been hoping for something scandalous or compromising, or at least expensive. But the gift of a tool kit was hardly something to indicate a hot affair.

Unfortunately in my case, this was more effective than a trunkload of diamonds. It suggested that Hardy Cates understood me, got me, in a way no man ever had. Not even Nick. That scared me almost as much as it pleased me.

"Nice," I said blandly, turning to hide my hot cheeks. I closed the tool kit and set it on the floor beside my desk.

Vanessa stayed at my desk until everyone else had gone back to work. I could feel her gaze on the back of my head. I ignored her, blindly studying my laptop screen.

"You really are bad with men, aren't you?" I heard her say in an undertone that no one else could hear. "I could have gotten him to give me something a lot better than that."

I convinced myself that the only decent thing to do was to thank Hardy for the gift. So I went up to his apartment after dinner that night, hoping he would be gone. My plan was to leave a bottle of wine and a note on the threshold, and avoid any actual contact with him.

But as I walked out of the elevator on the eighteenth floor, I saw Hardy punching the combination code on the door lock. He had just finished a workout — he must have gone to the fitness center on the sixth floor — and he was wearing sweatpants and a damp T-shirt that clung to every line of his body. He was built but not beefy, just . . . powerful. Ripped. I could see indentations of muscle all down his back. His biceps strained the sleeves of his shirt. The hair at the back of his neck was sweat soaked. A sheen of exertion covered his skin.

He was a big, steaming male, and I could almost smell the salt and fresh sweat and hot skin from where I stood. I felt the confusing, opposing pulls of repulsion and craving. I wanted to taste him. I wanted to put my mouth on him, any part of him. I also wanted to run as fast as possible in the opposite direction.

I managed to smile, clutching the bottle of wine against my front, as he turned to glance at me over his shoulder.

"Hey," he said softly, his gaze locking on mine.

"Hey." It seemed to take an absurdly long time to reach him, as if the hallway had become a conveyor belt moving in the opposite direction. When I finally got to him, I held out the wine bottle in an awkward motion. "Thank you," I said. "For the present. I love it."

He pushed the door open. "Come in."

"No, thanks, I just wanted to give you this —" Our fingers touched as he took the bottle from me, and I jerked my hand back.

He looked amused, a flicker of challenge in his eyes. "Don't you want to see how Todd's decorating turned out?"

"I . . . yes, I guess I could come in for a

minute." I followed Hardy into the apartment. He switched the lights on, and I almost gasped at the change in the place. It had been transformed into a rustic but sophisticated retreat. The rich earthy tones of the wood and upholstery played off the abundant row of windows. The furniture had been kept to a minimum, a few comfortable oversized pieces, including a deep sofa and chairs and a low, flat ottoman upholstered in caramel-colored leather. A stylized three-panel painting depicting a cattle drive had been mounted on one wall. Perfect.

"Whatever you paid Todd," I said, "it was worth it."

"That's what he told me." Hardy looked at the bottle appreciatively. "Napa. A mountain wine. I like those, especially the cabs."

"Did you ever end up going to a wine tasting?" I asked, flushing as I remembered how he had hoisted me up to the table in the wine cellar and stood between my —

"A few." Hardy set the bottle onto the counter. "I've learned a little here and there. Never got the retro-olfaction, though."

"It's very subtle. Sometimes it helps if you hold the wine in your mouth and let it warm to your body temperature . . ." As Hardy moved closer, I completely forgot what I was saying. My gaze went to the tanned skin of his throat, the damp hollow at the base of it. "So . . ." I said, "I need to get going. I'll let you take your shower now." The idea of him naked, with hot water running over all that hard flesh, all that compressed energy, frayed my composure even further.

"You haven't seen the rest of the apartment," he said.

"I'm sure it's great."

"You should see the bedroom, at least."

I saw a dance of mischief in his eyes. He was teasing me. "No, thank you."

Hardy leaned over me, all brawn and hormones, bracing a hand on the wall. "Has anyone ever told you," he asked conversationally, "that your eyes are the exact color of Dr Pepper?"

I laughed, disarmed. "Do you get far with lines like that?"

He seemed to relish my amusement. "Far enough, with the right woman."

"I'm not the right woman."

"You and Todd . . . you been friends for a long time?"

I nodded. "Since middle school."

A frown wove between his dark brows. "You ever go out with him?"

"You mean on a date? No."

His expression cleared, as if my answer confirmed something he'd been wondering about. "He's gay, then."

"Well, no. Todd's sort of 'anything goes.' He's had relationships with men and women. He's open to any possibility, because to him the outside of a person is just packaging. It's a pretty enlightened point of view when you think about it."

"I'm not enlightened," Hardy said flatly. "I'm only interested in packaging that includes breasts." And his gaze dipped briefly to my chest with an interest I found somewhat unwarranted, considering my lack of volume. He looked back into my eyes. "Haven, there's this thing I'm going to tomorrow night . . . they're reopening a theater —"

"The Harrisburg?" The nationally renowned theater had undergone a year-long reconstruction after the subterranean level had been destroyed by flood waters. The reopening would be attended by local and national celebrities, not to mention the Texas political and social elite. "I'm going to that with Todd."

"One of my partners made a donation on behalf of our company. So I've gotten roped into it."

I got the impression that Hardy had been about to ask me to go with him. Like on a date. I felt hot and suffocated at the thought.

I was not ready for a date with anyone, least of all him. "Maybe we'll see each other there." I tried to sound breezy. "But if we don't happen to cross paths . . . have a great night."

"You too."

"Okay. See you later." I turned and fumbled at the doorknob. He reached around me and grasped it.

"Let me get that for you."

I waited with panicked impatience, ready to flee. But Hardy paused before opening the door.

"Haven." He waited until I turned toward him, the front of my body aligned with his, not quite touching. The awareness between us was so intense that I could almost feel the pressure of him against my skin, the hardness and weight of him. I couldn't keep from wondering what sex would be like with him, if he would crush and hurt, if he would be gentle.

And then I wondered if he had ever hit a woman.

Somehow I couldn't imagine it, those powerful hands inflicting damage on someone more vulnerable than himself, rupturing vessels, leaving bruises. But Nick had taught me that unimaginable things were possible.

When I did gather the courage to try again,

it would not be with some excessively masculine creature. But maybe that was part of the attraction, knowing deep down that real feelings, real attachment, could never happen with Hardy.

I looked up into his eyes, mesmerized by the blueness. Even knowing how wrong it was, I wanted to melt into him, just flatten myself against that big, sturdy form and . . . let go. Breathe. Trust.

"Stay," he said softly, "and share the wine with me."

"You . . . you need to shower."

A slow grin crossed his mouth. "You can share the shower too."

"Right," I said darkly, while my mind filled with visions of soapy male skin and water-slicked muscles. "As if."

Hardy opened the door and let me escape. "Would have been fun," he called after me as I went down the hall.

And I had to hide a smile, not daring to look back.

After that I felt restless all night, my sleep fractured by dreams, and in the morning I woke up aching and moody. I realized that every encounter I had with Hardy Cates was beginning to feel like foreplay.

"Starlight Experience" was the theme of the

night, featuring singers and musicians all paying homage to the Gershwin brothers. At least five hundred people milled through the building while breezy, jazzy music filled the air. Gershwin was a perfect choice for the evening, giving it a feeling of spontaneous, thrown-together pleasures.

The Harrisburg actually consisted of two stages, the upstairs one about four stories high, a large traditional proscenium theater for spectacle productions. But the lower theater was the one I found more interesting. It was a modular stage with a segmented floor, each section mounted on its own independent pneumatic pistons. That way the floor could be reconfigured into any shape a production required. The walls were segmented too, allowing for a multitude of design possibilities.

Although I was immune to Todd in any romantic sense, I enjoyed the sight of him in a tux. Judging from the looks he got, most other people did too. He was sleek and feline, the tux hanging with elegant looseness on his lean body.

Todd had taken me shopping and picked out my dress, a simple long black sheath with a cowl neckline and black velvet straps. The front was relatively demure, but the back plunged so deeply that I couldn't wear anything underneath.

"That's the good thing about not having big breasts," Todd had told me. "You don't need a bra to look perky."

"I'm not worried about the front," I'd said. "Or looking perky. What worries me is that I'm feeling breezes in places where the sun doesn't usually shine."

But Todd had inspected my rear view and assured me that I wasn't revealing any posterior cleavage. Nothing would show, he said, as long as no one stood above me and looked straight down my back.

As I had expected, most of my family was there, including Dad, Liberty, and all three of my brothers. Liberty looked ravishing in a red silk gown, the shimmering fabric draped and twisted all around her voluptuous body.

"I can't stop looking at your wife," Todd told Gage. "It's like staring into a fire."

Gage grinned, sliding his arm around Liberty. The band began to play "Embraceable You," and Liberty looked up at him. "You want to dance," Gage said, interpreting her expectant glance, and she nodded. He took her hand and murmured, "Come on, then," in a low tone that made her blush. Their fingers tangled tightly as he led her away.

"She's got you well trained, boy," Todd called after them, and sat beside Jack and me. On the other side of the table, a never-ending parade of people came to pay homage to Dad.

"She's good for him," Jack commented, watching Liberty dance with his brother. "He's loosened up a lot since they got married. And I never thought I'd see Gage so crazy about anyone."

I grinned at Jack. "It'll be that way for you too. Someday you'll meet someone, and you'll feel like you've been hit on the head with a two-by-four."

"I feel like that every Saturday night," Jack informed me.

"Your date's a hottie," Todd said as Jack's girlfriend-du-jour made her way to our table, back from the ladies' room. "What's her name? Is that Heidi?"

Jack paled. "No. God, please don't call her that. That's Lola. She and Heidi had a public catfight last week."

"Over what?" I asked, and rolled my eyes as I saw the guilty look on my brother's face. "Never mind. I don't want to know."

"There's something else you probably don't want to know," Todd told me.

In response to my puzzled look, he nodded toward the other side of the table, where Dad was still holding court. My heart clutched as I saw Hardy Cates standing there shaking hands with him. Hardy didn't wear a tux with the languid ease of an aristocrat, but instead with the vague impatience of someone who'd rather be having a cold one with the boys. Leashed and restrained in civilized clothing, he seemed more a force of nature than ever.

My father was staring at him with narrow-eyed interest. As usual, he was as subtle as a pickax. And as usual, everyone held their breath when he spoke. "You plannin' to mess with the Travises?" Dad asked in a tone of amiable interest. "You tryin' to put something over on us?"

Hardy met his gaze squarely, a young scoundrel sizing up an old scoundrel, not without respect. "No, sir."

"Then why have you taken up livin' in my building?"

A slight smile touched Hardy's lips. "Travises aren't the only ones who want a view from the top floor."

I didn't have to look at my father's face to know he loved that. Loved it. On the other hand, he wasn't one to forget old scores. "All right," he said to Hardy. "You paid your respect to the big dog, you can go along now."

"Thank you. But you're not the Travis I came to see."

And Hardy looked at me.

I was being pursued, right in front of my family. I threw Todd a quick, desperate glance, pleading silently for help. But he was enjoying the show way too much.

While the collective gaze of the Travis clan focused on me, I looked back at Hardy. And in as normal a tone as I could manage, I said, "Hello, Mr. Cates. Are you having a good evening?"

"Hoping to."

A world of trouble lurked in those two words.

"Hey, Cates," Jack said, standing and clapping Hardy on the shoulder. "What do you say we go get a beer at the bar?"

Hardy didn't budge. "No, thanks."

"It's on me. I insist."

As if things weren't bad enough, Gage and Liberty returned to the table. And Gage, who was more than a little territorial where his wife was concerned, fixed Hardy with a stare that promised death.

Liberty seized Gage's hand and gripped it tightly. "Hardy," she said with a relaxed smile, "it's been a long time. How are you?"

"Great. You?"

"Wonderful," she said. "We have a little boy now. Matthew."

"I heard about that. Congratulations."

Gage stared at Hardy in a way that raised

the hairs on my arms. "What do you want?" he asked quietly.

Hardy's gaze turned to me, and held, as he answered. "I want to dance with your sister."

Before I could even answer, Gage said, "Not a chance."

And Jack said almost simultaneously, "I don't think so."

My father glanced at me from across the table and raised his brows.

And my brother Joe chose that moment to come up behind my chair and rest a hand on my shoulder. "We having a problem?" he asked of no one in particular.

I felt smothered by them, the men in my family, who were so determined to protect me that they weren't even considering my opinion on the matter. I pulled away from Joe's hand. "No problem," I told him. "Mr. Cates just asked me to dance. And I'm going to —"

"No way in hell," Joe said, putting his hand back on my shoulder.

Irritably I dug my elbow into his side. "I didn't ask for your opinion."

"Maybe you should," Joe muttered, giving me a hard look. "Need to talk to you, Haven."

"Later," I said, mortified. We were causing a scene. People were looking.

"Now," Joe insisted.

I stared at him in disbelief. "For God's sake," I said, "even for a family of crazy Texan control freaks, this is ridiculous."

Hardy had begun to scowl. "While you have a committee meeting to decide if you're allowed to dance," he told me, "I'll be at the bar."

And he sauntered off while I glared at Joe, who was usually the least interfering brother.

Of course, that wasn't saying much. But still.

" 'Scuse us," Joe said to the rest of the Travises, and he led me away from the table.

"What's going on?" I demanded in a taut whisper as we meandered through the crowd. "Why is it such a big deal if I dance with Hardy Cates?"

"The guy's trouble," Joe said calmly, "and everyone knows it. With all the men here to choose from, why give him a second thought? Are you *that* determined to push the family's buttons?"

"Newsflash, Joe: there are some things in life I get to decide without taking the family's buttons into consideration."

"You're right," he allowed after a moment. "But I'm still not going to keep quiet if I see you walking toward another hole in the ground. Not if there's a chance I can stop you from falling into it."

"Whatever I do or don't do with Hardy Cates, it's my business," I said. "I'll handle the consequences."

"Fine. As long as you understand that the chances of being set up and used are high."

I glanced at him sharply. "Why do you say that?"

"Two years ago, not long after you got married, I was called to do the *Texas Monthly* shoot for the piece they did on Cates. At his request. I spent the better part of the day with him. We talked about a lot of stuff, but what I realized near the end of the shoot was that every thread of conversation had led back to one person . . . he kept asking questions, digging up information, wanting private details . . ."

"About Liberty," I muttered.

"Hell, no, not about Liberty. About *you*."

"What?" I asked faintly.

"He said you two had met at the wedding."

My heart seemed to stop. "Did he tell you how?"

"No, but it made an impression on him, to say the least. So I made it clear you were off-limits. Told him you were married. And that didn't seem to matter to him one damn bit. He still wanted to know more. I got a bad feeling about it, even then." Joe stopped and looked down at me with eyes the same dark brown as my own. "And now you're coming off a divorce, and vulnerable, and he's after you."

"He's not *after* me, he just asked me to dance."

"He's after you," Joe repeated firmly. "Of all the women in this room, you're the one he went for. Why do you think that is, Haven?"

A wave of coldness went through me. *Shit.* Maybe I was being the woman in the Astrodome again. Maybe my attraction to Hardy was a form of self-destructive masochism.

"He's got some kind of plan," Joe said. "He wants to make his mark, get back at the Travises, get something from us. And he'll have no problem using you to do it. Because he's figured out there's no bigger turn-on for you than a guy your family doesn't approve of."

"That's not true," I protested.

"I think it is." Joe dragged his hand through his hair, looking exasperated. "For God's sake, Haven, find someone else. You want to meet guys, I know a ton of —"

"No," I said sullenly. "I don't want to meet anyone."

"Then let's go back to the table."

I shook my head. The idea of returning to my family's table like a chastened child was unbearable.

"You want to dance?" Joe asked.

That provoked a reluctant grin from me. "With my *brother*? No, that would be too pathetic. Besides, you hate dancing."

"True," Joe said, looking relieved.

"I'm going to the ladies' room to check my makeup," I said. "I'll be back at the table in a few minutes."

After Joe left me, I wandered disconsolately through the room. Obviously I shouldn't have gone to the theater opening. I should have stayed home. I needed to think about things, including the question of why, in spite of my better judgment and my family's conviction that it was a mistake, I was still attracted to Hardy Cates.

But before I was even aware I was doing it, I had gone to the bar.

It was easy to locate Hardy's tall, rangy form. He was half leaning against the bar, a rocks glass in his hand. It appeared he was talking to someone, although his shoulder blocked the view. I approached him hesitantly, tilting my head a little as I tried to get a glimpse of his companion.

He was talking to a woman. Naturally. It was inconceivable that a man with his looks wouldn't attract female attention. The woman was slim and busty and dressed in a sparkling gold gown. All that, along with her light blond hair, made her look like an awards show statuette.

I stiffened as I saw her face.

"Hi, Vanessa," I said weakly.

CHAPTER TEN

Vanessa Flint gave me a look I was familiar with, the one that said she didn't want to be interrupted. But her voice was warm and friendly. "Haven, how nice to see you here! Are you having fun?"

"Words can't describe it," I said. It was just not my night. Of all people for Hardy to hook up with, it had to be my boss from hell. Fate was trying to get it through to me that this wasn't going to work on any level.

Hardy set his glass on the bar. "Haven —"

"Hi, Mr. Cates," I said coolly. "Have a good night, you two. I was just leaving."

Without giving either Vanessa or Hardy a chance to react, I turned and pushed through the crowd. Nauseous and white-faced with fury, I acknowledged that my family was absolutely right about Hardy. He was trouble I didn't need.

I'd made it about halfway through the room when I felt him come up behind me,

251

his touch on my arm. I stiffened and turned to face him. His face was as hard as granite.

"Go back to Vanessa," I told him. "If she thinks I've taken you away from her, I'll be cleaning the office bathroom for the next week."

"I wasn't with her, I was having a drink. Was I supposed to wait alone in the corner while you were trying to make up your mind about me?"

"Not in the corner, no." I glared at him. "But you could have at least waited five minutes before finding a replacement."

"She wasn't a replacement. I was waiting for you. And it took you a hell of a lot longer than five minutes to decide if you wanted to dance with me. I'm not going to take that shit from you or your family, Haven."

"After the way you've behaved in the past, what do you expect? Flowers and a parade? They have every right to distrust your motives."

"What about you? What do you think my motives are?"

"I don't think you want me to answer that in front of all these people."

"Then we'll go somewhere private," he said through clenched teeth. "Because I'm going to have an answer, by God."

"Fine." My mind went blank, frozen in

white panic, as I felt him take my wrist. The last time I'd been handled by an angry man, I'd ended up at the hospital. But his grip, firm as it was, was not painful. I forced myself to relax and go along with him as he steered me through the crowd.

A female singer was crooning "Summertime," the dark, moody melody weaving around us like smoke.

I was in a daze as we made our way out of the room, past the crush in the lobby. We reached a set of doors, but we were forced to stop as someone stepped in our way. Gage. His eyes flashed like bottled lightning as he glanced over both of us, missing no detail, including the way Hardy was gripping my wrist.

"Do you need me?" Gage asked me quietly.

Hardy looked like he was ready to commit murder. "She's fine," he said.

My brother paid no attention to that, only kept his gaze on me. I felt a wave of gratitude for him, understanding how difficult it was for him to let me go off with a man he despised. But Gage knew it was my choice. He was there to offer help only if I wanted it.

"It's okay," I said to him. "I don't need anything."

My brother nodded, although it was obvious he was struggling not to interfere. As we left him, he looked as if he were watching me walk off with Lucifer himself. I knew Gage was afraid for me. He didn't trust Hardy Cates.

Neither did I, come to think of it.

Hardy pulled me past the set of doors, and around a corner, working deeper into the building until we finally stopped in some kind of maintenance stairwell, which smelled of concrete and metal and musty dankness. It was quiet except for a dripping sound, and the broken rhythms of our breathing. A light from somewhere above shed uncertain fluorescence over us.

Hardy faced me, looking huge and dark against a background of concrete. "Now," he said brusquely, "tell me what you wouldn't say back there."

I let him have it. "I think if I were anyone but a Travis, you wouldn't give me the time of day. I think you want to show my brother Gage that if he got Liberty, you're going to get back at him by sleeping with his sister. I think you have more hidden agendas than you can admit even to yourself. I think —"

I stopped with a gasp as he grabbed me. A wild feeling pumped through me, a mixture of fear and anger and, unbelievably, arousal.

"Wrong," he bit out, his accent heavy and

charred with scorn. "I'm not that complicated, Haven. The truth is, I've wanted you ever since I met you in that damned wine cellar. Because I got a bigger charge out of that five minutes than I have with any woman before or since. No secret plot against your family, Haven. No hidden agendas. Plain and simple, I'm just interested in screwing your brains out."

My face was stiff with offended bewilderment. Before I could string a few coherent syllables together, Hardy kissed me. I pushed at him, and his mouth lifted, and he muttered something that sounded obscene, but I couldn't quite hear it over the rampaging pulse in my ears.

He took my head in both his hands, fingers shaping around my skull. His lips found mine again. The taste and heat of him were unbearably sweet as his tongue sank into my mouth. The pleasure of it went screaming through me, hunger striking against equal hunger, creating fire. I opened to him, shaking so hard I could barely stand. His arm went around me, shielding my back from the cold press of concrete, the other hand running down the front of my body. I kissed him back, licking into his mouth the way he was doing with mine. I was feeling too much, losing control.

His mouth broke from mine, roughly searching the side of my neck. The rasp of his shaven jaw sent bolts of delight down to my stomach. I heard him mutter something to the effect that after going to a fancy college I should at least be smart enough to know when a man wanted to go to bed with me. Except that he said it a lot more crudely.

"I'm not a gentleman," he went on, gripping my body, his breath hot on my skin. "I can't get you into bed with fancy words or nice manners. All I can tell you is that I want you more than I've ever wanted a woman. I'd break any law to have you. If you'd gone with me that night we met, I would have taken you to Galveston and kept you there for a week. And I'd have made sure you never wanted to leave."

As the arm behind me tightened to arch my torso upward, I realized he'd pulled at the side of the dress until my breast was bare. He cupped the shallow weight, his thumb prodding the tip until it was tight and rosy, and then he bent to touch it with his tongue. I lifted, gasping, as he kissed the erect nipple, sealing his mouth over the taut flesh. He tugged rhythmically, sending washes of pleasure through me, licking between each soft pull. I held his head to me, tears stinging the corners of my eyes because it felt so good.

He moved upward and fastened his mouth to mine again, the kiss rich and drugging. "Let me into your bed," he muttered. "I'll give it to you any way you want it . . . long, slow, hard, easy . . . Hell, I'll even try to do it like a gentleman, if that's what gets you off. You think I want you because you're a Travis? I wish you were anyone but a fucking Travis. Your kind of people have looked down on me my whole life."

"I've never looked down on you," I snapped, shaking with frustration and desire. "If you knew anything about me, you'd never think that."

"Then what's the problem?" he growled. "Your ex-husband? You still got feelings for him?"

"No." My hands worked at the folds of his lapel, fingers clenching on the sleek fabric.

"Tell me you don't want me. Tell me, and I'll leave you the hell alone."

"I'm not good at this," I burst out. "My God, isn't that obvious? Nick is the only one I've ever slept with. I can't be casual about this."

I had never meant to admit that. But I was helpless, broken open, afraid I couldn't stand to be hurt the way Hardy was going to hurt me. Sex and pain and fear were all

257

mixed up in my head.

Hardy went still. In one blistering moment, everything changed. He forced my face upward, his hand cupping the back of my head. His eyes were blue even in the darkness as he stared at me. Slowly his grip gentled, turning protective, his free hand stroking the gooseflesh on my upper arm. I realized he was stunned. It hadn't occurred to him that I might be too inexperienced to know how to play the game.

"Haven . . ." The new softness in his voice made my trembling even worse. "I didn't know. I thought —"

"That I'm a spoiled River Oaks brat? A snob —"

"Hush."

"But I —"

"*Hush.*"

I fell silent and let him hold me. I was swallowed up in his embrace, clasped against that hard chest. Part of me wanted to escape. The other part of me craved this, being held, being touched. He stroked my hair, fingertips moving gently over the curve of my scalp. I felt something giving way, some inner tightness dissolving.

We swayed a little as we stood together, as if sensation were an ocean current pushing against us. Hardy nuzzled into my neck. I twisted to find his mouth, and he gave me what I wanted, kissing me with slow hunger until I was weak and dizzy. His arm was strong around me, cradling and supportive. With his free hand, he clenched his fingers into the loose folds of my dress, easing the knit fabric upward.

I jumped as his hand clasped my bare hip. He kissed my throat and said things I only half heard, endearments, reassurance, soothing me while he parted my thighs. He touched me, opening tenderly, one fingertip moving over layered flesh in teasing circles, smaller and smaller until he reached the center. I writhed helplessly as he caressed that one pulsing spot, over and over, and every time the callus on his finger crossed the wet surface of my clit, a pleasure-cry rose in my throat.

I melted on him, moaning, while the need for sex, to be filled, pulsed all through me. Turning my mouth to his, I let him kiss me as deeply as he wanted, welcoming the aggressive thrust of his tongue. His hand left me, and he reached for the fastenings of his pants . . . and it was then that disaster struck.

As I felt him so huge and hard against me, all the pleasure disappeared. Just . . . vanished. Suddenly all I could see, hear, feel, was that last time with Nick, the searing pain, the brutal thrusts eased only by the slick of my own blood. My throat and stomach pulsed with nausea, and the masculine body against mine was revolting, his weight unbearable, and I began to struggle without thinking.

"No," I panted, twisting away, shoving hard at him. "*No.* I don't want it. I don't want it. I —" I stopped myself by biting hard on my lip, realizing my voice was rising in a harsh echo.

"What is it?" I heard Hardy ask, his breath coming in rough pants.

I was shivering, hostile, every cell in my body geared up for self-preservation. "Leave me alone," I snapped. "Take your hands off me." I fumbled with my dress, trying to pull it into place, my fingers shaking violently.

"Haven —" His voice was ragged. "Did I hurt you? What is it?"

"I'm not into fucking in public places," I said coldly, edging toward the door. If he touched me again, I would fall apart . . . I would go crazy. "And I don't like being pushed."

"Like hell I was pushing you. You wanted it."

"Don't flatter yourself, Hardy."

He looked flushed and dangerously aroused and annoyed as hell. Slowly he began to restore his own clothing. When he spoke again, his voice was low and controlled. "There's a word, Haven, for a woman who does what you're doing."

"I'm sure you know a lot of interesting words," I said. "Maybe you should go tell them to someone else."

And before he could reply, I fled from the stairwell like an escapee from prison.

Somehow I found my way back to the modular theater, the sounds of dancing and laughter swirling around me. I was terrified by the realization of how much was wrong with me, that I couldn't tolerate the normal act of having sex with a man I was attracted to. And I was humiliated by the way I had just behaved. Hardy had no choice but to think I was a bitch, a cocktease. He would never want anything to do with me again. That thought sort of relieved me, but at the same time I wanted to burst into tears.

Todd found me immediately. He had been talking with a guy at the bar, his gaze leisurely sweeping the room, when he saw me come in. He came to me, his gaze focused on my pale face and kiss-swollen lips. "You look like you just banged the Dallas Cowboys," he said. "First and second strings."

"Please, can you call me a cab?" I whispered.

Concern warmed his blue-green eyes. "I'll take you home, sweetheart. Here, lean on me."

But I flinched as he tried to put his arm around my shoulders.

"All right," Todd continued pleasantly, as if he hadn't noticed my bizarre reaction, "why don't you take my arm, and we'll go out the side door?"

He drove me to 1800 Main in his BMW Coupe, asking no questions, maintaining a comfortable silence until we finally got to my seventh-floor apartment. He had decorated it with an eclectic mix of antique-shop furniture and a couple of his own cast-off pieces. Creams and whites were balanced by dark distressed wood. And Todd had added a few touches of whimsy, like covering the inside-facing panel of my front door with an antique bamboo hula-girl screen.

Taking one look at my wretched face, Todd reached for the green chenille throw on my sofa and wrapped it around me. I snuggled in the corner of the sofa, drawing my feet back to make room for him.

"Must have been some dance," Todd said, untying his bow tie. He left it hanging loose on either side of his neck, and relaxed on the sofa beside me, as graceful as a cat. "What happened?"

"We didn't dance," I said numbly.

"Oh?"

"He took me to a dark corner somewhere. A stairwell."

"Purely for my vicarious enjoyment, tell me . . . is he good?"

I could feel my face go crimson.

"*That* good?" Todd asked.

A shaky laugh escaped me. I wasn't sure I could put it into words. "You know how when someone kisses you, you can tell they're only doing it as a step to something else? Like they're just trying to get it over with? Well, Hardy kisses like it's the only thing in the world he wants to do. Each kiss is like a complete sex act." I closed my eyes for a second, remembering. "And he's a face-holder."

"Mmmn. I love that. So did one of your brothers find you?"

"No, it was me. I screwed it all up. I freaked out in the middle of it."

There was a long silence. "Freaked out how? What do you . . . Haven, take your hands down and look at me. This is Todd. Just say it."

"I got scared. More than scared. I pushed him away and ran out of there as fast as I could."

"Scared by what?"

"I felt his . . . you know, his . . ."

Todd gave me a sardonic glance as I hesitated. "Hard-on?" he suggested. "Package? Lap-taffy? Bait-and-tackle? Come on, Haven, let's not talk about this like a pair of tweenies."

I scowled defensively. "My conversations don't usually include the subject of erections."

"Too bad," he said. "All the best conversations do. Go on, sweetheart."

I took a deep breath. "While we were kissing, I felt his erection, and all the desire just disappeared. Poof. After what I went through with Nick, the feel of *that* has a lot of bad connotations for me."

"Went through what?" he asked quietly. "You've never told me. Although I've had my suspicions."

"The night I left Nick" — I looked away from Todd as I made myself say it — "we had rough sex."

"Rough sex?" Todd asked. "Or rape?"

"I don't know." I was drowning in shame. "I mean, we were married. But I didn't want to do it, and he forced me, so I guess —"

"It was rape," he said flatly. "It doesn't matter if you're married or not. If you don't want to do it and someone forces you, it's rape. Holy shit, I'd like to kill the bastard." Todd's face was dark with a fury I'd never seen in him before. But as he stared at me, his expression changed. "Haven, sweetheart . . . you know if a woman's ready, aroused, it's not going to hurt. Especially if the man knows what he's doing, which I have no doubt Hardy does."

"Yes, but even though my mind knows it, my body doesn't. So as soon as I felt that huge *thing* pressing against me, I couldn't stop myself from going into a blind panic. I felt positively nauseous. God." I wrapped myself tighter in the green chenille as if it were a cocoon.

"Haven't you talked about this stuff with the therapist yet?"

I shook my head. "We're still working on my boundary issues. And she's on vacation for the next two weeks, so I'll have to wait until she's back to help me deal with this."

"Sex isn't a boundary issue?"

I frowned at him. "I've had a lot more important things to worry about than sex."

Todd opened his mouth to reply, appeared to think better of it, and closed it again. After a moment he said, "So just when things were getting hot, you told Hardy to stop."

"Yeah." I rested my chin on my bent knees.

"And I . . . I wasn't very nice about it."

"What did he say? What was his reaction?"

"He didn't say much of anything. But I could tell he was pissed."

"Well, yeah, guys tend to get pretty frustrated when they're hung out to dry, sexually speaking. But the point is, Hardy didn't hurt you, right? He didn't try to make you do something you didn't want?"

"No."

"I'd say that means you're pretty safe with him."

"I didn't feel safe."

"I think at this point, safety isn't a feeling, it's a process. Starting with trust. Why don't you try telling Hardy some of things you've told me?"

"He won't be able to handle it. I know he won't. He'll be headed for the exit door before I can even finish telling him what a basket case I am."

"You're not a basket case," Todd said calmly, "and he's no fucking wimp, Haven. I think the reason you're drawn to him is that deep down you know he can handle anything you could throw at him."

"But what if he doesn't want to?"

"Here are your options: you can give him a chance to cowboy up, or you can walk away without ever finding out. And then you'll have to face this same deal with the next guy you're attracted to."

"Or . . ."

"Or what?"

I moistened my lips nervously. "I could practice with you first."

I had never seen Todd at a loss for words before. But his eyes widened, and his mouth opened and closed, fishlike, for at least ten seconds. "You're asking me to go to bed with you?" he finally managed to ask.

I nodded. "If I'm going to freak out or throw up in the middle of it, I'd rather it be with you. And if I can manage to get through it with you, I'll know I can do it with Hardy."

"Oh, shit." Todd started to laugh helplessly, grabbing my hand and kissing the palm. "Sweetheart. Haven. No." He kept my hand, laying his cheek gently against my palm. "I would love to help you through this, little friend, and I'm totally honored that you asked. But right now you don't want a fuck-buddy. You want a hell of a lot more than that. And somewhere, not far from here, there's a big, blue-eyed roughneck who's dying to show you a good time in bed. If I were you, I'd give him a try." I felt his smile press against the edge of my hand as he added, "If you can get past him being so ugly and scrawny, that is."

When he released my hand, I closed my fingers around my palm as if his kiss were a lucky penny. "Todd, when you danced with Liberty . . . did she say anything about Hardy?"

He nodded. "She told me in spite of that thing that went down with Gage's business deal, she doesn't see any danger in you and Hardy being interested in each other. Based on what she knows about him from the time they both lived in that little crap-hole town —"

"Welcome."

"Yeah, whatever." Todd was not a fan of small-town living. "Based on that, Liberty doesn't think he'd hurt you. She said Hardy had always gone out of his way to keep from leading her on, and he'd done what he could to help her. In fact, she thinks the two of you might even do each other some good."

"I can't imagine how," I said glumly, "when I can't manage to be around his erection without freaking."

Todd smiled. "A relationship is about more than just an erection. Although, if you ask me . . . wondering what to do with one is a nice problem to have."

After Todd had left I took a long bath, pulled on a pair of flannel pajamas, and poured myself a glass of wine. I wondered where Hardy was at that moment, if he had stayed at the theater after I'd left.

The temptation to call him was nearly overwhelming, but I wasn't certain what I wanted to say, how much I could bring myself to explain.

I resumed my place in the corner of the sofa, staring at the phone in its cradle. I wanted to hear Hardy's voice. I thought of those fevered minutes in the stairwell before I'd gotten afraid, when his hands and mouth had been all over me, slow and searching and tender . . . so good. So unbelievably good —

The phone rang.

Jolted, I set aside the wine, almost spilling it in my haste. I snatched up the phone and answered in breathless relief. "Hello?"

But the voice was not Hardy's.

"Hi, Marie."

CHAPTER ELEVEN

"Nick." I felt as if ice crystals had formed in my veins. "How did you get my number? What do you want?"

"Just to know how you're doing."

His voice was so familiar. The sound of it vaporized the past several months as if they had all been a dream. If I closed my eyes, I could almost believe I was back in the Dallas apartment and he would be coming back from work soon.

So I kept my eyes open, as if one blink would result in death. I stared at the weave of the cream sofa slipcover until each individual thread came into distinct focus. "I'm great," I said. "How about you?"

"Not great." A lengthy pause. "Still trying to make myself believe it's really over. I miss you, Marie."

He sounded contemplative. Something in his voice drew out a dark, seeping guilt from my heart.

"It's Haven," I said. "I don't answer to Marie anymore."

I thought that would provoke him, but he stunned me by saying, "Okay, Haven."

"Why are you calling?" I asked abruptly. "What do you want?"

"Just to talk for a minute." Nick sounded resigned and a little wry. "Are we still allowed to talk?"

"I guess so."

"I've had a lot of time to think. I want you to understand something . . . I never meant for things to get out of hand the way they did."

I gripped the phone so hard I was vaguely surprised the plastic didn't crack. I believed him. I had never thought Nick had wanted or planned to be the way he was. There were things in his background, his childhood, that had made him a damaged person. A victim, as surely as I had been.

But that didn't mean he was off the hook for the harm he'd done me.

I was filled with regret for what we'd lost . . . and what we'd never had. I felt sick and weary.

"Do you hate me, Haven?" Nick asked softly.

"No. I hate what you did."

"I hate what I did too." He sighed. "I keep

thinking . . . if we'd had more time together, if we could have been allowed to work out our problems instead of having your brother come in and push that divorce through so fucking fast . . ."

"You hurt me, Nick," was all I could say.

"You hurt me too. You lied to me all the time, about little things, big things . . . you always shut me out."

"I didn't know how else to handle you. The truth made you angry."

"I know. But it takes two people to make a good marriage. And I had a lot to deal with — being rejected by your family, having to work like a dog to provide for you — and you always blamed me for not being able to solve your problems."

"No," I protested. "Maybe you blamed yourself. But I never felt like that."

"You were never really *with* me. Even when we slept together. I could tell you were never really into it. No matter what I did, you never responded to me the way other women did. I kept hoping you'd get better."

Damn it, Nick knew how to get to me, how to reawaken the sense of inadequacy I'd struggled so hard to overcome. Nick knew things about me that no one else did. We would always be linked by our shared failure — it was part of our individual identities. It could never be erased.

"Are you dating anyone now?" I heard him ask.

"I don't feel comfortable talking about that with you."

"That means yes. Who is he?"

"I'm not dating anyone," I said. "I haven't slept with anyone. You don't have to believe that, but it's true." Instantly I despised myself for saying it, and for feeling that I was still accountable to him.

"I believe you," Nick said. "Aren't you going to ask about me?"

"No. I don't care if you're dating anyone. It's not my business."

He was quiet for a moment. "I'm glad you're okay, Haven. I still love you."

That brought tears to my eyes. I was so glad he couldn't see them. "I'd rather you didn't call me again, Nick."

"I still love you," he repeated, and hung up.

Slowly I replaced the phone in the receiver, and blotted the tears by doing a deliberate face-plant into the sofa. I stayed that way until I started to smother, and then I lifted my head and sucked in a deep breath.

"I thought I loved you," I said aloud, even though Nick couldn't hear me.

But I hadn't known what love was. And I

wondered how you could ever be sure, when you thought you loved someone, if you really did.

The next day, it rained.

During the occasional droughts, Houston got so dry that, as a local joke went, "the trees are bribing the dogs." But when it rained, it rained. And as a virtually flat city built around bayous, Houston had major drainage issues. During a heavy downpour, water collected high in the streets and flowed into storm drains, culverts, and bayous that directed the flow to the Gulf of Mexico. In the past, countless people had been killed by flash flooding, their cars overturned or swept away as they tried to cross the rising water. Sometimes flooding ruptured fuel pipelines, sewer lines, knocked out bridges, and made major roads inaccessible.

A flood watch was announced after lunchtime, and later it was changed to an actual warning. Everyone took it in stride, since Houston residents were accustomed to flash flooding and generally knew which streets to avoid during the evening commute.

Late in the day I went to a meeting at Buffalo Tower to discuss a new online system for processing maintenance requests. Vanessa had originally planned to go to the meeting, but she had changed her mind at the last minute and sent me instead. She told me it was mostly an information-gathering meeting, and she had more important things to do than talk about software. "Find out everything about the system," she told me, "and I'll have some questions for you in the morning." I was pretty sure there would be hell to pay if Vanessa had a question I couldn't answer. So I resolved to find out every last detail about the software program, short of memorizing the source codes.

I was relieved but puzzled that Vanessa had not mentioned one word about seeing me at the Harrisburg the previous night. And she didn't ask about Hardy. I tried to read her mood, but that was like trying to predict the weather, an iffy proposition at best. Hopefully she had decided to consider the subject as something beneath her notice.

Even though Buffalo Tower was only a few blocks from 1800 Main, I drove because the rain was coming down in sheets. The building was one of the older skyscrapers, a gabled red granite structure that reminded me of a 1920s-style building.

As I parked in one of the lower levels of the underground garage, I checked my phone messages. Hardy had called, I saw, and my stomach tightened. I pushed a button to hear his message.

"Hey." His tone was brusque. "We need to talk about last night. Give me a call when you get off work."

That was all. I listened to the message again, and I wished I could cancel the meeting and go to him right then. But it wouldn't take long — I would get through it as quickly as possible, and then I would call him.

By the time the software consultant, Kelly Reinhart, and I had finished, it was a few minutes past six. It might have gone on even longer, except there was a call from the security office to tell us that there had been some flooding in the lowest level of the garage. It was mostly unoccupied, since most people had already left for the day, but there were still one or two cars down there, and they should probably be moved.

"Shoot, one of them's mine," I said to Kelly, closing my laptop and sliding it into my briefcase. "I'd better go see to my car. Is it okay if I call you tomorrow about the last couple of points we didn't get to?"

"Sure thing," Kelly said.

"What about you? . . . Are you going to the garage too?"

"I didn't bring my car today, it's in the shop. My husband's picking me up at six-thirty. But I'll ride down with you in the elevator if you want company —"

"No, no . . ." I smiled and picked up my briefcase. "I'll be fine."

"Great. Okay. Call up here or go to the security office off the lobby if you have any problems." Kelly made a face. "The way this old building leaks, your car may be underwater by now."

I laughed. "Just my luck. It's new."

With most of the daytime occupants gone, the building was quiet and a little eerie, doors locked and windows darkened. Thunder was rumbling outside, making me shiver in my business suit. I was glad to be going home. One of my shoes was pinching, and the clasp of my side-zip pants was digging into my skin, and I was hungry. Most of all, I was anxious to reach Hardy and tell him how sorry I was for the previous night. And I was going to explain . . . something.

I entered the elevator and pressed the button for the lowest garage level. The doors closed, and the cab descended smoothly. But as I reached the bottom, the floor beneath me gave a strange lurch, and I heard pops and snaps, and then everything went dead. The lights, the hydraulics, everything stopped. I let out a startled yelp as I was left in complete blackness. Worse, I heard the continuous splash of water, like someone had turned a faucet on inside the elevator.

Concerned but not panicked, I felt for the panel beside the door, pushing a few buttons. Nothing happened.

"Phone," I said aloud, trying to reassure myself with the sound of my own voice. "There's always a phone in these things." My groping fingers found an elevator speaker phone with a push button, all of it embedded in the wall. I pushed the button, held it, but there was no response.

I counted myself lucky that I wasn't one of those people with elevator phobias. I was remaining calm. Methodically I went through my briefcase to find my cell phone. Something icy swept over my foot. At first I thought it was a draft, but a second later I felt the wet chill in my pumps, and I realized there were a couple of inches of water inside the elevator cab.

Carefully I pulled out the cell phone and flipped it open. I used it as a makeshift flashlight, shining the tiny glowing screen at my surroundings to see where the water was coming in.

Oily-looking water was spurting through the seam of the closed elevator doors. That was bad enough. But as I moved the glow of the cell phone upward, I saw that it wasn't just coming in through the bottom of the doors. It was coming through the top.

As if the entire elevator car were submerged.

But that wasn't possible. There was no way the shaft could be filled with eight or nine feet of water . . . wouldn't that mean most of the lower garage was flooded? That couldn't have happened in the time since I'd arrived at the building. But *shit* . . . an elevator shaft full of water would explain why all the electrical systems seemed to have short-circuited.

"This is crazy," I muttered, my heartbeat picking up anxious speed as I dialed the building's main number. It rang twice, and then a recorded message began to list extension numbers from the main directory. As soon as I heard the three digits for the security office, I punched them in. Another two rings . . . and then a busy signal.

Swearing, I redialed the main number and tried Kelly's extension. An answering machine picked up. *"Hi, this is Kelly Reinhart. I'm away from my desk, but if you'll leave a message at the tone, I'll return your call as soon as possible."*

I left a message, trying to sound professional but urgent. "Kelly, it's Haven. I'm stuck in one of the elevators on the garage level, and water's coming in. Do me a favor and let security know that I'm down here."

Water kept pouring in, swirling around my ankles.

As I ended the call, I saw that the low battery signal on my phone was flashing. With hardly any juice left, I wasn't going to take any chances. I dialed 911, watching my finger as if it belonged to someone else. And I listened, incredulous, as the line was picked up and directed to a recorded message. *"We are currently experiencing a high volume of calls. All circuits are busy. Please remain on the line until a dispatcher is available."* I held, waited for a minute that seemed to last a lifetime, and ended the call when it was clear nothing was going to happen. I dialed it again with excruciating care . . . *9-1-1* . . . and this time I got nothing but a busy signal.

My phone beeped to let me know the battery was almost dead.

With the water now midway up my calves and pouring in continuously, I stopped pretending that I was anything close to calm. Somehow I managed to bring the list of recently received calls to the phone screen. I pressed the return on Hardy's last call.

It rang. Once . . . twice . . . I gasped with relief as I heard his voice.

"Cates."

"Hardy," I choked, unable to get the words out fast enough. "It's me. I need you. I need help."

He didn't miss a beat. "Where are you?"

"Buffalo Tower. Elevator. I'm in an elevator stuck in the garage and there's water coming in, lots of water —" The phone beeped again. "Hardy, can you hear me?"

"Say it again."

"An elevator at Buffalo Tower — I'm stuck in the garage, in an elevator, and it's flooding, and I need —" The phone beeped and went dead. I was left in darkness once more. *"No,"* I half screamed in frustration. "Damn it. Hardy? Hardy?"

Nothing but silence. And gushing, splashing water.

I felt hysteria welling up, and I actually considered whether or not to give in to it. But since there was nothing to be gained by it, and I was pretty sure it wasn't going to make me feel any better, I shoved it back down and took deep breaths.

"People don't drown in elevators," I said aloud.

The water had reached my knees, and it was biting cold. It also smelled bad, like oil and chemicals and sewage. I pulled my computer from my briefcase, opened it, and tried in vain to get any kind of Internet signal. At least with the glowing screen open, it wasn't completely dark in the elevator. I looked at the ceiling, which was covered in wood paneling and tiny recessed lights, all out. Wasn't there supposed to be an escape hatch? Maybe it was concealed. I couldn't think of any way to get up there and search for it.

I waded to the side of the door and tried the phone panel again, as well as all the buttons, and nothing happened. Taking off one of my pumps, I used the heel to bang on the walls and shout for help for a few minutes.

By the time I got tired of pounding, I was submerged up to my hips. I was so cold that my teeth were chattering and the bones in my legs were aching. Except for the water pouring in, everything was quiet. It was calm everywhere except inside my head.

I realized I was in a coffin. I was actually going to die in this metal box.

I'd heard it wasn't supposed to be a bad way to die, drowning. There were worse ways to go. But it was so unfair — I had never done anything with my life that was worth putting in an obituary. I hadn't accomplished any of the goals I'd had at college. I'd never made peace with my father, not in a real sense. I'd never helped people who were less fortunate. I'd never even had decent sex.

I was certain that people facing death

should be occupied with noble thoughts, but instead I found myself thinking about those moments in the stairwell with Hardy. If I'd gone through with it, at least I would have had good sex for once in my life. But I'd blown even that. I wanted him. I wanted so much. Nothing was finished in my life. I stood there, waiting for my eventual drowning not with resignation but milling fury.

When the water had reached the bottom edge of my bra, I was tired of holding the computer up, and I let it sink. It submerged and floated to the elevator floor in water so polluted you could barely see the glowing screen before it shorted out and went dark. It was disorienting, the cold blackness all around me. Huddling in the corner, I leaned my head against the wall and breathed, and waited. I wondered what it would feel like when there was no more air left and I had to pull water into my lungs.

The sound of a sharp bang on the ceiling caused a start that went through me like a bullet. I turned my head from one side to the other, sightless and scared. *Bang.* Scraping, sliding noises, tools against metal. The ceiling creaked, and the entire elevator rocked as if it were a rowboat.

"Is someone there?" I called out, my pulse thundering.

I heard the muffled, distant sound of a human voice.

Galvanized, I pounded the elevator wall with my fist. "Help! I'm trapped down here!"

There was a reply I couldn't hear. Whoever it was kept working on the top of the elevator, wrenching and prying until a raw shriek of metal filled the air. A portion of the wood paneling was ripped back. I flattened myself against the wall as I heard cracking and splintering, debris splashing. And then the beam of a flashlight shot into the dark elevator cab, bouncing off the water.

"I'm here," I said with a sob, sloshing forward. "I'm down here. Is there any way you can get me out?"

A man leaned into the elevator cab until I could see his face and shoulders illuminated by the reflected light.

"You should probably know up front," Hardy said, widening the opening with a grunt of effort, "I charge a lot for elevator rescues."

CHAPTER TWELVE

"Hardy! Hardy —" he had come for me. i nearly lost it then. In the wild torrent of relief and gratitude, there were at least a dozen things I wanted to tell him at once. But the first thing that came out was a fervent, "I'm so sorry I didn't have sex with you."

I heard his low laugh. "I am too. But honey, there are a couple of maintenance guys with me who can hear every word we're saying."

"I don't care," I said desperately. "Get me out of here and I swear I'll sleep with you."

I heard one of the maintenance guys volunteer in a Spanish accent, "I'll pull her out."

"This one's mine, amigo," Hardy said affably, and he leaned farther into the elevator cab, one long arm extended. "Can you reach my hand, Haven?"

Standing on my toes, I strained upward. Our palms met, and his fingers moved downward to close around my wrist. But I was coated with slippery stuff, and my hand slid right through Hardy's grip. I fell back against the wall. "I can't." I tried to sound calm, but my voice was shredded. I had to stifle a sob. "The water's oily."

"Okay," he said quickly. "That's okay. No, don't cry, honey, I'm coming down. Stay on the side and hold on to the rail."

"Wait, you'll get stuck down here too —" I began, but Hardy was already lowering his feet and legs. He gripped part of the ceiling frame, eased himself down and hung for a moment. As he came into the cab with a controlled drop, the floor shifted and the level of water came up. I sloshed through the heavy water, leaping on him, climbing halfway up his body before he could even move.

Hardy caught me in a firm grip, one arm sliding beneath my bottom, the other strong and solid around my back. "I've got you," he said. "My brave girl."

"Not brave." My arms were locked in a death grip around his neck. I buried my face against him, trying to comprehend that he was really there with me.

"Yes you are. Most women would be in hysterics by now."

"I was w-working up to that," I said into

his shirt collar. "You just c-caught me early in the process."

He gripped me closer. "You're safe, sweetheart. It's all right now."

I tried to set my teeth against the chattering. "I can't believe you're here."

"'Course I'm here. Anytime you need me." He squinted up at the hole in the ceiling, where one of the maintenance men was angling a flashlight to help us see. "Manuel," he said, "you guys got a sump pump at the bottom of the shaft?"

"Nah," came the regretful reply. "It's an old building. Only the new ones got pumps."

Hardy's hand stroked up and down my shivering back. "Probably wouldn't make a difference anyway. Can someone shut off the main disconnect switch? I don't want this thing to start moving while we're getting her out."

"Don't need to, it's off."

"How do you know?"

"There's an automatic shunt trip."

Hardy shook his head. "I want someone to go to the machine room and make sure the fucker's really off."

"You got it, *jefe.*" Manuel used a two-way radio to get in touch with the supervisor running the security office. The supervisor said he would send their only available guard

287

to the machine room to shut off the mainline switch for all the elevators, and call back when it was done. "He says he can't get the cops," Manuel reported to us. "Nine-one-one is broke. Too many calls. But the elevator company is sending a guy."

"The water's getting higher," I told Hardy, my arms linked tightly around his neck, my legs clamped on his waist. "Let's get out *now*."

Hardy smiled and pushed my straggling hair back from my face. "It'll only take a minute for them to find the disconnect switch. Just pretend we're in a hot tub."

"My imagination's not that good," I told him.

"You've obviously never lived on a drilling rig." His hand rubbed over my shoulders. "Are you hurt anywhere? Any bumps or bruises?"

"No, I was just scared for a little while."

He made a sympathetic sound, gripping me closer. "You're not scared now, are you?"

"No." It was true. It seemed impossible that anything bad could happen while I was holding on to those solid shoulders. "I'm just c-cold. I don't understand where the water's coming from."

"Manuel says a wall between the garage and a drainage tunnel collapsed. We're getting runoff from some pretty big waterways."

"How did you find me so fast?"

"I was just heading home when you called. I hightailed it over here and got ahold of Manuel and his buddy. We took the service elevator to the level just above this one, and I popped the doors open with a bent screwdriver." He kept smoothing my hair as he talked. "The escape hatch on the elevator was a little harder — I had to knock a couple of bolts out with a hammer."

We heard some static and a garbled voice from the two-way radio overhead, and Manuel called to us. "Okay, *jefe*. Switch is off."

"Great." Hardy squinted at Manuel. "I'm going to hand her up to you. Don't let her fall into the hoistway — she's slippery." He pulled my head back until I was looking into his eyes. "Haven, I'm going to push you up, and then you get on my shoulders and let them pull you out. Got it?" I nodded reluctantly, not wanting to leave him. "Once you're on top of the elevator," Hardy continued, "don't touch any of the cables or drive sheaves or any of that shit. There's a ladder attached to the wall of the elevator shaft. Be careful while you're climbing — you're as slick as a greased hog on ice."

"What about you?"

"I'll be fine. Put your foot in my hand."

"But h-how are you —"

"Haven, quit talking and give me your foot."

I was amazed by the ease with which he lifted me, one big hand fitting under my bottom to boost me up to the two maintenance men. They gripped me beneath the arms and pulled me onto the top of the elevator, holding me as if they feared I might skid over the side. And I probably would have, I was so covered in slime.

Normally I could have clambered up the ladder with ease, but my feet and hands kept slipping on the metal. It required concentration and effort to make it to the landing, where Hardy had pried open the hoist doors. There were more people to help me, a couple of office workers, the security supervisor and guard, the newly arrived elevator technician, and even Kelly Reinhart, who couldn't stop exclaiming in horror, saying over and over, "I just saw her a half hour ago . . . I can't believe this . . . I just saw her . . ."

I ignored them all, not out of rudeness but single-minded fear. I waited beside the open doors and refused to budge, calling out Hardy's name anxiously. I heard a lot of splashing and some grunting, and a few of the foulest curses I'd ever heard in my life.

Manuel was the first to emerge, and his companion came next. Finally Hardy crawled out of the hoistway, dripping and covered with the same dark slime I was, his business clothes plastered to his body. I was certain he didn't smell any better than I did. His hair was standing up in places. He was the most gorgeous man I'd ever seen in my life.

I launched myself at him, wrapped my arms around his waist, and drove my head against his chest. His heart thudded strongly under my ear. "How did you get out?" I asked.

"I got a foothold on the handrail, did a pull-up on the top frame, and swung a leg up. I almost slipped back down again, but Manuel and Juan grabbed me."

"El mono," Manuel said as if to explain, and I heard a rumble of laughter in Hardy's chest.

"What does that mean?" I asked.

"He called me a monkey." Reaching into his back pocket, Hardy extracted a wallet and fished out some dripping cash, apologizing for the condition it was in. They chuckled and assured him the money was still good, and they all shook hands.

I stood with my arms clutched around Hardy as he spoke with the elevator technician and security office supervisor for a couple of minutes. Even though I was safe, I couldn't make myself let go of him. And he didn't seem to mind that I had attached myself to him, only ran his hand over my back now and then. A fire truck pulled up outside the building, lights flashing.

"Listen," Hardy said to the security supervisor, handing him a soggy business card. "We're done talking for now — she's been through enough. I've got to take care of her and get us both cleaned up. If anyone wants to know something, they can reach me tomorrow."

"Right," the supervisor said. "I understand. You let me know if I can help you in any way. Take care, y'all."

"He was nice," I said as Hardy guided me out of the building, right past the fire truck and a van with a camera crew emerging.

"He's hoping you don't sue his ass," Hardy replied, leading me to his car, which had been double-parked. It was a gleaming silver Mercedes sedan, and the inside beige upholstery was buttery and perfect.

"No," I said helplessly. "I can't get into that car when I'm all disgusting and dirty."

Hardy opened the door and manhandled me inside. "Get in, darlin'. We're not walking home."

I cringed every second of the short drive to 1800 Main, knowing we were ruining the interior of his car.

And there was worse to come. After Hardy parked in the garage beneath our building, we approached the elevator that went to the lobby. I stopped like I'd been shot, and looked from the elevator to the stairs. Hardy stopped with me.

The absolute last thing I wanted to do was to get back on another elevator. It was too much. I felt every muscle tense in rejection of the idea.

Hardy was silent, letting me struggle through it.

"Shit," I choked out. "I can't avoid elevators for the rest of my life, can I?"

"Not in Houston." Hardy's expression was kind. Soon, I thought, the kindness would turn to pity. That was enough to spur me forward.

"Cowboy up, Haven," I muttered to myself, and pushed the up button. My hand was shaking. While the elevator cab descended to the garage, I waited as if I were at the gates of hell.

"I'm not sure I actually thanked you for what you did," I said gruffly. "So . . . thank you. And I want you to know, I'm not usually . . . troublesome. I mean, I'm not one of those women who needs to be rescued all the time."

"You can rescue me next time."

That actually pulled a smile from me despite my anxiety. It was exactly the right thing to say.

The doors opened, and I just did it, made myself walk into the metal box, and I hunched into the corner as Hardy followed. Before the doors had closed, Hardy had pulled me into a tight-bodied clinch, length to length, and our mouths came together, and it seemed as if everything I had felt that day, anguish, anger, desperation, and relief, all surged to a flash point of pure white heat.

I responded with frantic kisses, pulling his tongue into my mouth, wanting the taste and feel of him all over me. Hardy gave a short, sharp pant, as if taken unawares by my response. He gripped my head in his hand and his mouth worked over mine, hungry and sweet.

In a matter of seconds we were at the lobby. The doors opened with an annoying beep. Hardy pulled away and tugged me out of the elevator, into the shining black marble lobby. I was sure we looked like a pair of swamp creatures as we went past the concierge desk to the main residential elevator.

David, the concierge, gaped as he saw us.

"Miss Travis? My Lord, what happened?"

"I had a little . . . sort of, well . . . accident at Buffalo Tower," I said sheepishly. "Mr. Cates helped me out."

"Is there anything I can do?"

"No, we're both fine." I gave David a meaningful look. "And there is *really* no need to tell anyone in my family about this."

"Yes, Miss Travis," he said, a little too quickly. And as we went to the residential elevator, I saw him pick up his phone and start to dial.

"He's calling my brother Jack," I said, trudging into the open elevator. "I don't feel like talking to anyone, especially not my nosy, interfering —"

But Hardy was kissing me again, this time bracing his hands on the wall on either side of me as if I were too dangerous to be touched. The hot openmouthed kiss went on and on, and the pleasure of it was overpowering. I reached up and let my hands follow the thick slope of his shoulders, the muscles bunched and rigid.

I was dimly amazed by the effect of my hands on him, the way his mouth locked on mine as if he were desperately feasting on something that might be taken away. He was aroused, and I actually wanted to touch him there, put my hand on that heavy bulge. My trembling fingers slid over the flat reach of his stomach, crossing the warm metal buckle of his belt. But the elevator stopped, and Hardy gripped my wrist, tugging it back.

His eyes were a hot, soft blue, his color high as if with fever. He gave a shake of his head to clear it, and pulled me from the elevator. We were at the eighteenth floor. His apartment. I went with him willingly, waiting at the door as he entered the combination. He misdialed, causing it to beep indignantly. I bit back a grin as he swore. He gave me a wry glance and tried again, and the door opened.

Taking me by the hand as if I were a small child, Hardy led me to the shower. "Take your time," he said. "I'll use the other bathroom. There's a robe on the back of the door. I'll fetch some clothes from your apartment later."

No shower had ever been as good as that one. I doubted any future ones would even come close. I turned the water temperature up to near-scalding, groaning with pleasure as it rushed over my cold, aching limbs. I washed and rinsed my body and shampooed my hair three times.

Hardy's robe was too big for me, trailing the floor by at least a half-foot. I wrapped myself in it, in the scent that was now becoming familiar. I tied the belt tightly, rolled the sleeves up several times, and looked at myself in the steam-slicked mirror. My hair had sprung up in curls. Since there were no styling tools other than a brush or comb, there was no help for that.

I would have expected to feel drained after what I'd experienced, but instead I felt alive, overstimulated, the soft terry of the robe abrasive on my tender skin. Wandering to the main room, I saw Hardy dressed in jeans and a white T-shirt, his hair still wet from his shower. He was standing at the table, pulling sandwiches and containers of soup from a paper bag.

His gaze took inventory of me from head to toe. "I had the restaurant send up some food," he said.

"Thank you. I'm starving. I don't think I've ever been this hungry."

"That happens sometimes after a trauma. Whenever there was a problem on the rig — an accident or a fire — we all ate like wolves afterward."

"A rig fire would be scary," I said. "How do they start?"

"Oh, blowouts, leaks . . ." He grinned as he added, "Welders . . ." He finished setting out the food. "You start eating. I'll run down to your apartment and get some clothes for you, if you'll tell me the combo."

"Please stay. I can wait for a while. This robe is comfortable."

"Okay." Hardy pulled out a chair for me. As I sat, I glanced at the television, which was showing the local news. I nearly fell off the chair as the anchorwoman said, ". . . and now more on the flooding. We've just learned that earlier this evening an unidentified woman was pulled from a flooded elevator in Buffalo Tower. According to security personnel on the scene, rising water in the lower level of the garage caused the elevator malfunction. Building employees said the woman seemed to be in good condition after the rescue and did not require medical treatment. We'll let you know more on this story as it develops . . ."

The phone rang, and Hardy glanced at the caller ID. "It's your brother Jack. I've already talked to him and told him you're okay. But he wants to hear it from you."

Oh, hell, I thought. Jack must have been just thrilled to find out I was with Hardy.

I took the phone from him and pressed the talk button. "Hi, Jack," I said in a cheerful tone.

"The thing you never want your sister to be," my brother informed me, "is an unidentified woman on the news. Bad things happen to unidentified women."

"I'm fine," I told him, smiling. "Just got a little wet and dirty, that's all."

"You may think you're okay, but you're probably still in shock. You may have injuries you're not even aware of. Why the hell didn't Cates take you to a doctor?"

My smile disappeared. "Because I'm fine. And I'm not in shock."

"I'm coming to get you. You're staying at my apartment tonight."

"No way. I've seen your apartment, Jack. It's a pit. It's so bad my immune system grows stronger every time I visit you."

Jack didn't laugh. "You're not going to stay with Cates after you've been through something this traumatic —"

"Remember our talk about boundaries, Jack?"

"Fuck boundaries. Why did you call him when you've got two brothers who work just a few blocks away from Buffalo Tower? Gage or I could have handled everything just fine."

"I don't know why I called him, I —" I darted an uncomfortable glance at Hardy. He gave me an unfathomable look and went to the kitchen. "Jack, I'll see you tomorrow. Do *not* come over here."

"I told Cates if he touches you, he's a dead

man walking."

"Jack," I muttered, "I'm hanging up now."

"Wait." He paused, and his tone became cajoling. "Let me come and get you, Haven. You're my baby sis —"

"No. Good night."

I hung up as the sound of swearing came through the receiver.

Hardy returned to the table, bringing me a glass filled with ice and fizzing liquid.

"Thanks," I said. "Dr Pepper?"

"Yes. With some lemon juice and a splash of Jack Daniel's. I thought it might help steady your nerves."

I gave him a quizzical glance. "My nerves are okay."

"Maybe. But you still look a little strung out."

It was delicious. I drank a few sweet, tart gulps, until Hardy touched my hand. "Whoa, there. Sip it slowly, honey."

There was a pause in the conversation as we ate vegetable soup and sandwiches. I finished the drink and exhaled slowly, feeling better. "May I have another?" I asked, nudging the empty glass toward him.

"In a few minutes. Jack Daniel's has a way of sneaking up on you."

I turned sideways to face him, hooking my elbow over the back of my chair. "There's no need to treat me like I'm a teenager. I'm a big girl, Hardy."

Hardy shook his head slowly, his gaze holding mine. "I know that. But in some ways you're still . . . innocent."

"Why do you think that?"

His reply was soft. "Because of the way you handle certain situations."

I felt a wash of heat over my face as I wondered if he was referring to how I had behaved in the stairwell. "Hardy —" I swallowed hard. "About last night —"

"Wait." He touched my arm as it lay on the table, his fingers gently tracing the tiny lattice of veins on the inside of my wrist. "Before we get to that, tell me something. Why did you call me instead of your brothers? I'm glad as hell you did. But I'd like to know why."

The heat went everywhere then, spreading over the naked skin beneath the robe. I was suffused with uneasiness and excitement, wondering how far I would dare to go with him, what he'd do if I told him the truth. "I didn't really think about it. I just . . . wanted you."

His fingers moved in a lazy, warm stroke from wrist to elbow, and back again. "Last night," I heard him murmur, "you were right to push me away. The first time shouldn't be in a place like that. You were right to call it off, but the way you did it —"

"I'm sorry," I said earnestly. "I'm really —"

"No, don't be sorry." He took my hand in his and began to play with my fingers. "I thought about it later after I'd cooled down a little. And I thought you might not have reacted like that unless you'd had some kind of . . . bedroom problems . . . with your husband." He looked at me, those blue eyes taking in every nuance of my expression.

"Bedroom problems" was putting it mildly, I thought. I floundered in silence, wanting more than anything to open up to him.

"Was he really your first?" Hardy prompted. "That's pretty unusual, this day and age."

I nodded. "I think," I managed to say, "in a weird way, I was trying to please my mother. Even after she was gone. I felt she would have wanted me to wait, she would have told me nice girls didn't sleep around. And I had so much to make up to her for. I was never the kind of daughter she wanted — or the one Dad wanted either. I felt I owed it to her, to try and be good." I had never admitted that to anyone before. "Later I realized that if I wanted to sleep with someone, it was my own business."

302

"So you chose Nick."

"Yeah." My lips quirked. "Not a great idea, as it turned out. He was impossible to please."

"I'm easy to please." He was still toying with my fingers.

"Good," I said unsteadily, "because I'm pretty sure I don't know how to do it right."

All movement stopped. Hardy looked up from my hand, his eyes bright with hunger. Heat. "I wouldn't —" He had to pause to take an extra breath. His voice was raspy. "I wouldn't have any worries on that account, honey."

I couldn't look away from him. I thought of being under him, his body inside mine, and my heart started thrashing. I needed to slow it down. "I'd like another Jack Daniel's, please," I managed to say. "This time no Dr Pepper."

Hardy let go of my hand, still staring at me. Without a word, he went to the kitchen and brought back two shot glasses and the bottle with its distinctive black label. He poured the shots in a businesslike manner, as if we were settling down for a game of poker.

Hardy tossed his shot back, while I sipped mine, letting the smooth, slightly sweet liquid warm the surface of my lips. We were sitting very close. The robe had parted to reveal my bare knees, and I saw him glance down at them. As his head bent, the light rippled over his dark brown hair. I couldn't stand it anymore, I had to touch him. I let my fingers brush over the side of his head, playing in the silky close-trimmed locks. One of his hands closed over my knee, engulfing it in warmth.

His face lifted and I touched his jaw, the masculine scrape of bristle, laying my fingers against the softness of his lips. I explored the bold shape of his nose, one fingertip drifting to the tantalizing crook at the bridge. "You said you'd tell me someday," I said. "How you broke it."

Hardy didn't want to talk about that. I could tell by the look in his eyes. Except that I had risked a lot by confiding in him, by being honest, and he wasn't going to back down from that. So he gave me a short nod and poured himself another shot, and to my regret, removed his hand from my knee.

After a long pause, he said flatly, "My dad broke it. He was a drinker. Drunk or sober, I think the only time he ever felt good was when he was hurting someone. He cut out on the family when I was still young. I wish to hell he'd stayed away for good. But he came back now and then, whenever he wasn't in jail. He would beat the hell out of Mama, knock her up, and light out again with every cent he could steal from her."

He shook his head, his gaze distant. "My mother's a tall woman, but there's not much to her. A strong wind could knock her over. I knew he'd kill her someday. One of the times he came back, I was about eleven — I told him don't even try, he wasn't going near her. I don't remember what happened next, only that I woke up on the floor feeling like I'd been stomped by a rodeo bull. And my nose was broken. Mama was beat up nearly as bad as I was. She told me never to go against Dad again. She said trying to fight back only made him mad. It was easier on her if we just let him have his way, and then he'd be gone."

"Why didn't anyone stop him? Why didn't she divorce him, or get a restraining order or something?"

"A restraining order only works if you handcuff yourself to a cop. And my mother thought it best to take her problems to her church. They convinced her not to divorce him. They said it was her special mission to save his soul. According to the minister, we should all make it a matter of prayer, that Dad's heart would turn, that he'd see the light and be saved." Hardy smiled grimly. "If

I'd had any hopes of being a religious man, they disappeared after that."

I was floored by the revelation that Hardy had been the victim of domestic violence too. But in a worse way than I had, because he'd only been a child. I restrained my voice to a careful monotone as I asked, "So what happened to your dad?"

"He came back a couple of years after that. I was a lot bigger then. I stood at the door of the trailer and wouldn't let him come in. Mama kept trying to pull me aside, but I wouldn't budge. He —" Hardy stopped and rubbed his mouth and jaw slowly, and wouldn't look at me. I was filled with the electrifying awareness that he had been about to tell me something he'd never told anyone before.

"Go on," I whispered.

"He came after me with a knife. Caught me in the side with it. I twisted his arm and made him drop the knife, and then I beat him until he promised to clear out of there. He never came back. He's in prison now." His face was taut. "Worst part about it was, Mama wouldn't talk to me for two days after."

"Why? Was she mad at you?"

"I thought so, at first. But then I realized . . . she was scared of me. When I was going ape shit on Dad, she couldn't see any difference between us." He looked at me then, and said quietly, "I come from bad stock, Haven."

I could tell he meant it as a warning. And I understood something about him, that he had always used this notion of being from bad stock as a reason to keep from getting too close to anyone. Because letting someone in close meant they could hurt you. I knew all about that kind of fear. I lived with it.

"Where did he cut you?" I asked thickly. "Show me."

Hardy stared at me with the glazed concentration of a drunken man, but I knew it had nothing to do with the Jack Daniel's. A flush had crossed the crests of his cheeks and the bridge of his nose. He tugged at the bottom of his T-shirt until it revealed the taut flesh of his side. A thin scar showed white against the silky tan. And he watched, transfixed, as I slipped out of my chair and knelt before him, and leaned between his thighs to kiss the scar. He stopped breathing. His skin was hot against my lips, his leg muscles so tense they felt like iron.

I heard a groan above my head, and I was plucked from between his knees as if I were a rag doll. Hardy carried me to the sofa, laid me out on the velvet upholstery, and knelt beside me while tugging at the belt of the robe. His mouth covered mine, burning and whiskey-sweet as he pulled the front of the robe apart. His hand was warm as he touched my breast, cupping beneath the soft curve, plumping it high for his mouth.

His lips covered the tight peak, and he drew his tongue over it in tender licks. I squirmed beneath him, unable to hold still. The nipple budded almost painfully, sensation darting to the fork of my body with every stroke and swirl. I moaned and put my arms around his head, my spine dissolving as he moved to the other breast. My fingers tangled in the silk of his hair, shaping to his skull. Blindly I urged his mouth back up to mine, and he took it savagely, as if he couldn't get deep enough.

The weight of his hand settled low on my stomach, spanning the soft curve. I felt the tip of his little finger resting on the edge of the dark triangle. Whimpering, I nudged upward. His hand slid lower, and as his fingertips played in the springy curls, my insides began to throb and close on the emptiness. Until that moment, I had never felt as if I could die from raw need. I moaned and pulled at his T-shirt. Hardy's mouth returned to mine, licking at the sounds I made as if he could taste them. "Touch me," I gasped, my toes curling into the velvet cushions. "Hardy, please —"

"Where?" came a devil-whisper, while he stroked the damp curls between my thighs.

I parted my knees, shaking all over. "There. There."

He gave a sigh that was almost a purr, his fingers nudging me open, finding heat and syrup, centering on the place that drove me wild. His mouth rubbed over my swollen lips, dragging gently. His hand slid from between my legs, and he gathered me in his arms as if he meant to lift me, but instead he just held me in a bundle of smoothness and trembling bones and gasping dampness. He dipped his head, kissing the arc of a knee, the plush give of a breast, the tight strain of my throat.

"Take me to bed," I said hoarsely. I caught one of his earlobes between my teeth, drew my tongue over it. "Take me . . ."

Hardy shuddered and released me and turned to sit on the floor facing away from me. He rested his arms on his bent knees and lowered his head, his breath coming in deep, harsh gusts. "I can't." His voice was muffled. "Not tonight, Haven."

I was slow to understand. Trying to think straight was like pushing past layers of filmy curtains. "What is it?" I whispered. "Why not?"

Hardy took an unnervingly long time to answer. He moved to face me, kneeling with his thighs spread. He reached out to cover me with the sides of the robe, the gesture so careful that it seemed even more intimate than what had gone before.

"It's not right," he said. "Not after what you've just been through. I'd be taking advantage of you."

I couldn't believe it. Not when everything had been going so well, when it seemed like all my fear had gone. Not when I needed him so badly. "No you wouldn't," I protested. "I'm fine. I *want* to sleep with you."

"You're in no shape to make that decision right now."

"But . . ." I sat up and rubbed my face. "Hardy, don't you think you're being a little high-handed about this? After getting me all worked up, you —" I stopped as an awful thought occurred to me. "This is payback, isn't it? For last night?"

"No," he said in annoyance. "I wouldn't do that. That's not what this is about. And in case you hadn't noticed, I'm as worked up as you are."

"So I'm not part of the decision? I don't

get a vote?"

"Not tonight."

"*Damn it,* Hardy . . ." I was aching all over. "You're going to let me suffer just so you can prove some completely unnecessary point?"

His hand slid over my stomach. "Let me finish you off."

It was like being offered an extra appetizer when the entrée wasn't available. *"No,"* I said, red-faced with frustration. "I don't want a halfway job, I want a full, start-to-finish sex act. I want to be regarded as an adult woman who has the right to decide what to do with her own body."

"Honey, I think we just proved beyond the shadow of a doubt that I think of you as an adult woman. But I'm not going to take someone who's just been through a near-death experience, bring her up to my apartment and give her alcohol, and then take advantage of her while she's feeling grateful. It's not happening."

My eyes widened. "You think I would sleep with you out of *gratitude?*"

"I don't know. But I want to give it a day or two to wear off."

"It's worn off already, you big jerk!" I knew I wasn't being fair to him, but I couldn't help it. I was being left high and dry, just at the point when my body was about to go up in flames.

"I'm trying to be a gentleman, damn it all."

"Well, now's a fine time to start."

I couldn't stay in his apartment another minute — I was afraid I'd do something to embarrass us both. Like throw myself on him and beg. Struggling off the sofa, I retied the belt of the robe around my waist and headed for the door.

Hardy was at my heels immediately. "Where are you going?"

"Down to my apartment."

"Let me get your clothes first."

"Don't bother. People wear robes when they're coming up from the pool."

"They're not naked underneath."

"So what? Are you afraid someone will be so overcome with lust he'll pounce on me in the hallway? I should be so lucky." I charged to the door and went out into the hallway. I was actually grateful for the surge of invigorating rage — it didn't leave much room for me to worry about the elevator.

Hardy followed, and waited beside me until the elevator doors opened. We went in together, both of us barefoot. "Haven, you know I'm right. Let's talk about this."

"If you don't want to have sex, I don't want to talk about our feelings."

He scrubbed his hand through his hair, looking confused. "Well, that's for damn sure the first time a woman's ever said that to me."

"I don't take rejection well," I muttered.

"It's not rejection, it's a postponement. And if Jack Daniel's makes you this ornery, I'm never pouring you another shot."

"It has nothing to do with the whiskey. I'm this ornery all on my own."

It seemed Hardy realized that no matter what he said, it was only going to aggravate me further. So he remained strategically silent until we reached my door. I entered the combination and stepped over the threshold.

Hardy stood looking down at me. He was disheveled and appetizing and sexy as all get out. But he wasn't apologetic.

"I'll call you tomorrow," he said.

"I won't answer."

Hardy slid a long, lazy glance over me, the folds of his own robe wrapped around me, the tight clench of my bare toes. A hint of a smile deepened one corner of his mouth. "You'll answer," he said.

I closed the door smartly. I didn't need to see his face to know there was an arrogant grin on it.

CHAPTER THIRTEEN

I showed up for work at eight-thirty the next morning and was immediately surrounded by Kimmie, Samantha, Phil, and Rob. They all expressed relief that I was okay, and asked about the flooding and what it had been like to be trapped in the elevator, and how I'd gotten out.

"I managed to call a friend of mine before my cell phone went out," I explained. "He showed up and . . . well, everything was fine after that."

"It was Mr. Cates, wasn't it?" Rob asked. "David told me."

"Our tenant Mr. Cates?" Kimmie asked, and grinned at my sheepish nod.

Vanessa came to my cubicle, looking concerned. "Haven, are you all right? Kellie Reinhart called and told me what happened last night."

"I'm just fine," I said. "Ready for work as usual."

She laughed. Maybe I was the only one who heard the condescending edge to it. "You're a trouper, Haven. Good for you."

"By the way," Kimmie told me, "we got a half-dozen calls this morning, asking if you were the woman in the elevator. I think the local media wants to make a deal out of the Travis angle. So I played dumb and said as far as I knew, it wasn't you."

"Thank you," I said, conscious of the slight narrowing of Vanessa's eyes. As much as I disliked my being a Travis, she disliked my being a Travis even more.

"All right, everyone," Vanessa said, "let's all get back to work." She waited until the others had left my cubicle before saying pleasantly, "Haven, come to my office and we'll have coffee while we go over your meeting with Kellie."

"Vanessa, I'm sorry, but I'm not going to be able to remember everything we went over."

"It's on your computer, isn't it?"

"I don't have the computer," I said apologetically. "It drowned."

Vanessa sighed. "Oh, Haven. I wish you'd be more careful with office property."

"Sorry, but it just wasn't possible to save it. The water was coming up and —"

"Look through your notes, then. You did

make notes, didn't you?"

"Yes, but they were in my briefcase . . . and everything in it was trashed. I'll call Kelly and try to reconstruct the meeting as well as I can, but —"

"Honestly, Haven, couldn't you have managed to hold on to your briefcase?" She gave me a look of gentle chiding. "Did you have to go into a panic and drop everything?"

"Vanessa," I said cautiously, "the leak in the elevator was more than just a puddle on the floor." Clearly she didn't understand what had happened, but the last thing you could tell Vanessa was that she didn't understand something.

She rolled her eyes and smiled as if I were a child telling stories. "With your flair for drama, there's no telling what really happened."

"Hey." A rich, easy voice interrupted us. Jack. He came to the cubicle, and Vanessa turned to face him. Her slim fingers gracefully tucked a lock of pale, perfect hair behind her ear. "Hello, Jack."

"Hello, yourself." He came in, surveyed me thoroughly, and reached out to pull me against his chest in a brief hug. I stiffened a little. "Yeah, I don't give a shit that you don't like to be touched," Jack said, continuing to hug me. "You scared the life out of me last night. I stopped by your apartment a couple of minutes ago, and there was no answer. What are you doing here?"

"I work here," I said with a crooked grin.

"Not today. You're taking the day off."

"I don't need to do that," I protested, conscious of Vanessa's stony gaze.

Jack finally let go of me. "Yes you do. Relax. Take a nap. And make sure to call Gage, Joe, Dad, *and* Todd . . . they all want to talk to you. No one called you at home in case you were sleeping."

I made a face. "Am I going to have to repeat the whole story four times?"

" 'Fraid so."

"Jack," Vanessa broke in sweetly, "I don't think it's necessary to make Haven take a day off. We'll take good care of her. And it might help to take her mind off the trauma of getting stuck on that elevator."

Jack gave her a strange look. "It was more than being stuck on an elevator," he told her. "My sister was trapped like a minnow in a bait bucket. I talked to the guy who pulled her out last night. He said the elevator cab was nearly full of water, and completely dark. And he didn't know any other woman who would have handled it as well as Haven did."

Hardy had said that about me? I was

pleased and flattered . . . and I was also fascinated by the quick, subtle contortions that
worked across Vanessa's face.

"Well, *of course* you should take the day
off," she exclaimed, startling me by putting
an arm around my shoulders. "I had no idea
it was that bad, Haven. You should have told
me." She gave me an affectionate squeeze.
The dry, expensive scent of her perfume,
and the feel of her arm around me, caused
my skin to crawl. "You poor thing. Go home
and rest. Is there anything I can do for you?"

"Thanks, but no," I said, inching away
from her. "Really, I'm okay. And I want to
stay."

Jack looked down at me fondly. "Get
going, sweetheart. You're taking the day off."

"I have a ton of stuff to do," I told him.

"I don't give a crap. It'll all be here tomorrow. Right, Vanessa?"

"Right," she said cheerfully. "Believe me, it
will be no problem to cover for Haven." She
patted my back. "Take care, sweetie. Call me
if you need anything."

Her high heels left deep, pointy gouges in
the office carpeting as she left.

"I really should stay," I told Jack.

His expression was intractable. "Go visit
Dad," he said. "He wants to see you. And it
wouldn't hurt either of you to try to talk like

a couple of civilized people for a change."

I heaved a sigh and picked up my purse. "Sure. I haven't had enough excitement in the past couple of days."

Sliding his hands in his pockets, Jack watched me with a narrowed gaze. His voice lowered. "Hey . . . Did Cates make a move on you last night?"

"Are you asking as a brother or a friend?"

He had to think about that. "Friend, I guess."

"All right." I continued in the softest possible whisper. "I made a move on him, and he turned *me* down. He said he didn't want to take advantage of me."

Jack blinked. "What do you know."

"He was really high-handed about it," I said, turning grumpy. "And that whole 'I'm the man, I get to decide' attitude doesn't play with me."

"Haven, he's a Texan. We're not generally known for our sensitivity and tact. You want a guy like that, go find yourself a metrosexual. I hear there's a lot of 'em in Austin."

A reluctant grin broke through my indignation. "I'm not sure you even know what a metrosexual is, Jack."

"I know I'm not one of 'em." He smiled and sat on the corner of my desk. "Haven, everyone knows I got no love lost for Hardy

Cates. But I have to take up for him on this one. He did the right thing."

"How can you defend him?"

His black eyes sparkled. "Women," he said. "You get mad when a man makes a move on you, and you get even madder when he doesn't. I swear, there's no winning."

Some men were partial to their daughters. My dad wasn't one of them. Maybe if we'd spent more time together, Dad and I could have found common ground, but he'd always been too busy, too driven. Dad had yielded the responsibility of daughter-raising to Mother's exclusive control, and no matter how she whittled and chipped, she had never been able to make a square peg fit into a round hole.

My attitude had worsened the harder Mother tried to make me into the right kind of daughter. The possessions that had been deemed unfeminine — my slingshot, my cap pistol, my plastic cowboy-and-Indian set, the Rangers hat Joe had given me — had either disappeared or were given away. "You don't want those," she had said when I complained. "Those things aren't appropriate for little girls."

Mother's two sisters had been sympathetic to her plight, since it was obvious nothing could be done with me. But I thought they had taken some secret satisfaction in the situation. Even though their husbands hadn't been able to afford to buy *them* a mansion in River Oaks, they had managed to produce my cousins Karina and Jaci and Susan, all perfect little ladies. But Mother, who'd had everything in the world she wanted, had gotten stuck with me.

I'd always known that I'd never have gone to Wellesley if my mother were still living. She had been a staunch antifeminist, although I wasn't sure if she even knew why. Maybe because the system had always worked well for her, a rich man's wife. Or possibly because she believed you could never change the order of things, men's natures being what they were, and she hadn't been one to knock her head against the wall. And many women of her generation had believed there was virtue in tolerating discrimination.

Whatever the reason, Mother and I had certainly had our differences. I felt guilty because her death had allowed me to have my own beliefs and go to the college I wanted. Dad hadn't been happy about it, of course, but he'd been too grief-stricken to argue about it. And it had probably been a relief for him to get me out of Texas.

I called Dad on my way to River Oaks to make sure he was at home. Since my car had been totaled by the garage flooding, I was driving a rental car. I was greeted at the front door by the housekeeper, Cecily. She had worked for the Travises for as long as I could remember. She'd been old even when I was a child, her face lined with grooves you could wedge a dime in.

While Cecily headed off to the kitchen, I went to Dad, who was relaxing in the family room. The room was flanked by walk-in fireplaces on each side, and was big enough that you could park a personnel carrier in it. My father was at one end of the room, relaxing on a living room sofa with his feet propped up.

Dad and I hadn't spent any real time together since my divorce. We had seen each other only for short visits, with other people present. It seemed we both felt that getting through a private conversation was more trouble than it was worth.

As I looked at my father, I realized he was getting old. His hair had gotten more white than gray, and his tobacco tan had faded, evidence that he was spending less time outdoors. And he had a sort of settled-in air, the look of a man who had stopped straining and hurrying to reach the next thing around the corner.

"Hey, Dad." I leaned down to kiss his cheek, and sat next to him.

His dark eyes inspected me carefully. "None the worse for wear, looks like."

"Nope." I grinned at him. "Thanks to Hardy Cates."

"You called him, did you?"

I knew where that was leading. "Yeah. Lucky I had my cell phone." Before he could pursue the line of questioning, I tried to divert him. "I guess I'll have a good story to tell my therapist when she gets back from vacation."

Dad frowned in disapproval, as I knew he would. "You're going to a head doctor?"

"Don't say 'head doctor,' Dad. I know it's what people used to call mental health professionals, but now it has a different meaning."

"Like what?"

"It's slang for a woman who's good at . . . a certain bedroom activity."

My father shook his head. "Young people."

I grinned at him. "I didn't come up with it. I'm just trying to keep you updated. So . . . yes, I'm going to a therapist, and she's helped me a lot so far."

"It's a waste of money," Dad said, "paying someone to listen to you complain. All they do is tell you what you want to hear."

As far as I knew, Dad knew approximately nothing about therapy. "You never told me about your psychology degree, Dad."

He gave me a dark look. "Don't tell people you're going to a therapist. They'll think something's wrong with you."

"I'm not embarrassed for someone to know I have problems."

"The only problems you got are the ones you made for yourself. Like marrying Nick Tanner when I told you not to."

I smiled ruefully as I reflected that my father never missed a chance to say I-told-you-so. "I've already admitted you were right about Nick. You can keep reminding me about it, and I can keep admitting I was wrong, but I don't think that's productive. Besides, you were wrong in how you handled it."

His eyes glinted with annoyance. "I stood by my principles. I'd do it again."

I wondered where he'd gotten his notions of fathering. Maybe he thought it was good for his children to have the authority figure he'd never had. His fear of ever admitting he was wrong, about anything, seemed like strength to him. It seemed like weakness to me.

"Dad," I said hesitantly, "I wish you could

be there for me even when I'm doing the wrong thing. I wish you could love me even when I'm screwing up."

"This has nothing to do with love. You need to learn there are consequences in life, Haven."

"I already know that." I had faced consequences Dad didn't even know about. If we had had a different relationship, I would have loved to confide in him. But that required a kind of trust that took years to accumulate. "I shouldn't have rushed into marriage with Nick," I admitted. "I should have had better judgment. But I'm not the only woman who's ever fallen in love with the wrong man."

"Your whole life," he said bitterly, "all you ever wanted was to do the opposite of what your mother or I said. You were more contrary than all three boys put together."

"I didn't mean to be. I just wanted your attention. I would have done anything to get some time with you."

"You're a grown woman, Haven Marie. Whatever you did or didn't get when you were a child, you need to get over it."

"I am getting over it," I said. "I'm done with expecting you to be any different from what you are. I'd like you to do the same for me, and then maybe the two of us could stop being so disappointed in each other. From now on, I'll try to make better choices. But if that means doing something that pisses you off, so be it. You don't have to love me. I love you anyway."

Dad didn't seem to hear that. He was intent on finding out something. "I want to know what's going on with you and Hardy Cates. Are you taking up with him?"

I smiled slightly. "That's my business."

"He's got a reputation," Dad warned. "He lives at one speed: wide-open. Not cut out for marrying."

"I know," I said. "Neither am I."

"I'm warning you, Haven, he'll run roughshod over you. He's a no-account East Texas redneck. Don't give me another reason to say 'I told you so.'"

I sighed and looked at him, this parent who was always convinced he knew best. "Tell me, Dad . . . who would be the right guy for me? Give me an example of someone you'd approve of."

Settling back comfortably, he drummed his thick fingers on his midriff. "George Mayfield's boy, Fisher. He'll come into money someday. Good character. Solid family. Nice-looking too."

I was aghast. I had gone to school with Fisher Mayfield. "Dad, he has the blandest, *limpest* personality in the entire world. He's the human equivalent of cold spaghetti."

"What about Sam Schuler's son?"

"Mike Schuler? Joe's old buddy?"

Dad nodded. "His daddy's one of the best men I know. God-fearing, hardworking. And Mike always had the best manners of any young man I ever met."

"Mike's turned into a pothead, Dad."

My father looked offended. "He has not."

"Ask Joe if you don't believe me. Mike Schuler is single-handedly responsible for the annual income of thousands of Colombian ganja farmers."

Dad shook his head in disgust. "What's the matter with the younger generation?"

"I have no idea," I said. "But if those are your best suggestions, Dad . . . that no-account East Texas redneck is looking pretty good."

"If you start up with him," my father said, "you make sure he knows he'll never get his hands on my money."

"Hardy doesn't need your money," I took pleasure in saying. "He's got his own, Dad."

"He'll want more."

After having lunch with my father, I went back to my apartment and took a nap. I woke up replaying the conversation we'd had, and brooding over his lack of interest in any real father-daughter communication. It depressed me, realizing I wasn't ever going to get the same kind of love from him that I was willing to give. So I called Todd and told him about the visit.

"You were right about something," I said. "I do have a pathetic daddy complex."

"Everyone does, sweetheart. You're not special."

I chuckled. "Want to come over and have a drink at the bar?"

"Can't. Got a date tonight."

"With who?"

"A very hot woman," Todd said. "We've been working out together. What about you? Sealed the deal with Hardy yet?"

"No. He was supposed to call today, but so far —" I stopped as I heard the call waiting beep. "That might be him. I've got to go."

"Good luck, sweetheart."

I clicked over to the second call. "Hello?"

"How are you feeling?" The sound of Hardy's drawl slow-blistered every nerve.

"Fine." My voice sounded like a squeaky balloon. I cleared my throat. "How are you? . . . Any pulled muscles from yester-day?"

"Nope. Everything in working order."

I closed my eyes and let out a breath as I

absorbed the warm, waiting silence between us.

"Still mad at me?" Hardy asked.

I couldn't hold back a smile. "I guess not."

"Then will you go out to dinner with me
tonight?"

"Yes." My fingers curled tightly around the
phone. I wondered what I was doing, agree-
ing to a date with Hardy Cates. My family
would have a fit. "I like to eat early," I told
him.

"So do I."

"Come to my apartment at six?"

"I'll be there."

After he hung up, I sat quietly for a few
minutes, thinking.

I knew Dad would say I had no idea what
I was getting into, going out with Hardy
Cates. But when you started dating someone, you could never be sure what you were
getting into. You had to give someone a
chance to show you who he really was . . .
and believe him when he did.

I dressed in jeans and high heels and a
daffodil-colored halter top with a sparkly pin
anchoring one strap to the bodice. Using a
straightening iron, I worked on my hair until
it was shiny and the ends were all turned up.
Since the weather was humid, I used a min-

imum of makeup, just a touch of mascara and cherry-colored lip stain.

It occurred to me that I was a lot more nervous about the idea of sleeping with Hardy than I had been with Nick as a virgin. Probably because with the first guy, you figured you got a beginner's pass. With the second one, however, something more would be expected. It hadn't helped that I had recently taken a women's-magazine quiz entitled "Are You Good in Bed?" and my score had put me in the category of Inhibited Babe, and had given all kinds of suggestions for enhancing my "carnal abilities," most of which sounded unsanitary, uncomfortable, or just plain unsightly.

By the time I heard the doorbell ring, a few minutes before six, the tension had collected until my entire skeleton felt like it had been fastened with tight metal screws. I opened the door. But it wasn't Hardy.

There stood my ex-husband, dressed in a suit and tie, perfectly groomed and smiling. "Surprise," he said, and grabbed my arm before I could move.

CHAPTER FOURTEEN

I reeled back, trying to break free, but he followed me across the threshold. Nick's smile never wavered. I knocked his hand away from me and faced him, trying to keep the alarm from showing on my face.

I was in the middle of a nightmare. I thought it couldn't be real, except that misery and fear and anger were swarming over me like insects, and that feeling was all too familiar. It had been my reality for almost two years.

Nick looked healthy, fit, a little heavier than he'd been during our marriage. The new roundness of his face emphasized a boyishness that wouldn't sit well as he aged. But overall he gave the appearance of a clean-cut, prosperous, conservative guy.

Only someone who knew him like I did would be aware of the monster inside.

"I want you to leave, Nick."

He gave a bemused laugh, as if my quiet

hostility were coming out of left field. "My God, Marie. I haven't seen you in months, and that's the first thing you say?"

"I didn't invite you here. How did you find my apartment? How did you get past the concierge?" David never let nonresidents into the building without first getting approval.

"I found out where you were working, and I went to your office. Just talked to your manager, Vanessa — she told me you lived here in the building. She gave your apartment number and said to go right on up. Nice girl. Said she'd show me around Houston whenever I want."

"You two have a lot in common," I said tersely. Damn Vanessa! I had told her enough about my past to make her aware that I was *not* on good terms with my former husband. No surprise that she would make use of any opportunity to cause trouble.

Nick ventured farther into my apartment.

"What do you want?" I asked, backing away.

"Just thought I'd drop by and say hi. I'm in town to interview for a job with an insurance company. They need an estimator. I'm sure I'll get it — I'm totally the best guy for the position."

He was interviewing for a job in Houston?

I was sick at the thought. A city with a population of two million was still not big enough for me to share with my ex-husband.

"I'm not interested in your career plans." I tried to keep my voice steady. "You and I have nothing to do with each other anymore." I moved toward the phone. "Leave, or I'll have to call for building security."

"Still the drama," Nick murmured, rolling his eyes. "I came to do you a favor, Marie, if you'd let me talk long enough to —"

"Haven," I snapped.

He shook his head, as if he were confronting a small child who was having a temper tantrum. "Okay. Christ. I have some things that belong to you. I'd like to give them back."

"What things?"

"Stuff like a scarf, a purse . . . and that charm bracelet you got from your aunt Gretchen."

I'd had my lawyer request the return of the bracelet, and Nick had claimed it was lost. I had known better, of course. But the chance to have it back caused a stab of longing. That little piece of my past meant a lot to me.

"Great," I heard myself say casually. "Where is it?"

"Back at my hotel. Meet me tomorrow, and I'll bring it."

"Just send it to me."

He smiled. "You can't have something for nothing, Haven. You can have your things back, including that bracelet — but you have to meet me in person. Just to talk. A public place is fine, if that's what you want."

"All I want is for you to leave." I wondered when Hardy would show up. Probably any minute now. And then there was no telling what would happen. Sweat gathered between my skin and clothes, making the fabric adhere in salty patches. "I'm expecting someone, Nick."

But instantly I knew that was the wrong thing to say. Instead of making him leave, it guaranteed that he would stay. Nick wanted a look at the next man in line.

"You said you weren't dating."

"Well, now I am."

"How long you known him?"

I stared at him coldly, refusing to answer.

"Does he know about me?" Nick pressed.

"He knows I'm divorced."

"You fucked him yet?" His tone was soft, but there was contempt and anger in his gaze.

"You have no business asking that."

"Maybe he'll have better luck thawing you out than I did."

"Maybe he already has," I shot back, and

had the satisfaction of seeing his eyes widen in surprised fury.

I saw movement, someone coming to the doorway . . . Hardy's long, lean form. He paused for a moment, assessing the situation. And his eyes narrowed as Nick turned to face him.

I knew Hardy realized immediately who my visitor was. He could tell from the angry bruised weight of the air, and the bleached whiteness of my face.

I had never expected to make direct physical comparisons between the two men. However, with both of them in the same room, it was impossible not to. Objectively speaking, Nick was more handsome, with smaller, more chiseled features. But Hardy's roughcast good looks and self-assurance made Nick look callow. Unformed.

As Nick stared at Hardy, his aggressive stance softened, and he actually moved back a half step. Whatever kind of man Nick had been expecting me to date, it wasn't this. My former husband had always felt superior to everyone — I had never seen him so visibly intimidated.

It struck me that Hardy, a seasoned, high-octane male, was the authentic version of what Nick was always pretending to be. And because Nick knew deep down that he was a fraud as a man, he occasionally gave in to the explosive rages that I had been a casualty of.

Hardy walked into the apartment and came to me without hesitation, brushing by Nick. I quivered as he slid his arm around me, his eyes dark blue as he stared down at me. "Haven," he murmured. The sound of his voice seemed to unlock a tight clamp around my lungs — I hadn't been aware that I'd been holding my breath. I took in some air. His grip tightened, and I felt some of his vitality jolt into me like an electric current.

"Here," Hardy said, pressing something into my grasp. I looked down at the offering. Flowers. A gorgeous burst of mixed colors, rustling and fragrant in tissue wrapping.

"Thank you," I managed to say.

He smiled slightly. "Go put them in water, honey." And then, to my disbelief, I felt him pat my bottom familiarly, right in front of Nick. The classic male signal of *this is mine*.

I heard my ex-husband take a swift breath. Darting a glance at him, I saw the glow of anger begin at his shirt collar, rising fast. There had been a time when that flush of fury would have heralded untold misery for me. But no longer.

I felt a strange mixture of emotions . . . a knee-jerk uneasiness at the sight of Nick's anger . . . a twinge of annoyance at Hardy . . .

but mostly a sense of triumph, knowing that no matter how badly Nick wanted to punish me, he couldn't.

And although I had never especially liked the fact that Hardy was so physically imposing, I relished it at that moment. Because there was only one thing a bully like Nick respected, and that was a bigger bully.

"What brings you to Houston?" I heard Hardy ask casually as I went to the kitchen sink.

"Job interview," Nick replied in a subdued tone. "I'm Nick Tanner, Haven's —"

"I know who you are."

"I didn't catch your name."

"Hardy Cates."

Glancing back, I saw that neither of them had moved to shake hands.

The name rang a bell for Nick — I saw the flicker of recognition on his features — but he couldn't quite put it in context. "Cates . . . wasn't there some trouble between you and the Travises a while back?"

"You could say so," Hardy replied, sounding not at all regretful. A deliberate pause, and then he added, "Getting friendly with one of 'em, though."

He was referring to me, of course. Pushing Nick's buttons on purpose. I sent Hardy a warning glare, which went completely unnoticed, and I saw the quiver of outrage run across Nick's face.

"Nick was just leaving," I said hastily. "Goodbye, Nick."

"I'll call you," Nick said.

"I'd rather you didn't." I turned back to the sink, unable to look at my ex-husband for another second.

"You heard her," came Hardy's murmur. And there was something else, some brief exchange of words before the door closed firmly.

I let out a shuddery sigh, unaware that I was gripping the bunched flower stems until I looked down and saw a smear of blood on the fleshy pad beneath my right thumb. A thorn had punctured it. I ran some water over my hand to clean it, filled a vase, and settled the flowers in it.

Hardy came up behind me, gave a quiet exclamation as he saw the blood on my hand.

"It's okay," I said, but he took my hand and held it under the water. When the tiny wound was rinsed, he reached for a paper towel and folded it a couple of times.

"Keep pressure on it." He stood facing me, gripping the paper towel against my palm. I was so unsettled by Nick's visit that I couldn't think of a thing to say. Unhappily

I acknowledged that I couldn't throw out my past like an old pair of shoes. I would never be free of it. I could move on, but Nick would always be able to find me, walk back into my life, remind me of things I would have given anything to forget.

"Look at me," Hardy said after a minute.

I didn't want to. I knew he would read my face far too easily. I couldn't help remembering what Todd had said about him . . . *"You watch his eyes. Even when he's doing his regular-guy routine, he's taking measure, learning, every damn second . . ."*

But I forced myself to meet his gaze.

"Did you know he was in town?" Hardy asked.

"No, it was a surprise."

"What did he want?"

"He said he had some old things of mine that he wanted to give back."

"Like what?"

I shook my head. I wasn't in the mood to tell him about Aunt Gretchen's bracelet. Certainly I wasn't about to explain that I'd left it behind because I'd been beaten up and thrown out on the front steps of my own home. "Nothing I want," I lied. I tugged my hand from his and removed the paper towel. The bleeding had stopped. "What did you tell Nick at the door?"

"I said if he showed up here again, I'd kick his ass."

My eyes widened. "You didn't really, did you?"

He looked smug. "I did."

"You arrogant . . . Oh, I can't believe you just took it upon yourself to . . ." I sputtered into silence, fuming.

Hardy wasn't a bit sorry. "That's what you want, isn't it? Not to see him again?"

"Yes, but I don't want you making decisions for me! I feel like I've spent my life surrounded by dominating men — and you'll probably turn out to be the worst of them all."

He had the nerve to smile at that. "You can handle me. I told you before, I'm tame."

I gave him a dark glance. "Yeah, like a buck-strapped rodeo horse."

Hardy's arms went around me. He bent his head, and his low voice caressed my ear. "I guess you got your work cut out for you."

A baffling wave of heat went through me, something rooted in excitement, too intense to name. And with that came a touch of queasiness, and I felt scared and all twisted up with desire.

"Worth a try, isn't it?" Hardy asked.

I wasn't entirely sure what we were talking about. "I . . . I'm not trying anything with you until you promise to stop acting so high-handed."

He nuzzled behind my ear. "Haven . . . do you really think I'd stand aside politely while another man comes sniffing around my woman? If I let that happen, I wouldn't be a man. And I sure as hell wouldn't be a Texan."

I wasn't breathing well. "I'm not your woman, Hardy."

Both his hands curved around my scalp, angling my face upward. His thumbs stroked over my cheeks. He gave me a look that dismantled my brain and set off an erotic flush that covered me from head to toe. "That's something we're going to fix."

More arrogance, I thought dimly. But much to the shame of my politically correct self, it was a huge turn-on, sending heat mainlining through every vein. My fists clenched reflexively in his shirt.

It was a beautiful light-gray shirt that probably cost the equivalent of the average mortgage payment. And I saw my finger had left a bright red splotch of blood on it.

"Oh, no."

"What?" Hardy looked down at my hand. "Damn, it's bleeding again. We need to get you a Band-Aid."

"I don't care about my hand, it's your

shirt! I'm so sorry."

He seemed amused by my concern. "It's just a shirt."

"I hope I haven't ruined it. Maybe it's not too late if I soak it in the sink . . ." I began on the placket of buttons, wincing at the sight of the bloodstained fabric. "It is a silk blend? Maybe I shouldn't try to wash it."

"Forget the shirt. Let me see your hand."

"Is it dry-clean only? What does the tag say?"

"I never read the tag."

"Such a man." I undid another button . . . another. My fingers slowed, but didn't stop.

I was undressing him.

Hardy didn't move, just watched me, his amusement evaporating. His chest went rigid beneath the blinding-white undershirt, his breath coming faster as I made fumbling progress.

I tugged the hem of the shirt free of his jeans, the thin fabric crumpled and warm from his body.

Such a man. A good-looking, over-the-top male, trying so hard not to seem dangerous . . . he was absolutely tantalizing. My hands shook as I reached for the cuffs of his sleeves, pushing the buttons through the crisp starched layers of fabric.

Hardy remained still as I tugged the shirt

from his shoulders. When the shirt reached his wrists, he moved as if he were dreaming, slowly pulling his arms from the sleeves. He tossed the garment to the floor and reached for me.

I went weak as his arms enclosed me, his mouth descending with hot, searching pressure. I reached around his back, beneath the T-shirt, finding the powerful muscles on either side of his spine.

His lips slid to my throat, exploring gently until I squirmed and arched to get closer to him. Excitement roared through me, and I stopped thinking, stopped trying to control anything.

Hardy lifted me until I was sitting on the small kitchen island, my legs dangling. I shut my eyes against the artificial glare of the overhead lights. His mouth came to mine, tender and devouring, while his hands closed over my thighs and stroked them apart. God, the way he kissed. It had never been like this with Nick, or anyone, this urgent heat that melted me at the core.

My clothes felt too tight, the halter top cinched over my breasts, and I tugged frantically at the straps to be rid of it. Hardy pushed my hands away. I felt him working at the straps, unhooking the closures at the back.

The halter top loosened and fell to my waist. My breasts felt heavy, achy, the tips turning hard as they were exposed to cool air. Hardy slid an arm behind my back to support my faltering weight. He bent over me, his mouth hot as he navigated the pale slope of my breast. His lips traveled slowly to the deep pink crest. A moan swelled in my throat as he suckled, nibbled, moving from one breast to the other. Gasping, I held his head to me, the hair like thick silk, the scent of him as fresh as vetiver.

He pulled me up, his arm amazingly strong, and he cradled my head in one hand to feed on my mouth again. His fingers clamped on a nipple still damp from his tongue.

I clutched at him, so close, needing more, just a little more . . .

He seemed to understand. Murmuring against my throat, Hardy pulled at the fastenings of my jeans, unzipped them, began to tug them down over my hips.

Then something in me snapped.

I went cold for no reason, as if I'd just been dropped into a glacier lake. I saw Nick's face, felt Nick's arms around me, his legs pushing between mine. There was a bolt of pain in my chest, like the beginning of a heart attack, and my gut roiled.

I came apart, crying out and shoving at him, nearly falling off the island. Hardy caught me, lowering my feet to the floor, but I was too far gone at that point, snapping at him, *no get away don't touch me don't,* and I kicked and pushed and clawed away from him like a wild thing.

I must have blanked out for a moment, because the next thing I knew, I was curled up on the sofa, and Hardy was standing over me.

"Haven, look at me," he said, and kept repeating it until I obeyed. I saw blue eyes, not hazel. I focused on them desperately.

Hardy had draped his discarded button-down shirt over my naked chest. "Take a deep breath," he said patiently. "I'm not going to touch you. No, sit still. Breathe."

My stomach was cramping so painfully, I was certain I was going to throw up. But gradually the jerky breaths eased into longer ones, and the sickness faded. Hardy gave a curt nod when my breathing returned to something approaching normal. "I'll get you some water. Where are the glasses?"

"To the right of the sink," I croaked.

He went to the kitchen area, and I heard the tap running. While he was gone, I pulled his shirt on and wrapped it around myself. I was clumsy, trembling with aftershocks. As I realized what had just happened, how I had freaked out on him, I wanted to die. I buried my head in my arms. I had thought everything was fine. It had felt so good, but all the excitement and pleasure had turned to panic.

Something was really, really wrong with me. And I knew if I couldn't be close to this man, now, I was never going to be close to anyone. I was never going to be okay.

Swamped in despair, I huddled in the corner of the sofa. Hardy sat on the coffee table, facing me. Silently he gave me the glass of water. My mouth had gone as dry as dust, and I drank thirstily. But after a few swallows, the sick feeling threatened to come back, and I set the glass aside.

I forced myself to look at Hardy. He was pale under his tan, his eyes electric blue.

My mind was a complete blank. What the hell should I say to him? "I didn't think I was going to do that," I heard myself mumble. "I'm sorry."

His gaze locked on me. "Haven . . . What kind of problem are we dealing with?"

CHAPTER FIFTEEN

I *really* didn't want to get into that. I wished Hardy would go away and leave me the privacy for tears. I wanted to cry and go to sleep, and never wake up. But it was pretty clear Hardy wasn't going anywhere until he got an explanation. And God knew I owed him one.

I gestured clumsily to a chair on the other side of the table. "If you wouldn't mind . . . I can talk about it easier if you sit over there."

Hardy shook his head. The only sign of emotion on his face were the twin lines notched between his brows. "I can't," he said in a husky voice. "I think I might know what you're going to tell me. And I don't want to be far away from you when you say it."

I looked away from him, shrinking into the folds of his shirt. I could only talk in fits and starts. "What just happened was . . . Well, I behaved that way because . . . I have some leftover problems from my marriage. Because Nick was . . . abusive."

The room was deathly quiet. I still couldn't look at him.

"It started out in little ways," I said, "but it got worse over time. The things he said, the demands . . . the slapping, screaming, punishing . . . I kept forgiving him, and he kept promising never to do it again . . . but he did, and it got worse, and he always blamed me for causing it. He always said it was my fault. And I believed him."

I went on and on. I told Hardy everything. It was awful. It was a train wreck happening right in front of me and I couldn't do anything about it, except that not only was I watching, I was also the train. I confessed things that in a saner moment I would have had dignity or sense to filter out. But there was no filter. All my defenses were down.

Hardy listened with his face averted, his profile shadowed. But his body was tense all over, the stark relief of jutting muscles in his arms and shoulders more eloquent than words.

I even told him about the last night with Nick, the rape, being thrown out, the barefoot walk to the grocery store. While I talked, I cringed at the ugliness of what I'd been through.

There was a certain relief in it though. An ease. Because I knew that with all the baggage I was unloading, any chance of a relationship with Hardy was vanishing. Syllable by syllable. No man would want to deal with this. And that was for the best, because it was obvious I wasn't ready for a relationship anyway.

So this was goodbye.

"I didn't mean to lead you on," I said to Hardy. "I knew from the beginning I was playing with fire, having anything to do with you. But —" My eyes watered, and I blinked fiercely and talked in a rush. "You're so good-looking and such a good kisser and I wanted you so much last night that I thought I could go through with it, but I'm too screwed up and I just can't do it, I can't."

I fell silent then. My eyes wouldn't stop leaking. I couldn't think of anything else to tell Hardy, except that he could go if he wanted. But he stood and went to the fireplace and braced a hand on the mantel. He stared into the empty space. "I'm going after your ex-husband," I heard him say softly. "And when I finish, there won't be enough left of him to fill a fucking matchbox."

I'd heard louder and more colorful threats, but never one delivered with a quiet sincerity that raised all the hairs on the back of my neck.

Hardy turned to look at me then. I felt myself blanch as I saw his expression. It was not the first time I'd been alone in a room with a man who had murder in his eyes. This time, thankfully, the violence wasn't directed at me. All the same, it made me fidgety. "Nick's not worth going to jail for," I said.

"I don't know about that." Hardy stared at me for a moment, registering my uneasiness. His expression deliberately softened. "The way I was brought up, 'he needed killing' is an airtight legal defense."

I almost smiled at that. I let my shoulders slump, feeling drained in the aftermath of my personal catastrophe. "But even if you did, it wouldn't change the way I am now. I'm broken." I blotted my eyes with a shirt-sleeve. "I wish I'd slept with someone before I married Nick, because at least then I'd have some good experience with sex. As it is, though . . ."

Hardy watched me intently. "That night of the theater opening . . . you had a flashback when I was kissing you, didn't you? That's why you took off like a scalded cat."

I nodded. "Something in my mind clicked, and it was like I was with Nick, and all I knew was that I had to get away or I would be hurt."

"Was it always bad with him?"

It was mortifying, talking about my pitiful sex life. But at this point I had no pride left. "It started out okay, I guess. But the longer the marriage went on, the worse things got in the bedroom, until I was mostly just waiting for it to be over. Because I knew it didn't matter to Nick if I was enjoying it or not. And it hurt sometimes when I was . . . you know, dry." If a person could have died of embarrassment, I should have been laid out on a mortuary slab right then.

Hardy came to sit on the sofa beside me, laying one arm along the back of it. I flinched at his nearness, but I couldn't look away from him. He was ridiculously virile in that damned white T-shirt, with that long body and those sun-baked muscles. Any woman would have to be out of her mind not to go to bed with him.

"I guess it's over now," I said bravely. "Right?"

"Is that what you want?"

My throat clenched. I shook my head.

"What do you want, Haven?"

"I want *you,*" I burst out, and the tears spilled over again. "But I can't have you."

Hardy moved closer, gripping my head in his hands, forcing me to look at him. "Haven, sweetheart . . . you've already got me."

I looked at him through a hot blur. His eyes were filled with anguished concern and fury. "I'm not going anywhere," he said. "And you're not broken. You're scared, like any woman would be, after what that son of a bitch did." A pause, a curse, a deep breath. An intent stare. "Will you let me hold you now?"

Before I even realized what I was doing, I had crawled into his lap. He gathered me close, cuddling and soothing, and the comforting felt so good that I almost wished I could keep crying. I nuzzled into the fragrant skin of his neck, finding the place where the shaven bristle of his jaw began.

He turned his mouth to mine, easy and warm, and that was all it took to start me simmering again, my lips parting to welcome him.

But even as I responded to his kiss, I felt the intimate pressure of him beneath me, and I stiffened.

Hardy drew his head back, his eyes molten blue. "Is it this?" He nudged upward, the hard ridge pushing against me. "Feeling that makes you nervous?"

I squirmed and nodded, turning scarlet. But I didn't try to move off him, just sat there quivering.

His hands traced down my shoulders and

arms, caressing me through the shirt. "Should I visit the therapist with you? Would that help?"

I couldn't believe he'd be willing to do that for me. I tried to imagine it, me and Hardy and Susan discussing my sex problems, and I shook my head. "I want to fix it now," I said desperately. "Let's just . . . let's go into the bedroom and do it. No matter what I say or even if I freak out, just hold me down and keep going till it's finished and —"

"*Hell* no, we're not going to do that." Hardy looked almost comically appalled. "You're not a horse to be broken to saddle. You don't need to be forced, you need —" He drew in a quick breath as I shifted my weight on his lap. "Honey," he said in a strained voice, "I don't do my best thinking when all the blood leaves my brain. So you should probably sit next to me."

A warm pulse throbbed where we pressed, our flesh fitting exactly. I realized I wasn't quite as nervous, now that I'd had a few moments to get used to him. I settled a little deeper on him.

Hardy closed his eyes and made a guttural sound. I saw the color heighten in his face. And I felt a rearing response in the thick pressure beneath me.

Hardy's lashes lifted, his eyes bluer than

usual against his rich rosewood tan. He glanced at the front of my shirt — his shirt — where it gaped open to reveal the space between my breasts. "Haven . . ." His voice was hoarse. "We're not going to do anything you're not ready for. Let's get you dressed, and I'll take you out to dinner. We'll have some wine, and you can relax. We'll figure this out later."

But later was too late. I wanted to figure it out right then. I felt the heat coming off him, and I saw the mist of sweat on his throat, and I longed to kiss him. I wanted to give him pleasure. And please, God, I wanted at least one good memory to replace one of the bad ones.

"Hardy," I said tentatively, "would you . . . indulge me a little?"

A smile touched his mouth. He reached out and pulled the sides of the shirt closed, and used the backs of his fingers to stroke my cheek. "A little," he said, "or a lot. Just tell me what you want."

"I feel like . . . if we went to the bedroom right now, and just tried some things, I . . . I could handle it as long as you took it slow."

His hand stilled. "What if you have a flash-back?"

"I don't think it would bother me as much as it did before, because now I've told you everything and I know you understand what my problem is. So I would just tell you if I got afraid."

He stared at me for a long moment. "You trust me, Haven?"

I ignored a twinge of nerves in my stomach. "Yes."

Without another word Hardy plucked me from his lap, set me on my feet, and followed me to the bedroom.

My bed was an old-fashioned brass one, the sturdy, stately kind that weighed a ton and didn't move an inch. It was covered in cream linen, and the pillows were made of lace taken from antique wedding dresses. In the feminine surroundings of my bedroom, Hardy looked even bigger and more masculine than usual.

Such a normal act, two people going to bed together. But for me it was invested with far too much significance, too much emotion, too much everything.

The air-conditioning imparted a soft chill to the room, the lace on the pillows fluttering like moth wings as the ceiling fan turned overhead. An antique Victorian lamp shed amber light across the bed.

I tried to seem casual, sitting on the bed and working at the tiny straps of my high-heeled sandals. I wished I weren't stone-cold sober. A glass of wine might have loosened me up a little. Maybe it wasn't too late. Maybe I should suggest —

Hardy sat beside me, reached for my foot, and unfastened the miniature buckle. He squeezed my bare foot and ran his thumb along the arch before taking off the other shoe. Sliding an arm around me, he eased us both back onto the bed.

I waited tensely for him to start. But Hardy only held me, warming me with his body, fitting an arm beneath my neck. One hand traveled over my back and waist and hips, up to the nape of my neck, as if I were a skittish animal. And it went on until the petting and soothing had lasted longer than any sex act I had ever engaged in with Nick.

Hardy spoke against my hair. "I want you to understand . . . you're safe. I'm not going to hurt you in any way. And if I do something you don't want, or you start to feel scared, I'll stop. I'm not going to lose control." I flinched as I felt a tug at the front of my jeans and heard the snap being unfastened. "I'm just going to find out what you like."

My fingers curled into his T-shirt as his hands ventured inside the loosened waist of my jeans. "I want to find out what you like too."

"I like it all, darlin'," he whispered, peeling my clothes off as if he were unwrapping a bandage. "I told you, I'm easy to please."

His breath fell on me with a sweet burn as he drew his mouth over my throat and breasts. He knew what he was doing, taking his time. "Relax," he murmured, his fingers gliding over my straining limbs.

I clutched at his T-shirt, trying to pull it off. He helped me, stripping away the layer of thin cotton and tossing it to the floor. His skin was as brown as cinnamon against the antique-white bed linens. There was a light mat of hair on his chest, so unlike Nick's smoothness. I put my arms around his neck and kissed him, gasping as my breasts pressed into the warm, tickling hair.

Hardy caressed and explored as if he were intent on discovering every detail of my body. I realized he was playing with me, lifting and turning me, pressing kisses in unexpected places. He was so strong, his body sleek and beautiful in the muted light. I crawled over him and rubbed my nose and chin into the springy-soft fur of his chest. I trailed my fingers to his midriff, where the skin was satin-smooth and taut over bands of muscle. And lower, to the edge of his jeans . . . and lower still, to the part of him I was nervous of.

Watching my face, Hardy eased slowly onto his back, allowing me to explore him. I touched him over his jeans, hesitantly tracing the jut of his erection. His breath roughened, and I sensed how difficult it was for him to hold himself in check. My fingers wandered to the base of the shaft, where the flesh was weighted and tight-mounded, and I heard him give a soft grunt. A dart of excitement went through me as I realized how much he liked that, and I did it again, circling my palm over the taut denim.

A laughing groan escaped him. "You're trying to torture me, aren't you?"

I shook my head. "Just trying to learn you."

He pulled me farther over his chest, guided my head to his, and gave me another of those insatiable kisses, until I was rising and falling with the rhythm of his breathing as if I were floating on ocean waves. He reached down to his jeans and unfastened them.

I hesitated and slid my hand down to grip him gingerly. At this point there was no doubt that Hardy was built to scale all over. It was, as Todd would say, quite a package. But instead of greeting the discovery with a hallelujah, I grimaced. "You're a lot for me to manage," I said doubtfully. "I wish I could start with something smaller and gradually trade up."

"Can't help you there, honey." Hardy sounded breathless. "That one's not available in a mid-sized edition." He urged me over to my front, and I felt his mouth on my back, kissing and nibbling along my spine. But I stiffened as I remembered how Nick used to take me from behind. His favorite position. All the thumping excitement died away, and I broke out in an anxious sweat.

Hardy's mouth lifted from my skin, and he turned me to face him.

"Scared?" he murmured, his hand skimming over my arm.

I nodded with a mixture of defeat and frustration. "I guess I don't like it that way, with you behind me. It reminds me of —" I stopped, wondering bleakly if I was ever going to get Nick out of my head, if I would ever be able to forget what he had done. The bad memories had been woven into the fabric of my body, threaded through every nerve. Nick had ruined me for life.

Hardy continued to stroke my arm. There was a distance in his gaze, as if he were turning a thought over in his mind. I realized he was considering how to handle me, how to slip past my defenses, and that made me feel apologetic and wary.

His hand wandered from my arm to my

chest, his fingertips circling the breasts that Nick had complained were too small.

Damn it. There was no way the good feeling was going to come back. I couldn't stop thinking about my ex-husband, or my own inadequacies. "It's not working for me," I choked out. "Maybe we should —"

"Close your eyes," he murmured. "Lie still."

I obeyed, my fingers knotting into fists by my sides. The lamplight shone dull orange through my lids. His mouth descended, trailing kisses from my chest to my stomach. His tongue slipped inside the tight hollow of my navel, and I squirmed in response. His hand settled on one of my knees. "Easy," he whispered again, sliding lower until my eyes flew open. I jerked and pushed at his head.

"Wait," I gasped. "That's enough, I can't . . ." I was blushing furiously, trembling all over.

Hardy's head lifted, the soft light running over his hair like liquid. "Am I hurting you?"

"No."

His hand came to my stomach, rubbing in a warm circle. "Did I scare you, honey?"

"No, it's just . . . I've never done that before." Needless to say, Nick had never been interested in any activity that would enhance my pleasure rather than his.

Hardy contemplated my red face for a moment. A new glint entered his eyes.

Softly, "Don't you want to try it?"

"Well, someday, I guess. But I like to take these things in steps. I think I should get used to the regular stuff before going to the advanced —" I broke off with a little yelp as he bent over me again. "What are you doing?"

His voice was muffled. "You work on a plan for taking it in steps. Let me know when you got it figured out. In the meantime . . ."

I squeaked as he pinned my legs, holding them wide.

Hardy gave a low laugh, *enjoying* my discomfort. There was no doubt about it — I was in bed with the devil. "Give me five minutes," he coaxed.

"This is not up for negotiation."

"Why not?"

"Because —" I twisted and panted. "Because I'm about to die of embarrassment. I — *No*. I mean it, Hardy, this is —" My mind went blank as I felt him lick deep into that vulnerable, secret place. I managed a feeble push against his head. There was no dislodging him. "Hardy —" I tried again, but the delicate moist strokes opened the seam of closed flesh, and the pleasure was so acute I couldn't think or move. He followed the sensation to its center, using the tip of his tongue, and then he breathed on the throb and ache, steam fanning across wet skin. My heartbeat slammed so fast that I could barely hear his mocking whisper over the blood-rhythm in my ears.

"Still want me to stop, Haven?"

My eyes were wet. I was strung tight with pleasure, shaking with it, but it wasn't enough. "No. Don't stop." I was shocked by the sound of my own voice, so hoarse and low. And even more shocked by the way I cried out as he slid in one finger, and then another, stretching the glazed softness, while his mouth searched the furled flesh. The sensation was excruciating, my hips hitching upward and falling back. But release kept skittering out of reach, maddening in its elusiveness.

"I can't," I groaned. "I can't do it."

"Yes you can. Just stop trying."

"I can't stop trying."

His wicked fingers began a slow in-and-out slide. I sobbed as a surge began, my flesh rippling, closing. His knuckles wriggled deeper. His tongue flicked steadily, and his mouth . . . his mouth . . . I was gripped by an overpowering swell, every heartbeat, breath, impulse, guided into violent tumbling spasms. I arched into the intense pleasure, my trembling hands secured around his head.

Hardy pushed his fingers as deep as possible and his tongue circled to catch the last few twitches of release. When his touch was withdrawn, I whimpered and reached for him, tugging him upward. He rolled me to my side and put his arms around me, and kissed the tear smudges at the corners of my eyes.

We were quiet for a minute, my bare feet tucked between his, his palm warm on my bottom. I felt the urgency beneath his stillness, like the false lull of the bull pen before the animal exploded out of the chute.

My hand stole to the open waist of his jeans. "Take these off," I whispered.

Still breathing heavily, Hardy shook his head. "That's enough for tonight. Let's quit while we're ahead."

"Quit?" I repeated in groggy surprise. "No, there's no quitting now." I kissed his chest, relishing the masculine texture of him, the warm fur against my lips. "If you don't make love to me, Hardy Cates, I'll never forgive you."

"I did make love to you."

"All the way," I insisted.

"You're not ready for all the way."

I gripped him and ran my fingers up and

down the silky, hard-sprung length. "You can't tell me no," I told him. "It would be bad for my self-esteem."

I rubbed my thumb over the broad tip, slow circles that drew out a slick of moisture. A quiet groan escaped him, and he buried his mouth in my hair. Reaching down, he pried my fingers away. I thought he was going to tell me to stop. Instead he said in a muffled voice, "My wallet is in the kitchen. I'll go get it."

I understood instantly. "We don't need a condom. I'm on the pill."

His head lifted, and he looked at me.

I gave an awkward shrug. "Since Nick never wanted me to have them, they became sort of an issue with me. I feel more in control . . . safer . . . when I take them. And the doctor said it wouldn't hurt me. So I never miss a day. Believe me, we're covered. Even without any other protection."

Hardy rose and braced his weight on one elbow, looking down at me. "I've never done it without a condom."

"Ever?" I asked, bemused.

He shook his head. "I never wanted to take a chance on getting someone pregnant. I didn't want the responsibility. I always swore if I did have kids, I wouldn't leave them the way my dad did."

"You've never had a girlfriend who went on birth control?"

"Even then, I always used a condom. I've never been a fan of the trust-the-woman method."

Perhaps some women would have taken offense at that, but I understood all too well about trust issues. "That's fine," I said, leaning up to kiss his chin. "Let's do it your way."

Hardy didn't move, however. He kept staring at me with those vivid eyes, and I felt something intimate and visceral flourish between us, a sense of connection I found more than a little alarming. It felt as if all the rhythms of my body and his had been set to one invisible metronome.

"You gave me your trust," he said. "Damned if I can't do the same."

I eased to my back, and my breath quickened, and so did his.

He undressed and pressed against me. He was gentle . . . so gentle . . . but I could feel the power and weight of him, and I tensed. He nudged more strongly until we both felt the snug, supple yielding, softness giving way to hardness. Me, taking him inside. Opening to him. The blue eyes turned drowsy, pleasure-clouded, his lashes throwing spiked shadows on his cheeks. He entered me by slow inches, giving me time to adjust, to span the heavy invasion. I turned my face against his arm, my cheek tucked against taut muscle.

When I'd taken all of him I could, Hardy coaxed me to lift my knees, spread them wider, and he gave me even more. So tight, wet, my body offering lubricious welcome. I saw the concern on his face being replaced by lust. I loved the way he stared at me, as if he wanted to eat me alive.

I wriggled, uncomfortable with all that fullness inside me, and Hardy shivered and gasped out a few words that sounded like, *Oh God please don't move Haven baby please . . .*

"Feel good?" I whispered.

Hardy shook his head, struggling to breathe. His face was flushed as if with a high fever.

"No?" I asked.

"Felt good a half hour ago," he managed to say, his accent slurry like he'd just done about ten tequila shots. "Fifteen minutes after that it was the greatest sex I've ever had, and right about now . . . I'm pretty sure I'm in the middle of a heart attack."

Smiling, I pulled his head down to mine and whispered, "What happens after the heart attack?"

"Not sure." His breath whistled through

his teeth, and he dropped his head to the pillow beside mine. "Hell," he said desperately, "I don't know if I can hold on to this."

I drew my hands over his sides, his back, the muscles coiled and strong beneath my fingertips. "Don't hold back."

He began a careful rhythm, rooting out pleasure from the intimate channel where we were joined. One of his thrusts stroked a sensitive place, deep and low, and at the same time his body pressed the front of mine at just the right angle. A *zing* of delight went through me. I jerked in surprise and dug my fingers into Hardy's hips.

He lifted his head and smiled into my wide eyes. "Did I find a sweet spot?" he whispered, and did it again, and again, and to my everlasting embarrassment I couldn't keep quiet, groans climbing in my throat until my hips shuddered against his.

This time the spasms weren't as intense, but they were long and slow, pulling at the length of him until he came. He buried the pleasure sounds in my mouth, and kissed me, and kissed me, stopping only when we were both oxygen deprived and completely spent.

I was filled with an overpowering drowsiness after that. I dozed for a while, with his body still tucked inside mine, and I discovered that the sleep after good sex was almost better than the sex itself. I woke later with him hard inside me, not thrusting, just wedged deep, and his hands were wandering everywhere, stroking and massaging. I lay on my side, one leg hitched over his hip. I wanted, needed him to move, but he kept me impaled and still. I gripped his bicep, his shoulder, trying to pull him over me. He resisted, letting me wriggle like a worm on a hook.

"Hardy," I muttered, sweating at the roots of my hair. "Please . . ."

"Please what?" He licked at my upper lip, then the lower one.

I rocked against him and pulled my mouth free long enough to gasp, "You know."

He pressed his mouth into my neck. I felt the curve of his smile. Yes, he knew. But he continued to hold me locked against him while I clenched over and over, pulling at the deep pulse of him. Finally he gave me a hint of a thrust, more a suggestion of movement than an actual rhythm. It was enough though. It tipped me past the flash point, inner muscles contracting to gather sensation, and I came in rough shivers. Hardy drove upward in one strong shove and held, filling me with lustrous heat.

He continued kissing me in the aftermath,

his lips wandering sweetly while his fingertips coasted over my chin and cheeks and throat. After a while he pulled me out of bed and into the shower. Feeling drugged, I leaned on him as he washed me. His hands were gentle as he soaped and rinsed my body. Slippery, veiled in steam, I rested my cheek against the hard plane of his chest. He reached down and slipped two fingers inside me. I was sore and swollen, but it felt so good that I couldn't help pushing my hips forward. I heard a low crooning sound in his throat, and his thumb swirled tenderly around my clit. With infinite skill, he eased me into another climax, while the hot water rained over me and his mouth ate at mine.

I barely remembered drying off and going back to bed, only that I was soon drifting to sleep with his solid presence beside me.

But some time later, I woke from a nightmare, my body alarmed by the awareness of a man sleeping nearby. I woke with a start, thinking for a moment that I was back with Nick, that I hadn't escaped after all. There was movement beside me, a masculine weight, and I sucked in my breath sharply.

"Haven," came a dark murmur. The sound calmed me. "Bad dream?" His voice was sleep softened and thick, like crushed velvet.

"Uh-huh."

His palm stroked a circle on my chest to soothe my rocketing heartbeat.

I sighed, and quieted in his arms. His lips moved down to my breasts, kissing the tender, hardened tips. I put my arms around his head, his hair soft against my inner wrists. He worked his way down slowly. My knees bent, and I felt his hands grip my ankles like warm, living manacles. Even in the darkness, I saw the broad span of his shoulders and the outline of his head, anchored between my thighs. He lapped at me languidly, feeding off my pleasure, sending me into long, helpless shudders.

And when I fell asleep this time, there were no more dreams.

CHAPTER SIXTEEN

I knew I looked like hell when I went into work the next morning, with dark circles under my eyes and whisker burns on my throat. I didn't care. I felt more at peace than I had in months. Years. Maybe ever.

I could still feel the imprint of Hardy's body on mine, not to mention a trace of soreness that reminded me of all we'd done. And despite all the things I could and should have been worrying about, I decided to enjoy the simple human satisfaction of having been thoroughly made love to.

"Call in sick," Hardy had whispered in the morning. "Spend the day in bed with me."

"I can't," I had protested. "They need me at work."

"*I* need you."

That had made me grin. "You've had enough for now."

Hardy had pulled me up on his chest and kissed me lustily. "I haven't even gotten started," he'd said. "In fact, I've been holding back on account of you being out of practice."

We had finally agreed that we would both go to work, since it was Friday and we both had things that needed to be done. But at five-thirty that evening, the weekend would start.

Before Hardy had left that morning, I made him a five-egg omelet with cheese and spinach, a rasher of bacon, and three pieces of toast. He'd eaten every crumb. In response to my comment that he'd cleaned out the contents of my refrigerator, Hardy had replied that satisfying me took a lot of work, and a man had to keep his strength up.

Smiling, I went into my cubicle and opened my laptop. I reflected that I was in such a good mood, nothing could spoil it.

Then Vanessa appeared. "I've sent you some e-mails about the latest maintenance contracts," she said without preamble.

"Good morning, Vanessa."

"Print out the attachments and make copies. Have them on my desk in an hour."

"Absolutely." I watched as she turned to leave. "Wait, Vanessa. There's something we need to discuss."

She looked back at me, stunned by my crisp tone, not to mention the absence of the word "please." "Yes?" she asked with dangerous softness.

"I don't want you giving out my personal information to people. So if anyone asks for my home address or home number, do *not* give it to them unless you've checked with me. I think from now on that should be standard office policy for everyone's protection."

Her eyes widened dramatically. "I was trying to do you a *favor,* Haven. Your ex-husband said he had some things he wanted to return to you. Evidently you left him in such a hurry, you forgot to pack everything." Her voice turned soft, as if she were trying to explain something to a small child. "Don't try to put me in the middle of your personal problems. That's not professional."

I swallowed hard, longing to inform her that I hadn't *left* Nick, I'd been beaten up and thrown out. But one of Vanessa's favorite tricks was to make accusations in her gentlest voice until I ended up saying things I hadn't meant to say. I wasn't going to fall for it anymore. And there were some things in my private life that were going to stay private.

"You didn't do me a favor," I said calmly. "Nick doesn't have anything I want. And you're not in the middle of anything, Vanessa."

Vanessa shook her head and gave me a cool glance overlaid with pity. "He told me a few things. About how he'd been treated. He was very charming. A little sad, actually."

I suppressed a bitter smile. How *he'd* been treated? That was what a narcissist did. He turned around and accused you of doing what he'd done, and he could be so convincing that you might even end up doubting yourself. I was sure Nick had told people that I'd treated him badly, that I'd walked out on him. But I couldn't control what he said, or whether others believed him or not.

"He can be charming," I allowed. "Every spider knows how to spin a web."

"There are two sides to every story, Haven." Condescension dripped from every syllable like rancid honey.

"Of course there are. But that doesn't mean both sides are valid." I probably should have shut my mouth right then. But I couldn't keep from adding, "And some people *are* all bad, Vanessa. I wouldn't wish Nick on any woman." *Even you,* I thought privately.

"I never realized how naïve you are," my boss said. "I hope someday you learn to look at the world with a little more sophistication."

"I'll work on that," I muttered, and

swiveled in my chair until my back was facing her.

It was not a surprise when Nick called in the middle of the day. I had already figured he'd gotten my work number from Vanessa. But the sound of his voice still caused my stomach to turn over.

"How was your date last night?" Nick asked. "I bet there wasn't much conversation going on after I left."

"Don't call me at work," I replied shortly. "Or at home, for that matter."

"There's only one thing a woman wants from a gym rat like that," Nick continued, "and it has nothing to do with talking."

I smiled a little, enjoying the fact that my ex-husband was so intimidated by Hardy. "He's not a gym rat," I said. "He happens to be very intelligent. And a good listener — which is a nice change."

Nick didn't seem to notice that last comment. "You didn't even go out. You stayed in the apartment and let him ball you all night, didn't you?"

I wondered if Nick had watched my apartment. That gave me the creeps. "That's not your business," I said.

"I wish you'd have been half so willing to give it out while we were married. Put a wedding ring on you, and you turn frigid."

Once that comment would have hurt. And I might have even believed that I was frigid. Now I knew better. And I knew Nick for exactly what he was, a narcissist who was incapable of caring about anyone but himself. I could never change him, or make him aware of his own flaws. Nick wanted what he wanted . . . he didn't understand himself any better than a shark was aware of why it wanted to kill and eat. It just did.

"Well, thank God you're rid of me," I said. "Do us both a favor and don't call again, Nick."

"What about your things? What about that bracelet from your aunt —"

"If it means having to see you again," I said, "it's not worth it."

"I'll throw it in the fucking garbage," he threatened. "I'll pull it apart and —"

"I've got work to do." And I hung up on him, feeling triumphant and disgusted at the same time. I decided not to tell Hardy, or anyone, about the call from Nick. It would take little provocation for Hardy to track my ex-husband down and wipe him off the planet. And while I wouldn't have minded having Nick gone for good, I wouldn't be too crazy about visiting Hardy behind bars.

■ ■ ■ ■

Over the next two weeks I learned a lot about Hardy. We spent every possible minute together, not by any plan or design. It was just that he had become the person I most wanted to be with. And the puzzling thing was, he seemed to feel the same way.

"It's almost too easy," I told Todd on the phone one night, while I was waiting for Hardy to come home from work. "There are no mind games. He calls when he says he's going to. He shows up on time. He really listens to me. He's sort of, well, perfect. It's kind of worrisome."

"No one's perfect. You're leaving something out. What is it? He must be hung like a cocktail weenie."

"No. If anything, he's too much the other way."

There was a pronounced silence.

"Todd? Are you still there?"

"Yeah. I'm just trying to think of a good reason to continue our friendship."

I grinned. "Jealousy is so unattractive, Todd."

"It would help if you could tell me one thing that's wrong. One flaw. Bad breath? Warts? Some condition that requires anti-fungal spray?"

"Would chest hair be a flaw?"

"Oh, yeah." Todd sounded relieved. "I can't stand a chest rug. You can't see the muscle cut."

I thought it best not to argue, even though I disagreed. There was something infinitely comforting and sexy about being held against a broad, hairy chest.

"Haven," Todd said, sounding more serious. "Remember what I told you about him."

"The thing about not being a simple guy? About being twisty twisted?"

"Yeah, that. I stand by my gut feeling. So be careful, sweetheart. Have fun, but keep your eyes open."

Later I pondered what it meant to keep your eyes open in a relationship. I didn't think I was idealizing Hardy . . . it was just that I liked so much about him. I liked the way he talked to me, and even more, the way he listened. I especially liked how tactile he was. He gave impromptu shoulder rubs, pulled me onto his lap, played with my hair, held hands. I hadn't been brought up in a physically affectionate family — Travises put a high premium on personal space. And after my experiences with Nick, I had never thought I could stand being touched again.

Hardy had charmed me more than anyone

I'd ever met. He was engaging, playful . . . but always and foremost a man. He opened doors, carried the packages, paid for dinner, and would have been mortally offended by the suggestion that a woman do any of those things. Having lived with a husband who had spent most of his time inflating his own fragile ego, I appreciated Hardy's self-assurance. He had no problem admitting that he'd made a mistake or that he didn't understand something, only turned it into an opportunity to ask questions.

I had seldom, if ever, met a man with such an endless reserve of energy, or such keen appetites. Privately I acknowledged my father had probably been right about Hardy wanting more . . . and it didn't stop at money. He wanted respect, power, success, all the things he must have hungered for when the world had considered him a nobody. But the world's opinion hadn't crushed him. There had been something in him, a drive fueled by pride and anger, that had insisted he deserved more.

He was not unlike my father, who had also started from nothing. The thought was a little scary. I was getting involved with a man who might turn out to be as much of an ambitious, driven hard-ass as Churchill Travis. How did you handle a guy like that? How did you keep it from happening?

I knew Hardy thought of me as sheltered. Compared to him, I probably was. When I had traveled overseas, I had gone with college friends and stayed in nice hotels that were paid for with my father's credit card. When Hardy had gone overseas, he had worked on offshore rigs in places like Mexico, Saudi Arabia, and Nigeria. Fourteen days on, fourteen off. He'd learned to adapt quickly to foreign cultures and customs. And it struck me that this was the same way he was approaching Houston society. Learn the customs. Adapt. Find your way in.

We talked far into the night, exchanging stories about growing up, past relationships, things that had changed us. Hardy was open about most things, but there were a few subjects he was not willing to discuss. His father, for example, and whatever he'd done to land in prison. And Hardy preferred to keep his mouth shut about his past love life, which made me rampantly curious.

"I don't understand why you never slept with Liberty," I said to him one night. "Weren't you tempted? You must have been."

Hardy settled me more comfortably on his chest. We were in his bed, a California king-sized piled with pillows stuffed with Scandia down. It was covered in acres of eight-hundred-thread-count sheets, and bed-spreads of raw silk.

"Honey, any man over the age of twelve would be tempted by Liberty."

"Then why didn't you?"

Hardy stroked the line of my spine, gently investigating the shallow hollows. "I was waiting for you."

"Ha. Rumor has it you were plenty busy with the ladies of Houston."

"I don't remember any of them," he said blandly.

"Beebe Whitney. Does that name ring a bell?"

Hardy gave me an alert glance. "Why do you mention her?"

"She was bragging to Todd about having slept with you on her divorce-moon."

He was quiet for a moment, his hand sift-ing through my hair. "Jealous?"

Hell, yes, I was jealous. In fact, I was aston-ished by the amount of emotional poison that came from imagining him in bed with Beebe in all her spray-tanned perfection.

I nodded against his chest.

Hardy rolled me to my back and looked down at me. The lamplight played over his strong features, a stray gleam catching the faint smile on his lips. "I could apologize for all the women I knew before you. But I'm not going to."

"Didn't ask you to," I said sullenly.

His hand slipped under the sheet, gently sweeping over me. "I learned something from every woman I've been with. And I needed to learn a lot before I was ready for you."

I scowled. "Why? Because I'm complicated? Difficult?" I fought to keep my breathing steady as he cupped my breast and shaped it.

He shook his head. "Because there's so much I want to do for you. So many ways I want to please you." He bent to kiss me, and brushed the tip of his nose against mine in a playful nudge. "Those women were just practice for you."

"Good line," I said grudgingly.

His hand covered my heart with light, warm pressure. "Ever since I can remember, I wanted to get somewhere, be someone. I'd see other sons of bitches who had it all — an expensive car, a big house, a beautiful woman. And I told myself, 'Fuck 'em. Someday I'll have it all too, and I'll be happy.' " His mouth twisted. "But the past couple of years, I finally got the things I wanted, and it wasn't enough. I was still a miserable bastard. When I'm with you though . . ."

"What?" I prompted.

"When I'm with you, I feel like I finally have what I need. I can relax and be happy." He traced an idle pattern on my chest. "You slow me down."

"In a good way, you mean?"

"In a good way."

"I never slow anyone down," I said. "I'm not a restful person."

A lazy grin crossed his mouth. "Whatever you do works for me."

He lowered over me, kissing my throat, murmuring that I was beautiful and he wanted me. I shivered as the light pelt on his chest dragged softly across my breasts.

"Hardy?"

"Mmmn?"

I put my arms around his neck. "Sometimes I get the feeling that you're holding back, in bed."

He drew back to look down at me, his gaze caressing. "I'm taking it slow with you," he admitted.

"You don't have to," I said earnestly. "I trust you. If you show me what you want, I'll do it. I mean, whatever you and Beebe did . . ."

His lips twitched with rueful amusement. "Damn it all. Forget her, honey. I spent one night with her and never went back for seconds."

"Well, regardless," I said, filled with a competitive spirit. "You don't have to be careful with me. I can take it."

The hint of amusement broadened into a smile. "Okay."

I tugged his head down. Reaching his mouth, I kissed him ardently. He responded without hesitation, searching the depths of my mouth until we were both gasping.

Hardy lifted me to my knees, facing him, his hands clasped beneath my arms in a strong but solicitous hold. His gaze was blistering, but his voice was gentle. "You want to try something new, Haven?"

I gulped and nodded, my hips riding forward in a subtle sway. He noticed. I saw how aroused he was, and it made me giddy with desire. His hands slid to my wrists. He raised my arms, and guided me to grip the top of the tall louvered headboard. My breasts lifted with the movement, the tips contracting.

Hardy stared steadily into my eyes until I was drowning in the depths of blue. His breath was hot against my lips. "Hold on," he whispered, clamping my fingers on the headboard.

And then came scalding minutes of intimacy . . . of skillful torment that led to fever. Fever that led to sweetness. He was everywhere, all around me, inside me. Somehow I survived, but just barely. By the time Hardy had finished with me, my fingernails had dug crescents into the headboard, and I couldn't remember my own name. I collapsed slowly into his arms, every limb quivering with release.

"Just you," Hardy said when he got his breath back. "All I want is you."

I felt like I was falling through clouds as he lowered me into the down pillows. Falling hard and fast. And there didn't seem to be a thing I could do about it.

CHAPTER SEVENTEEN

"Let me get this straight," I said to Jack, standing at his apartment door. "You're not going to cut Hardy any slack even though he *saved my life* two weeks ago? What does he have to do for you to treat him politely? . . . Come up with a cure for cancer? Save the world from an asteroid?"

My brother looked exasperated. "I didn't say I wasn't going to be polite. I can do that much."

"Gee, that's big of you."

That night Hardy and I were going to a rigs-to-reefs party, which was being sponsored jointly by a couple of major oil companies.

Rigs-to-reefs was a program in which companies chopped off the tops of their used platforms and left them on the ocean floor to create an artificial reef. Since the entire Gulf of Mexico was mud bottom, the rigs created a supportive environment for the fish.

Despite protests from naturalists, fish seemed to like the abandoned platforms. And oil companies loved the program because it saved them millions in lieu of platform recovery. So they had donated an exhibit to the Houston Aquarium to display how much, in their opinion, rigs-to-reefs benefited the Gulf.

My family would be at the exhibit opening. And I had done my best to make it clear that not only would I attend with Hardy Cates, but I expected the Travises to behave like reasonable human beings. Apparently that was asking a lot. I had called Joe, who had informed me darkly that I was being used by Hardy, just as he had predicted. And now Jack was being stubborn. I certainly didn't expect anything different from my father, whose opinions were as unalterable as his blood type.

That left only Gage to worry about . . . but I felt certain he would be decent to Hardy, if only for my sake. He'd indicated as much when I had talked to him after the elevator incident.

"All I said was," Jack continued, "Cates doesn't get extra credit with the Travises just for doing what any guy would have done. I told you before, if you'd called me or Gage, either of us could've gotten you out of that elevator just fine."

"Oh. I get it."

His eyes narrowed. "What?"

"You're mad because you didn't get a chance to do macho stuff and show off. You can't stand for anyone else to be a hero. You're the head caveman, and no one's club is bigger than yours."

"Damn it, Haven, quit fighting like a girl. It has nothing to do with the size of my club." He glanced up and down the hallway. "Come inside for a minute, will you?"

"No, I don't have much time to get ready. I'm going up to my place. I only wanted to stop by and tell you to be nice to my —" I broke off abruptly.

"Your what?" Jack demanded.

I shook my head, disconcerted. God knew what word or phrase I should apply to Hardy. "Boyfriend" sounded so high-schoolish. And inappropriate, since Hardy was far from a boy. Lover . . . well, that was old-fashioned and melodramatic. Significant other? Friend with benefits? No, and no.

"My date," I said, and gave him a warning frown. "I'm serious about this, Jack. If you're a jerk to him tonight, I'm going to skin you like a buffalo."

"I don't get what you're asking for. If you

want my approval, you're not getting it. I don't know enough about the bastard yet . . . and what I do know isn't consistent."

My temper ignited at his assumption that my love life depended on his good opinion. "I don't want your approval," I said curtly. "Just basic good manners. I'm just asking you not to be an asshole for two hours. Think you can manage that?"

"Shit," Jack muttered, drawing the word out to a full two syllables. "Bossy as you're getting, I almost feel sorry for the guy."

The aquarium had a nice view of the Houston skyline from a third-floor ballroom lined with glass windows. There was a reception for at least six hundred people, who entered a foyer with a large cylindrical tank, went to a shark-voyage ride, and browsed past exhibits designed to imitate a shipwreck, a sunken temple, a swamp, and a rain forest.

The concerns I had over attending a reception with Hardy were gone within five minutes of arriving. He was relaxed and fun, chatting easily with people, taking me around. As Hardy introduced me to his business partners and their wives, and several other friends, I realized he was far from an outsider in this crowd. Although he hadn't yet become part of the established circles like my family's, he was part of a group who ran the smaller, more nimble companies that were finding new niches to fill.

Hardy and I even knew some of the same people, a few of whom laughingly advised me that he would be a good catch for a woman who could manage to keep him in line. I realized that in his deceptively lazy way, Hardy was working the crowd as adeptly as anyone I had ever seen. He seemed to know everyone's name, and he had the knack of focusing on the person he was talking to as if he or she were the most important person in the room.

At the same time, Hardy was an attentive date, getting me a drink from the bar, keeping a light hand on my back, whispering things to make me laugh. As we stood in a group and talked, he idly straightened a kink on the gold chain of my evening bag as it dangled from my shoulder.

I had wondered how Hardy would treat me when we were with other people, if he would want me to act as his satellite. That was what Nick had always demanded. But to my surprise, Hardy didn't seem to mind me having my own opinions. When the conversation turned to oil shale, for example. One of Hardy's business partners, a geophysicist named Roy Newkirk, was talking enthusiastically about the possibilities of developing shale as an alternative to conventional oil. But I said I'd read that it would be as bad for the environment as open-pit mining. And furthermore, the processing of shale would dump huge amounts of carbon dioxide into the atmosphere, which I thought was criminal. Unless one thought that global warming wasn't coming along fast enough.

Roy received my comments with a forced smile. "Hardy, didn't I warn you not to date a woman who reads?"

Hardy seemed amused by my outspokenness. "Keeps the arguing to a minimum," he replied. "No point in trying when I know she's going to win."

"I hope I didn't annoy you," I murmured to Hardy afterward. "I'm sorry I didn't agree with Roy."

"I like a woman who speaks her mind," Hardy replied. "Besides, you were right. Technology is nowhere near where it needs to be, for the extraction to be worth it. As things stand, it's bad for the environment *and* it's too expensive."

I gave him a speculative glance. "If technology made the process cheaper but it was still bad for the environment, would you go for it?"

"No —" he began, but before he could explain why, we were interrupted by a booming laugh. A heavy hand on my shoulder turned me around.

"Uncle T.J.," I exclaimed. "It's been a while, hasn't it?"

T.J. Bolt wasn't really my uncle, but I'd known him since I was born. He was Dad's closest friend, and I suspected he'd always had a crush on my mother. He liked women a little too much, having been married five times. T.J. was one of the more colorful characters in the oil patch.

As a young man in East Texas, T.J. had gotten his start by working at a drilling equipment supplies company. Somehow he'd found the money to buy land and mineral rights for some productive fields, and he'd used the profits to buy more land, and more. He had his fingers in a lot of pies. And he was courted by landmen from every major development company, all eager to negotiate for potentially priceless leases.

I'd never seen T.J. without his signature white beaver-felt hat with five-inch brim and a six-inch crown. A Western hat of those dimensions would have looked ridiculous on a regular-sized man, but T.J. was a mountain of a human being. He was taller than Hardy, and outweighed him by at least half again. One of his beefy wrists was weighted with a yellow-gold and diamond Rolex. A sausage-sized forefinger sported a gold nugget ring shaped like Texas.

Even as a child I had been subjected to T.J.'s disconcerting habit of kissing females of all ages on the lips. Tonight was no exception. He planted a wrinkly kiss on me, smelling like saddle leather and sweet cologne and La Unica cigars. "What's my favorite girl doing," he boomed, "keeping company with this rascal?"

"Evening, sir," Hardy said with a smile, reaching out to shake his hand.

"You've already met Mr. Cates?" I asked T.J.

"We did some talkin' on my Gregg County property," T.J. allowed. "Couldn't quite settle on terms." He winked at me. "Man's gotta have deep pockets, dealing with me."

"T.J. doesn't want the pockets," Hardy said ruefully. "He wants the whole pair of pants."

The old man chuckled richly. He put a fleshy arm around me and squeezed. He gave Hardy a meaningful glance. "You treat this little girl right," he said. "She was brought up by the greatest lady ever to grace the state of Texas."

"Yes sir, I will."

After T.J. left us in his shambling, gouty stride, I turned to Hardy. "Why couldn't you

393

come to terms with him?"

Hardy shrugged slightly, his smile wry. "It all got hung up on the bonus." Seeing my incomprehension, he explained. "When the landowner signs the lease, he usually gets a bonus from the buyer. Sometimes he's entitled to a pretty substantial one, if the land looks good and there are producing wells nearby. But the bonus is always low if the land doesn't warrant it."

"And T.J. wanted a big bonus?" I guessed.

"Bigger than any sane man would pay. And I believe in calculated risks, but not crazy ones."

"I'm sorry he wasn't willing to be reasonable."

Hardy shrugged and smiled. "I'll bide my time. It'll work out sooner or later. And God knows I've got enough on my plate already." He regarded me with impeccable politeness. "Feel like going home now?"

"No, why would I —" I broke off as I saw the glint in his blue eyes. I knew exactly why he wanted to go home.

Demurely, I said, "We haven't seen the whole exhibit yet."

"Sweetheart, you don't need to see the rest of the exhibit. I can tell you anything you want to know about rigs-to-reefs."

My smile turned into an outright grin. "So

you're an expert?" Having become familiar with his solid recall of facts and details, I wasn't all that surprised.

"Ask me anything," he said readily.

I toyed with a button on the front of his shirt. "Do the rigs actually do anything to enhance the fish population?"

"According to a biologist who works for the Marine Science Institute, yes. The reefs attract some fish, but there's no way you can get such huge numbers to come randomly from all over the ocean to gather at the rig. So fish are definitely being created there." He paused and asked hopefully, "Heard enough yet?"

I shook my head, staring at the front of his throat, where the skin was smooth and brown and appetizing. I loved the sound of his voice, the thick honey of his accent. "Does the rig still belong to the oil company after they cut the top off?" I asked.

"No, it's donated to the state, which takes title to it. Then the company donates half the savings to the Artificial Reef Program."

"How long does it take for the fish to come to the . . . the structure they leave in the water?"

"It's called a rig jacket." Hardy fingered the edge of the flutter sleeve on my dress. "After the rig jacket's been toppled and placed for about six months, you get all kinds of plants and invertebrates attaching to it — a lot of hard coral recruits near the top, where there's more light, and then the fish come along." He leaned closer to me and let his mouth touch the tip of my eyebrow. "Want to hear about the food chain?"

I breathed in his scent. "Oh, yes."

His hand came to my elbow, stroking gently. "There's a little fish swimming along, and then comes a big hungry fish . . ."

"Haven!" A high, cheerful voice cut in, and I felt a pair of small arms wrap around my waist. It was Liberty's little sister, Carrington, her pale gold hair hanging in two neat braids.

I hugged her and bent to kiss the top of her head. "Carrington, you look so stylish," I said, viewing her miniskirt and clogs.

She flushed in pleasure. "When are you going to come for a sleepover at my house again?"

"I don't know, sweetie. Maybe —"

"You're here with *Hardy?*" she interrupted, having glanced at my date. She went to hug him, chattering all the while. "Haven, did you know Hardy drove my mama to the hospital the night I was born? There was a storm, and it was flooding everywhere, and he got us there in an old blue pickup."

I glanced at Hardy, smiling. "He's pretty good at rescuing people."

His gaze turned wary as we were joined by two more people — Gage and Liberty.

"Hardy," she said, reaching out for his hand, pressing it affectionately.

He flashed her a grin. "Hi, Liberty. How's the baby?"

"Fine. Matthew's at home with his grandfather. Churchill likes to look after him." Her green eyes twinkled. "He's the cheapest babysitter we've got."

"Liberty," Carrington said, tugging at her hand, "do you want to come see the piranhas? There's a whole big tank of them over there."

"Okay," she said, laughing. "Excuse me, y'all. We'll be right back."

As Liberty left, Gage contemplated Hardy for a moment. Tension strung through the air, until my brother reached out to shake Hardy's hand. "Thank you," Gage said. "I owe you for helping my sister out of that elevator. If there's anything I can do to repay you —"

"No," Hardy said at once. He seemed to be caught somewhat off guard by Gage's sincerity. It was the first time I had ever seen a trace of awkwardness in him. "You don't owe me a damn thing. I . . . after the stunt I pulled with your biofuel deal . . ."

"You more than made up for that two weeks ago," Gage said. "Haven's safety — and happiness — mean everything to me. As long as you're good to her, you've got no problem with me."

"I understand."

I didn't like being discussed as if I weren't there. "Hey, Gage," I asked, "have you seen Jack yet? He was supposed to be here tonight."

"He's here. He met an old girlfriend at the bar. Looks like they're getting reacquainted."

I rolled my eyes. "You could form a chain from here to El Paso with Jack's old girlfriends."

Just then I heard the ring of a cell phone, and Hardy reached inside his jacket pocket. Glancing at the number, he did a quick double blink. "Excuse me," he said to Gage and me. "I have to take this one. Would you mind if I —"

"Go right ahead," I said immediately.

"Thanks." Hardy flipped the phone open and moved through the crowd to a door that led to an outside wraparound balcony.

Left alone with Gage, I smiled up at him uncertainly, wondering if I was about to get a lecture.

"You look great," my brother said, running an appraising gaze over me. "You look happy."

It had been a long time since anyone had said that to me. "I am happy," I admitted, feeling a little sheepish. "Gage, I'm so sorry if it makes things difficult for you, me taking up with someone from Liberty's past . . ."

"It doesn't make things difficult for me," Gage said gently. He surprised me by adding, "You can't always choose who you're attracted to. When I first met Liberty, I thought she was one of Dad's side dishes — and I'm sorry to say I behaved like an asshole." He smiled wryly. "But even then, there was something about her that got to me, every damn time I saw her." He slid his hands in his pockets and frowned slightly. "Haven, considering how Cates helped you at Buffalo Tower, I'm sure as hell inclined to give him a break. But if he hurts you . . ."

"If he hurts me, you have my permission to beat the tar out of him," I said, making him grin. I drew a little closer, mindful of the possibility of being overheard. "If it doesn't work out, though . . . I'll be okay, Gage. I'm stronger than I was a few months ago. He's helped me get over some of the problems I had after Nick. So no matter what he does in the future, I'll always be grateful to him for that."

Hardy returned, and I knew from looking at him that something was terribly wrong. There was no expression on his face, but he was chalk-white under his tan, and he had the distracted tension of a man whose mind was working on a multitude of levels.

"Haven." The voice, too, was different, as flat and scratchy as a sheet of sandpaper. "I just got a call from my mother. There's some family stuff I've got to deal with, and it can't wait."

"Oh, Hardy . . ." I wanted to pull him close, do something to ease him, comfort him. "Is she okay?"

"Yeah, she's fine."

"We'll leave right now —"

"No," Hardy said at once. Hearing the unnecessary force in his own voice, he made an effort to relax. "This isn't the kind of thing you need to be bothered with, honey. I need to handle it alone."

Gage broke in. "Is there anything I can do?"

Hardy nodded. "Please take care of Haven. Make sure she gets home safe." He looked at me, his eyes opaque. "I'm sorry. I hate to leave you like this."

"Will you call me later?" I asked.

"Of course. I —" He stopped, as if words

had failed him, and he glanced at Gage once more.

"I've got Haven," Gage said immediately. "Don't worry about her."

"Okay. Thanks."

And Hardy left us, his head bent, his strides eating ground as if he were preparing to plow through obstacles ahead.

"Maybe one of his brothers is sick, or was in an accident," I fretted.

Gage shook his head. "No telling. Except . . ."

"Except what?"

"If it was something like that, I think he would have said so."

I was swamped in worry for Hardy's sake. "He should have taken me with him," I muttered. "I *hate* being left out of things. And it's not like I'm going to have a good time here when I know he's out there dealing with some mystery problem. I should be with him."

I heard my brother sigh. "Come on, let's go find Liberty and Carrington. I'd rather be watching a tank of man-eating fish than wondering what trouble Hardy Cates might be getting into."

CHAPTER EIGHTEEN

I had asked the concierge to call me when he saw Hardy arrive at 1800 Main. "No matter what time it is," I had told him. If he thought that was a little strange, or wondered why I wasn't expecting Hardy to call me himself, he didn't say a word.

Checking the phone messages, I saw nothing but two hang-ups, both of them from a Dallas number. It had to be Nick. I had cut all ties to the other people I had known in Dallas, the people I'd worked with at the Darlington, and the people in Nick's circle who had known me as Marie. Nick was furious with me for rejecting him, for showing no interest in getting Gretchen's bracelet back. For going on with my life. I hoped that ignoring him would cause him to back off. If he persisted in trying to get in touch with me, I would be forced to do something about it. Maybe a restraining order?

Except I remembered Hardy's cynical

comment . . . *"A restraining order only works if you handcuff yourself to a cop."*

I wondered what Hardy was doing at that moment, what kind of problem he was dealing with. I was sorely tempted to call him, but I figured the last thing he needed was his cell phone ringing while he was in the middle of some difficult situation. So I took a long bath and put on sweatpants and an oversized T-shirt, and I tried to watch TV. I must have clicked through a hundred cable channels, but there was nothing good on.

I slept lightly, my ears pricked for any sound. And then it came, the phone giving one shrill ring before I grabbed it and pressed the talk button. "Yes?"

"Miss Travis. Mr. Cates just came through the lobby. He's in the elevator now."

"Great. Thank you." I glanced at the clock and saw that it was about one-thirty in the morning. "Um, did he seem okay? Did he say anything?"

"No, Miss Travis, he didn't say anything. I guess he seemed . . . tired."

"Okay. Thanks."

"No problem."

I hung up and sat with the phone in my lap, willing it to ring. But the damn thing was silent. I waited until I was certain Hardy had had enough time to reach his apartment, and then I called his main line. I got a voice message.

Flopping back on the sofa, I stared at the ceiling with bleary impatience. Unable to stand it any longer, I called Hardy's cell phone.

Another recording.

What was going on? Was he all right?

"Let him alone," I said aloud. "Go to bed. Let him sleep. He'll call tomorrow when he feels like talking."

But I wasn't listening to myself. I was too worried about Hardy.

I paced around my apartment for another fifteen minutes, and then I called again.

No answer.

"Crap," I muttered, scrubbing my eyes with half-closed fists. I was tense and tired and uneasy. No way was I going to get any sleep until I made sure Hardy was okay.

Just a quick knock at his door. Maybe a hug. Maybe a cuddle in bed. I wouldn't ask him to talk. No pressure. I just wanted him to know I was there if he needed me.

Sticking my feet into a pair of hard-soled slippers, I left my apartment and took the elevator to the eighteenth floor. It was cold in the elegantly sterile atmosphere of the hallway. Shivering, I went to the threshold and rang the bell.

Stillness. Silence. And then a scrape of movement inside the apartment. I waited, waited, and realized incredulously that Hardy wasn't going to answer. My face tightened in a scowl. Well, that was too damn bad. I would stand at his door and ring the bell all night if necessary.

I pushed the button again.

I had a sudden, terrible thought that maybe Hardy wasn't alone. What other reason could there be for his refusal to see me? But I couldn't make myself believe —

The door opened.

I was confronted with a version of Hardy I had never seen before. It was mostly dark in his apartment, a faint illumination coming from the living room where the skyline bled an artificial glow through the row of long windows. Hardy was dressed in a white T-shirt and jeans, his feet bare. He looked big and shadowy and mean. And I got a strong, acid-sweet whiff of cheap tequila, the kind you went for when you wanted to get really hammered, really fast.

I had seen Hardy drink before, but never to excess. He had told me he didn't like to feel out of control. What he hadn't said, but I had understood, was that he couldn't tolerate the idea of being vulnerable, physically or emotionally.

My gaze traveled from his dark face to the empty shot glass in his hand. A crawly feeling went across my shoulders. "Hey," I managed to say, my voice coming out in a wheeze. "I wanted to see if you were okay."

"I'm okay." He looked at me as if we were strangers. "Can't talk now."

He began to close the door, but I stepped over the threshold. I was afraid to leave him by himself — I didn't like the blank, weird look in his eyes. "Let me fix you something to eat. Eggs and toast —"

"Haven." It seemed to take all his concentration to speak. "I don't need food. I don't need company."

"Can't you tell me something about what happened?" Without thinking, I reached out to stroke his arm, and he flinched backward. As if my touch were repulsive. I was stunned. It was quite a reversal for me, after all the times I had done that to other people, jerking away from them in a startle reflex. I had never considered how it might have made them feel.

"Hardy," I said softly. "I'll go. I promise. But first tell me what happened. Just a few words, so I'll understand."

I could feel the anger radiating off him. It was too dark for me to see the color of his eyes, but the shine of them was almost malevolent. Anxiously I wondered where the real Hardy had gone. He seemed to have been replaced by an evil twin. "I don't know how the fuck you could understand," he said thickly, "when I don't."

"Hardy, let me in," I said.

He continued to block me. "You don't want to come in here."

"Oh?" I forced a skeptical half-smile. "What's in there that I should be afraid of?"

"Me."

His answer sent a ripple of uneasiness through me. But I didn't move. "What did you do tonight?" I asked. "What did your mother call you for?"

Hardy stood with his head lowered. His hair was rumpled as if he'd tugged at it repeatedly. I wanted to smooth those gleaming dark locks and settle my hand on the taut back of his neck. I longed to soothe him. But all I could do was wait, with a patience that had never been easy for me.

"She asked me to bail my father out of jail," I heard him say. "He was taken in tonight for a DUI. He knew better than to call her. I've given him money over the past two years. I pay him to stay the hell away from Mama and the boys."

"I thought he was in prison. But I guess . . . he's out now?"

Hardy nodded, still not looking at me. His free hand clenched the doorframe. I felt a little curl of repulsion in my stomach as I saw how brutally strong those fingers were.

"What did he do," I asked gently, "to get himself in prison?"

I wasn't sure Hardy would answer. But he did. Sometimes the closest-held secrets in the world can be pried out by the right question at the right time.

Hardy spoke in the flat, hopeless whisper of a criminal in a confessional. I knew I was hearing things he'd never said to any living being. "He did fifteen years for aggravated rape. He's a serial rapist . . . godawful things to women . . . never gave him parole, they knew he hadn't changed. But the term was finally up, and they had to let him out. He'll do it again. I can't stop him. I can't watch over him every minute. I can barely keep him away from my family —"

"No," I said scratchily, "it's not your job to be his keeper."

"— my brothers are taking after him. Bad blood coming through. I had to bail Kevin out last month, had to pay off a girl's family, keep them from pressing charges —"

"That's not your fault," I said, but he was beyond hearing.

"Evil bastards, all of us. No-good

white trash —"

"No."

Each breath scraped audibly in his throat. "Before I left Dad at a hotel tonight, he told me —" He stopped, shaking from head to toe. He swayed on his feet.

God, he was so drunk.

"Told you what?" I whispered. "What is it, Hardy?"

Hardy shook his head, backing away. "Haven." His voice was low and guttural. "Get out. If you stay . . . I'm not in control. I'll use you. Hurt you, understand? Get the hell out."

I didn't think Hardy was capable of hurting me, or any woman. But the truth was, I wasn't completely sure. At that moment he seemed like nothing so much as a large, suffering animal, ready to tear apart anyone who came near him. And this was too damned soon after my divorce from Nick. I was gun-shy. I was still dealing with my own anger, my own fears.

But there were certain moments in life when you had to step up to the plate or lose your chance forever. If Hardy was capable of hurting me, I would find out now.

Every vein in my body was lit with the burn of adrenaline. I got dizzy with it. *All right, you bastard,* I thought with grimness and fury and love. Absolute scalding love, in that moment when he most needed it and least wanted it. *Let's see what you've got.*

I walked into the darkness and closed the door.

Hardy was on me the second after the lock clicked. I heard the thump of the shot glass as he dropped it. I was gripped, spun around, pushed against the door by two hundred pounds of hard-breathing male. He was shaking, his hands too tight, his lungs laboring. He kissed me with bruising force, lewd and whole-mouthed, going on for minutes until the tremors had eased and his erection was grinding against me. Every emotion, anger, grief, self-hatred, need, had found an outlet in pure hundred-proof lust.

He pulled at my T-shirt and sent it flying to the side. As he ripped his own shirt off, I moved blindly toward the living room, not to get away from him but to find a more comfortable place than the entryway floor. I heard a possessive growl, and I was grabbed from behind.

Hardy pushed me over the back of the sofa, bending me forward. He yanked the waistband of my sweatpants down. Gooseflesh rose all over, and I felt the weight of panic like a block of ice in my stomach. This was so much like what Nick had done. Another flashback was hovering, waiting to strike. But I gritted my teeth and braced my feet, and stiffened every muscle.

As Hardy stood behind me, I felt the brush of burning skin, a heavy shaft against my backside. I wondered if he was too far gone to recall that I was afraid of doing it this way, that this was how I'd been raped. Maybe he was doing it on purpose, to punish me, to make me hate him. One of his hands ran over my frozen spine, and I heard his breathing change.

"Go on, damn you," I said. My voice cracked. "Go on and do it."

But Hardy didn't move except for the hand on my back. His palm glided up and down, and then around my waist to my stomach. He bent farther over me, his other hand cupping my breast. His mouth came to my shoulders, my spine, and he was groaning and kissing me while his fingers worked down below, opening me. I could only breathe in gasps, my body relaxing, yielding. I pictured his hand with those star-shaped scars on them . . . the last time we'd been in bed I'd made a project of kissing each tiny mark. And remembering, I went wet, responding helplessly to the touch, scent, warmth, that had become familiar.

"Do it," I said again, panting.

He seemed not to hear, intent on fondling the soft pleated flesh beneath his fingers. His legs pressed between mine, widening my stance.

The last traces of fear melted away. I pushed my hips back, quivering as I felt the stiff length of him. But he wouldn't give it to me, only massaged with agonizing gentleness until I clawed the velvet sofa, my breath coming in sobs.

Darkness wrapped around us, cool and cradling, while he centered himself. I whimpered, my entire being focused on the place where he pressed me, inner muscles working in anticipation.

He thrust forward, and I came from the thick-skewering pleasure, and he rooted deep while his hand stayed on my sex, stroking and stroking. He took me down to the floor, kneeling, pulling me against his chest. My head tipped back on his shoulder. I was raised and lifted, moaning in rhythm with the full slippery pitch of flesh into flesh until the delight broke and spread and flooded me with fresh heat.

Hardy let me rest on his thighs, his arms locked around me. When my breathing had slowed, he carried me into the bedroom. His grip was tight. He was in a dominating mood. And it was primal and even a little threatening, but at the same time I was aroused beyond belief, which stunned me. I would have to figure out why . . . I needed to understand . . . but I couldn't think with his hands on me. He knelt on the bed, reaching beneath my bottom to hoist my hips off the mattress.

I was filled in a slow plunge, one of his hands going to the wet triangle between my thighs. The steady pumping and teasing, while he kept me lifted and supported, sent me hurtling into new sensation, cresting, easing, surging again. When my pleasure had finally spun out, Hardy pushed me flat, my arms and legs spread wide, and he spent inside me with violent pulses. I curved my arms around him, loving the feel of his shuddering body over mine.

Gasping, he rolled us both to our sides. I heard my name carried on a taut breath. For a long time he held me to him. His hands compressed my body at slow intervals, molding me closer.

Resting my head in the crook of his arm, I slept for a little while. It was still dark when I awoke. I felt from the tension in Hardy's body that he was awake too. I rocked slowly against the insistent throb of his erection, my temperature rising. His mouth came to my neck and shoulder, kissing the soft skin, tasting.

I pushed at his shoulders, and he went over easily, letting me straddle him. Gripping his sex, I positioned him and sank down. I heard the faint whistle of his breath through his teeth. He steadied my hips with his hands, letting me find a rhythm. He belonged to me absolutely . . . I knew it, I felt it in that moment of masculine surrender. I was riding him, giving it to him, and he groaned and arched his hips to meet every downward pump. His hands slid up my thighs to the center, caressing with his thumbs until I came, and that set him off too. He stiffened beneath me, the pleasure spiking. His hand closed behind the nape of my neck as he pulled me down to kiss him. A forceful kiss, flavored with desperation. "It's okay," I whispered afterward in the quiet room, feeling the need to comfort him. "It's okay."

Morning was nearly over by the time I awoke. The covers had been drawn up carefully around me, and my discarded clothes had been retrieved and draped neatly over the back of a chair. I called out sleepily for Hardy, wanting him to come back to bed. But as I was greeted with silence, I realized he'd left me alone in his apartment.

I rolled to my stomach, wincing a little as I

felt an accumulation of tiny strains and pulls. An embarrassed grin spread across my face as I remembered the previous night. I might have thought it had been a long erotic dream, except that my body was letting me know it had definitely happened.

I felt curiously light and buoyant, almost feverish with happiness.

The night had been different from anything I had ever experienced before. Sex on a new level . . . deeper, more intense, opening me emotionally as well as physically. And it had affected Hardy the same way, which had probably scared the crap out of him.

I realized Nick had always regarded sex as a kind of annexation. I had never been an individual to him, certainly not someone whose thoughts or feelings mattered. Which meant that when Nick had sex with me, it had really been nothing more than a form of masturbation.

Whereas Hardy, even in his wildness, had made love to my mind and body, to *me*. And he had let me in past his defenses, however unwillingly.

I no longer believed in the idea of soul mates, or love at first sight. But I was beginning to believe that a very few times in your life, if you were lucky, you might meet someone who was exactly right for you. Not because he was perfect, or because you were, but because your combined flaws were arranged in a way that allowed two separate beings to hinge together.

Hardy would never be the easiest man to have a relationship with. He was complex and strong-willed and rough-edged. But I loved those qualities about him. I was more than willing to take him exactly as he was. And it didn't hurt that he seemed equally game to take me on my own terms.

Yawning, I went to the bathroom, found Hardy's robe, and tugged it on. The coffeemaker was all set up in the kitchen, with a mug and a clean spoon laid out. I pushed a button, and the air filled with the cheerful gurgle of brewing coffee.

I picked up Hardy's phone and dialed his cell number.

No answer.

I hung up the phone. "Coward," I said without heat. "You can run, Hardy Cates, but you can't hide forever."

But Hardy managed to avoid me all Saturday. And while I wanted badly to talk to him, pride wouldn't let me chase after him like a lovestruck skink, a Texas lizard which was known to lunge and circle around the male it was interested in. I figured I could afford to be patient with Hardy. So I left a couple of casual messages on his machine, and decided to wait him out.

Meanwhile, I got an e-mail from Nick.

CHAPTER NINETEEN

"The whole thing is crazy," I said when Susan had finished reading Nick's e-mail. I had printed it out and asked her to take a look at it during our Saturday therapy session. "He's turned everything backward. Upside down. It's like Alice in Wonderland."

It was ten pages long and filled with accusations and lies. I had felt dirty and tainted after reading it, but most of all, outraged. Nick had recast our entire marriage, with himself as the victim and me as the villain. According to Nick, I had been an insane, histrionic, and unfaithful wife, and he had tried in vain to pacify me and my moods and rages. And in the end, when he had lost his temper with me, it was because I had pushed him to the edge, by rejecting his honest efforts to fix our relationship.

"What pisses me off the most," I continued heatedly, "is how detailed and convincing it is . . . like Nick believes his own crap. But he doesn't, does he? And why would he write this to me? Does he actually think I'm going to buy any of this?"

Susan's brow was furrowed. "Pathological lying is the MO for a narcissist . . . they're not interested in the truth, only in what gets them what they want. Which is attention. Supply. So basically Nick is trying to get a reaction from you. Any kind of reaction."

"Like, me hating him is just as good a supply as me loving him?"

"Exactly. Attention is attention. The only thing Nick can't tolerate is indifference. That creates what's called 'narcissistic injury' . . . and unfortunately this e-mail is sending strong signals in that direction."

I didn't like the sound of that. "So what happens when Nick gets a narcissistic injury?"

"He may try to frighten you in some way, which to him is another form of supply. And if you refuse to react, it may very well escalate the situation."

"Oh, great. Does that mean more phone calls? More unexpected visits?"

"I hope not. But yes, probably. And if he's angry enough, he may want to punish you."

There was silence in Susan's small office while I digested the information. It was so unfair. I had thought that divorcing Nick would be enough. Why did he have to pull this crap with me? Why did he expect me to go on being a supporting player in the movie of his life?

"How do I get rid of him?" I asked.

"There's no easy answer. But if I were you, I would save this e-mail and document every interaction with him. And try to go no-contact, no matter what he does. Refuse gifts, don't answer e-mails or letters, and don't discuss him with anyone who might approach you on his behalf." Susan looked down at the e-mail, frowning. "If a narcissist is made to feel inferior to something or someone, it eats away at him until it's relieved. Until he feels he can walk away as the winner."

"But we're divorced," I protested. "There's nothing to win!"

"Yes there is. He's fighting to retain his image of himself. Because without that image of superiority and dominance and control . . . Nick is nothing."

The session with Susan had not done a lot for my mood. I felt anxious and angry, and I wanted comfort. And since Hardy was still not answering his cell phone, he had moved close to the top of my shit list.

When my phone finally rang on Sunday, I

checked the caller ID eagerly. My hopes were deflated as I saw it was my dad. Sighing, I picked it up and answered morosely. "Hello?"

"Haven." Dad sounded gruff and self-satisfied in a way I didn't like. "I need you to come over. There's something we have to talk about."

"Okay. When?"

"Now."

I would have loved to tell him I had something else going on, but no convenient excuses sprang to mind. And since I was already bored and moody, I figured I might as well go see him.

"Sure thing, Dad," I said. "I'll be right over."

I drove to River Oaks, and I found Dad in his bedroom, which was the size of a small apartment. He was relaxing in a massage chair in his sitting area, punching buttons in the control panel.

"Want to try it?" Dad offered, patting the arm of the chair. "Fifteen different kinds of massage. It analyzes your back muscles and makes recommendations. It also grabs and stretches the thigh and calf muscles."

"No, thanks. I prefer my furniture to keep its hands to itself." I smiled at him and sat in a nearby, ordinary chair. "So how's it going,

Dad? What do you want to talk about?"

He took his time about answering, taking a moment to enter a massage program into the chair. It began whirring and adjusting the seat position. "Hardy Cates," he said.

I shook my head. "No way. I'm not talking to you about him. Whatever it is you want to know, I'm not —"

"I'm not asking for information, Haven. I know something about him. Something you need to hear."

Every instinct urged me to leave right then. I knew my father kept tabs on everyone and would have had no compunction about digging up dirt from Hardy's past. I didn't need or want to hear anything that Hardy wasn't ready to confide. Besides, I was pretty sure I knew what Dad was going to tell me: about Hardy's father, and his prison time, and the DUI arrest. So I decided to stay and hear Dad out, and put him in his place.

The room was quiet except for the whirring of mechanical gears and rollers. I summoned a cool smile. "All right, tell me."

"I warned you about him," Dad said, "and I was right. He sold you out, honey. So it's best to put him out of your mind and go find someone else. Someone who'll be good to you."

"Sold me out?" I stared at him in bewilderment. "What are you talking about?"

"T.J. Bolt gave me a call after he saw you with Cates on Friday night. He asked me what I thought, about you taking up with a rascal like Cates, and I told him."

"What a pair of busybodies," I said in annoyance. "Good Lord, with all the time and money each of you has, you can't think of anything better to talk about than my love life?"

"T.J. had an idea to expose Cates for what he is . . . to show you what kind of man you're keeping company with. And after he told me about it, I agreed. So T.J. called Cates yesterday —"

"Oh, *hell,*" I whispered.

"— and offered him a deal. He said he'd sign the lease contract Cates offered him a while back, and forgo the bonus completely. *If* Cates promised to drop you for good. No dating, no socializing of any kind."

"And Hardy told T.J. to go screw himself," I said.

My father gave me a pitying glance. "No. Cates took the deal." He leaned back in his massage chair, while I absorbed the information.

My skin was prickling and crawling. My mind rejected it — Hardy would never have taken such a deal. Not after the night we'd spent together. I knew he had feelings for me. I knew he needed me. It didn't make sense for Hardy to throw it all away. Not for some leases he would have probably gotten in time, anyway.

What the hell was going on in Hardy's head? I had to find out. But first . . .

"You manipulative old coot," I said. "Why do you have to go messing around in my private life?"

"Because I love you."

"Love means respecting someone else's rights and boundaries! I'm not a child. I'm . . . no, you don't even think of me as a child, you think of me as a dog you can lead around on a leash and control in any way you —"

"I do not think of you as a dog," Dad interrupted, scowling. "Now, settle down and —"

"I'm not going to settle down! I have every right to be furious. Tell me, would you pull this kind of crap with Gage or Jack or Joe?"

"They're my sons. They're men. You're a daughter who's already gone through one bad marriage and was likely headed for another."

"Until you can treat me like a human being, Dad, our relationship is over. I've had it." I stood and slung my bag over my shoulder.

"I've done you a favor," Dad said irritably. "I just showed you that Hardy Cates isn't good enough for you. Everyone knows it. He knows it. And if you weren't so hardheaded, you'd admit it too."

"If he really agreed to this deal with T.J.," I said, "then he doesn't deserve me. But neither do you, for doing something so rotten in the first place."

"You're going to shoot the messenger?"

"Yeah, Dad, if the messenger can't learn to keep his interfering ass out of my business." I walked toward the doorway.

"Well," I heard my father mutter, "at least you're through with Hardy Cates."

I turned back to scowl at him over my shoulder. "I'm not through with him yet. I won't be gotten rid of without finding out the reason. A *real* reason, not some half-baked business deal you and T.J came up with."

There was no one I could talk to. I had been warned by everyone, including Todd, that this was exactly what I should expect from Hardy Cates. I couldn't even call Liberty, because he had done something similar to her once, and she couldn't say it was out of character. And I felt like such an idiot, because I still loved him.

Part of me wanted to curl up into a ball and cry. Another part was ripping mad. And another part was busy analyzing the situation and trying to figure out the best way to handle it. I decided to cool down before I confronted Hardy. I would call him tomorrow after work, and we would talk everything out. If he wanted to break everything off between us, I would deal with it. But at least it wouldn't be done third-party, by a couple of manipulative old geezers.

The office was unusually subdued when I went in at eight on Monday morning. The employees were quiet and busy. No one seemed inclined to share details about their weekend as we usually did. No water-cooler gossip, no friendly chitchat.

As lunchtime approached, I went to Samantha's cubicle to ask if she wanted to go get a sandwich with me.

Samantha, usually so vivacious, looked shrunken and despondent as she sat behind her desk. Her father had died about two weeks earlier, so I knew it would take some time before she was back to her old self.

"Want to go out for lunch?" I asked gently. "It's on me."

She gave me a wan smile and shrugged.

"I'm not hungry. But thanks."

"Let me at least bring you a yogurt or a —" I stopped as I saw the glitter of a tear beneath one of her eyes. "Oh, Samantha . . ." I went around to her side of the desk and hugged her. "I'm sorry. Bad day, huh? Thinking about your dad?"

She nodded and rummaged for a tissue in her desk drawer. "Partly that." She blew her nose. "And partly . . ." Her slender hand reached across the desk and nudged a sheet of paper to me.

"What is this? A billing sheet?" I frowned curiously. "What's the problem?"

"My weekly paycheck is on direct deposit, every Friday. So I checked my account balance last week, and it was a lot lower than I expected. Today I logged on to the office computer and found out why." She smiled crookedly. Her eyes pooled again. "You know that huge flower arrangement the company sent to my father's funeral? The one with all your names on the card?"

"Yeah." I almost didn't want to hear what she was going to say next.

"Well, it cost two hundred dollars. And Vanessa took it out of my paycheck."

"Oh, God."

"I don't know why she'd do something like this," Samantha continued. "But I've made

427

her mad somehow. I think it was those days I took off after Dad died . . . she's been weird and cold to me ever since."

"You took those days off to go to your father's funeral, Sam. No normal person would hold that against you."

"I know." She gave a shaky sigh. "Vanessa must be under a lot of pressure. She told me it was the worst possible time for me to be absent from work. She seemed so disappointed in me."

I was filled with volcanic rage. I wanted to storm through the office like Godzilla and trample Vanessa's desk underfoot. If Vanessa wanted to attack and belittle me, I could handle it. But to crush poor Samantha right after the death of a beloved parent . . . it was too much.

"Don't tell her I complained," Samantha whispered. "I couldn't handle getting in trouble right now."

"You won't get in trouble. And Samantha, that two-hundred-dollar deduction was a mistake. It's going into your account right away."

She gave me a doubtful glance.

"It was a mistake," I repeated. Pulling out a clean tissue, I dabbed at her eyes. "The office is paying for those flowers, not you. I'm going to fix this, okay?"

"Okay." She managed a smile. "Thanks, Haven."

The intercom pad on my desk beeped. Since the office was furnished in an open-cubicle system, anything Vanessa said on the intercom was audible to everyone.

"Haven, come to my office, please."

"No problem," I muttered, leaving Samantha's cubicle and heading to Vanessa's corner office. I deliberately took my time, trying to compose myself before confronting my boss. I knew I was probably going to get fired for what I was about to say, and that afterward I would probably be the victim of a highly effective smear campaign. But that didn't matter. I could get another job. And the damage Vanessa would do to my reputation wasn't nearly as important as standing up to her.

By the time I reached Vanessa's office, she had pressed the intercom button again. *"Haven, come to my —"*

"I'm here," I said, going directly to her desk. I didn't sit, just stood and faced her.

Vanessa stared at me as if I were an ant crawling up the wall. "Wait at my door, please," she said in a detached tone, "until you're invited in. Haven't we gone over that enough times for you to remember, Haven?"

"I'm setting aside the rules for a few minutes. This is important. There's been a mistake with the billing sheets. It needs to be fixed."

Vanessa was not accustomed to anyone else setting the agenda. "I don't have time for this, Haven. I didn't call you to the office to talk about the billing sheets."

"Don't you want to know what it is?" I waited. When it was obvious she wasn't going to answer, I shook my head slowly. "No, because you already know. It wasn't a mistake, was it?"

A curious, chilling smile spread across her lips. "Okay, Haven. I'll play. What is it?"

"Samantha's been charged for the flowers the office sent to her father's funeral." I waited for any kind of reaction, a slight widening of the eyes, a flicker of shame, a frown. Anything. But Vanessa showed all the emotion of a department store mannequin. "We're going to fix it, right?"

An excruciating silence passed. Silence was one of Vanessa's more effective weapons . . . she would stare at me until I felt myself collapsing like a tower of blocks, and I'd say something, anything, to fill the unnerving wordless void. But I held her stare. The silence drew out until it was actually sort of funny. But I managed to outwait her.

"You're out of line," she informed me. "How I choose to manage the employees is none of your business, Haven."

"So taking that money out of Samantha's paycheck is some kind of management technique?"

"I think you'd better leave my office right now. In fact, take the day off. I've had more than enough of you and your bratty attitude."

"If you don't agree to put that money into Samantha's account," I said, "I'm going to Jack."

That got a reaction. Her face darkened, and her eyes flashed. "You spoiled bitch," she said, her voice taking on a crisp edge. "Nick's told me all about you . . . how you use people, how selfish you are. How you lie and manipulate to get your way. Lazy, cheating, whiny little parasite —"

"Yeah, that's my PR from Nick." I wondered if she had actually gone out with my ex-husband. Good Lord, what was it like when two narcissists went on a date? "But that's not what we were talking about, is it? Are you going to give the money back, or should I go to Jack?"

"You dare say one word to him, and I'll unload. By the time I finish telling him what you really are, he'll be as disgusted by you as I am. He'll tell you where to —"

"Vanessa," I said quietly, "he's my brother.

Are you really so arrogant that you think you could turn him against me? You think he'll take your side over mine? Jack is loyal. You can trash me all you want, and it won't do you any good with him."

Her face was starting to look splotchy, rage bringing up red patches that seemed to float on top of her skin like oil slicks on water. But somehow she managed to keep her tone controlled. "Get out of my office, Haven. And don't come back. You've just been let go."

I was calm on the surface even though my heart had been galvanized into a rocketing pace. "That's what I thought you'd say. Bye, Vanessa."

I went to my desk to get my purse. As I reached my cubicle, I was bemused to see Samantha, Rob, and Kimmie all standing there, wearing identical blank expressions. If I hadn't been so distracted, I might have thought it was funny, the way they all looked. "What's going on?" I asked, going into my cubicle. I stopped short as I saw Jack beside my desk. He was staring down at the intercom pad, his color high and his mouth hard.

"Hey, Jack," I said in bewilderment. "What are you doing here?"

He answered slowly. "I came to take you

out to lunch."

Kimmie moved closer to me and touched my arm. "The intercom was on," she murmured.

Vanessa must have forgotten to turn it off when I had barged into her office. And Jack and the others had heard every word.

Jack picked up my purse and handed it to me. "Come on," he said gruffly.

I went with him, blanching as I realized we were heading to Vanessa's office.

Opening the closed door without a knock, Jack stood in the doorway and gave her a hard stare.

My boss's face went blank. "Jack," she said in surprise. And then she gave him a warm smile, and she looked so poised and pleasant that I was astonished by the change in her. "How nice to see you. Come in, please."

My brother shook his head, his dark eyes cold. And he said three words in a tone that left no room for negotiation. "Pack your things."

I spent the rest of the afternoon with Jack, explaining how Vanessa had tried to bully and gaslight me, and that she was now likely doing the same thing with Samantha. By the time I had finished, Jack had stopped shaking his head and swearing, and simply looked sick.

"Sweet Jesus, Haven . . . why didn't you say anything to me before now?"

"I didn't want to be a prima donna. I wanted what was best for the company, and I knew she'd done good work for you in the past."

"Fuck the company," he said. "People matter more than business. I don't care how good the manager is if she behaves like a damn terrorist behind the scenes."

"At first I hoped Vanessa would get better over time, or that we'd work out some kind of system we could both live with. But I've come to realize that kind never gets better. There's no working things out. She's like Nick. A malignant narcissist. She doesn't feel any more remorse over hurting a fellow human being than you or I might feel about stepping on an ant."

Jack's mouth was set in a grim slash. "You meet a lot of that type in the business world. And although I hate to say it, some of that behavior . . . being ambitious and ruthless and selfish . . . can get you pretty far in some companies. But not mine."

"Are you really going to get rid of her?"

He nodded at once. "She's gone. I'll have to replace her now." A meaningful pause. "Any ideas?"

"I can do it," I said readily. "I'm not saying I'll be perfect. I'll make mistakes. But I know I can handle the responsibility."

A smile spread across my brother's face. "You're singing a different tune than when you started."

My answering smile was wry. "I've been on a fast learning curve lately."

We discussed the office situation a while longer, and then the conversation turned to personal matters. I couldn't help telling Jack about my falling-out with Dad. About T.J. and Hardy, and the lease deal.

Jack was satisfyingly irate about the whole thing, saying they were all assholes. He also agreed with me that I needed to get to the bottom of Hardy's behavior, because it didn't make sense. "T.J.'s got some prime property," he said, "but he's not the only game in town. And your boy Hardy can go shopping anywhere he wants. He may want those leases, but he doesn't need 'em. So I'd say this is Cates's way of breaking up with you. He's done something he knows will force *you* to call it off."

"The passive-aggressive jerk," I said. "If he wants to break up with me, he'll have to do it face-to-face."

Jack grinned. "I almost pity the bastard. Okay — you handle Cates, and I'll set Dad straight on a few things."

"No," I said automatically, "don't do anything about Dad. You can't fix my relationship with him."

"I can block or run interference."

"Thanks, Jack, but I don't need blocking, and I *really* don't need any more interference."

He looked annoyed. "Well, why did you waste all that time complaining to me if you didn't want me to do something about it?"

"I don't want you to fix my problems. I just wanted you to listen."

"Hang it all, Haven, talk to a girlfriend if all you want is a pair of ears. Guys *hate* it when you give us a problem and then don't let us do something about it. It makes us feel bad. And then the only way to make ourselves feel better is to rip a phone book in two or blow something up. So let's get this straight — I'm not a good listener. I'm a guy."

"Yes you are." I stood and smiled. "Want to buy me a drink at an after-work bar?"

"Now you're talking," my brother said, and we left the office.

It was early evening when I returned to my apartment. I felt better after a drink and a couple of hours in Jack's easygoing presence.

The thing that surprised me was his lack of condemnation for Hardy, especially given his earlier stance on the subject.

"I'm not for or against him," Jack had informed me, tilting back a long-necked beer. "Here's how I'm looking at this deal with T.J.: Hardy's either done the wrong thing for the wrong reason . . ." Another big swallow. "Or the wrong thing for the right reason."

"How could there possibly be a right reason for what he did?"

"Hell, I don't know. Give him a chance to explain himself, is all I'm saying."

"Todd thinks Hardy is conniving and twisted," I'd said morosely.

For some reason that had made Jack laugh. "Well, you oughta be used to that, coming from the Travis family. There's not a one of us — with the exception of Gage — who isn't as twisted as a duck's dick. And the same goes for Todd."

"You're scaring me," I said, but I hadn't been able to restrain a rueful smile.

I continued to smile as I went into my apartment, but I was nervous, thinking about seeing Hardy. As I saw the continuous blinking of the answering machine, my heart gave a little jolt. I went to the machine and pressed a button to hear the message.

Hardy's voice. "I need to see you. Please

call me when you get in tonight."

"Okay," I whispered, closing my eyes briefly. But I opened them right away, because something had caught my attention. A glitter and gleam next to the phone base. Perplexed, I reached out for the object, and was astonished to discover it was a charm bracelet. Aunt Gretchen's. But how had it gotten there? It had been in Nick's possession. Nick —

Before I could make a sound, someone came up behind me, and a hand clamped on my neck. The barrel of a handgun pressed cold and hard against the side of my head. I knew who it was even before I heard his gloating voice.

"Got you now, Marie."

CHAPTER TWENTY

When you suddenly find yourself in a dangerous situation, your brain splits into two parts, the part that's actually going through the situation, and the part that stands back and tries to understand what's happening. And those parts are not necessarily sharing information with each other. So it took a few moments for me to focus on what Nick was saying.

". . . can't ignore me, you bitch. You can't keep me away if I want to see you."

He wanted me to know he was all-powerful. He wanted to prove I couldn't beat him.

My mouth had gone so dry I could barely talk, while sweat broke out on my face. "Yeah," I said in a suffocated voice. "You definitely found a way to see me. How'd you do it? You couldn't have figured out the combination."

"I used an override key."

Each apartment in the building had two

override keys, in case of emergency, or in case someone forgot his or her touch-pad number. One set of all the residential keys was kept in a room behind the concierge desk. The other set was locked away in the management office.

"Vanessa gave it to you," I said in disbelief. That was illegal. It could get her prosecuted. Did she hate me so much that she would risk going to jail just to stick it to me after she'd been fired?

Apparently so.

"I told her I needed to drop some things off."

"Well, you did," I said faintly. "Thanks for the bracelet. But you didn't need to bring the gun, Nick."

"You've been ignoring me —"

"I'm sorry."

"— treating me like I mean nothing to you." The gun jabbed my temple hard enough to leave a bruise. I stayed still, my eyes watering. "I sure as hell mean something now, don't I?"

"Yeah," I whispered. Maybe he had come here with the sole intention of scaring me. But he was working himself up as he always had, letting his temper build. Once he started getting angry, it was an avalanche. You couldn't hold it back.

"You fucking ripped me off in the divorce, and left me in Dallas, with everyone asking about what happened, where you were . . . What do you think that did to me, Marie? Did you give a shit about what I was going through?"

I tried to remember what Susan had told me, that a narcissist needed to walk away feeling like the winner. "Of course I did," I said breathlessly. "But everyone knew you could do better. Everyone knew I wasn't good enough for you."

"That's right. You'll never have it as good as you did with me." Nick shoved me hard, and I slammed against the wall, my breath knocked out. The gun pressed against my skull. I heard the click of the safety being turned off. "You never tried," he muttered, urging his hips against my backside. A wave of nausea went through me as I felt the bulge of his erection. "You never did enough. It takes two to make a marriage, and you were never fucking *in* it, Marie. You should have done more."

"I'm sorry," I said around fitful gulps of air.

"You left me. Just walked away from that apartment in your bare feet, like goddamn white trash, to try to look as pitiful as possible. To make me look bad. And then you got

441

your asshole of a brother to push a divorce through. Just throw a handful of cash at me, and expect me to disappear. Legal papers and all that shit don't mean a thing to me, Marie. I can still do what I want with you."

"Nick," I managed, "we'll sit down and talk as long as you want if you'll just put the gun aw —" I broke off with a grunt of pain as I felt a blunt white explosion behind my ear, and heard a tinny high-pitched sound. A thin, hot trickle of liquid ran behind my ear and down my neck. He had hit me with the butt of the gun.

"How many men have you fucked?" he demanded.

No good answer to that one. Anything I said would lead to the subject of Hardy, and Nick's sense of humiliated fury would go into full swing. I had to pacify him. Soothe his injured ego.

"You're the one who matters," I whispered.

"Damn right about that." His free hand gripped my hair. "Dressing like a whore, cut your hair like a whore. You used to look like a lady. Like a wife. But you couldn't handle that. Now look at you."

"Nick —"

"Shut up! Everything you say is a lie. Every time you took one of those pills, it was a lie.

I was trying to give you a baby. I wanted us to have a family, but all you wanted was to leave. Lying slut!"

He used his grip on my hair to drag me down to the floor. His temper had heated to full boil, and he was shouting more filthy words, jamming the gun against my head. My mind, my emotions, disengaged from what was happening, the intimate violence that was coming. Just like before, only now with a gun at my head. I wondered dazedly if he would pull the trigger. His body crushed mine as he used his weight to pin me down. His breath was rank and boozy as he muttered near my ear. "Don't scream, or I'll kill you."

I was stiff, all muscles bitterly tensed. I wanted so badly to survive. My mouth flooded with the flavors of salt and metal. The familiar-awful touch of his hand paralyzed me as he started to drag the hem of my skirt up.

We were both so absorbed in our savage struggle, one bent on inflicting harm, one resisting body and soul, that neither of us heard the door open.

The air vibrated with an inhuman sound, and the entire room exploded, chaos unfolding. I managed to look up, my neck twisting painfully, and a brutal form was rushing toward us, and the gouge of cold metal left my skull as Nick raised the gun and fired.

Silence.

My ears were temporarily numb, my body resounding with the force of my terrified heartbeat. The smothering weight was gone. I rolled to my side and opened my blurry eyes. Two men were brawling in a pounding, choking, jaw-cracking dogfight, sweat and blood flying.

Hardy was on top of Nick, pummeling over and over. I could see the fight draining out of Nick as damage accumulated, bones fracturing, skin rupturing, and still Hardy wouldn't stop. There was blood everywhere — Hardy's left side was drenched and welling crimson.

"Hardy," I cried out, lurching up to my knees. "Hardy, *stop*."

He didn't hear me. He had lost his mind, every impulse and thought bent on destruction. He was going to kill Nick. And judging from the rate his own blood was pouring out, he would kill himself in the process.

The gun, knocked out of Nick's hand, had skittered a few yards away. I crawled over and picked it up. "Hardy, leave him alone now! That's enough! It's over. Hardy —"

Nothing I said or did was going to matter. He was on an adrenaline-fueled rampage.

I had never seen so much blood. I couldn't believe he hadn't passed out yet.

"Damn it, Hardy, I need you," I shouted.

He paused and looked over at me, panting. His eyes were slightly unfocused. "I need you," I repeated, staggering to my feet. I went to him and pulled at his arm. "Come with me. Come to the sofa."

He resisted, looking down at Nick, who had passed out, his face swollen and battered.

"It's okay now," I said, continuing to tug at Hardy. "He's down. It's over. Come with me. Come on." I repeated the words several times, coaxing and commanding and hauling him to the sofa. Hardy looked ashen and haggard, his face contorting as the murderous instinct faded and pain began to hit him. He tried to sit, ended up collapsing, his fists suspended in midair. He'd been shot on his side, but there was so much blood, I couldn't see the exact location or extent of the damage.

Still holding the gun, I ran to the kitchen and grabbed some folded dishtowels. I set the gun on the coffee table and ripped Hardy's shirt open.

"Haven," he said through thready breaths, "did he hurt you? Did he —"

"No. I'm fine." I wiped at the blood and

found the wound, a surprisingly small, neat hole. But I couldn't see an exit wound, which mean the bullet had gone in and possibly ricocheted, doing damage to the spleen, liver, or kidney . . . I wanted to burst into tears, but I forced them back and placed the pad of dishtowels over the wound. "Hold still. I'm going to put pressure on your side to slow the bleeding."

He let out a groan as I pushed downward. His lips were turning gray. "Your ear —"

"It's nothing. Nick hit me with the gun, but it wasn't —"

"I'll kill him —" He was trying to rise from the sofa.

I shoved Hardy back down. "Stay *still,* you idiot! You've been shot. Do not move." I put his hand over the folded dishtowels to maintain the pressure while I dashed to get the phone.

I called 911, David, and Jack, while keeping the dishtowels clamped tightly on the wound.

Jack was the first to reach my apartment. "Holy shit." He took in the scene before him, my ex-husband stirring on the floor, Hardy and me on the sofa. "Haven, are you —"

"I'm fine. Make sure Nick doesn't do anything else."

Jack stood over my ex-husband with an expression I'd never seen him wear before. "As soon as I get the chance," he told Nick in a deadly quiet voice, "I'm going to drop you in your tracks and gut you like a feral hog."

The paramedics arrived, followed soon by the police, while the building security guards kept anxious neighbors from coming in. I wasn't aware of the exact moment Nick was taken out of the apartment by the police, I was too absorbed in Hardy. He drifted in and out of consciousness, his skin clammy, his breathing weak and fast. He seemed confused, asking me at least three times what had happened, and if I was okay.

"Everything's fine," I murmured, stroking his tumbled hair, gripping his free hand firmly while a paramedic inserted a large bore needle for an IV. "Be quiet."

"Haven . . . had to tell you . . ."

"Tell me later."

"Mistake . . ."

"I know. It's okay. Hush and be still."

I could tell he wanted to say something else, but the other paramedic put him on high-flow oxygen and applied patches for a cardiac monitor, and fitted him with a stabilizing board for transport. They were fast and efficient. What EMS professionals call the "golden hour" had started: the time be-

447

tween when a victim was shot and the time he arrived at a trauma center for treatment. If more than sixty minutes passed before he got treated, his chances of survival started to drop.

I rode with Hardy in the ambulance while Jack drove to the hospital. It was only for Hardy's sake that I managed to stay outwardly calm. Inside, I felt an anguish that seemed too great for a human heart to withstand.

We arrived at the ambulance entrance, and the paramedics lifted Hardy on a gurney up to the building floor, which was slightly higher than the floor of the ambulance.

Liberty and Gage were already at the trauma unit, having been alerted by Jack. I guessed the rest of my family wouldn't be far behind. I hadn't given a thought to how I must have looked, all wild-eyed and blood-stained, but I gathered from their expressions that my appearance was a cause for concern. Liberty put her jacket over my shirt and cleaned my face with some baby wipes from her purse. When she discovered the lump behind my ear, she and Gage insisted that I get it looked at, despite my howls of protest.

"I'm not going anywhere, I'm going to stay right here until I find out what's going on with Hardy —"

"Haven." Gage was in front of me, his steady gaze boring into mine. "It's going to be a long time before they've got any news. They're checking his blood type, doing CT scans and X-rays . . . believe me, you're not going to miss a thing. Now let someone look at that hard head of yours. Please."

I was cleaned and bandaged, and sent back to the trauma unit waiting room. As Gage had predicted, there was no news. Hardy was in surgery, although no one would tell us what it was for, or how long it would last. I sat and stared blindly at the television in the corner of the room, wondering if I should call Hardy's mother. I decided to wait until I found out something about his condition — hopefully something reassuring — that I could relay along with the news that he'd been hurt.

As I waited, guilt sucked me down like quicksand. I had never imagined Hardy would suffer for my past mistakes. If only I had never gotten involved with Nick . . . if only I had never started a relationship with Hardy . . .

"Don't think that." I heard Liberty's gentle voice beside me.

"Don't think what?" I asked dully, drawing up my knees to sit cross-legged on the hard plastic chair.

"Whatever it is that's put that look on your face." Her arm slid around my shoulders. "You're not to blame for any of this. You're the best thing that's ever happened to Hardy."

"Oh, obviously," I muttered, casting a glance at the doors leading to surgery.

She squeezed me a little. "When I saw the two of you at the rigs-to-reefs party the other night, I couldn't believe the difference in Hardy. I've never seen him look so relaxed and happy. Comfortable in his skin. I didn't think anyone could ever do that for him."

"Liberty . . . something's gone wrong the past couple of days. Dad and Uncle T.J. —"

"Yes, I know about that. Churchill told me. He also told me about something that happened today, which you really need to hear."

"What is it?"

"I think Churchill should be the one to tell you." She nudged me to look toward the visitors' entrance, where my father and Joe were just coming in. Liberty stood and motioned Dad over to us, and he eased into the chair beside me. And in spite of all my anger and feelings of betrayal, I leaned against him and put my head on his shoulder, breathing in his leathery Dad-smell.

"What happened, Punkin?" he asked.

I kept my head on his shoulder as I told him. Every now and then his hand came up and patted my arm gently. He seemed bewildered that Nick would have done something so crazy, and asked what had happened to drive him off the deep end. I thought of explaining that Nick had always been that way, that his abuse had destroyed our marriage. But I decided to save that particular conversation for a better time and place. So I just shook my head and shrugged and said I had no idea.

And then Dad surprised me by saying, "I knew Hardy was going to come see you tonight."

I lifted my head and looked at him. "You did? How?"

"He called me around five today. Said he was sorry he'd agreed to the lease deal, and he'd already told T.J. it was off. He said he hadn't been thinking straight on Saturday, and it had been a mistake on both sides — us for offering, and him for accepting."

"He was right," I said shortly.

"So the deal is off," Dad said.

"Oh, no it isn't!" I scowled at him. "You're still going to keep your end of it. You make sure Hardy gets the leases at the fair price he offered, and tell T.J. to forget the bonus. And if you do that, I'll be willing to give you another chance at a normal father-daughter relationship."

I was determined that for once in his life, Hardy Cates was going to have it all.

"And you're going to keep on seeing him?"

"Yes."

My father smiled slightly. "Probably a good thing, considering what he told me about you."

"What? What did he tell you?"

My father shook his head. "He asked me to keep it private. And I'm done interfering. Except . . ."

I gave an unsteady laugh. "Except what? Damn it, Daddy, why do you have to quit interfering when you finally have something I want to hear?"

"I can tell you this much. I've had two men approach me about their feelings for my daughter. One of 'em was Nick. And I didn't believe a word he said. Not because you're not worth loving. Nick just didn't have it in him. But Hardy Cates . . . for all that he's a rascal and a born redneck . . . I believed him today. He wasn't trying to sell me something. He was just telling me like it was. I respected that. And whatever you choose to do about him, I'll respect that too."

■ ■ ■ ■

Two hours passed. I paced, sat, watched TV, and guzzled burnt-tasting coffee flavored with powdered creamer and fake sweetener. When I thought I was going to explode from the tension of not knowing anything, the door opened. A tall white-haired surgeon stood there, his gaze sweeping the room. "Any family for Hardy Cates?"

I shot over to him. "I'm his fiancée." I thought that might get me more information. "Haven Travis."

"Dr. Whitfield."

We shook hands.

"Mr. Cates used up all his luck on this one," the surgeon said. "The bullet nicked the spleen, but no other organs were damaged. Almost a miracle. I'd have expected the bullet to bounce around a little more, but thankfully it didn't. After we removed the bullet, we were able to do a relatively simple suture repair on the spleen and salvage it completely. Given Mr. Cates's age and excellent health, there's no reason to expect complications of any kind. So I'd say he'll be in the hospital for about a week, and then it'll take about four to six weeks more until he's all healed up."

My eyes and nose stung. I passed a sleeve

over my eyes to blot them. "So he won't have any problems from this in the future? No gimpy spleen or anything?"

"Oh, no. I'd expect a full recovery."

"Oh, my God." I let out a shuddering sigh. It was one of the best moments of my life. No, the absolute best. I was electrified and weak, and breathless. "I'm so relieved, I actually feel sort of queasy from it. Is that possible?"

"It's either relief," Dr. Whitfield said kindly, "or the waiting room coffee. Most likely the coffee."

The hospital rule was that intensive care patients could have twenty-four-hour visitation. The catch was, you could only stay fifteen minutes per hour, except in special circumstances as approved by the nursing staff. I asked Gage to pull whatever strings he could to make sure I could come and go at will. My brother seemed vaguely amused by this, and reminded me about how I had once objected to using power and money to get special treatment. I told him that when you were in love, hypocrisy won out over principle. And Gage said he certainly understood that, and he went and got me special permission to stay with Hardy as long as I wanted.

I dozed in a reclining chair in Hardy's room most of the night. The problem was, a hospital was the worst place in the world to sleep. Nurses came in hourly, exchanging IV bags, checking the monitors, and taking Hardy's temperature and blood pressure. But I welcomed each interruption, because I loved hearing about how well he was doing, over and over again.

At daybreak Gage came to the hospital and told me he was going to drive me back to my apartment so I could shower and change. I didn't want to leave Hardy, but I knew I looked like something the cat dragged in, and it was probably a good idea for me to clean up some.

Hardy had woken up when I came back at seven, and he was not pleased, to say the least, to find himself in a hospital bed and hooked up to monitors. I walked in to hear him arguing with a nurse, demanding that she take the IV out, and categorically refusing the pain medicine that he obviously needed. He didn't want to be poked and prodded, he said. He felt fine. All he needed was a bandage and an ice pack.

I could tell the nurse was enjoying the argument with the big, blue-eyed male who was at her mercy, and I didn't blame her a bit. He looked lost, a little anxious, and utterly appetizing.

And he was mine.

"Hardy Cates," I said, coming into the room, "you behave, or I'll step on your tube."

The nurse seemed taken aback by my un-sympathetic bedside manner.

But Hardy's gaze met mine in a moment of bright, hot voltage, and he relaxed, reassured in a way that cooing sympathy could never have done. "That only works if it's a breath-ing tube," he told me.

I went to the tray on the bed-table and picked up the Vicodin tablets the nurse had been trying to get him to take, along with a cup of water. "Take these," I said. "No argu-ing."

He obeyed, shooting a glance at the nurse, whose eyebrows were slightly raised. "She's little," he told her, "but she's mean."

The nurse left, no doubt wondering why such a hunk hadn't been able to find a nicer girlfriend. When the door had closed, I fussed over Hardy a little, straightening the covers and readjusting his pillow. His gaze didn't stray from my face.

"Haven," he muttered, "get me out of here. I've never been in a hospital before. I can't stand being hooked up to all this crap. All I need is —"

"Surrender to the process," I told him, "and you'll get out of here a lot quicker." I kissed his forehead. "Will you behave if I get in there with you?"

Without hesitation, Hardy maneuvered himself over to the side, grunting in pain at the effort. I slipped off my clogs and climbed in carefully, resting in the crook of his arm. He sighed deeply, a sound of contentment.

I nuzzled gently into his warm neck, breathing him in. Hardy smelled antiseptic, medicinal, like he'd been sprayed with eau-de-hospital. But underneath the sterilized blankness I found the familiar fragrance of him.

"Hardy," I murmured, stroking his wrist, "why did you take that stupid deal from Dad and T.J.? And why'd you call it off?"

His hand found mine, long fingers folding over my palm. "I went a little crazy after I saw my dad on Friday night."

"Really? I hadn't noticed."

"I bailed him out and dropped him off at a motel with some money. And I told him to get lost. But what I didn't tell you . . . I should have . . . is that he and I talked for a few minutes. And he said —" Hardy stopped, gripping my hand more tightly.

I waited as he took a few unsettled breaths.

"He got pissed when I told him what I'd do

to him if he ever called Mom again," Hardy muttered. "He said that was funny coming from me, because . . . I was the reason they'd gotten married. Mom had stopped going out with him, but then she had to go back to him because she was pregnant. It was my fault she ended up with the son of a bitch. Her whole life has been hell because of me. She's suffered —"

"No. Hardy . . ." I lifted up and stared into his dark blue eyes. My chest ached with sympathy. "You know that's not right. You know it wasn't your fault."

"But it's a fact that if I hadn't come along, Mom wouldn't have married him. And once he got her, her life was ruined."

I understood Hardy's feelings even if I didn't agree with his logic. But his anguish and irrational guilt couldn't be solved with convenient platitudes. He needed time, and love, to come to terms with the truth. And I had more than enough of both to give him.

Hardy kissed my head. His voice was deep and rough. "I hate being his son. I hate the half of me that's him, and I can feel it, that part that's a bad, low, worthless son of a bitch, and when Churchill and T.J. came to me with that deal, I thought why the hell not. I was going to have to leave you anyway.

Because I loved you too much to drag you down with me."

My hand crept up to caress the rigid line of his jaw. "Why'd you change your mind?" I whispered.

"After I calmed down a little and had a chance to think, I figured . . . I love you enough to try and deserve you. I would do anything, be anything, for you. Last night I went to your apartment to beg you to give me another chance. I was shaking in my boots, thinking you might not forgive me for Friday night."

I flushed as I remembered the long, erotic hours with him in the darkness of his bedroom. "Of course I . . . I mean, there's nothing to forgive." My voice lowered to an abashed whisper. "I wanted to do all that with you."

His body had turned so warm, I wondered if he was blushing too. "I thought it might have been too much for you. I pushed you too hard. And after what you'd been through with Nick . . . well, I was afraid you wouldn't want me in your life anymore. So I was coming to your apartment to tell you how sorry I was. How gentle I would be from now on. And even if you don't want me now, I wish you'd just . . . let me be near you, at least. In case you ever need me for anything."

I had never heard him so utterly humble, never imagined it was possible. I guided his face to mine until our noses almost touched. "I need you for a lot of things, Hardy. A lifetime's worth of things."

He kissed me with surprising strength, his mouth warm and demanding.

"I love you," I whispered. And it was a testament to the man's considerable vigor that in spite of blood loss, drugs, and a distinctly unromantic hospital setting, he put some serious moves on me.

"Don't," I said with a shaky laugh as his free hand wandered boldly over my front. "We'll set off the cardiac monitor. And they'll kick me out for compromising your recovery."

But Hardy paid no attention, of course, doing exactly as he pleased.

"You know," I said, arching a little as he kissed my neck, "I told the hospital staff I was your fiancée, so they'd let me stay in here with you."

"I'd hate to make a liar out of you." Hardy smoothed my hair back. "But after what happened last night, you're feeling grateful, and I don't want to take advantage. So tomorrow, when the gratitude's worn off . . . I'll probably ask you to marry me."

"I'll probably say yes," I told him.

Hardy brought my forehead to his, and I was lost in the brilliant blue depths of his eyes.

"Soon?" he whispered against my lips.

"As soon as you want."

It occurred to me in retrospect that I probably should have been nervous about getting married again, in light of my past experiences. But everything was different with Hardy. His love came with no strings attached, which I thought was the greatest gift one human being could give to another.

"You know," I told him on our wedding night, "I'm just as much me when I'm with you, as I am without you."

And because Hardy understood what I meant, he pulled me into his arms, against his heart.

Epilogue

"He's on the phone, Mrs. Cates," Hardy's secretary says. "But he said to send you in as soon as you got here."

I'm at Hardy's high-rise office on Fannin, an aluminum and glass building that looks like two puzzle pieces put together. "Thanks," I tell the secretary, and I go to my husband's door and let myself in.

Hardy is at his desk, his suit jacket tossed carelessly over a chair. His tie is loose and his shirt sleeves are rolled up over heavy-muscled forearms, as if he's tried to make himself more comfortable in the confining business attire. *Roughneck,* I think, with a pang of possessive pleasure.

We've been married for nearly a year, and I still can't get used to the fact that he's mine. It's nothing like the marriage I had with Nick in any way, shape, or form. Nick is no longer a threat to me or anyone, having been convicted of two counts of aggravated assault and sent to Texarkana. And Vanessa Flint ended up leaving Houston. The last I heard, she was the assistant manager at a fertilizer company in Marfa.

I don't spend much time dwelling on the past. One of the blessings human beings take for granted is the ability to remember pain without re-feeling it. The pain of physical wounds is long gone for both Hardy and me. And the other kind of hurt, the damage done to our spirits, has been healed. We are careful with those scarred places in each other. And we delight in a marriage that the two of us are creating, deepening, every day.

". . . want you to pin 'em down on exactly what kind of fluid they're planning to pump into that crack," Hardy says.

I bite back a grin, thinking by now I should be used to the filthy-sounding oil business lingo.

". . . I'm less concerned with the flow rate than the additives they use." Hardy pauses to listen. "Yeah, well, I don't give a damn about stimulation technology secrets. It's *my* ass the EPA will come after if there's ground water contamination, and —"

He breaks off as he sees me, and a slow, dazzling smile crosses his face, the one that never fails to make me a little light-headed. "Let's finish this later," he says into the phone. "Something's come up. Okay."

Setting the phone aside, Hardy walks around the desk. He half sits, half leans on the edge, and reaches to pull me between his thighs. "Brown-eyed girl," he murmurs, kissing me.

"Stimulation technology?" I ask, looping my arms around his neck.

"Ways of getting hard-to-reach oil out of low permeability reservoirs," he explains. "You inject fluids into the wellbore hole until they widen underground cracks enough to let the oil out." His hands coast over my sides and hips. "We're working with a new hydraulic fracturing group."

"You could have finished your conversation," I tell him.

"I wouldn't want you to be bored."

"Not at all. I love hearing you talk about business. It always sounds so risqué."

"I don't know exactly what risqué means," Hardy returns, his hand wandering down to my bottom, "but I think I've done it a few times."

I mold myself against him. "Suggestive of sexual impropriety," I explain. "You've been risqué your entire adult life."

His blue eyes sparkle. "But now only with you." He kisses me slowly, as if the point needs demonstrating. "Haven, sweetheart

. . . how did the appointment go?"

We've been talking lately about the possibility of having a baby. Hardy seems willing but cautious, while I've been feeling what must be a biological imperative. I want a baby with him. I want our own family. And whatever life has in store for us, I know we'll deal with it together.

"The doctor said I'm perfectly healthy and good to go," I tell him. "Now the rest is up to you."

He laughs and grips me closer. "When do we start?"

"Tonight?" I tilt my head back languidly as his lips slide along my throat.

"How about lunch hour?"

"No way. I want mood music and foreplay."

I feel the curve of his smile against my skin. But as he lifts his head and looks into my eyes, his grin fades. "Haven . . . I don't know if I'm going to be a good father. What if I don't do it right?"

I am touched by Hardy's concern, his constant desire to be the man he thinks I deserve. Even when we disagree, I have no doubt that I am cherished. And respected. And I know that neither of us takes the other one for granted.

I have come to realize you can never be

truly happy unless you've known some sorrow. All the terrible things Hardy and I have gone through in our lives have created the spaces inside where happiness can live. Not to mention love. So much love that there doesn't seem to be room for bitterness in either of us.

"I think the fact that you're worrying about it at all," I say, "means you'll probably be great at it."

Hardy smiles and pulls me safe and secure into the shelter of his body. He holds me tightly, and it feels good. It's what I need. "That does it," he says, his voice muffled in my hair. "It's going to be lunch hour for you, honey. Get your purse. We've got time for foreplay, but not for mood music. Unless you can find something on the car radio on the way to the apartment."

I turn and find his lips, and discover that it's nearly impossible to smile and kiss at the same time. I have no intention of arguing. "Who needs mood music?" I say.

And a few minutes later, we're heading home.

AUTHOR'S NOTE

Dear Friends,

As I researched *Blue-Eyed Devil* and contemplated the personal journey of my heroine Haven Travis, I became amazed by how widespread the issues of abuse and narcissistic personality disorder are, and how seldom they are discussed in the media. I think part of the problem is that victims of verbal and emotional abuse — which can occur at home, in the workplace, or in any kind of relationship — are so accustomed to what they think of as "normal" behavior, they aren't aware of what "normal" really is.

No person has the right to bully, slander, or control someone else. No person has the right to diminish or harm another person in any way.

I have found a few Web sites that I think are very informative about abuse and personality disorders. They contain links, articles, and resources for anyone interested in finding out more about these problems.

www.abusesanctuary.blogspot.com
www.controllingparents.com
www.narcissism.101.com

There is also a National Domestic Violence Hotline, which has a Web site as well as a phone number.

(800) 799-SAFE
www.ndvh.org

Also, I would like to encourage anyone who has long hair and is thinking of getting a short cut, like Haven Travis did, to check out the Locks of Love program. It is a wonderful nonprofit organization that gives hairpieces to children suffering from medical hair loss.

Locks of Love
2925 10th Avenue N
Suite 102
Lake Worth, FL 33461-3099
(561) 963-1677
Toll-Free Information Line: (888) 896-1588
www.locksoflove.org

I hope you enjoyed *Blue-Eyed Devil,* and as always I appreciate the support and friendship of so many readers.

Wishing you happiness always,

Lisa

ABOUT THE AUTHOR

Lisa Kleypas is the RITA-Award winning author of 20 novels. Her books are published in fourteen languages and are bestsellers all over the world. She lives in Washington with her husband and two children.

The employees of Thorndike Press hope you have enjoyed this Large Print book. All our Thorndike and Wheeler Large Print titles are designed for easy reading, and all our books are made to last. Other Thorndike Press Large Print books are available at your library, through selected bookstores, or directly from us.

For information about titles, please call:

(800) 223-1244

or visit our Web site at:

http://gale.cengage.com/thorndike

To share your comments, please write:

Publisher
Thorndike Press
295 Kennedy Memorial Drive
Waterville, ME 04901